KYN KRONICLES BOOK 2

SHADOWS SOUL

JAMI GRAY

Cover Art: Deranged Doctor Design, www.derangeddoctordesign.com
Publisher: Celtic Moon Press Revised edition, 2018
ISBN: 978-1-948884-18-1 (ebook) ISBN: 978-1-948884-19-8 (print)

First edition, June 2012, Black Opal Books ISBN: 978-1-937329-48-8 (ebook)
ISBN: 978-1-937329-49-5 (print)

SIGN UP FOR FREE READS FROM JAMI!

Join Jami's newsletter to be the first to hear about new releases, free books, special prices and other nifty events.

Sign up at: https://www.subscribepage.com/jami-gray-books

What Readers Say...

About Arcane Transporter:
"Taking a refreshing approach to fantasy magic, this fast-paced, economical thriller is told from a highly likable perspective." —Red Adept Editing

About PSY-IV Teams:
"This story is an emotional roller coaster, from betrayal, anger, fear, love..." —InD'tale Magazine

About the Kyn Kronicles:
"...a fantastic paranormal action novel is quite possibly the best book I've read this year. I could not put it down, and had to exercise serious self-control to keep from staying up all night to finish it." —The Romance Reviews

About Fate's Vultures:
"...if you like your characters with a bit more bite, with secrets, with hidden agendas, and all those sorts of things, and your worlds are a far more deadlier place, then this is for you." —Archaeolibrarian

ALSO BY JAMI GRAY

ARCANE WONDERLAND

Last Call

Bitter Spirits

Rune & Tonic

ARCANE TRANSPORTER

Ignition Point (*Prequel Novella*)

Grave Cargo

Risky Goods

Lethal Contents

Collision Course

Blind Spot

Terminal Drift

THE KYN KRONICLES

Shadow's Edge

Shadow's Soul

Shadow's Moon

Shadow's Curse

Shadow's Dream

Shadow's Fall

Tangled in Shadows (*Short Story Collection*)

FATE'S VULTURES

Lying in Ruins

Beg for Mercy

Caught in the Aftermath

Fear the Reaper

PSY-IV TEAMS

Hunted by the Past

Touched by Fate

Marked by Obsession

Fractured by Deceit

Linked by Deception

BOX SETS

PSY-IV Teams Box Set I (Books 1-3)

The Collapse: Fate's Vultures (Books 1-4)

The Kyn Kronicles Box Set (Books 1-6)

Arcane Transporter Box Set I (Books 1-3)

Arcane Transporter Box Set II (Books 4-6)

So many to thank, so little space—
This one goes to Donna Jo, because you understand how hard it is to believe in the light after a long dark journey!
As always, much love and gratitude to my knight in slightly muddy armor and the Prankster Duo—thanks for keeping that lantern lit and making sure there wasn't a train attached!
And because none of this would be possible without them—huge thanks to the 7 Evil Dwarves—I wouldn't have made it through this one without you guys!
For my readers—huge hugs and thanks for all your encouragement and comments! It verifies that someone out there is really reading this!
Finally—for all those survivors who fight to make it past the nightmares—your strength paves the way for those who follow you—thank you for never giving up!

CHAPTER 1

Blood dripped into her eyes. Raine McCord raised a hand to brush it away, smearing the warm wetness across her face. Around her the world shimmered feverishly, sunlight glinting off the snow draped forest. She stumbled over a fallen log. Pain screamed through tattered nerve endings and down her right leg before the overload caused it to go limp. Collapsing to her side, she tried to protect her injured right shoulder. With a groan, she used her left hand to push up to her knees.

She knelt there, head down, eyes closed, trying to breathe through the never-ending dizziness. Instincts screaming, she struggled to lift her heavy head and forced her eyes open. *Get up! Move!*

A strange silence filled the winter forest. Under the white barked tress, patches of snow clung to the forest floor as faint whimpers and ragged breathing filled her ears. Dead leaves and fallen twigs scraped against her tender palms as she ignored the chill and dug her bloodied hands into the wet, cold dirt.

Inadvertent sounds whispered on the icy air as she

dragged her battered body along the ground. Somewhere behind her a branch cracked. Jerking to look back she found only drag marks smeared with crimson marking her path. Turning forward, she blinked, trying to clear her vision as it wavered between gray and bright white.

Aiming for the large, dark shape looming just out of reach she began to move, inch by agonizing inch. The indistinct shape slowly became the remains of a fallen tree, large enough to hide behind. She managed to crawl behind its dubious shelter before her arms and knees gave out, sending her face first into the cold, wet earth.

The rattling shivers from earlier were now a bone deep weariness. Still, she pulled her knees to her chest, curling into a ball, each slow movement torture. Soft pain-filled noises broke the silence. *Quiet. She had to be quiet.* She stuffed her fist against her bruised lips, hoping to mute the piteous sounds as the swirling darkness and cold dragged her relentlessly under.

Her dreams included strangely soothing chants and curiously subdued drumming. It was a new experience. Generally, her nightmares involved cages, mad scientists, and monsters. At least the forest motif remained familiar. Rough edges dug into her spine. Trying not to be obvious, Raine reached behind her and found—tree bark?

Slitting her eyes open, she was met with a curtain of dark, matted hair. Hazy light filtered through the strands. She rolled over and stared into a latticework of branches complete with leaves dancing in soft green light.

This wasn't right. Well, more not right than the fact she was lying at the foot of a freaking huge tree.

The towering branches continued their hypnotic sway in the still air. *How did leaves dance without wind?*

Gingerly she sat up, brushing her hair out of her face, her hand snagging on a twig. Pulling the tangled mass forward, she studied the crushed sticks and leaves snared in the inky strands. Flowing white sleeves fell back from her arms as she pushed the mess back.

White? Flowing? What the hell? She didn't own a white, flowing anything. Jeans, leather, and steel, that's what she was comfortable in.

The crackle of dried leaves heralded the arrival of a new player. All her thoughts on weird clothing disappeared under a rush of adrenaline. She instinctively moved into a crouch, reaching for her weapons. A streak of panic hit when she found nothing.

Unarmed, all she could do was wait.

A wolf emerged from the shifting shadows, its fur blending from white to gray to black. Its amber gaze strangely calm as it padded forward then sat, like a dog. Not once did its attention waver.

She carefully eased back until the great oak pressed against her spine, not once breaking eye contact with the waiting animal.

Unsure of where she was, she dropped the protective mental barrier that lay between her magic and the everyday world and her senses flared to life. The natural magic in the surrounding fauna became a visible palette of shifting colors. A recently discovered talent that had nothing to do with her Fey bloodlines and everything to do with her time spent as a lab rat.

She reached for her magic, only to have it slip through her psychic fingers like mist. Startled, she tried again even as the strange wolf continued to watch her. Frustrated when her magic escaped again, she muttered, "What the hell?"

She eyed the wolf, possible options cascading through her mind. She reached back and dug physical fingers into the rough edges of the tree bark. That was definitely real. She stared at the watching wolf—escape or confront?

As if reading her mind, he gave her a canine grin full of very pointed teeth.

She grimaced. "Yeah right, Mr. Big Bad Wolf. Do I look like I'm wearing a little red hood?" She was surprised at how hoarse her voice was. Only one thing left her throat this raw. Small problem—she couldn't remember anything requiring that much screaming.

"Red is not your color, Raine."

At the mocking female voice, Raine jerked her head up so fast everything did a slow, stomach-churning spin. Once the world resettled, she dared to look around. Other than the wolf and the tree behind her, everything remained shrouded in shadows and mists.

A woman stepped out of the shadows. "You need to come back." She moved to the wolf and scratched behind one gray ear. She was tall, taller than Raine's own five-foot-five frame by a good couple of inches. Various shades of blonde were drawn into a simple braid. Deep brown eyes sparkled with some inner amusement. "You can't stay here."

"I don't know where here is."

The blonde tilted her head in a strange bird-like manner. "Here is where you go to heal, to get away from the rest of the world. Think of it as your own personal garden of Eden."

Raine couldn't stop the snort of disbelief or the bitter twist of her mouth. "This is the first time my Eden doesn't look like hell, so I'm not so sure this is all my doing."

Impatience passed over the strong-boned face. "Regardless, you need to go back now."

The snappy tone didn't sit well with Raine. Rising from her crouch, she hid the shakiness of her legs behind a sneer. "How am I supposed to get back?"

This place set her teeth on edge and getting out of here was quickly becoming priority number one.

Frustration tightened the woman's lips. "Don't you know how to do this? It's your spirit you've trapped here." Her voice carried sharp impatience. "Make the decision to come back to yourself. If you don't, you'll die." She crossed her arms as a flash of understanding washed through her face. "Ah. Perhaps that's what you want then?"

Raine curled her hands into useless fists, the hair along her arms rising as danger circled. "If this is my Eden, who the hell are you?"

"Tala Whiteriver, and you, Raine McCord, are dying." Tala's voice stayed unmoved and melodic, yet something in the undertones sent shivers racing down Raine's spine.

"Follow." Tala turned away, her voice floating back, the challenge unmistakable. "If you have the courage."

The wolf rose to its feet, his tongue lolling out in obvious canine laughter. Tala's figure disappeared into the thick surrounding shadows. The wolf turned and followed his mistress into the haze.

Not one to ever back down, Raine left the sheltering tree, each step steadier than the last. Gray shifting shadows curled around her as the drums and chanting made a comeback. When she came to the glade's edge, the sounds turned insistent, driving. A few more steps took her into the mist of dark shadows.

They wrapped around her like ghosts and pulled her forward. A strange fear spiked deep in her bones. She tried to brush the phantom mists away, but they clung tight. Obviously whatever this was, it didn't want her to leave. She stopped struggling and noticed the ghostly bindings began to fade as she pressed forward. The only way to tell she was on the same path as Tala and the wolf was the flash of a tail up ahead.

"Try to keep up." Tala's voice drifted back. "There's no woodcutter coming to save you."

Raine's teeth snapped together. She really disliked this woman.

The dense gray soup compromised her sense of direction. Flashes of fur became her guide. Time passed—she wasn't sure how much. The fog grew lighter and the disturbing shadows dissipated. When the wolf disappeared between one blink and the next, she stepped up her pace and abruptly broke free of the shadows. Light blinded her, while the chanting and drumbeats took up a resonant pulse in her bones.

"Show me how strong you are, warrior girl." Tala's whispered taunt cut through the chaos of noise and blinding glare of light.

A strong shove from invisible hands sent Raine stumbling forward. She fell into endless darkness. Panic left a metallic taste in her mouth. Blood rushed through her veins, following the beat of the unseen drums. Colors became a dizzying kaleidoscope, while sonorous chanting infiltrated her mind like a thousand voices.

Wrenching agony choked off her frustrated scream as every bone in her body shattered at once. Acid replaced the blood in her veins as the chanting swelled until it swallowed her agonized consciousness, sucking her into the terrifying abyss.

CHAPTER 2

Something held Raine down. No matter how much she fought, she couldn't get free. She couldn't be tied down, not again. Raking out, she felt her nails score someone's skin, but her movements were weak and uncoordinated. Every muscle felt insubstantial. And she hurt. *Oh gods.* The last time she had hurt like this, she woke to find herself strapped to a lab table, changed in ways she still didn't understand. The scientists couldn't have gotten her again. They were dead.

She heard a whimper from somewhere.

"Raine, you have to stop."

She knew that voice. The low-pitched tone arrowed to her soul, lodging deep. She stilled. It couldn't be *him*. She was too far from home and he wanted nothing to do with her. *A hallucination maybe?*

She dragged air into her lungs, feeling her body quiver like a trapped animal. The scent of cool wind cutting through leaves and green things deep in the forest curled its way inside her. That scent belonged to one man. "Gavin?" His name came out on a mere whisper of sound.

She pried her heavy lids open, wondering if her mind had finally broken.

"Hey." Jade green eyes dark with concern stared back. Not cold, not angry, but worried.

That wasn't right. Maybe she was still dreaming?

Her hallucination kept talking, "You need to lie still, okay?"

She tried to nod, only to stop when a spike of pain slammed through her skull. She couldn't hold back her harsh groan.

No moving her head. Instead, she let her gaze travel around—slowly, so she wouldn't pass out from the reeling images. The drums and chanting were gone, replaced by the snap, crackle of a nearby fire. Which would explain the dancing light in the darkened room.

The touch of a cool cloth drew her attention back to the man next to her. She studied him, some unacknowledged part of her starving for the sight of him. His auburn hair was pulled back, leaving his high cheekbones and strong jaw line exposed.

She hadn't seen him in three months, a deliberate move on her part. Her guilt over what had happened to him was a handy tool in avoiding contact. So, why was he here now? And where exactly was here?

Gently trailing the cloth over her brows, along her burning cheeks, he only stopped when he reached her chin.

Little rivulets of water trickled down her neck, but not wanting to break this strange spell, she remained mute. With her luck, anything she said would turn his concern to anger. She wanted to enjoy what she could for now. Dark circles hung under his eyes and his face seemed a bit thinner. Sure signs he hadn't been taking care of himself.

He moved the cloth down her neck, gently running it

over the collar-like scar on her neck. "You remember anything?" His question was soft.

She closed her eyes, shutting his distracting presence out while she pulled her memories together. She recalled being summoned into her boss's office at Taliesin Security in Portland, Oregon, and being given her a new assignment by Mulcahy. He wanted her to play bodyguard. Not to some high profile human. Nope, she was to protect an even higher profile Kyn—Cheveyo.

Head of the Magi House, Cheveyo was responsible for all the witches, shamans, and wizards residing in the Northwest. He had been asked by the head of the Southwest Magi House to come to Arizona and assist her on an existing problem.

Four hours later, Raine had boarded a private plane with the most powerful witch in the Northwest, who just also happened to be her current mentor and pain in the ass. With no security to run through, she was able to keep her weapons. A definite perk of private air travel. They left Portland's slushy snow and freezing temperatures to land under clear skies in Phoenix's balmy, sixty-seven degrees.

She followed Cheveyo to the waiting rental car, then proceeded to check the vehicle for any hidden threats, magical or practical. Only then did she let him put their bags in the trunk.

She began navigating her way through Phoenix despite taking exception to the GPS's assurance that taking a right wouldn't send them careening off the overpass. After her rather loud disagreement with the stupid computer, Cheveyo took over the navigation and directed her out of Phoenix and toward Flagstaff.

At one point, they stopped for gas while he rechecked his directions. Walking into the busy convenience store, she noted the bevy of feminine attention he garnered. His Native American heritage was apparent in his straight black collar length hair, which framed a strong face. Being taller than most men only added to his quiet, compelling presence.

When those same glances landed on her, they quickly shied away. Unlike Cheveyo, she could never be mistaken for anything other than what she was—lethal. She looked young, most Kyn did, but her eyes held too much darkness. Hell, she hadn't even flashed any of her scars thanks to the long sleeves of her jacket and her turtleneck tucked into faded jeans. Even her jacket served to hide the various blades lying at her wrists and back.

As Cheveyo had chatted with the clerk, Raine kept her face professionally blank scanning their surroundings without being obvious about it. A crucial skill when guarding someone.

Directions in hand, they continued into the mountains. Turning off the highway, they drove along the winding roads that seemed to lead to nowhere. Winter was in full display, with snow dusting the tall trees and covering the ground in a thin, white blanket.

They bumped along a dirt road, long enough for dusk to fall. As sunlight faded, she caught movement from her left and stomped on the brakes. A deer turned panicked eyes her way before bounding away. A shiver of unease worked its way down Raine's spine, but nothing else came out of the woods.

She turned to warn Cheveyo, when her blood iced. The air grew heavy, thick. Malice riding through the deepening shadows like an insidious mist. She scrambled out of the car, trying to pinpoint what was heading their way.

Unreasoning fear blossomed, but there was nothing to

fight. The fear expanded, deepened, until it choked her. Standing back to back with Cheveyo's, they pulled on their combined magic to set a protection circle in place. Before the last piece fell, darkness slammed into them.

That was when her memories twisted into nightmares.

She remembered flying through the air, her body's trajectory abruptly halted by a tree. The cracking of her ribs lost in the impact. She barely got her feet under her as she landed. She tried to locate the threat, yet there was nothing to fight. She lost sight of Cheveyo, but could hear his voice, thunderous and commanding, calling in a language she didn't recognize. The darkness was so complete she couldn't see her own hands.

That was when she recognized the threat was the overwhelming darkness and whatever hid inside its inky depths. It was so thick it left her enhanced vision useless. Normally able to register heat in various shades of orange and red, there, in that unnatural darkness, all she saw was endless emptiness.

Honed instincts warned her that whatever they faced was targeting Cheveyo. Ignoring the screaming protests of her ribs, she dropped into a crouch, her hands grasping the hilts of her boot blades. Drawing them out, she whispered the command to trigger the protection spells on her weapons.

As her magic flared, outlining the blades in blue-white flames, the devouring darkness paused. She began to straighten when it rushed her. Unable to brace, it hit her, the impact stealing her breath, leaving her unable to scream. Unseen fingers ripped through skin and bone, tearing her magic from the bones of her soul.

Her blades fell into the opaque stew. Their light flickered out like fading stars as she desperately tried to protect her magic, slamming the shields Cheveyo had been teaching her into place. It didn't stop the clawing fingers. They scored through old scars, shattering her defenses with agonizing speed. By sheer luck, she managed to reinforce her critical inner barriers with hastily cobbled pieces of her magic.

Claws closed over her right thigh, on top of a recently acquired burn scar, and snapped the bone in half. For a singular moment, she had the stupid thought that it didn't hurt as bad as expected, then a wildfire of pain seared through her leg, driving her to the ground.

The destructive hands clamped on her shoulder, slamming her into an unyielding surface. The agony of her bones breaking barely made a dent to the chorus of pain her battered body wailed.

That inhuman grasp disappeared and her torn body fell to the forest floor. Time passed, and when she could finally raise her head, the darkness was seeping away through the trees. Her vision faded in and out, but she could swear there was someone standing just on the edge of the clearing.

"Cheveyo?" Her voice came out weak and unsteady. The only answer was a chilling laugh that followed her into unconsciousness.

"I woke up and began crawling." Ending her retelling, Raine swallowed hard and opened her eyes, unable to meet Gavin's gaze.

Shame coursed through her. It didn't matter if she was one of the most feared warriors in the Kyn society. Whatever that darkness was had been so fast, so destructive, it left her choking in debilitating fear, her vow to protect Cheveyo fracturing under the threat. It managed to reduce her to the child who'd been chained to a lab table.

"Whatever you're thinking, stop." The command came

out sharp, verging on cruel. Gavin grasped her chin, forcing her to meet the merciless demand of his gaze. "You can't fall apart."

She winced. He had no right to judge. He hadn't been there.

His face grew grim. "We need to find Cheveyo and figure out what the hell is going on here."

She jerked her chin out of his hand. The abrupt movement sent blades of pain flaring through her head. "How did you get here?"

"You didn't check in." He absently traced the inked Celtic markings circling her left shoulder. "Mulcahy ordered Xander and me down here to find out what was happening."

Her lip curled into a sneer at her uncle's perception of her abilities.

Catching it, Gavin's lips twitched. "He gave you three days before he sent us in."

Fine, maybe her uncle wasn't being a complete dick. At least he sent in Xander, she was the best tracker in the Northwest. "So Xander found me."

Gavin shook his head. "We got a call en route that Tala Whiteriver found you."

Recognizing the name, Raine blinked. "Blonde? Tall? Has a pet wolf?"

His eyes narrowed and tension tightened his jaw. "You met her?"

"In a manner of speaking." She went to raise her right hand to rub her aching head only to find she couldn't. Looking down, she finally noticed the splint. "She was in my dream."

She turned back to Gavin, only to catch a shadow rising behind him. Her body moved before her mind clicked in. She was half way out of the bed before he stopped her.

Firelight flared and illuminated the tall blonde in question. “Sorry to startle you.” The mocking tone undermined the words. “I’m glad to see you made it.”

“Not like you gave me much of a choice.” Raine tried not to groan as Gavin helped her lay back down.

The tinkling of Tala’s laughter floated through the air. That laugh was dangerous. It rang around Raine, pressing her to drop her guard and relax her defenses. The false sense of security had her refocusing on her mental shields. The woman must have some Fey running through her blood to pull off such glamour against another Kyn. Especially one with Fey blood. *Tricksy, very tricksy.*

Tala moved around Gavin to lay her hand across Raine’s sweat beaded brow. “Good try, warrior, but you need the rest.”

Warmth seeped into her bones, leaching the pain away, allowing her muscles to relax. She could feel her eyes growing heavy. “No, don’t want to sleep,” her voice slurred.

“*Shh.*” Tala’s voice was soft. “You need it.”

Gavin’s fingers stroked down her arm, and Raine clenched his hand tightly.

He squeezed back. “I’ll be right here.”

She let her eyes flutter closed. There was a brush of warmth on her forehead, but it was so faint maybe she imagined it. Regardless, it made her feel safe. Holding his hand, she fell into the waiting darkness.

CHAPTER 3

When Raine opened her eyes, sunlight was drifting across her face. The spicy scent of burning wood layered the air. She lay in a comfortable bed, and it took a minute to realize it no longer hurt to breathe. Moving her head slowly, she released a small sigh of relief when nothing complained.

She let her attention roam around the silent room. This was not the same place of drums and firelight. There was a simple wooden dresser with a mirror, sitting on the same wall as a partially opened door.

Rolling to her side to sit up, she pushed away the patchwork quilt. Remembering the splint on her right arm, she stopped short. She looked down and found her arm bare, no splint in sight. Weird. Although Kyn healed much faster than humans, it still took time to heal the kind of damage she sustained. Testing her arm, she used it to prop herself up. It was sore, but held. She rolled her shoulder to find the same there. Sore, but movable.

Time to test her leg. She sat up, the oversized T-shirt riding high on her thighs. A lingering scent teased the edges of her mind, but it disappeared the memory of her thighbone snapping in half rose. Ghostly echoes of pain crawled over her body. She focused on keeping her breathing under control as she ran a shaky hand over her undamaged thigh. Well, undamaged if you didn't count the weird hand-shaped scars from her last adventure. She took her time getting to her feet, not letting go of the bed until her shaky legs steadied. Unwilling to trust her balance, she used the dresser to hobble to the door.

Passing the mirror her reflection brought her up short. Hell, she could give the Grim Reaper a run for his money. Wincing she tried to smooth the tangled mess of her long, dark hair. It didn't take her long to give up. Her gray eyes were sunk in bruised shadows and her cheekbones pressed white against her abnormally pale skin. The too large T-shirt revealed the old scar collaring her neck, but the colorful artwork ringing her upper arms was hidden under the short sleeves. Thankfully, there seem to be no new scars in her existing collection.

Turning away, she pulled the door open. The sound of voices drew her down the carpeted hallway. She stopped in the entryway to lean against the wall and eyed the three people seated in the living room.

Gavin's long frame was slumped into a big easy chair, his booted feet stretched toward the fireplace with its merrily snapping flames. Seeing new lines in his face, probably brought on by recent exhaustion, she fought the urge to offer comfort knowing damn well he'd push her away. He didn't appear to be listening to the conversation of the room's other two occupants.

Tala sat on the edge of a small couch, elbows resting on jean clad knees. Her face was somber and one hand absently combed between the ears of the black and gray wolf resting its head on her knee. "There were no clues left around the car. As good as Cheveyo is, he can't just disappear into thin air."

"There was a blood trail." The comment came from the woman curled on a larger sofa across from Tala. Between the mesmerizing tattoo tracing delicate patterns from temple to chin on the right side of her face, and her wild hazel eyes shot through with gold, Xander was nowhere near forgettable. "Granted most of it was Raine's, but there was a small amount of Cheveyo's on the other side of the car."

Tala's knuckles whitened on the wolf's ruff, her mouth curving down into a frown. "A small amount means he wasn't gravely injured." Her voice carried a sharp edge.

"Maybe," Xander agreed, her gaze watchful. "He might not have taken a physical beating like Raine, but that doesn't mean he isn't seriously hurt. We still don't know what left the dent in the car's hood."

The witch opened her mouth to answer, when Gavin broke in, proving he was listening regardless of appearances. "Does it matter?" He aimed his attention at Tala, pining her with a steely glare. "We need to know why you asked Cheveyo to come down."

Raine moved forward, the hardwood floor creaking underfoot and snapping Gavin's attention to her. Taking in her appearance, his gaze narrowed. An unwelcome shimmer of female vanity woke, but she shoved it away. Granted, she wasn't at her best, but still...

Whatever had attacked her and Cheveyo had managed to kick her, but at least she was still standing. So was Cheveyo. She clung to that belief even as lurking shame and fear curled in her belly. Gritting her teeth, she tamped them both down. Damn it, she would get through this, and so would Cheveyo.

Caught in her thoughts, she was startled into taking a quick step back when she Gavin suddenly stood in front of her, his hand out to help. At her visible retreat, his hand dropped. Obviously taking her reaction wrong, he stiffened slightly and a shadow passed over his face leaving it unreadable.

Misery flashed through her and unable to deal with her unstable emotions hidden, she retreated behind her familiar blank face. "What the hell is going on?" She looked beyond him to include Xander in her question.

She took a step, stumbled, and her hand automatically reached out to brace. Gavin caught her before she could fall. His arm curled around her waist as she clutched at his arm. He drew her shaking body closer, his heat warming her cool skin. Another kind of heat flared, and burning her fear to ash and leaving her wanting something she didn't deserve.

"What are you doing out of bed?" His growl sent unsettling vibrations down her spine even as he pulled her in tight.

Uncomfortable awareness washed through her as she tilted her head back and snapped, "My job."

He caught her furious gaze with and his lowered his head. "You're barely able to stand," his rough voice scraped over her nerves

Realizing how close his mouth was, the heat inside her body went up a notch. Memories of their last shared kiss seared across her brain. Her breath caught and her tongue nervously wet her lower lip. The revealing movement on her part caused an equally apparent reaction in him. One she couldn't miss feeling. Her gaze widened and her traitorous body melted. A discrete cough reminded her they had an audience.

Gavin wasn't done chewing her ass out. "You're too weak to be out of bed."

Weak? She hissed at him like a cat. No one called Raine McCord weak. "Let me go!"

He snarled under his breath, but dropped his arms and stepped back.

She forced her legs to work and aimed for the nearest couch. Unfortunately, it was already occupied by Tala. Raine considered the longer trek to Xander's couch, but nix it when the room took a slow spin. She took a seat next to the smart-ass witch.

"Nice to see you up, Sleeping Beauty," Xander's greeting cut through the tension filled air.

Breathing through her body's numerous complaints, Raine sat back carefully and flipped Xander a one-finger salute.

Not taking offense, a small answering smile played around Xander's mouth.

"Any word on Cheveyo?" Raine shifted another pillow to her right side, trying to get comfortable.

Next to her, Tala shook her head, but Gavin answered, "No, we were just getting to why Cheveyo was invited down here in the first place." Settling in his chair, his attention turned to the witch.

Tala's fingers continued to move over the wolf next to her. "I asked him to come down and consult on a situation I'm dealing with."

Raine stayed quiet. Based on her experiences with the Kyn leaders, demanding a straight answer from Tala would get them nowhere. In fact, such an approach would generally garner the opposite reaction. If anyone could get information from the witch, it would be Gavin. He was a damn pied piper of females.

Not easily discouraged, Gavin pushed. "And that situation would be?"

Tala took her time answering. "Someone's murdering innocents under my protection."

Her response dropped in to the room, its ripples brushing against the protective instincts of the three hunters. Xander straightened, her golden gaze sharpening, while the sudden stillness of a waiting predator fell over Gavin. For Raine, the words were the phantom touch of a cold finger on her neck. She fought the urge to shiver as her skin pebbled.

Killing in its varied forms was not a mystery to any of Tala's visitors. They were elite Kyn warriors, known as the Wraiths. An ancient collection of races, the Kyn co-existed with their human cousins. Most humans considered the Kyn mere fairy tales. Unfortunately, when those fairy tales came to violent, vicious life, mortal authorities didn't stand a chance. That's when the Wraiths were called in.

"Start at the beginning," Gavin demanded with a startling abruptness.

Tala's lips tightened and her spine snapped straight at his command.

Noting her reaction, he visibly gritted his teeth before adding, "Please."

Her pursed lips relaxed fractionally, but her spine remained ramrod straight. "A couple weeks ago, Daniel, one of our younger witches, went missing. His pickup truck was found abandoned on the side of the highway between Flagstaff and Page, in the middle of reservation land. The truck was perfectly fine, nothing wrong with the engine or tires. There was no sign of a struggle and his cell phone was on the passenger seat with a full charge."

"Did you have someone try to track him?" The question came from Xander.

Tala nodded. "We had one of our local shifters come in. He tried to track Daniel, but the scent disappeared a few feet from the truck."

"That doesn't make sense." Xander frowned. "Scent can't just disappear. There should've been some sort of trail."

"I agree with you, but I was told the trail 'went blank.'" Grim amusement played over Tala's face. "Since tracking is not my forte, I have to take him at his word."

Before Xander could push, Gavin interrupted, "What happened after this Daniel disappeared?"

"For a week, nothing," Tala answered. "We searched everywhere, used every tool we had. We couldn't find him. His parents swore he wouldn't just take off. He was trying to save money to go to school next year. Most of the families out here struggle to keep food on the table."

Raine finally spoke up. "Was he the only one to disappear?"

"No." Tala's hand stilled on her wolf, her lashes coming down to veil a sudden spark of checked anger. "He's the fourth one in the last three months."

Raine was stunned as Tala's unexpected response. "Four?"

"Four." Strain crept through Tala's voice. "Two witches, one wizard, and one shaman. They're a combination of male and female, between the ages of eighteen and forty-two. None of them seem to have anything in common, other than the fact that they live around here." She raised her chin, guilt and anger struggling over her face. "We're being hunted and we have no idea who's hunting us. Protecting my people is paramount, so I turned to an old friend for help."

"Cheveyo," Raine murmured.

Tala's gaze dropped to the wolf at her feet. "Daniel's body was found the day before I called Cheveyo. We identified him with dental records."

Raine was surprised to see Tala battling for emotional control. It was unusual for the head of a Magi House to be so transparent. Maybe Tala was as young as she looked, a rarity among the Kyn. But if that was true, had Tala had been given the position at too young an age?

Normally the most powerful, most controlled, and sometimes the most ruthless member of a Kyn House became the one in charge. Tala Whiteriver did not seem to fit the mold. Yeah, she could shred a person with words alone, but she wore her emotions too close to the surface.

Or maybe Tala was a damn good actress who lured Cheveyo here for some other reason. *Cynical much?* Maybe, but she was still breathing, wasn't she? Either way, something was definitely going on here. "What happened to Daniel?"

Tala lifted her head and Raine suppressed an instinctive flinch at the raw emotions turning Tala's eyes into bottomless pits of night. "They broke every bone, then they nailed him in place and skinned him alive." Her voice was eerily blank. "From what the coroner could tell, he was alive during the entire process. Cause of death was a slit throat."

Silence ticked through the room. The image Tala painted hung like a smothering shroud.

"It would require a great deal of magic to keep someone alive and aware through all of that." Gavin's voice was matter of fact in its tone. "Most people pass out from the overload of pain."

"True." Raine met his gaze. "Whoever is doing this would need someplace well hidden, well insulated, and they'd need the right tools. Not to mention they would have to have a strong control of dark magic, otherwise it could turn on them."

Tala made a choking sound, bringing both of their attention back to her. Something that sounded like a cross between a sob and dry laugh escaped. "Those were just the physical signs. There was more."

Picking up the reluctance in her voice, Gavin's green eyes sharpened. "What do you mean, 'more'?"

Faint color dusked her cheeks. "I needed answers, so I brought in a necromancer."

Raine hid her shock. Bringing in a necromancer meant Tala had been desperate. Most witches stayed as far away from what was considered dark magic as they could. The whole three-fold law tended to be a karmic bitch. The belief that what you did would come back to you threefold put a damper on how far most witches were willing to go to achieve desired results. Which was why they left the darker territory to the wizards, or so she had been told.

"A necromancer would cost you," Gavin said.

A mocking smile touched Tala's mouth. "Everything costs, witch. Even you know that." Arrogance tightened her face. "I did what I felt was needed."

Raine tried to keep the sarcasm out of her voice. "Was the information worth it?" At Tala's furious look Raine figured she hadn't succeeded.

"If Mulcahy hadn't vouched for you both, I would send you back. You forget who you are."

Before Raine could rip her a new one for her snide

comment, Xander's calm voice cut through the charged silence. "Tala, Mulcahy sent us because we're the ones who will stand before what is hunting your House. It's what we're trained to do."

Tala sneered. "Perhaps he should have sent someone more capable of doing their job." Her brown eyes raked over Raine. "Someone who could actually protect Cheveyo."

Raine took the well-deserved hit, but it didn't put a damper on her mouth. "Maybe he would have made a better decision, if he had known what exactly he was sending his chief magi into."

Tala's face colored with fury. "If I knew what we were facing, I wouldn't have called Cheveyo in, you bitch."

"But you did." Gavin's hard voice jerked Tala's focus to him. "What did the necromancer find out?"

"Nothing!" she hissed. "Not a damn thing!"

Tala's answer rang false to Raine. "What do you mean nothing? Shouldn't Daniel's spirit have been able to give you something?"

Tala rubbed her face with a shaky hand. "There was no spirit left."

Coldness settled into Raine's bones. That was impossible. There had to be traces, especially with such a horrific death. Sometimes a spirit wouldn't remember the whole traumatic death experience, but small pieces, enough so those left behind could find justice for them.

Xander broke through Raine's thoughts. "What do you mean?"

The witch's brittle laugh was short and cutting. "There was no soul, no spirit, no magic left in Daniel. Whatever butchered him managed to eradicate his very essence. Power like that belongs to one monster." She visibly swallowed. "It's called *Nomâhtsé'héōò Adanata*."

"Soul Stealer," Gavin's translation carried an aching hollowness.

Tala flinched as if slapped. Even Xander shivered.

Raine reeled in shock. "What in the hell is going on here? Why would anyone in your area raise a Stealer?"

"Why else?" Tala slumped forward, her anger draining away, leaving her face lined with stress and fear. "Revenge."

CHAPTER 4

The next morning, dressed in another oversized T-shirt, Raine huddled under a woven blanket while her toes curled against the wooden deck. Ducking her head, she drew the lingering scent of wild forests and something unique to its owner deep inside, finding comfort.

The sound of the sliding patio door opening was followed by a stronger version of the tantalizing scent as Gavin joined her. She watched warily as he leaned against the railing, crossing his arms over his broad chest. Sighing, she tried to stop her shiver as his heat curled around her. He faced her with serious, but watchful eyes.

Looking out to the yard, she avoided his penetrating stare and tried to ignore the feelings ricocheting inside her. She hated indulging in emotions, but this man tripped her every switch. The roiling mass caused a familiar confusion—something she wasn't ready to deal with. She felt weak, physically and emotionally. A dangerous combination with an even high price tag, one she wasn't willing to pay.

The silence stretched, tightened. He finally spoke. "Cassandra sends her regards."

White-knuckling the blanket, she nodded stiffly. "How's she doing?" It came out husky and she winced at the stupidity of her lame question. "Look, Gavin—"

He didn't let her finish. "You want to explain where you've been, Raine?" His voice was level, no accusations, just a simple question.

Too bad she didn't have a simple answer.

She shrugged, trying to release the tension riding her shoulders. "Finally took that vacation everyone kept saying I needed."

"Vacation?" A world of disbelief echoed in his voice.

"Yeah, you know those things we get four weeks each year for? One of those."

His derisive snort almost brought a smile to her lips. "You don't do vacations. That would be like a shifter going vegetarian." His dry humor had her looking at him. His arms dropped to rest on the porch railing. His intense stare belied his casual pose. "Xander told me what happened with Alexi. I'm sorry."

She felt her face smooth out as memories crashed through her—the feel of soft skin giving beneath raking claws, the need for blood, and snippets of searing pain made her breath catch in her chest. Alexi, a psychotic demon halfling, had teamed up with an equally self-absorbed mad scientist in an attempt to take out those she held responsible for her lover's death. Too bad Gavin ended up paying the price for Raine's misdeeds.

"I'm not." She forced herself to meet his gaze and say the words she should have had the balls to say weeks earlier. "If anyone should apologize it should be me. I'm sorry. More than you'll ever know, I'm sorry you paid the price."

One dark eyebrow arched. "You're apologizing? Raine

McCord? Thought the word didn't exist in your vocabulary?"

His sarcasm set her teeth on edge, but she took the deserved hit. "Yeah, I am. If I had paid attention, I would have stopped her before she turned you over to Lawson. If I had told you everything, instead of hiding it, maybe I'd have put the pieces together faster." Months of guilt tore its way to the surface. Why did it seem that everyone else paid for her mistakes? "If I had hit the lab earlier instead of waiting, I could have stopped what she did to you."

His harsh laugh was as good as a physical slap. "Good gods, Raine, you have the biggest ego ever."

Reeling from his accusation, her confusion morphed into a safer emotion, anger. Her eyes narrowed, fury overriding her lingering guilt. "Don't you dare call me egotistical!"

In a blink he went from an angry man to a silent predator, invading her space as he stalked her into a corner. Trapping her between his body, the railing and the cabin wall, he loomed over her.

Lowering his head until his auburn strands tangled with her black hair, he stared into her eyes from inches away. "It's not all about you, Raine." His nearness triggered an internal earthquake. "You did your job. The demon bitch's lover was a traitor, and you followed orders. A lover you didn't even know about. Best friend or not, you aren't responsible for her state of mind. You didn't introduce her to Lawson and make them the fucked up duo they became." Hard hands grasped her shoulders giving her a short, frustrated shake. "It wasn't your hand shooting some trippy ass drug into my bloody veins. It's not your mind trying to figure out what the hell they unlocked!"

"I'm sorry!" The ragged words were torn from her throat, her heart.

Suddenly she was jerked up, his low growl rumbling through his chest just before his lips closed over hers. The blowtorch of heat seared through her. Her hands released their death grip on the blanket to latch on to his shoulders. The contrast of the cold air against her over-heated skin sent shivers coursing over her body.

Her low moan broke free. Need had her dragging him closer, trying to crawl inside the man she should know better than to hold on to. All the promises she made herself in the past couple of months flew by the wayside. The flaring inferno erupting deep within drowned the quiet voice of sanity.

He dragged her closer, bringing her to her tiptoes. Her body begged for his touch, and she struggled to press herself against every inch of him. As her lips parted under his teasing tongue, he delved in, sparking wildfires in the lower half of her body. Losing herself in the kiss, she couldn't stop her tongue from dueling with his, revealing her unrelenting desire for control, even here.

He answered her demands with a series of sharp nips that stoked her needs even higher. Her body arched against his, searching for something just out of reach. His fingers tangled in her hair, the sharp tug adding another layer of need as he tilted her head back for better access. Just as she managed to free her own hands in retaliation, the sound of a discreet cough dropped like snow down her spine.

Stiffening, she tried to step back, but was locked into place by Gavin's hand in her hair. Her fist curled against his chest as he kept her head immobile, locking their gazes together.

"Yeah, Xander?" Gavin's voice rumbled in his chest, making it vibrate.

Raine's body's answering reaction set her teeth on edge.

"When you two are done with your discussion, we need to plan." The underlying laughter in the other woman's voice made Raine glare at the man holding her captive.

He kept his mesmerizing gaze on her face. "We're almost done."

A small snicker and a muttered, "Take your time," was quickly followed by the sound of the sliding door closing.

A taunt silence wrapped around them. She couldn't read his face but his intense regard made her uncomfortable. Tilting her head to the side, she pulled against his grip. A small flash of what could have been humor raced across his face. His very tempting lips twitched. Maybe she had a head injury? It would explain why her hormones decided to pick now for a full-on riot.

Giving a soft sigh, he let her step back, her hair unraveling from his hand.

Unable to think, much less come up with something cutting or witty, she bent down and picked up the fallen blanket. Wrapping it around her shoulders she tried to step around him, only to be stopped by his hand curling around her arm.

"You and I, Raine, we're not done with our discussion." His clear intent scared her more than any words he could have said.

CHAPTER 5

TALA NAVIGATED THE UNPAVED ROADS AS SHE DROVE THEM TO THE scene of the attack. Raine knew finding something Xander missed was a long shot, but Raine wanted to come back. Correction, she didn't want to come back, but the dread reducing her muscles to jelly meant sucking it up and doing her job.

Dressed in Gavin's T-shirt and her own jeans, Raine almost felt back to normal. Her leather jacket concealed the two wrist blades, and the knives tucked inside her boots were better than a security blanket. Their reassuring presence eased the small ball of fear generated by her impending return to the scene of the crime.

In the back, Tala's wolf forced Raine and Xander to share half the back seat so he could stick his head out the window. The open window allowed crisp, cold air to drift through the car, even as the heater valiantly tried to fight back.

Shoving a wall of fur out of her face, Raine asked, "What's his name?"

Tala shot her a look through the rearview mirror, eyebrows raised.

Raine tilted her head at the shaggy passenger. "Your wolf?"

"Ash." Tala's attention went back to the road. "His name is Ash, and he doesn't belong to me."

"Just doggy sitting, then?"

"Ash belongs to himself." Another quick glance in the mirror. "Like any wild thing, he chooses who to be with."

Ash turned his head. Meeting the unspoken challenge in his amber gaze, Raine's dormant wildness rose to answer. She held his stare, fighting the urge to bear her teeth. After a few tense moments, Ash huffed. It sounded suspiciously like a laugh. Before she realized what was happening, he leaned in and licked her from chin to forehead before hanging his head back out the window.

"What the hell?" She used her sleeve to wipe the dampness from her face.

Chuckling, Xander shook her head. "He thinks you're a pup."

"I so don't understand furry dynamics," Raine groused. "Pup I'm not."

Xander snorted. "Ain't that the truth, kitty cat."

This time, Raine didn't stop her frustrated growl.

Xander's hazel eyes were more gold than normal. "It's a dominance thing, McCord, a question of who'll back down first. In this case, Ash just has better control." She scratched behind the wolf's ear. "Besides, you're not a wolf."

"Or a shifter." Gavin joined the conversation from the front passenger seat even as he kept his attention on the road ahead.

Xander caught Raine's flinch and lifted her eyebrows in silent question.

Raine answered with a sharp shake of her head even as she snapped at Gavin, "You're not the only one trying to handle new and improved skills."

His shoulders tensed before he turned to pin her in place with a hard stare. Dark lenses hid his gaze, but something dangerous moved across his face.

Tala's, "We're here," earned a silent sigh of relief from Raine even as she added another conversation to her 'important things to talk about' list for Gavin.

All four Kyn piled out of the truck, Ash happily following. Raine trailed the others into the clearing as she shifted into professional mode. All the messy emotional crap was shoved to the back burner.

She walked the scene, trying to superimpose her memories on her surroundings. *The deer jumped out there. The car stopped about here. She and Cheveyo fought about here.*

She stopped, and did a slow turn, analyzing attack and defense positions. Over there, between those two trees, the night shadows would successfully hide an unseen attacker. Especially if your victims were busy scanning their surroundings.

She eyed the trees, moving closer to the spot and idea blooming. Under Cheveyo's relentless poking and prodding, she discovered a unique twist to her magic—an ability to track magical signatures. It wasn't common among the Kyn, and he used some esoteric explanation on how her little quirk worked, but she likened it to visualizing a living tapestry. Every thread unique, each allowing her to trace it back to someone or something specific.

Here's hoping the months of training with Cheveyo were about to pay off.

Lowering her mental shields enough to bring the tapestry to glowing life but not leave her vulnerable, she watched the signatures of her companions flare then settled into the overall undulating fabric of the world surrounding her.

Ash and Xander's threads mixed easily with the natural world, most likely due to their animal natures. Tala's held a bright gold hue, the color sharp and distinct. Witches, Raine discovered, straddled magic and nature instinctively, which accounted for the overall brightness of their colors.

Gavin's signature told a different story. It wove through the whole, complete with the bright edge exclusive to witches, but the blue strands fluctuated with darker flecks. His magic created its own path, warping the power around him. The closest example of such weird phenomena was her own altered magic.

Shaking off her curiosity, she reached for her magic. Nothing answered. Her breath stalled. Clenching her fists, she tried again. Nothing. Narrowing her focus, she reached deeper. *There!* She gathered the fragile energy, anchoring it before spinning a tendril through her shield's opening, searching for any residual traces of her attackers.

An unnatural, oily blackness clung close to the trees. Moving forward, she noticed the closer she got, the more the sense of wrongness grew. Intent on tracing it, she reached out with psychic fingers. Inky tendrils curled around her psychic touch leaving burning icy in its wake as it burrowed through her magic.

With an unexpected suddenness, her unruly magic raged to life. Her muscles locked as she fought for control even as she tried to fend off the faint traces of tainted power. A low, ache set up shop at her temples.

Before she could tighten her grip on her power, her memories rushed forward like a sucking wave, forcing air from her chest as debilitating fear found a foothold. Frantic, she reached for the protection of her magic only to have it slipped through her fingers like mist.

Her heart slammed against her chest. Reeling, she frantically tried again, desperate to find the magic needed to weave a defense. Through her rising panic, she caught a spark and snagged the delicate strand. It was so faint, but the effect was instantaneous.

Her power flared white hot, obliterating the black tendrils. Unfortunately, it also sliced her psychic probe short, sending a sharp pain ripping behind her eyes. When her vision cleared, the edges were white and blurry and where her magic once sat felt hollow. Clammy sweat coated her skin and her knees were weak. A firm grasp on her arm kept her from falling.

"Raine? What happened?" From Gavin's tone, it wasn't the first time he'd asked.

She shook her head. Something was wrong with her magic. The haunting memory of cold, painful fingers plucking her apart left nausea threatening to rise. Without her magic, going up against this thing was suicidal.

Unsettled, she wrenched away from Gavin and stumbled towards the car, her gaze darting around the clearing. Across from her, a rust colored stain about ten feet up a tree trunk snagged her attention. Memories collided with reality. Painful echoes of slamming into the tree left her cradling her still-sore ribs.

She took an unsteady step forward, forcing her gaze to the forest floor, trying to stem the nightmares in her mind. Small drops of blood spotted the dead leaves and branches scattered over the ground. Agony spiked through her leg and she could feel the ghostly hands snapping bone.

Struggling to find her way out of the past, she spun around. Through her reeling vision a broken branch, about two feet down from the first stain, sent searing pain blazing through her shoulder.

It was over, damn it! She screwed her eyes shut and clung to the silent mantra, trying to find a way free of the maelstrom of memories.

An unexpected sting on her lower lip snapped whatever spell held her. Her eyes opened to find Gavin cupping her face, his eyes dark with worry. He leaned in and gave her another sharp nip. Air shuddered out of her stalled lungs, loosening the bands tightening her chest. He raised his head, watching her carefully.

"What the hell?" she rasped, her tongue tracing over her stinging lip.

His hands dropped to curl around her upper arms, holding tight. "You were stiff as a board, not breathing."

"So you bit me?" She tried pulling back, but he wouldn't let go.

"I was going to slap you, but that left your hands free. I didn't want to get slapped back." Wicked male amusement curled his lip. "Besides, biting works faster than CPR."

Narrowing her eyes, she stomped on his foot.

Chuckling, he released her and stepped back.

She turned to find Tala and Xander huddled near the weirdly shadowed trees. Not wanting to rehash what just happened, Raine raised her voice, keeping it firm. "That thing threw me all the way across the clearing." She jerked a thumb at where the blood still stained the ground behind her. "It held me there and took pieces of me."

Tala began walking closer. "What pieces?"

Since Raine didn't have an answer to that question, she forced her legs to move and resumed her study of the clearing. She found the drag marks first. She followed them. Blood smeared here and there as if an injured animal tried to crawl away. An old emotion, one she thought long gone, rose. Mortified shame rose, but she kept to the trail, hearing the others follow behind.

Minutes passed, and a clinical part of her was amazed at how far she managed to crawl despite her injuries. She finally came to the fallen tree she hid behind and stopped. She turned to study the path she made when crawling, trying to step outside the morass of her emotions, to pretend it wasn't her attack she was tracking, but someone else's.

With her emotions locked down, the details began to bug her. "Why didn't it follow me?" she mused out loud.

Xander came up on her side. "It had what it wanted."

"I don't think so." Raine cocked her head, thinking it through. "It had Cheveyo, but it wanted to chase, to play." She remembered that. "It wasn't done with me, yet."

"It almost killed you," Gavin growled.

She looked at him. "Almost doesn't count in our world. It's a hunter. It should have kept going until I was dead. It didn't."

"It's on a leash," Tala chimed in.

Raine nodded, recalling the brief glimpse of someone who was not Cheveyo before she passed out the second time.

"So how strong do you have to be to keep something like this on a leash?" She was amazed at how steady her voice sounded. No outward sign of the fractures threatening her sense of self. Ironic that she would panic at the thought of losing the twisted magic she spent years cursing. Now she wanted it back, every frightening piece of it.

"If it's a Soul Stealer, you'd have to be really damn strong," Tala said quietly.

Gavin folded his arms across his chest. “Who fits that description in your Houses?”

Tala opened her mouth to answer, but branch snapped nearby. Xander raised her hand for silence. Gavin, Xander and Raine spread out in front of Tala, their Wraith training coming to the fore. Ash crouched at Tala’s side, his muzzle flared in a silent snarl. Raine palmed a wrist blade just as two forms slinked out of the surrounding forest.

The concealing shadows fell away to reveal two oversized wolves, one dark and one light. They stopped short and sat at the edge of the clearing. Before Raine could move, a man with a rifle cradled in his arms stepped clear of the forest. “Tala!”

Short and stocky, he fit every preconceived notion Raine held of a rancher. His barrel chest was covered in a faded, long-sleeved, blue-green plaid shirt with a gray thermal underneath. Worn jeans met the scarred leather of well-used boots.

The man stepped in front of his two furry bodyguards and continued forward, his worn felt cowboy hat shading his expression.

Gavin and Raine shifted to block his path to Tala, while Xander stepped back next to Ash.

The rancher stopped a few feet away, the glimmer of his white teeth startling in the tanned face. “Whatcha doin’ here, Tala?”

“I should ask you the same thing, Tomás.” The witch pushed her way between Gavin and Raine. “Step back and let me introduce the Southwest Alpha of the Red Thunder Pack, Tomás Chavez.”

Raine snagged Tala’s arm, halting her before she could step closer to Tomás.

Tala stiffened, raking her with a death glare.

Unimpressed with Tala's temper, Raine didn't remove her hand. "He's armed, you aren't. Considering what's happened, I'd rather not lose a second magi."

A sharp pain at her wrist left Raine's arm momentarily numb, allowing Tala to jerk free. The witch stepped into Raine, her extra couple of inches allowing her to stare down into Raine's face. "I'm never unarmed, girl."

Not bothering to shake the numbness from her arm, Raine leaned in to whisper back, "Neither am I." She gave Tala a feral smile.

Tala looked down their bodies to find Raine's blade poised delicately above her kidney.

Raine held still, knowing she had no business taunting the witch, but unable to help it. Before she could step back, Tala surprised her with a quick kiss. Startled, Raine stumbled back, her blade falling to the ground. *What the fuck was that?*

Tala's laughter rang out while Raine crouched down to pick up her blade and hide the furious blush searing her face. When her blade was back in its wrist sheath, and the stupid heat in her face was under control, she glared at the still laughing witch.

"Oh gods, Raine," Tala gasped. "Your expression was priceless!"

Rattled and off kilter, Raine snapped, "Glad to amuse." She didn't dare look at Gavin or Xander. Hell, it was all she could do, not to slap Tala, a move more suicidal than threatening her with a blade.

Chuckling, Tala continued toward Chavez. "Tomás, let me introduce you to our visitors. This is Gavin Durand, Xander Cade, and Raine McCord."

Moving his rifle to his side, Tomás held his hand out to Gavin. "Pleased to meetcha."

At some point during Raine's exchange with Tala, Xander managed to move to Raine's side. Probably worried she'd need to step in and keep the witch from killing her, Raine thought with grim amusement.

Tomás offered Xander his hand. "Ms. Cade."

Raine found Xander's reaction interesting. The other woman shook the dark-haired man's hand, but kept her eyes focused over his shoulder, avoiding direct eye contact.

Tomás turned to Raine. "Ms. McCord."

She met his gaze without hesitation, even as the electric tingle she associated with all shifters ran up her arm. Going by the slight widening of Tomás's eyes, she wasn't the only one who felt that little jolt.

Introductions done, Tala asked her question again. "What's going on?"

"I'm missing a wolf." Tomás's voice carried a rough edge, the anger lying just under the surface reflected in his tense jaw.

Tala searched his face. "Who?"

"Jeremiah Davis."

"Did you go to the authorities?" Gavin asked, drawing Tomás's attention.

The older man snorted. "Son, out here the human authorities deal with the humans and we deal with our own. As long as you can pass for human, most agencies are comfortable pretending the Kyn are humans with a few—" he made quote marks with his fingers "—special skills."

Xander asked, "If you can't pass?"

"There are still varmint laws on the books in this state." Darkness settled over the alpha's face as tension crackled in the air. "A wolf is just another varmint, regardless of the skin it's in," he continued. "Especially if certain respected people claim to be losing cattle to rabid wolf packs."

As the bitter bite of his words faded into the strangely silent forest, the two wolves sitting behind the alpha moved to his side. An uncanny intelligence shone in both canine gazes, and Raine realized she was staring at the alpha's guards.

With heavy sigh, Tomás banked his churning energy, dialing it down.

Gavin got their conversation back on track. "What was Jeremiah doing?"

Tomás grimaced. "Following a lead on Daniel."

"He's your tracker?" Xander asked. When he nodded, she continued, "He told Tala there was no scent to track. That it disappeared. So what lead was he following?"

Obviously not used to being questioned, a soft growl escaped Tomás. "The absence of a scent is as telling as a scent, girl."

The clear condescension in the alpha's answer left Raine worried she would have to pull Xander back. Raine didn't need the headache of explaining to Mulcahy why Xander flipped out and attacked the Southwest Alpha.

Instead of backing down, Xander's voice went soft which somehow made it more menacing. "Our chief magi is missing, our Wraith was attacked, and we've come down here to help. Only we're being kept in the dark. We can't do our job if we don't have all the information. So if my questions displease you, take it up with my alpha, Warrick."

Raine silently cheered Xander. Shifters managed to corner the dominant male market, which made being female a bit of a bitch—no pun intended.

While Xander and Tomás engaged in a silent battle of wills silence stretched and tightened.

"Enough!" Gavin snapped.

When both shifters' heads swiveled toward him, Raine softly snorted. There was no missing how close the two wolves' animalistic sides were riding under their skin. Neither Xander's bright gold gaze nor Tomás's disturbingly dark one were anywhere near human.

"We need to focus, people," Raine interjected. "Where did your tracker do his vanishing act?"

Tomás flicked a hand back to the forest behind him. "About a mile out from here." He deliberately turned his shoulder to Xander and rested a hand on the lighter wolf's head, before continuing. "Carlos and Andrew reported it."

Looking to the wolves, Raine asked, "Carlos and Andrew?"

The lighter wolf sat back, tongue hanging out. The darker wolf remained standing, staring at her.

Tomás nodded. "The boys tracked him to a spot back there. Unfortunately, like I said before, the scent trail disappeared." Frustration carved deep lines in his craggy face. "There are some signs of a struggle, but no blood and no trail out of the clearing."

"Can we ask what brought you our way?" Xander's voice held no trace of her earlier anger.

Tomás answered in a similarly even tone. "Voices carry in the woods, Ms. Cade." Giving Raine an unreadable look, he added, "Besides, big cats aren't native to these woods."

CHAPTER 6

Xander closed in on Raine's side, but Raine gave a sharp shake of her head. "Is it a problem?" She kept an eye on Carlos and Andrew, her muscles coiled as she waited for his answer. In the small part of her brain not currently worried about becoming a tasty wolf treat, she wondered if she'd get a chance to explain any of this to Gavin. The low growls emanating from the darker wolf moved her odds closer to *probably not.*

Tala stood off to the side, watching but offering nothing. Raine figured the witch hoped Tomás would strip a few pieces off her hide.

The alpha wolf didn't move. When he finally spoke, his gravelly tone grated along her nerves. "No. No problem, Ms. McCord."

"If you all are done comparing who has bigger teeth, can we move on to figuring out what in the hell is going on out here?" Gavin's frigid voice cut in.

Hearing the fury riding under it, Raine shot him a quick look. Catching sight of the cold remote mask he wore, she winced. Yep, he was half past pissed.

"We should split up," Xander offered. "One group can start from where Jeremiah's scent disappeared and the other where Raine and Cheveyo were attacked."

Xander's suggestion triggered a question from Raine. "Mr. Chavez, did you or your men notice anything different about where Jeremiah was taken from?"

"Different how?"

Explaining magic sucked. Trying to explain an unknown ability to someone familiar with magic was even worse. Raine did her best to keep it simple. "Just different. Echoes of something that didn't belong, maybe?"

The alpha's puzzled stare meant she was bungling it.

Fortunately, Xander rode to Raine's rescue. "In the clearing were there residual traces of magic? Similar to faint scent markers? Something that felt off or missing?"

The lighter wolf shifted on his haunches, drawing his alpha's attention. Tomás cocked his head, listening to something no else could hear. Xander once explained the ability to hear your pack, regardless of the form they wore, was a nifty perk of being the top dog.

"Carlos says near one side he thought there might have been a dead rabbit or something. The scent of rotted flesh was old, really old." Tomás's lips flattened. "He was going to go and investigate, but when he stepped forward to search the temperature dropped slightly. Then we heard you."

"Why do you ask, Raine?" Anger still frosted Gavin's voice.

She absolutely hated when he used that tone with her, and her sharp reply made that abundantly clear. "The traces of whatever magic attacked Cheveyo and me left a twisted echo of itself behind."

"You see magic?" Tala's voice was carefully neutral.

Raine stiffened. "I've been working with Cheveyo in the last few months learning to trace magical signatures. This was unlike anything I've run across."

Something in the solemn look Tala and Tomás shared made her nervous. Tala turned back to Raine, giving her a considering look. "Were you able to track the traces just before you..." here she paused, as if searching for a word, "... froze?"

Giving Tala a short nod, Raine was grateful the witch hadn't chosen another, more accurate word.

Tala blew out a silent breath. "We need to see what you can sense where Jeremiah disappeared." She tucked a loose strand of hair behind her ear. "In the meantime, I have to meet with a couple of people."

"Take Gavin," Tomás ordered.

Tala shook her head. "I don't think so." Her sly smile left Raine bracing for whatever came next. No doubt, it was going to piss her off. Sure enough, Tala didn't disappoint. "He's seems to be the only one who can keep our little kitty cat under control."

Yep, before everything was said and done, Raine was going to hurt the Southwest Magi. She'd figure out a believable story for Mulcahy later.

CHAPTER 7

Xander and Tala headed back to the car accompanied by Ash and Carlos, the lighter of the alpha's two wolves. Gavin stayed close to Raine while Andrew kept pace with Tomás. The group backtracked to the second site.

Gavin didn't say a word or touch her. It didn't bother her—much. Her headache was morphing into a distraction she couldn't afford. Their ever-growing laundry list of necessary conversations simmered between them, leaving her concentration in shambles. As soon they were alone, Gavin would no doubt corner her for answers. *Oh joy!*

It didn't take long for them to reach the second site where Jeremiah pulled his disappearing act. Tomás stopped. "This is it."

Without a word, Gavin and Raine moved to opposite sides.

Taking a deep breath, she lowered her shields once again. Emptiness yawned shredding her confidence. Closing her eyes, she blocked out the whisper of doubt and pictured herself pushing against a solid mental door. It slowly gave way. The effort left sweat beading on her forehead.

Anticipating a wild rush of magic, she braced. Only nothing came. No familiar brush of fur under her fingertips indicating the leopard dwelling deep inside was awake. Not even a growl. Forcing her panic down, she reached into the seemingly empty space. A few heart stopping beats later, she felt delicate cobwebs brushed against touch. She went to grasp them, only to have them disintegrate into mist.

Her heart clenched as her magic slipped away. She couldn't function without it. Wild and unpredictable it may be, but it was hers. Utilizing every ounce of discipline she possessed, she tried again. This time, she coaxed and pleaded, attempting to lure the fragile power in.

Slowly, it answered wrapping around her wrist and palm, and twining through her fingers. Gathering it with every trick Cheveyo had shown her, she managed to send it outward.

Opening her eyes, relief filled her. The scenery was once more a surreal tapestry. Needing a focal point to start her search, she found Gavin's unique signature.

"See anything?" Tomás's voice came from behind and had her turning to find him and Andrew watching her.

"Give me a minute," she muttered. The dizzying colors settled until she could pick out the three men.

Tomás and Andrew stood to her right with Gavin behind them. Near the young ash trees, something snagged her attention. Like the flickering flame of a candle brushed by a breeze. Narrowing her eyes, she tried to bring whatever it was into focus. It didn't help. Ignoring her watchers, she moved closer.

The flicker came again.

For a moment, she caught a glimpse of something dark

hiding under the flowing colors. Instinctively she sent her magic in pursuit. It proved to be a bad move. With no warning, she was slammed with a cold so deep, her bones ached and her blood froze. Even the air in her lungs iced over.

Images flickered across her mind's eye like a bad reel of film. There was no logic to them, just bits and pieces. First, a wolf, swallowed by an immense shadow, then a man's face twisted in pain under a mask of blood. Whatever held her in its web dragged her deep until she was drowning in devouring darkness. Her body fought for air, but the invading magic and the cold held her paralyzed.

Brilliant light detonated, heat searing away the cold and darkness. The whisper of an unexpected voice swept across her mind, bringing a new power into play. The attacking darkness continued to pummel her in unrelenting waves.

Unable to rely on her magic, she reached for the only defense left, her leopard. A whirlwind of claws and teeth answered her call. They ripped through the cloying magic, shredding it, keeping it at bay, until she could slam her mental door closed. With her shields firmly in place, the warmth of the new power disappeared.

She opened her eyes to find in Gavin's arms once again. Light pierced her brain and the world shifted as she was lifted off her feet.

"I'm taking her back to Tala's." Gavin's deep tone rumbled next to her ear. "I don't know what the hell is going on, but this is the second time it's taken her out."

She missed Tomás's reply since she was trying not to throw up from the pounding in her head. Her body's barely healed injuries added their complaints to the mix. Mortified by the soft moans she couldn't stop, she curled closer to Gavin. His heat slowly penetrated the cold enveloping her limbs as his arms tightened around her. Oblivion nipped at the edges of her mind, but she fought it, trying to think because that voice she heard just before she got her shields in place? She could have sworn it belonged to Cheveyo.

CHAPTER 8

ONCE AGAIN, RAINE WOKE UP IN A STRANGE BED, DRESSED IN Gavin's long T-shirt and her underwear. Third time was the charm because this time she wasn't alone and she was warm. Heat poured from whoever lay behind her, cocooning her. Strong arms held her in a loose prison of latent strength. A strange contentment filled her. Half asleep, she snuggled back into the shelter being offered, letting her battered mind float.

"If you don't stop moving, you can go find your own bed." Gavin's low voice rumbled in her ear leaving chills in its wake.

Stiffening, she came wide-awake as it hit her. *She was in bed. With Gavin.* Oh, this wasn't good! Her dry mouth left her voice scratchy. "Wh—what happened?"

His arms tightened then eased. "I was hoping you could tell me."

Right, okay, she could do that. She let her breath escape in a slow exhale as she let her muscles uncoil. Unwilling to disturb the growing sense of intimacy, she kept her voice soft. "There was something like what we found at the first site."

"You followed it?" His question was equally quiet.

Clearing her throat, she whispered, "I tried."

She felt him move behind her, then he was gently turning her over. Lying on her back, her legs tangled with his, she found her hands pressed against his bare chest as he leaned over her, trapping her in his heat.

"What happened?" He searched her face, his scrutiny making her nervous. "Something's wrong. What are you hiding?"

She worried her lip, not wanting to answer, but the last time he asked such a question, she lied in an attempt to protect him. It backfired in horrific fashion, landing him in the hands of a demented scientist. After Raine fought to bring him back from the drug-induced madness, she swore never again. Despite her vow, it took everything she had to meet his gaze and give him the truth.

"I think," she swallowed hard choking down the lump in her throat. "I think when the Soul Stealer attacked me, it took something."

Confusion washed over his chiseled features. "What?"

She licked her dry lips and something hot sparked in his eyes as he followed the small movement. "My magic—" Her voice broke. "It doesn't respond right—if at all."

He arched an eyebrow. "Magic is, Raine. It exists and if it's there, you have it."

She gave a sharp shake of her head. "Every time I open my shields, it gets harder. Putting them back is almost impossible." Her fingers dug into his chest. "When I draw on my magic, it's not there."

He caught her wrists, holding her twitching hands still. "You can't lose your magic."

"You're sure about that, because I'm not." Frustrated, she pulled against his hold. "Don't forget, I know damn good and well how our abilities can be twisted and changed." Being a living experiment for warped human scientists taught her that lesson the hard way.

"Changed, yes, but take it away completely?" He shook his head as he let her go and rolled until he was lying next to her. "Dr. Lawson's injection ruptured my shields and twisted my magic into something new. It didn't take anything away, just increased what was already there."

Knowing it was time, she decided to tackle one of the topics she avoided to this point. "Yeah, well they didn't just level up my magic," she made the admission reluctantly. She kept her gaze adverted as she plowed through the whole truth. "My mother was a Fey Witch, and she never shared who my father was." She snuck a look at him from under her lashes. "The scientists that took us, they gave me a parting gift."

His face closed down. "What kind of gift?"

Instead of telling, she decided to show him. She lifted her left hand and reached down inside where her other half waited. Urging the faint brush of fur forward, she struggled to keep her transformation slow, breathing through the resulting ache as her bones shifted and reformed.

Finished, she looked up to find Gavin no longer lying next to her. Instead, he was crouched over her in eerie stillness. His gaze locked on her hand that was now a black, fur covered paw. She held her breath, waiting for his rejection. He used one long finger to trace from her retractable claws to her very human elbow, sending shock racing through her. His small touch upended her world.

"Kitty cat, uh?" His voice came out rough, but a small smile curved his lips.

His unexpected reaction left her speechless. Where was his anger, his revulsion? She wasn't a shifter, had never been a shifter, until after the human scientists had finished their macabre games. Letting her arm shift back, she tried to untangle her body from his.

He thwarted her struggles by settling over her, trapping her legs with his, as he kept his upper body poised above her. Unless she was willing to hurt him, she wasn't going anywhere. Desire kindled and began a slow burn. The rasp of his bare skin set of a series of anticipatory shivers. The thin materials of his boxers and her panties didn't offer much in the way of protection. Tucked close against the clenching muscles in her lower stomach lay hot, hard proof that turning furry did not a turn him off.

"Gavin." Mesmerized by his unnerving and disturbingly intimate gaze, his name came out on a husky plea.

He lowered his head, his hard chest pressing into hers, one delectable inch at a time. The first soft brush of his mouth had her hands curling over his shoulders as she tried to drag him closer. His tongue traced her trembling lips until they parted, letting him in. He teased and tempted.

Spiraling need left her writhing beneath him. Her body stretched into a taunt line as he shackled her wrists and locked them over her head. When he raised his head, there was no missing the desire flushing his skin and turning his gaze into green fire. Her nipples peaked against the soft material of the oversized T-shirt. He released one wrist and cupped her aching breast. The heat of his palm as he lifted her aching flesh to thumb the peaked nipple had her spine arching in blind need.

Plunging her free hand into the silky stands of his hair, she tugged, needing his mouth back. "Kiss me, dammit!" Her demand came out on a groan.

His throaty chuckle stoked the raging fire higher. He shifted and his tongue traced a fiery trail from the base of her throat to curl just below her ear. One more destructive stroke before he released her breast to run his hand down her body and along her bare thigh. He skimmed his fingers over her sensitive skin, forcing her T-shirt up.

He was taking too damn long! With a growl, she forced him to his back with a very cat like move. She needed him—now. Need his taste, his heat that filled all those hollow cracks.

Fire raced through her veins as his mouth took over, teasing one moment, demanding the next. His tongue plundered and she answered. Gentleness fell by the wayside, replaced by ravenous hunger as desire wiped all but instinct and need away.

She crawled up his body, her tongue tangling with his, and straddled his waist, feeling the cool air of the room against her legs. It provided a startling contrast to the heat of his hands as they held her hips below the red lace edges of her high-cut bikini underwear.

Unable to keep her hands still, she ran her nails down his shoulders and over the planes of his chest, one she fantasized about for months. His low, appreciative groan filled the room when she trailed kisses down his strong jaw and along his neck. His muscles flexed as he arched into her touch.

She slid her hands down his sides, tracing delicate patterns, following the path of her wandering hands with her mouth, tasting him. His hand tangled in her hair holding her still as she indulged. Forcing her eyes open, she rolled her gaze upward as her tongue traced one male nipple. His green eyes darkened as the heat flared, but his hand didn't loosen.

“Raine, we need to stop.” Under her tongue she felt the rumble of his deep voice.

He wanted to stop? What the hell? Ignoring him, she focused on tormenting the man at her mercy. The impulse to mark him rode her hard. Giving in, she nipped.

Using his fist wrapped in her hair he gave a sharp tug. The small pain caused her to snarl and she curled her nails into his waist in protest. He held her fascinated for months and now he was here, under her. A situation she never thought would happen. She wasn’t stupid. If they stopped now, who knew when they’d be able to pick this back up?

“Raine.” This time her name was a reprimanding growl.

Please gods, don’t say he wanted to talk! Lifting her head, she found him watching her, determination clear in his flushed face. She narrowed her eyes. Determined to keep him distracted she stroked one teasing finger along the edge of his boxers.

With a growl, he rolled her beneath him and locked her hands above her head in one tight grip. He wrapped his free hand around her jaw, holding her still as he gave her one last, punishing kiss. “Enough.” He nipped her lip in erotic punishment, then with reluctance apparent in every move, pushed away from her to sit on the edge of the bed. “We’re expected downstairs.”

Disgruntled and frustrated, she rolled to her side and propped her head on a hand, watching the light play over his auburn hair brushing his shoulders. Without thinking, she reached out to trace the tattoo decorating his shoulder. “They can wait.”

“No, they can’t.” Capturing her wandering fingers, he brushed his lips over her knuckles, easing the sting of his answer. “It’s not healthy to keep an alpha waiting.” Desire faded under an unsettling seriousness. "We aren't done talking."

Damn it! Just when she thought she was safe. She yanked her hand away. "And when we are?" She'd be shocked and mortified at her behavior later, right now she ached.

He rose, the thin material of his boxers stretched to a breaking point. His dark chuckle drew her gaze up to catch a very male smile curving his lips. "Don't worry, baby. I promise to finish what we started." He moved to the dresser across the room and snagged a white T-shirt from the top drawer. Tugging it over his head, his voice was muffled as he added, "Somewhere private, where I don't have to worry about having an audience."

"What audience?" she grumbled as she sat up. Damn male was hell on her logic. She tugged her T-shirt down and brushed her tangled mass of hair back from her face.

"We're in Chavez's house," he explained as he grabbed a pair of jeans from a nearby chair and tugged them on.

Riveted by the denim gliding over long legs and then covering one of the best asses she'd ever seen, his words barely penetrated. When they did, a stupid blush burst to life. Damn shifters and their stupid hearing. Made privacy a thing of legend.

She swung her legs over the bed's edge just as another pair of jeans smacked into her back. Turning with an angry hiss, she snatched them up. "How long have we been here?"

"You were out a few hours."

Shoving her feet into her jeans, she stood and pulled them up, wiggling to get them up the last inch or so. Turning around, she caught Gavin ogling her ass, desire carving sharp angles into his face. Narrowing her eyes, she wagged a finger at him. "Uh-uh, Gavin. We're being summoned, remember?"

Stomping over to the light wood dresser, she found a hair tie right next to her boot blades. Behind her, he made a non-committal noise. Using the mirror, she pulled her hair back and met his gaze in the reflective surface. She watched him warily as he stepped close until the heat of him pressed against her spine.

He held her gaze with his equally serious one. "Tell me something."

Finished with her hair, she dropped her hands, please to see they remained steady. Keeping the minute distance between them, she turned and settled back against the dresser, folding her arms across her chest. "About?"

He placed his hands on the dresser, effectively caging her. His tantalizing scent wrapped around her until her fingers itched to touch. "I want to know why."

Confused, she frowned. "Why what?"

"Why now?" Color rode high on his cheekbones. "Why, after all these months, are you letting me touch you, hold you?"

Thrown by his unexpected question, she stuttered, "I—you—"

He cut her off. "You've driven me crazy since the minute I arrived." Self-mockery twisted his face into a grimace. "I waited for you, Raine." His harsh, almost painful laugh made her flinch. "I was stupid enough to believe that whatever this thing was that we started, would have you coming to me."

His words sliced against her heart. "I didn't think you wanted me around," shaky though it was, she finally found her voice.

With a disgusted snort, he straightened and stepped back. "So things get shitty and you run?"

Hurt and anger flared as his accusation stung deep. "I didn't run."

"What would you call it then?" His hands curled into fists at his side. "Do you remember our conversation outside of the Governor Hotel? Where you swore you would face whatever came with me?"

The memory was etched in her brain. Heading to a fancy party to eliminate suspects in a series of murders. Making the decision to share her past with him, fearing it would be enough for him to walk away. Only to find that instead of leaving her, he asked for a promise. '*If I'm going to get through this with you, you need to start facing things. Can you do that?*'

She nodded. "You were in no shape to keep hunting, but I could. I did." Her throat ached. "I got them both. For you."

"But you left, Raine." Something eased in his hard features, but his voice remained hard. "You stayed away."

Seeing the pain of her decision in the depths of his eyes, she tried to explain. "Because it was my fault, and there was no way you'd want me around as a reminder."

He cocked his head. "Says who? You?" She opened her mouth to respond but he held up a hand, cutting her off. "Don't ever make the mistake of making my decisions for me."

She compressed her lips mutinously, but her mind whirled. Was it easier to believe he wouldn't want her, than to believe he would? The shaming answer was, yes. After losing her mother and almost losing her mind in the cruelty of the labs, she locked her emotions down. Those few individuals she let in hadn't gotten far. Gavin was different. He got in deep, so deep it scared her.

Instead of giving him a chance to prove he would

cherish her gift, she'd taken it back, leaving him before he could leave her. In doing so, she screwed up. Again. *When would she get it right?*

Her shoulders slumped and she licked her dry lips. "I'm sorry." It came out as a whisper. Clearing her throat, she offered the only excuse available. "I warned you, I suck at relationships."

He quirked an eyebrow. "Is that what we have? A relationship?"

The ground under her feet might be shaky, but she knew one thing—if her answer didn't matter to him, they'd be having sex right now instead of "talking". So, if there was still a chance he'd take her, she'd risk it. "I hope so."

For a moment, silence reigned. Then, coming to a decision, he closed the distance between them. One hand curled around her neck, tugging her in. Using his waist for balance, she rose on tiptoes and met his kiss even as the bands around her heart loosened. She expected to be punished for her lack of faith, but the gentleness of his touch left her undone. Expecting him to punish her for her lack of faith, she was undone by the gentleness of his caress. Under the ever-present desire, something precious and fragile bloomed.

Ending the kiss, he held her as she rested her forehead against his chest. Closing her eyes, she absorbed his presence, the steady beat of his heart, as her riotous emotions calmed. Finally, she leaned back enough to see his face. "Are we okay?" She couldn't hide the worry in her voice.

He brushed his thumb across her lower lip, igniting butterflies. "For now." An enticing promise lurked in his eyes as he let her go and stepped back. "I'll figure out how you can make it up to me later."

Her stupid blush came back in full force, but it did nothing to stop the wicked images his promise evoked. Since going back to bed was no longer an option, she sighed and began searching for her boots.

"Got another question for you."

She stopped her search and looked at him. "Okay, might have an answer for you."

"What's going on between you and Cheveyo?"

A strange intensity emanated from him, leaving her on edge. She spotted her boots half hidden behind an end table and a chair. Taking a seat on the chair, she answered his question with one of her own. "You know I'm studying under Cheveyo, right?"

He gave a short nod. "Just not sure how that came about."

She grimaced as she pulled on one boot. "Okay, let's back up a bit. What do you know about what happened with Alexi?" Determine to keep her vow, she wasn't risking omitting any details.

He studied her. "From what I heard, you and the little psycho demon ripped into each other pretty good. However, since you're here and she's not, I can guess the ending."

Shoving the disturbing memories back into a corner, she snorted. "Considering who I faced, I utilizing what tools I could was my smartest move." She rubbed her suddenly chilled arms. "So, I decided to embrace my inner kitty cat, as you call it. I also made sure Mulcahy would be able to track her down and finish the job, if she actually managed to kill me."

His mouth tightened in disapproval. "What the hell did you do?"

"What I needed to." She dropped her eyes and gave an

uncomfortable shrug. "I used blood magic to leave a tracer behind." She kept her gaze on getting her other boot on.

"That was pretty damn stupid."

His criticism rankled, even if it was warranted. Jerking her head up, she snapped back, "Well fucking excuse me! I figured if I couldn't stop her, I'd make sure someone else could." Pushing to her feet, she moved to the dresser, frustration eating at her temper.

"It didn't matter." Heavy silence descended as she pulled in a shaky breath and picked up the blades. "Alexi had the same plan. So, by the time Xander, Ryder, and Cheveyo showed up, she was dead and I wasn't far behind." Catching his sharply indrawn breath, she held up her hand, putting a stop to whatever was coming out of his mouth. "Cheveyo brought me back."

"Brought you back?" Skepticism and something that sounded suspiciously closed to jealousy colored his voice. "How exactly?"

She liked hearing that small bite. Even if he was back to being pissed at her. How warped was that? "I'm not sure, but according to him we're tied together. He said the spell was given to him by some old medicine man years ago."

Hands grasped her shoulders and spun her around. "Tell me what the spell does, Raine." His voice was low and dangerously even.

Refusing to be intimidated, she lifted her chin. "It creates a doorway between two Kyn, allowing them to use each other's magics for defense or offense."

His eyes narrowed. "That means he can pull whatever he wants from you, whenever he wants, and vice versa?"

She shook her head. "It only works if the other gives permission. Otherwise, you're out of luck."

"Have you considered maybe that's what is interfering with your magic? Not the Soul Stealer?"

"You think Cheveyo's pulling on my magic?" He gave her a grim nod and she pondered that for a moment. "Maybe, but I'm not sure."

He searched her face. "Would you know if Cheveyo was dead?"

She nodded. "No doubt, but he's not. In fact, this last go around, right before I got my shields up, I swore I heard him."

Gavin let her go and paced away, shoving his hands through his hair. "Could you use your connection to figure out where he is?"

"I don't know. I haven't tried opening that doorway, and with my magic not responding right, I'm not sure I can."

"Fine," he replied. "Then let's get Tala and see if she can help us push that door open."

Raine was shaking her head before he finished. "Oh hell no. I don't want that witch poking around in my head." She bent and slid her blades inside her boots.

Gavin didn't back down. "It can't matter what you want. Cheveyo is missing and you're our only link. We need to use our tools."

His words were a sharp slap, jerking her upright, but she kept her face averted so he wouldn't see her flinch. Hearing him say that hurt. Logically, she understood. To save their magi required using whatever and whoever they could. Their job demanded they put aside their personal feelings and do what they were sworn to do.

Unfortunately, his words scraped against old resentments birthed by her uncle, Ryan Mulcahy. As the head of the Northwest Fey House and Captain of the

Wraiths, he considered her a tool, simply something to be used. That well-honed anger rose.

Gavin took a step towards her, his brow furrowed. She jerked away and slid around him, staying out of reach. Without looking at him, she got to the bedroom door and yanked it open. "You're absolutely right. What I want can't matter."

CHAPTER 9

Early evening light flowed over wood floors, casting soft shadows as Raine stalked down the hallway, following the low murmur of voices and the subtle clinking of dishes. She stopped inside the entrance to a large kitchen where Tomás and a couple of men sat at a long, scarred wooden table. At the stove, a woman about Raine's height stirred something in a large pan. A spicy aroma filled the air. Raine's stomach gave an audible growl.

Conversation stopped, and Tomás looked up. "Raine." His gaze focused over her shoulder. "Gavin. Come on in and have something to eat."

Gavin slipped by her, his body deliberately brushing hers, leaving chills behind. He took an empty chair next to a dark haired male who seemed familiar. With no choice, Raine took the remaining seat across from Gavin.

The woman at the stove turned, holding an empty plate, while flashing a quick smile at her. "Chili and cornbread?"

"Please," she answered.

The woman nodded, raised an eyebrow at Gavin. When he repeated Raine's answer, she turned back and began dishing up the food. She was dressed in what Raine was coming to think of as standard western wear—faded jeans, boots, and a T-shirt. Her brown hair was pulled back in a serviceable ponytail, and her skin held a light tan sprinkled with freckles.

"My wife, Lizbeth," Tomás said. "She's a great cook, but if you don't like spicy food you may want to take it easy."

With a quiet laugh, Lizbeth set the full plates in front of Raine and Gavin, her hazel eyes open and friendly. "I kept it tame this time, no worries."

As Gavin and Raine ate, Tomás introduced the other two men at the table. "This is Eric, my foreman."

Judging by the gray streaking through his brown hair, Eric was older than Tomás. A crooked nose sat among the weathered lines on his smiling face as he held out a scarred, tanned hand. "Hello."

Taking his hand, Raine noted the calluses, but no flare of electricity. Eric wasn't a shifter, but that was the best she could determine with her erratic magic.

"And you've met Andrew." Tomás indicated the younger man next to Gavin.

The dark haired wolf shot them both a nod and then went back to his food.

"Were you able to get in touch with Tala and Xander?" Gavin directed his question to Tomás.

The alpha nodded. "They'll be here in about twenty minutes."

Eric pushed back from the table, empty dishes in hand. "If y'all will excuse me, I need to get back out to the yard. I have a few more things to do." He nodded to the table in general then his dishes to the sink. A few minutes later, he left.

Lizbeth took over Eric's chair and stirred her bowl of chili. Worry clear in her furrowed brow. "Tomás explained you're here to help catch whoever took that poor child, Daniel."

Tomás traced a gentle finger over the back of his wife's hand as it rested on the table. They shared a look until a sad smile broke over Lizbeth's face.

She turned her hand over to entwine her fingers with her husband's and turned back to Gavin and Raine. "My heart goes out to his parents. It's so hard to lose child."

Echoes of sorrow hung heavy in Lizbeth's voice, and Raine knew at some point, Lizbeth, too, had lost a child.

"Were you able to pick anything up at the last site, Raine?" Andrew asked with a slight, exotic accent, drawing attention from Lizbeth's quiet grief.

Unable to place it, Raine focused on her half-eaten chili and shrugged. "Snatches of images, nothing that made any sense."

Tomás eyed her. "Same thing you found at the other site?"

"Same magical traces." She recalled the images of the wolf and the bloodied face of a man. "Do you have a picture of your missing wolf?"

"Jeremiah?" Lizbeth frowned. "I think so. Let me go check." She pushed away from the table and left the kitchen.

Andrew caught Raine's gaze and held it, his challenge clear. Since she faced bigger and meaner things than this alpha's second, she refused to drop her eyes. Andrew gave her a grim smile before turning to watch Lizbeth walk back into the room.

"Here you go." She handed over a picture.

It was a group shot of five men. Raine recognized Tomás and Andrew standing behind a dark haired youth about eighteen. The kid was holding something shiny toward the camera. There was a blond man to the right of Tomás. The last male was a younger version of the one she saw with a bloodied face.

"It was taken about six years ago." Lizbeth stood behind Raine, pointing out faces. "Tomás, Andrew." She pointed to the blond. "That's Carlos." Her finger moved to the man next to him, confirming Raine's guess. "That's Jeremiah."

Raine cleared her throat. "The kid in front?"

Tomás's wife tensed before blowing out a small breath. "My son, Brett." Her voice was shaky, but level. "He just won first place in a rodeo." Her finger brushed over the image. "He died just after this was taken."

Raine handed the photo back, sympathy keeping her voice soft. "I'm sorry for your loss."

A return of that small, sad smile echoed the grief in Liza's hazel eyes. "Me, too."

Tomás cleared his throat regaining Raine's attention. "Recognize anyone?"

She gave a sharp nod. "Jeremiah. I saw him bloodied, but fighting. I don't know if he's still alive."

"This normal for you?" Andrew bit out.

"Which part?" she snapped back. "Getting my ass handed to me by some shadow monster? Seeing fleeting images that don't make sense? Or playing with dark magic that seems to have a taste for me?"

"Any of it." Andrew's smile was a baring of teeth. "All of it."

Rage bubbled up, comforting in its familiarity. "Lately it

seems to be par for the course." Uncaring of the trouble her mouth created, she struck back at him. "How normal is it for you, wolf boy? Besides the Stealer, what else do you have running around here that you can't seem to hunt down?"

Andrew snarled and lunged halfway out of his chair.

Gavin's sharp, "Raine!" was shouted over Tomás's equally sharp reprimand to his wolf.

Tomás kept a restraining hand on Andrew's shoulder while Raine sat back, her hands close to her blades. She appear unconcerned, but it wouldn't take much to draw her weapons.

"Enough!" Gavin's growl would do any shifter proud. He kicked out with one foot, pushing Raine's chair back a few inches. "Back off, Raine."

She shifted her focus, opening her mouth to tell him where to shove it, when phantom fingers closed around her throat in a gentle warning.

The unexpected touch left her blinking in shock. Gavin's gaze narrowed as she fought to keep her face blank. He held her startled gaze. She gave a brief nod of acquiescence. Those ghostly fingers relaxed and gave a gentle brush before disappearing altogether.

They were definitely continuing this conversation later. Especially since it appeared he managed to acquire a few new talents.

"Y'all need to settle back down," Tomás ground out, bringing Andrew to heel.

Raine slumped back in her chair, crossing her arms across her chest.

The alpha focused on Raine and Gavin. "Someone want to explain to me how y'all figure it's a Stealer?"

Gavin explained the lack of any spirit remnants in Daniel. "Soul Stealer is what came to mind."

"Could be other things," Andrew cut in, his previous anger banked.

"Like?" Gavin asked.

"Lots of legends in these parts." Andrew picked at his food. "The People still tell stories."

"Any in particular we should know about?" Gavin rested his arm on the table, waiting with deceptive casualness.

Andrew looked up, studying both Raine and Gavin. After a few moments, came to some sort of decision. "The Native American tribes have stories of spirits, angry and vengeful, which can be summoned and commanded to do tasks for their masters. Once the spirit is captured, the body remains an empty shell."

"None of that explains what happened to Daniel," Gavin said.

Raine didn't miss the tightness around Andrew's eyes. They were missing something. "Where do these spirits come from?"

"According to the legends, when someone dies before their time, their spirit stays behind." Andrew's voice was neutral as he stirred the chili on the plate in front of him. "Those spirits can be harnessed and used by a summoner."

His demeanor set off Raine's alarms. His movements were too casual, too controlled.

"Before their time?" she echoed. "Does the death need to be accidental or deliberate?"

The wolf's dark eyes were shuttered. "Either."

"So how many spirits could a summoner control?"

"Depends on the summoner."

The more Andrew spoke, the more dread curled in the

pit of her stomach. "Say the summoner loses control of these angry, vengeful spirits, do they just move on?"

Andrew's hand whitened as it tightened on the fork. "No."

When he didn't elaborate, she prodded, "What do they do?"

The wolf gave her a very unfriendly look. "They can turn on the summoner, or on those who still living that they hold responsible for their deaths."

"These spirits, who do the stories say raise them?" Gavin cut in. Nice to see he was catching the same strange undercurrents.

Tension tightened the air as Andrew shared an unreadable look with his alpha. Whatever the answer, she knew it couldn't be good.

"Witches." Tomás was the one who answered. "Chindis are raised by witches."

Politics were such a bitch. It would be so nice if just once, things could be a simple case of hunt down the murdering psychopath, kill it, and live happily ever after.

A heavy silence fell over the kitchen. After a few moments, Andrew went back to his dinner, while Gavin and Raine followed suit.

Plate empty, Raine thanked Lizbeth, and walked to the sink to rinse her dishes. Through the window, she caught sight of the approaching Jeep. "Tala and Xander are here," she informed the others. Drying her hands on the small towel, she leaned her hip against the counter, arms folded across her chest.

Gavin walked toward her, with plate in hand. He caught her look and gave her a slight nod.

Taking a deep breath she waded in. "Alpha Chavez, what do you believe is happening here?"

Tomás leaned back in his chair, his face still and serious. "To be honest, Ms. McCord, I'm not sure." His tone matched her formality. "However, I have to give consideration to each theory."

Each theory? "Just how many theories do you have?"

Tomás' lips thinned. "Soul Stealer is one. Chindis are a second." He gave a soft snort before raking a hand through his hair. "Hell, for all I know, we could have a good old fashion human serial killer with a taste for black magic."

The water shut off behind her. "Human?" Gavin asked. "Why would a human have it out for the Kyn in your territory?"

"Land." Strangely it was Lizbeth who answered. "Land is valuable and the prices have sky-rocketed in the last few years. Between the Red Thunder Pack and the lands deeded to the reservations, the Kyn hold a great deal of it."

"Wouldn't that mean if a human developer wanted your land, they would have to know about the Kyn?" Gavin pressed.

Lizbeth nodded. "It's not unheard of for a human with money to have enough contacts in the upper levels of government and military to have some concept of the Kyn's existence."

There was no arguing that. Raine continually wondered how long the Kyn were going to be able to keep their existence from the general population. The world was becoming smaller at an increasingly faster rate. If the Kyn didn't choose to reveal themselves soon, someone else was going to do it for them.

The doorbell rang and Andrew went to answer it. Moments later, muted voices reached the kitchen. Lizbeth rose from her seat. "Go, Tomás." She picked up her husband's dishes and headed to the sink, passing Raine and

Gavin. "Talk to Tala. See if you can figure out what's happening."

Raine shot Lizbeth a sharp look, but the woman's back was to her. She wondered if she was the only one who heard the faint underlying thread of sarcasm in Lizbeth's voice.

CHAPTER 10

Raine and Gavin followed Tomás into the open living room where Tala was making herself comfortable on an overstuffed leather couch. The two Heads of House exchanged greetings as Tomás took a seat in one of two armchairs. Raine caught a glimpse of Carlos disappearing down the other side of the hall toward the bedrooms.

Andrew led Xander into the living room before taking a seat on the brick ledge of the fireplace between the seated magi and alpha. Xander claimed the empty end of Tala's couch. Raine chose to lean against the entryway wall, where she could watch all the players.

As everyone settled in, Gavin disappeared only to return with an extra chair from the kitchen, Lizbeth trailing behind. She sank into the remaining armchair next to Tomás.

Gavin set the chair in front of Raine, turned it around, and straddled it. Folding his arms over the back, he looked between Tala and Xander. "Did you get anywhere?"

Tala shook her head, strands of hair escaping her braid. "We went to talk to the victims' families." Lines of exhaustion etched her face. “There wasn’t much more they could share.”

“Wasn’t much more they wanted to share,” corrected Xander, which earned her a dark look from Tala. Xander shrugged, addressing Gavin and Raine. “I’m not sure what’s going on here, but there seems to be some tension between the Houses.”

“Some tension?” Andrew let out a short, humorless laugh. “Hell, I’m surprised Jeremiah’s family let you in the door.”

“They didn’t actually.” Xander shot the other shifter a look. “Someone care to explain why?”

Raine decided to stir the pot. “I believe the Magi and Lycos Houses have a few relationship issues.”

Tomás avoided looking at Tala, his voice empty. “Our pack has no issues with Magi Whiteriver.”

Tala gave as good as she got, her response equally bland. “I have no issues with the Red Thunder Pack.”

Not about to let it go, Raine kept pushing. “Who does have issues then, Magi?”

Jaw clenched, Tala glared at Raine. “It’s not relevant.”

“Why don’t you let us make that determination?” Gavin cut through the tension, his patience obviously stretched thin. “Let’s start with an explanation of what kind of political mess we’ve stepped into.”

“It’s not so much political,” Tala reluctantly answered, her long fingers tapping absently against her knee. “It’s more cultural. Do any of you know much about the Native American people of this area?”

All three Wraiths held silent, so she continued, “Shamans are the native equivalent to earth witches. However, the native peoples have a long history of negativity toward the term ‘witch.’ For them, a witch is a negative being—someone who brings misfortunes to those who cross their paths."

"In my House, those who come from Native American backgrounds tend to walk the shamanistic path of their forefathers. They keep themselves very separate from the other witches. They have no quarrels with the Lycos House as shape shifters populate their oral histories."

"So the shamans accept Kyn who deal with natural magic?" Gavin asked.

Tala nodded. "For them, natural magic is neither good nor bad, it just is. It's a part of the natural world, and as long as the practitioner respects it, they have no quarrels."

That accounted for the majority of the Kyn, but it left two distinct groups out of the equation. Curious, Raine asked, "What about the Amanusa and the wizards, then?"

Tala's gaze shifted to Tomás who answered, "They are considered unnatural and are to be avoided at all costs."

Shock coursed through Raine. She wasn't the only one. In front of her, Gavin's shoulders tightened. Without censoring, she blurted, "You can't be serious?"

Based upon Tala's blank expression and Tomás's hard one, they were, which left Raine stunned. Since long lifespans equaled long memories, some grudges never died and prejudices could run deep. Yet, the Kyn tended to accept their own, especially since they were vastly outnumbered by humans. Like everything else in the universe, balance was crucial—light to dark, mortal to immortal.

Four main groups made up the Kyn community: the Fey, the Lycos, the Magi, and the Amanusa. The Amanusa housed what humans termed "demons." The Magi encompassed both witches—those who leaned toward natural magic and embraced the three-fold law—and wizards. The wizards were the witches' darker counterparts. They relied on spells and darker magics, and harming none was a "suggested" guideline. In Raine's experience, most wizards were seduced by the power—the more they had, the more they needed.

"Is it just the shamans who refuse to interact with the wizards and the demons?" Gavin's icy question sliced through the daunting silence. "Or is this par for the course for the Southwest Kyn?"

Gavin's unusual verbal attack made Raine blink in surprise. Questioning the heads of Kyn Houses was never a smart move. Not that it stopped her, but his approach tended to be more politically savvy than anything she ever managed.

His tone triggered a growl from the alpha even as Tala coolly admonished, "You have no right to question how our territory is run."

"I beg to differ." Raine took Gavin's back, laying a hand on his shoulder. She found it strange to be the calm one in the room. "Your answer either gives us a new starting point or eliminates one." She watched the witch and the alpha carefully. "So, the question is, do you share the shamans' views?"

"No," Tala bit out. "The relationship between the younger generation of witches, wizards, and shamans is much stronger than the older generations."

Raine turned to Tomás. "And you, Alpha Chavez?"

Tomás's growls faded, but the amber tint in his eyes remained. "No. The Red Thunder pack does not hold to those beliefs."

Andrew's quiet snort drew everyone's attention. He raised his chin in defiance. "The pack may not hold to the beliefs, but there are some who do so privately."

That was to be expected. No matter if human or Kyn, any diverse group would have issues. Yet one House remained unmentioned. "The Fey," she murmured. "What's their stand on all of this?"

"The Fey keep to themselves," Tala said. "Their numbers are pretty small here. Most prefer to stay in Colorado."

Gavin drew the conversation back on point. "Anyone in particular we should be looking at?"

Tala shook her head. "I brought Cheveyo here to try and determine who would hold such enmity with my House."

Eyes turned to Tomás who gritted out, "Don't have a clue."

Gavin shot to his feet, frustration boiling around him as he paced. Raine resumed her leaning position against the wall worried about the speculation on his face. That worry proved well founded when he said, "Perhaps we don't need names." He held Raine's gaze, but directed his words to Tala. "If we gave you a link to Cheveyo, could you follow it, Tala?"

Even expecting his suggestion, fear and anger surged. Raine fought it back, keeping her body relaxed and unconcerned.

Tala wasn't blind to the tension between them. "What kind of link?" Hope was a bright spark in her voice.

Stealing Gavin's thunder, Raine fed it fuel. "Cheveyo and I share a mental link he established a few months back." She turned from Gavin to Tala, not missing the edge of some undefined emotion flitting across the witch's face.

"I'll need more details than that." Her mocking tone was back in force, grating over Raine's nerves.

"He tied his life-force to mine to negate a death spell cast by a psychotic half demon." Outwardly, Raine was back to being coldly in control, but buried deep under that mask, fear seared a hole in her stomach. Or maybe, it was the chili.

Calculation sparked in Tala's eyes. "We could use it."

Raine's fear dug deeper. Nope, not the chili after all.

Not done, Tala added, "As long as he answers when we come knocking." The witch's lips tightened and her eyes narrowed. "However, I'm not sure how it will affect you."

Xander, who had been strangely silent through the whole conversation, cleared her throat. "What do you mean?"

Tala gave a nonchalant shrug. "There are quite a few possible outcomes. The best scenarios, we reach Cheveyo and are able to feed him enough magic for him to break free. Or, the link reacts like a telephone line and we follow it to where he's being held."

Raine wasn't taken in by the witch's studied casualness. When it came to dealing with magic, nothing was ever that simple. "What happens when I play conductor?"

"Depends on how strong you are." Tala's smile was chilling. "I've seen how stubborn you can be, so I'm sure you're strong enough to handle all that power. You'll be fine."

Considering how twitchy her magic was lately, Raine wasn't so sure. "If I can't channel the magic, it'll burn me out, right?"

"Maybe." Tala's cold smile faded. "If you fail, that would be the best scenario you'd face."

Ice settled in Raine's veins. Facing death was nothing new. It wasn't that she had a death wish, but it shocked her what she was willing to do to ensure she kept breathing. That willingness is what allowed Cheveyo to tie them together.

On the positive side, binding herself to Cheveyo meant gaining a certain amount of control over the twisted magic that she called hers. That control gave her a measure of peace she hadn't felt in a long while. She wasn't all that anxious to give it up just yet. "Worst case scenario?"

Sympathy crept through Tala's haughty demeanor. "Your soul will be unable to find its way back to your body. If you manage to survive, you'll be a vegetable."

A heavy shroud of silence dropped over the room as Raine fought the urge to squirm under the weight of everyone's stares. Well, one bright note—being a vegetable outranked being stark raving nuts. It wasn't like she had much of a choice. Cheveyo risked his life to save hers, could she really do any less?

Crossing her arms over her chest, she bared her teeth in a semblance of a smile. "When do we start?"

Tala gave a long slow blink. "Tonight. We need to go back to my house."

Of course they did, because like most earth witches, Tala's home base was a loaded power reserve. The more powerful and older the witch, the deeper the well. Which was why most high-ranking witches didn't bother living with a personal guard—unlike the alpha shifters.

Raine let out a soft sigh and pushed away from the wall. "Fine." Giving the alpha and his silent mate a respectful nod, she said, "Thank you, Alpha Chavez, for your hospitality and help."

Xander rose from the couch muttering, "Guess the meeting's over then."

Raine gave a sharp smile. "No point in wasting time."

They weren't going to get any more answers here, too many egos in the room. Gods, she hated politics. They were such a waste of time, and right now Cheveyo didn't have the luxury of waiting for them to wade through the political swamp of the Southwest Shifters and Magi.

"Fair warning," Gavin stood as well, cruel practicality lacing every word. "Our priority is to retrieve our magi and keep him safe. Whatever is hunting you and yours will have to wait."

Andrew snarled, his voice coming rough and dark. "You were invited down to help us with this threat."

"No, we weren't." Raine didn't bother hiding her malicious glee. "Cheveyo was. *We* are here to protect our magi from any and all harm."

Her implied threat was unmistakable. If these Kyn continued to keep needed information hidden, then they would be treated accordingly. For now, the Wraiths had one purpose—find Cheveyo and keep him safe, at any cost. Regardless of who stood between them and him.

The tension rose to a screaming point, but the three Wraiths—Gavin, Raine, or Xander—didn't waver. It was time to let these chiefs decide their next move.

"Fine." Tala snapped, rising from the couch. "Tomás, Lizbeth, I'll call you later."

Tomás rose as well. "Please do." He turned to Gavin and Raine. "While Tala is helping you find your missing magi, I'll be contacting Mulcahy."

Unable to help it, Raine laughed. "Please do, Alpha Chavez."

Even Gavin's lips curved, while Xander lowered her head to hide her grin. If Tomás thought threatening to sic Mulcahy on them would yank them in line, he was bound for disappointment. As captain of the Wraiths, Mulcahy would have never sent them down if he didn't trust them to do their job.

Knowing she was pushing it, Raine added, "Let him know we'll contact him in the next day or so."

Based on the roil of angry power surrounding the alpha, her dismissive tone managed to get under his skin. Before the claws came out, Gavin took her arm, pushing her toward the front door. He gave Tomás a nod as he crowded Raine out of the house, with Xander and Tala following behind.

CHAPTER 11

By the time they pulled into Tala's driveway, the inky blanket of darkness stretched through the sky. As they walked to Tala's front door, Ash trotted out of the surrounding woods to follow them inside. Ash and Tala headed to her room, leaving the others to the back bedrooms down the hall.

"Get changed and meet us up in Raine's room," Gavin ordered Xander softly.

With a quick nod, she moved ahead. When Gavin turned to disappear into Raine's room, the blonde shifter caught Raine's eye and raised an eyebrow suggestively. Raine flipped her a one-finger salute before closing the door on Xander's quiet chuckle.

Gavin sat at the end of the bed, with his elbows on his knees and his chin resting in his hands. She let him have his silence, knowing he would talk when he was ready. Instead, she moved around him, arranging a couple of pillows against the headboard. Taking off her boots, she let out a quiet sigh as she leaned back. She closed her eyes, the weariness washing through her.

Thanks to the two rounds with the Soul Stealer, or whatever the hell it was in the woods, and her still-healing body, she wasn't feeling her best. The last few days—hell, the last few hours—left her feeling like road kill. She needed a minute to shore up her defenses before heading back for more with tonight's little adventure.

Falling into that weird in-between state where sleep and awareness blended into a soft unreality, she could hear Gavin's even breathing. If she concentrated enough, she could hear Xander moving around in her room across the hall. Her mind wandered, letting the noises fade into the background.

Instinctively she reached out to her magic. It was there, just out of reach. Using the mental exercises Cheveyo drilled into her, she followed a familiar mental path. Working her way deeper behind her psychic shields, she searched for the reason behind her power's sudden shyness. The trail brought her to a barred door.

The brush of fur under her hand heralded the arrival of her leopard. She looked down to find its attention focused on the door. A warning brushed across her psychic nerves leaving her instincts humming.

She studied the door. It appeared to be solid metal, the locking mechanism similar to those found on old bank vaults. If it followed logic, the spiked wheel would control the locking bar on the other side.

Ignoring the low warning rumble from her leopard, she inched closer and reached out. Before her hand could touch the surface, her leopard fully formed between her and the door. The flash of sharp canines nipped at her fingers.

"Fine, I get it. No touching." Instead, keeping distance between her palms and the door, she skimmed the surface. The air was strangely warm and thick against her skin.

Nerve endings tingled as if she played with static electricity. A low level dread formed in the pit of her stomach. Whatever lay behind this door was powerful. Curling her fingers into fists, she rubbed them on her thighs. "Damn it."

Something told her that to get to Cheveyo, she needed to get beyond this door. She looked around and found the glimmering strand of her magic, faint and wispy, trailing under the door. She reached for it, only to have it fade. Battling back her frustration, she tried coaxing it. Nerve-wracking moments passed before it began to twine around her. It was frighteningly insubstantial.

She needed to strengthen it if she planned on surviving whatever waited on the other side. Her leopard wove around her legs and she watched, stunned, as her magic responded, twisting closer. Looking into the silver eyes of her cat, she thought it through.

Taking a step back, she put space between her and her inner kitty cat. Her magic started to fade. She stepped back to her leopard, feeling it brush against her legs. The glimmer of magic stopped its disappearing act.

Okay, that was helpful, but was it enough?

Deciding it would have to be, she reached for the door. A grim thought hit before should touch it. What if Cheveyo wasn't Cheveyo anymore? If she opened the door, and whatever held Cheveyo managed to destroy him, what would she be inviting in?

"Stop scaring yourself, idiot," she muttered.

Maybe she should wait for Tala. Hopefully, the witch knew what the hell she was doing.

A light knock shattered her concentration, snapping her back to the real world.

Gavin's voice was low. "C'mon in."

Xander stepped into the room as Raine rubbed her tired

eyes. Pulling her feet back, she made room for Xander to sit on the end of the bed next to Gavin.

Xander aimed her serious gaze at Raine. "Are you ready for this?"

"Honestly?" Raine shrugged. "I don't know, but it's not like we have much of a choice." She kept her voice as quiet as Xander's, neither wanting Tala to overhear their conversation.

"There's always a choice," Xander chided.

"Not this time." A small smile twisted Raine's lips. "I owe Cheveyo, not just for what he did for me, but because it's my job to keep him safe."

"This wasn't entirely your fault," Gavin said. "You got sent into a job unprepared. Can't fight what you don't know is out there."

"Maybe, but I have to finish it." She appreciated their support, but they knew as well as she did that trying to save Cheveyo was a nonissue. Wraiths were trained to keep the darker nightmares of Kyn world in check. Whatever held Cheveyo qualified.

"Fine." Under her delicate facial tattoos, Xander's jaw hardened. "What are our options?"

Gavin pinned Raine with an unbending look, something disturbingly deep moving in its depth. "We need to be there for whatever Tala's planning."

Not about to argue, she agreed. "Given, but you won't exactly be able to help. It's just Tala and me taking the trip in my head."

Determination carved his face into harsh angles. "I'm tagging along."

She didn't try hiding her sarcasm. "And, how exactly, are you planning on doing that?"

"Tala's not the only witch in the house." His teeth

flashed in a grin that would do any shifter proud. "I'm going to mirror you."

Xander shot him a sharp look. "You sure you can do that without letting Tala know?"

He shook his head, "She'll know, no way to hide it."

Raine held her hand up, bringing their attention back to her. "Hold up. How do you mirror me and what's it going to cost?"

"Mirroring," Gavin explained, "occurs when a witch sends part of themselves into another by merging two pieces of individual magic together." At Raine's continued skepticism, he clarified. "Basically, I'm going to tag along. I'll be able to add my strength to yours, but you'll be the one in control." When she arched her eyebrows, he continued, "Think of two magical threads twisting together."

"They make a stronger cord," she murmured, her heartbeat picking up the pace. "So you're going to use empathic magic for this?"

His nod triggered the beginnings of panic. Empathic magic meant he would be able to access her on an intimately deep level. It wasn't just disconcerting, it was frightening.

How would she handle him seeing into shadows even she wasn't ready to deal with? What if he saw into her darkness, then decided she wasn't worth fighting for? It was a distinct possibility. Things between them were so new, if—no, when she screwed up again, they could shatter under the strain. Hell, if this bond worked both ways, he wouldn't be able to his ultimate decision from her.

She shook her head, eyes wide.

"Raine, listen to me." His voice broke through her panic, proving he knew her well. "It's a surface link, just enough to lend you strength when needed. I'll be the anchor as you pull Cheveyo out. As long as we both maintain our inner shields, the tie won't be that deep."

She forced her breathing to calm, using the quiet confidence of the man in front of her as an example. Gavin was a damn good witch, if anyone could pull this off, he could. Her inner barriers would hold. They'd held through worse. She could do this.

Ignoring the sneering little voice whispering, *'Yeah, right,'* she cleared her throat. "Okay, fine. You can mirror me. We'll explain to Tala it's for added strength. What's Xander's part?"

"I'm the fall back option," Xander supplied gleefully.

Raine assessed the shifter. If something went wrong, Xander would sever the connection between Raine and Tala. It was a solution they didn't take lightly. To break the psychic connection between Tala and Raine, Xander would have to make a very difficult, possibly lethal decision. Yet every Wraith knew sacrifices were sometimes needed to save the primary.

Diffusing the choking tension with dark humor, Raine quipped, "Pick the one that will involve the least amount of paperwork."

Xander snorted and shook her head.

Raine's small smile faded as she voiced her biggest concern. "Say we open this door between Cheveyo and me and get some kind of link established. How are we going to hold it without whoever has him catching on?"

"If Cheveyo is like most Heads of House, then he's strong enough to keep his inner barriers up," Xander said. "Nothing short of a nuclear blast of magic will bring it down."

"So I, what?" Raine asked. "Hide out inside his mind?"

"If there's enough of Cheveyo left, he can help me create

an illusion the two of you can hide the connection behind," Gavin offered.

She narrowed her eyes. "I'm not sure I like this plan all that much. It leaves me a little too vulnerable on too many fronts."

How in the hell was she supposed to protect her inner barriers from Gavin, keep her remaining magic from getting sucked out by whatever was holding Cheveyo, and hold a connection to the witch, all without burning through her meager power?

Gavin grabbed her chin and forced her to meet his gaze. "I'm going to be right there, Raine. Between the two of us we can do this. Understand?"

She blinked, the command in his voice dragging a reluctant nod from her. Great. Along with saving Cheveyo, now she would be worried about making sure Gavin made it out as well. He held her chin for a moment longer, searching for something. Whatever he wanted, he must have found, because satisfaction flitted across his face before he let her go.

Tala's voice drifted through the door. "If you all are ready, we can begin."

"We'll be there in just a minute," Xander answered, never taking her gaze from Gavin and Raine. They all listened to Tala move down the hall.

Xander lowered her voice. "We call Mulcahy tomorrow." Her hazel eyes gleamed with wicked amusement as she got up from the bed and moved to the door. "You can give him an update."

Raine swung her legs over to follow. "Oh, joy! Can't wait."

CHAPTER 12

In the living room Tala had pushed her furniture to the edges, leaving a large open space with a half-finished salt circle. Four fat, unlit candles stood at each compass point—red, white, blue, and green. From the worn pattern on the hardwood floor it was clear this wasn't the first time such a circle had been laid out.

Tala appeared in the entrance from the kitchen, an old, but sharp, blade in one hand and a purple candle in the other.

"Raine, you need to be in the center." She waved the knife to indicate direction. "Xander and Gavin can sit on the outside. Just don't mess the salt line."

Ash pushed past her to sit between the fireplace and an outside edge of the circle.

Gavin shook his head. "We're all going to be inside the circle."

The witch drew up short, her spine snapping straight. "Excuse me?"

His only reaction to her haughty tone was a little smirk. The same one that drove Raine crazy when he directed it at her. With it now aimed at the witch, Raine found it kind of sexy. "I'm mirroring Raine for added strength." His statement bordered on a taunt. "Xander will stay inside the circle in case she's needed."

A furious silence filled the room, but Tala didn't take her gaze off of Gavin. "I see."

Raine was certain the other woman understood every unspoken word.

Tala's smile was all false sweetness. "Then you won't mind if I keep Ash in the circle as well?"

Game on. Tala's personal guardian would give the witch a few seconds of warning should Xander be forced into action.

"Agreed." Xander's quiet voice cut through the power play between the two witches. Raine shot her a questioning look and received a shrug in response. "I have no issues with Ash being in the circle. The more the merrier."

Figuring Xander knew her own limits, Raine let it go.

Tala gave a sharp nod. "Shall we get started then?"

Gavin gestured Raine forward. One by one they entered the circle. Tala took her place in the center, setting the purple candle and the knife on the floor nearby. Raine settled in front of her, while Xander and Ash picked their spots. Gavin followed, taking care to close the salt circle before settling in behind Raine.

She could feel him like a solid wall of heated strength, lending her focus. Keeping her attention on the candle's flame, she took deep, even breaths until her racing thoughts slowed, then stilled. Doubts were chased out. Awareness of her surroundings began to blur and fade. Her sole focus became the beckoning flame as she gathered her will into the waiting stillness.

Tala began to chant, her melodic voice lulling Raine

deeper. The reddish orange cast of the flame bled to a faint blue. Tala's voice deepened before slowly multiplying until there was nothing but the sound of a captivating chorus sucking Raine into the heart of the flame. Blue faded into an intense flash of white, leaving Raine blind.

Blinking furiously, she tried to bring her surroundings into focus. Tala's voice drifted to her like the faint song of water over rocks. As the incandescence faded, images took shape.

She stood on a gravel path snaking through a surreal forest made of watercolors that bled together to create a constantly changing terrain. The shifting colors made her slightly nauseous, but the images drew her. If she watched long enough, she might be able to figure out what they were.

Hands closed on her shoulders, pulling her attention from the ever-changing scenery. "Raine?"

She shook her head, dislodging the hypnotic pull of the forest. Turning, she faced Gavin, relieved to find him looking fairly normally—if a little fuzzy on the edges.

He smiled at her. "Ready?"

At her nod, his image faded more, causing a spurt of panic. She snagged his arm.

"It's okay." His voice was calm, his green eyes nearly glowing. "I'm not going anywhere, just muting my presence so I'm harder to sense."

"Sorry." She forced her hand to open, letting him go. Gavin became a faint shadow. She turned back to the weird forest and tested her inner barriers, relieved to find they were holding strong.

Lowering her primary psychic shields, she allowed Gavin to link with her. With him in place, she focused on her magic and finding the traces of energy binding her to

Cheveyo. She moved along the gravel path as her magic played hard to get. Once again, she had to cajole it to answer.

Steeling herself against the doubt now dodging her every step, she drew the faint colors of her magic close. They wrapped around her, sinking deep as she tried to strengthen it. Thanks to Gavin, she could feel a slight boost in her energy as magic began to vibrate against her skin.

The air in front of her shimmered, forcing her to a stop. Narrowing her gaze, she centered her concentration. Slowly, the shimmer—hovering about eye level—reformed into a multi-hued curtain. It was a tapestry of colors, some like weak nightlights, others with stronger glows. She was unsurprised to find that the weaker lights seemed to be hers, while the stronger ones belonged to Cheveyo and Gavin.

This is where she needed to take her time and pick the right threads. Pick the wrong ones, and she'd end up snared in her own wild magic, unable to find her way back. The fear of losing not just herself, but Gavin, in the powerful tapestry rose. Taking a deep breath, she let it become a faint discordant note in Tala's background choir.

"You need to hone in on your ties to Cheveyo." Gavin's voice slid through her, like a calm breeze.

Using the familiarity she gained through weeks of studying under Cheveyo, she tried to locate the colors she associated with the magi and his magic. The moving tapestry pulsed and twisted, but, finally, she found his deep earth tones. They undulated like storm clouds, reflecting the dangerous part of Cheveyo hidden beneath the deceptively calm exterior he presented to the world.

Slowly, the powerful magi's magical signature brightened until the others faded into the background. She reached for it, only to stop as something scrapped against her mental walls.

Sensing her hesitation, Gavin asked, "What's wrong

She wasn't sure. Something felt...off. With no way to verbalize her feelings, she didn't try. Instead, she gathered the magic. Cheveyo's earth tones were interwoven with another color. Peering closer she found a thin streak of silver. *Mine.* She continued to follow the interconnected line and discovered a distinctive blue flowing next to her silver.

Realization seared through her. By mirroring her, Gavin's magic would merge with hers until they appeared as one person. She spun to face Gavin as the true implications hit with stunning force. Should they survive this, some part of him would forever exist within her.

Gavin's image sharpened until he was solid. "It goes both ways, Raine." His seriousness was reflected in the weight of knowledge in his gaze.

She felt dizzy as her world shook. She tried to keep her voice steady. "Are you sure about this?"

Did he really understand what this meant? How tied they would be? Sometimes it seemed he could barely tolerate her. Hell, sometimes she could barely tolerate herself.

He stroked her cheek and a small unreadable smile twisted his lips. "We're going to be fine." Reading her disbelief, he added, "Remember to keep your barriers up. Surface link, remember?"

She glared. "That seems awfully close for a surface link."

She could swear he was laughing at her, even if his expression remained unchanged. "You can still keep your secrets." As he faded back into the surreal surroundings, he softly added, "For now."

Snorting, she turned away. She'd deal with the fallout later. Taking a deep breath, she dropped her secondary barriers enough to merge Gavin's magic with hers. Blue sank into silver until only a light tint remained. Strength spread through her. Familiar power bloomed and the strange wildness that haunted her for years settled into place.

Relief loosened her shoulders as determination steeled her spine. Pulling her secondary shields into place, she once again reached for Cheveyo's thread.

CHAPTER 13

Grabbing hold of her tie to Cheveyo set Raine's world spinning. The magic pulled her along the gravel path with such speed the strange watercolor forest blurred. She thought she caught a flash of her leopard racing beside her, but could only hold on as the magic drew her forward.

The background noise of Tala's voice rose to a cacophony until the words pounded through Raine's blood and bones. Noise and magic crested, threatening to fracture her.

Then, as if a switch was thrown, all fell silent. She found herself on her knees, one hand buried in the fur of her leopard, the other supporting her weight as gravel pressed against her palm. Her breath tore in and out of her lungs like an old fashion bellow, the noise loud in the deafening quiet. Slowing her breathing, she raised her head to see where they were.

The watercolor forest had thinned, disappearing into a deepening darkness. The old bank vault door was back, along with the low level dread. Tearing her gaze away from the intimidating door, she searched for Gavin. She found his faint shadow behind her. Reassured, she turned back to the door. Once through, she couldn't acknowledge Gavin's presence, needing to keep it as hidden as possible.

A rustling noise to her right announced Tala's arrival. Raine pushed to her feet as the blonde witch stopped in front of her. Irritated, Raine's tone was short, "You're here. Why?"

The small taunting smile Raine was really beginning to hate flashed to life. "Don't worry, kitty cat, I won't be following you in. Consider me back up."

Raine didn't bother to hide her derision. "It's thanks to you Cheveyo's in this situation in the first place." She almost missed the flash of hurt running through the witch's dark eyes.

"It doesn't matter what you think," Tala shot back.

Raine let her own mocking smile free. "Actually it does matter. My loyalties lie with my magi. His safety comes first. If I decide you're more of a hindrance than help, I have the right to refuse your offer."

Anger tightened the skin across Tala's high cheekbones, and something in her expression actually gave Raine pause. The witch's voice cut bone deep. "You don't get a choice in this, McCord. You will go in, give what help you can to Cheveyo and bring me the information necessary to get him back. Wraith or not, you do answer to me, because your continued existence depends on how I end this spell."

For the first time since meeting Tala, Raine saw what set the other woman apart and made her the Magi for the Southwest Kyn. A small spark of respect flared to life at Tala's threat. Here was the ruthlessness necessary for running a House, backed with the power to enforce her will regardless of the consequences.

Raine held her tongue as she studied the woman. Rarely

did she underestimate others, but this time she let her personal feelings interfere with her perceptions. Not a smart move and one she'd make damn sure not to do again. She sketched a small bow. "Understood, Magi."

Raine hid her smile at the surprise Tala was unable to hide. The witch's threat was very real, but Xander wasn't sitting in that circle for moral support either. Between Gavin and Xander, Tala wouldn't be walking away from the circle if Raine wasn't. It was a strange sort of comfort.

Leaving Tala on the path, Raine moved to the barred door. Each step closer increased the sickening weight boiling in her stomach. Stopping before the spike wheel, she took a deep breath and slowly reached out. Static electricity ran over her, raising the fine hairs on her body. The sensation of pushing through a thick paste coated her hands. Hearing the low growl from her leopard, she braced, setting her skin to the metal.

For a moment, nothing happened, then her palms began to burn, as a needle-sharp pain arrowed into her bones. Rising above the pain, she concentrated on turning the wheel to unlock the door. The burning grew in intensity, bringing tears to her eyes.

The deafening screech of metal scraping against metal raked her ears. She swore she could feel the warm trickle of blood easing from her abused eardrums. In defense, she drew on her magic, trying to block out the pain in her head and hands. Suddenly it felt as if Gavin's hands covered hers, helping to unlock the door. With a final clink of metal tumblers, the door released.

Rubbing her aching palms on her thighs, she hesitated before checking out the damage done to her hands. Although the shards of agony still echoed through her fingers, no blemish showed.

Shaking her head, she stared at the door in front of her. Closing her eyes, she gathered her magic and settled her cat back to its familiar place. Then she allowed Gavin's power to merge a bit deeper. On some distant level, she marveled at the sense of completion the joining brought.

Holding tight to Cheveyo's thread, she reinforced her barriers, opened her eyes, and shoved open the door wide. A soft swirling gray mist filled the other side.

Stepping through her feet hit a smooth, unseen surface. The mist curled around her, clinging to her like spider webs. She moved forward, following Cheveyo's pull. Once inside, she refused to turn around, worried she would lose her sense of direction. Instead, she let the magic guide her.

Caught inside the haze, time became static. Her nose twitched at the hint of moisture and spicy smoke. The damp scent took on hints of stone while the caustic smoke coated the back of her throat. Muted noises emerged, spiked with occasional sharp tones. No matter how much she concentrated, she couldn't make out the words, or figure out if it was one person or many.

The floor beneath her feet became uneven, causing her to step with care, caution beating inside her skull. She was getting close, but the gray mist still obscured her sight. Straining, she listened to the rise and fall of sound. Reaching out, she hissed as a sharp edge of stone etched fire against her palm. Moving with even more caution, she traced her hands over the stone walls only to discover she was in a cave.

Between one blink and the next a blur of flames and shadows replaced the gray mist.

Instincts held her still. She tightened her hold on Cheveyo's magic, her stomach lurching as it dragged her forward. Off balance, she braced herself as she fell. The impact knocked the breath from her body. As she concentrated on rebooting her lungs, she could feel rough stone cutting into her back. She tried to rub her chest but discovered her arms were being held down. Not wanting to alert whatever was out there that she was conscious, she peeked under her lashes. The quick check revealed her legs were in the same boat.

Panic crested and phantom screams rang through her head. Reality warped with the past sending searing pain along her wrists, ankles, and neck where iron bands shackled her in place. The surrounding stone morphed into white walls, and the smoke disappeared under the smells of antiseptic. The distorted voices changed into cold, clinical tones. Hollow footsteps came closer, and a craggy face topped with gray hair floated in front of her. The man's smile should have been comforting, if you could ignore the empty pools of darkness staring down with gleeful evil.

Flames raced through her veins, eating into her bones. Screams choked her, but she held them back, unwilling to give her tormentors that small victory. Fingers plucked inside her, pulling, tugging. The searching digits didn't hurt at first, then the pain from their scraping and clawing began to multiply, until each tug became another lash with a hot poker. With no ability to physically get away, she reached for her shields with a frantic desperation.

They slammed into place, leveling the painful barrage until it began to ebb. Closing her eyes she took stock. Her limbs were weak and trying to move took a hell of a lot of effort. Still, she managed to work some give in the restraints on her left hand. Rope, she was bound with rope. The smoke-clouded air made breathing difficult, but heat wafted from her right. Turning her head, she slit her eyes open.

Thanks to the firelight from a burning campfire, her surroundings danced into hazy focus. Light flickered over her tanned arm revealing the raw rope burns on her very masculine wrist.

Tanned arm? When had that happened?

Clarity struck like lightning. She was in Cheveyo's body. A small sense of accomplishment sparked. Okay, that was good, but where in the hell was he? Trepidation slid its icy fingers in deep.

The flickering firelight shifted over a shadow approaching her—no, approaching Cheveyo—whoever. Letting her lashes drift down, she kept her breathing light. Straining her ears for clues, she battled back the frantic thoughts scraping inside her brain. The sound of a something rasping against rock a few feet from her head had her fighting not to flinch. Cheveyo's body was weak, which meant her chances at breaking free and fighting her way out was not an option. Besides if she was in the driver's seat, where was her damn passenger?

The heat from the fire on her face leached away, only for the bone deep cold she associated with the Soul Stealer to crash in. Before the tidal wave of fear could rip her under, something yanked her back, deeper into Cheveyo's body. The cavern and cold disappeared, replaced by some weird landscape coated with a wispy, drab mist.

The phantom grip released her and she collapsed under a draining weakness reaching all the way to her spirit.

"Good gods, girl. Didn't I teach you better than that?"

The sound of Cheveyo's sharp voice jerked her head up. Scrambling to her knees, she met the disgruntled gaze of her mentor. "Obviously not," she snapped back.

A small grimace that might have been a strained smile appeared on his tired face. It should have made her feel better, but he didn't look good. Weariness and pain left deep niches around his mouth and eyes, drawing his skin tight over his high cheekbones. His normal bronze skin was a pale olive. Gone was the fierce, dominating magi. In his place was a hard, battle-weary warrior.

"Cheveyo," she started, but he waved his hand cutting her off.

"I know—we have to get me out of here, yadda, yadda..." He raked a hand through his collar-length hair, as he slid down some invisible wall to sit across from her. Placing his hands on his upraised knees, he just looked at her.

His assessment made her uncomfortable.

"Didn't expect me to answer your knock?" A faint thread of humor twisted through his words.

His question threw her back to when he first created their bond. Her concerns on how linked they would be had resulted in his reassurance that the only way the door would open was if she knocked and he answered.

"Actually we were hoping you would."

He raised an eyebrow. "We?"

Before she could respond, the feel of nails scoring her skin left her scrambling to her feet. She spun around to face the thick barrier of fog behind her, hissing as another scrape ripped against her magic. Cheveyo's hand on her arm stopped her from stepping forward.

"Raine." He turned her away from the fog, his six-foot-six frame towering over her.

She didn't let it stop her from yanking from his hold. "What?" Screw respecting authority. Right now, they were in deep shit and needed to get out.

The humor lighting his eyes made her worry he was reading her mind. "Who else are you working with?"

Paranoia flashed through her mind. Was this really Cheveyo, or some sort of illusion created by the ones holding him? If it was just her at risk, that was one thing, but she was tied to Gavin and Tala. Being responsible for others sucked. She shrugged, watching him closely. "Why do you care? Isn't the important thing to get you out?"

He reached for her, his movements cautious as if he didn't want to spook a skittish animal. Instead of touching her, he used one long finger to trace over the silver lynx resting on her throat. Suspended from a leather strap, it was the charm he had given her last year. The same one he used to track her down when she went to confront Alexi.

He raised his eyes from the charm to her face. "You still wear it."

It wasn't a question, so she didn't answer.

He let out a soft sigh, dropping his hand. "I gave that to you last year for Talbot's ball at the Governor Hotel. It was a stunning addition to the lovely leather bustier and skirt combo you were wearing that night." A slightly wicked bent of humor peeked out. "Besides it made an even lovelier leash in tracking you to your rendezvous with Alexi."

Yep, she was definitely dealing with Cheveyo. No one else could be so damn confusing as far as she was concerned. Gavin's image popped into her head, causing her to self-correct.

Reassured she was facing nothing more threatening than her mentor, she answered his first question. "Gavin and Tala are waiting on us."

His quick step back and the donning of a damn good poker face was more of a reaction than she expected.

Tilting her head, she gave him a considering look. "What is up between you and that witch?"

A surprised snort escaped him. "I take it you and Tala won't be going out for coffee anytime soon?"

"Not damn likely." She shot him a feral grin. "Unless the coffee comes with arsenic."

A short bark of laughter escaped him. "I would have loved to watch you two meet."

She narrowed her eyes. "You aren't answering my question."

Implacable arrogance colored his voice. "And I'm not going to, so don't ask again."

"Fine." But Raine wasn't done yet. "Can we trust her?"

He gave a short nod. "As much as anyone."

She let it go. Another gouge against her magic, a little deeper this time, brought her attention back to the barrier behind her. The mist flared with silvery blue and brown. "What is it doing?"

"Trying to break through the wall you and Gavin have in place."

She turned back to Cheveyo. She hadn't told him Gavin was helping with the protection.

He obviously read her expression correctly. "You didn't have to." He indicated the magical barrier. "I know your magic. I know mine."

"Right. Then let's get the hell out of here." She went to move around him, but stopped when he remained where he was. "Cheveyo?"

"It won't work this way," he said, his expression inscrutable.

Frustration ate at her, between his non-answers and the Soul Stealer's attempt to shred her, her patience was wearing thin. "Fine, then what will?"

"That wall you two have up won't last much longer. Once the *Nomâhtsé'héõò Adanata* tears through, the chances of you and Gavin being trapped here with me increase significantly." There was no fear, no defeat, in his voice, just a statement of fact. "If the Stealer gets through, so do the others."

Her pulse spiked. "Others?"

His exhaustion became unmistakable. "The summoner not only managed to raise a Soul Stealer, but they've trapped the spirits of Tala's murdered witches."

"Chindis," she muttered.

He nodded. "If you know the term, you know what we're dealing with."

She sighed. "Not really. We're still trying to piece it together. Tala and Tomás aren't exactly fonts of information." Another testing rake of pain left her clenching her fists.

Cheveyo uttered a phrase in a liquid sounding language, and the sensation of being clawed bloody, faded.

Realizing they were working against a clock, she grabbed his arm. "Come on. We'll talk about it once we're out of here."

He pried her hand from his arm. "No, Raine. There's no getting me out of here."

His words, more than anything, sent fear skittering along her skin. "We're not leaving you here, Cheveyo. It's not an option."

Something flickered in his obsidian eyes. "I don't expect you to. Whatever spell is being used, it's not one I know. The bond between my spirit and body is fraying. If you succeed in getting my spirit on the other side of the wall, my body will die and I'll be trapped on this plane. I'm really not into being a ghost just yet. For now, retreat is the only option." He shrugged his wide shoulders. "I can hold on a bit longer."

Shaking her head, she tried to ignore the insidious worry burrowing deep in her mind. "I don't think you understand. This link you and I have, we're going to make it work for us. Your magic has been drawing on mine, which tells me you're struggling harder than you're letting on."

Surprise flitted briefly across his face. "I was unaware—"

"I know." She waved off his words. "I'm not concerned about that right now. We have a plan, but you have to get to the other side of the damn door." She had no clue how to get back to the door, but she started to walk away from the pulsing wall.

"What damn door?" Cheveyo reluctantly followed.

She didn't answer. The dull mists curled around her feet as she followed Gavin's pull. For once, she would trust Gavin to lead and pray he wouldn't lose her.

CHAPTER 14

THE FEEL OF CLAWS TEARING AT HER SKIN AND THE HAUNTING chorus of angry wails chased her through the thickening fog. At some point, she grabbed Cheveyo's hand, dragging him behind her. The driving sense of urgency increased with each step. Gavin's tugs refused to let her slow. Here in this other place, there was no sense of time.

The fog pulled back and she stumbled to a stop in front of the old-fashioned safe door. The scrabble of clawed feet on stone came from behind them as the Soul Stealer and its chindi minions closed in. Another hit struck and she felt the protective barrier buckle. Her breath hitched and a cold sweat broke out.

She looked back to Cheveyo, worry gathering. Whatever battle he waged was creating a serious toll. His skin held a gray tint, while his chest pumped furiously. Peering into the roiling fog behind them, she tried to make out their pursuer. "Come on, old man."

Cheveyo glared back.

She ignored his anger, considering he was entitled to it. Especially since he'd been slowing the monster's assault by lying down numerous obstacles as they ran. A dangerous, but necessary move. She needed to reinforce their tie, but didn't have time.

Think. She needed to think. If she opened the door, she would lead the Stealer to Gavin and Tala, probably losing Cheveyo in the process.

A strong metaphoric tug from Gavin yanked her forward until she stumbled, an answer flaring to life. *Shit! Right, Gavin!*

Worried about the Soul Stealer and company ripping her magic away, her internal walls were locked down tight. Keeping not just the monsters out, but Gavin as well. To increase her strength, and by proxy, Cheveyo's, she needed to let Gavin in. Problem was, if she created an opening, the Stealer could crash the party.

With an unnatural suddenness, the wispy fog surged forward, reaching for her and Cheveyo. The protective veil began to shred under invisible claws, leaving her no choice. With each slash, the pain of psychic rendering sent her to her knees, and she lost what little control she held.

Her shields came down with a crash and Gavin surged in, his magic weaving with hers at an incredible speed. Silver-blue fire hit the Cheveyo's threads, reinforcing the magical ties into a thick rope.

She blinked at Cheveyo's wordless shout and realized she was on her feet in front of that blasted door.

Gavin's voice was an urgent whisper in her head, "Now, Raine! Get it opened now!"

Trusting Cheveyo to cover her back and Gavin to hold their hunters off, she grasped the metal lever, bracing for the pain. It didn't come. She yanked—hard. The bar separated and the heavy door began to inch open.

Gavin shoved through the widening crack. His green

eyes glowed as he shot her a sharp look before taking a position between her and Cheveyo.

A ringing filled her ears just as another swipe of pain tore through her, bringing a choked scream to her throat.

The door opened a bit more, giving a glimpse of Tala on the other side. Caught in some unseen wind, her blonde hair blew wild and a gold glow outlined her body. An undulating curtain of the same glow hovered just outside the door.

On some level, Raine recognized Tala's spirit was unable to cross the door's threshold. Raine's understanding of the metaphysical might be limited, but she knew enough to grasp the concept of being a conduit. Reaching through the doorway, the gold glow curled around her wrist like a scarf and she dragged Tala over. "You okay?"

Tala nodded, and taking her at her word, Raine rushed to the two men.

The gray fog snapped at Cheveyo's magic as it burned like solar flares along his body, but failed to find purchase. Behind him stood Gavin, glowing with his own power. Unconsciously, she stepped between the two of them. The hand still wrapped in Tala's magic fell on Cheveyo's left arm, while her other hand caught Gavin's right wrist.

The minute all three touched, an eerie silence descended. Then, like the muted thunder of a tsunami, a wave of power swept through her. The combined magics of Cheveyo, Tala, and Gavin collided like the titans they were, shoving Raine back. Completely unprepared, she tumbled into the abyss.

Desperate for an anchor, she reached out only to find nothing. Even her scream was noiseless, swallowed by the emptiness tearing her apart. The bonds of magic holding her together disappeared under the flood of power.

Into the roaring void came a lifeline.

"Raine!" Gavin's shout snagged her like a fish on a line.

Unable to breathe and fighting back panicked fear, she concentrated on his voice. He called again, and she struggled through the solid waves of darkness, praying she was heading in the right direction. One moment she swam through a pitiless void, the next dancing lights left her blinded.

Her lungs found air in a harsh rasp that filled her ears, drowning out all other sounds. Blindly, she reached out, mutely appealing for rescue. A strong hand wrapped around her wrist, and pulled her free of the chaotic waves. Keeping her desperate grip, she scrambled out of the sea of power, stumbling to fall against a solid chest. Strong arms held her tight as she focused on the mechanics of breathing.

The rumbles under her ear soon coalesced into Gavin's rough tones. "Breathe, Raine. Just like that. Come on back, baby."

A shudder worked through her as she burrowed closer to his heat. Gods, she felt so cold. If this is what channeling power entailed, count her out. Never fucking again did she want to go through that.

But this—having Gavin hold her—was nice. So was the encroaching feeling of safety his presence brought. Taking one last deep breath into her aching chest, she raised her head.

Gavin stroked her back, watching her intently, as if he could see deep inside her, past skin and bone. It made her uncomfortable. Hell, she didn't even dare look that deep into herself.

Reluctantly she stepped back, and he let his hands drop. "I'm—" Her throat felt shredded. "I'm okay, I think." She took another careful step back, looking around. Just behind Gavin's shoulder stood Cheveyo, speculation filling his face. She looked away, feeling color rise to her cheeks. "What happened?"

Tala's mocking voice floated through the air causing Raine to search for the witch. "I knew you were too stubborn to die, little cat."

A growl rumbled in the back of Raine's throat. "Where are you?"

A faint, blurred image of the witch emerged next to Cheveyo. The woman waved her fingers at Raine.

Raine snarled back.

"Enough." Cheveyo's voice was exasperated. "We don't have time for this."

Tala's image wasn't crystal clear, but it was good enough for Raine to catch the hint of hurt Cheveyo's curt words invoked.

That tiny vulnerability left Raine empathizing, especially as she found herself on the tail end of such tones from Gavin more than she cared to remember. "What's next?"

"You, Tala, and Gavin are going back on the other side of that door and locking it behind you," Cheveyo growled.

Gavin tensed.

"Think again, oh mighty one." For once the sarcastic rejoinder didn't come from Raine, or even Gavin. Instead, Tala who glared at Cheveyo, hand on her hips, mouth drawn into a deep frown.

Raine shot a look at Gavin, who only shrugged.

Cheveyo crowded Tala, who, unsurprisingly, did not step back. "Excuse me?"

Wow, the arrogance in those two words could make the arctic look like the Caribbean. Tala didn't flinch. Instead, she moved until her golden image pressed against Cheveyo's. The resulting light show mesmerized Raine and she almost missed Tala's response.

"You heard me, you stubborn ass." Tala faced down Cheveyo. "You are going to hold on to this binding so we can track you down through this little tie you've got with the hellcat over there."

Raine figured hellcat was a nicer description than others, and she couldn't help her little grin that broke out. It was refreshing to see someone else go toe to toe with Cheveyo.

Cheveyo blinked slowly, obviously picking up on the hint of jealousy in Tala's voice. When he dragged Tala's blurry image forward and slammed his mouth down on hers, Raine couldn't stop her childish snicker as Tala thoroughly enjoyed the moment.

Gavin cleared his throat and Raine's muttered, "Spoilsport" was lost under his, "Can we focus for a second? Please?"

Cheveyo lifted his head and shot them a dark look. In his arms, Tala's golden glow took on a hint of rose. "Fine." Cheveyo's voice was still rough. "What was the next step in your brilliant plan?"

Gavin cocked an eyebrow. "Originally, we were going to take you and Raine back through the door without the Soul Stealer following."

"Not an option anymore," Raine cut in.

Gavin shot her a look. "Why not?"

"Because it would sever my soul from my body." Cheveyo didn't react to Tala's tiny gasp.

Gavin studied the older man for a moment. "We need to keep the ties between you and Raine intact in order to pinpoint your location. I'm assuming if this thing finds it, it'll use it to drain you both?"

Cheveyo nodded grimly.

"How do we hide it?" Raine wasn't worried about making it through the door. She was more worried about hiding her magic.

"Illusion," Gavin stated.

Raine rolled her hand in a gesture for him to expand.

He sighed. "If Cheveyo helps, I can create an illusion that nothing has changed. When the Stealer sees him, Cheveyo will seem weaker than he is."

She thought back to those ghostly fingers on her throat back at the alpha's house. "Another one of your new superpowers?"

His expression cooled, arrogance adding a sexy vibe—if you went for that kind of thing. His tone was just as remote. "Thanks to Dr. Lawson's little psychedelic cocktail, yes it is, kitty cat."

How the hell did he manage to make that annoying term so sexy? "Fine. You and Cheveyo do the Copperfield thing, and then what? Tala and I slip out the door?"

At his intense regard, heat swam under her skin, but she refused to look away, knowing if she did, he'd take it as a win.

Not missing her challenge, his lips twitched. "You worry about keeping Cheveyo's thread secure and follow Tala out."

"And you?" The question escaped before she could censor.

His slow smile stole her breath. Then he traced one finger down the side of her face. "I'll be right behind you."

This time she didn't stand a chance against the blush riding along her cheekbones. His answer triggered a very disturbing mental image and set off a flutter of those damn butterflies currently nesting in her stomach. Gritting her teeth, she dropped her gaze.

A whip of fire scored her chest and she gasped, her hand rising to deflect the unseen blow. "The Stealer's close." Too damn close.

Cheveyo's head snapped up as Gavin's arm curled around her waist. With no warning, he took her into the roiling magic and dropped her into the clearing before the door.

As the world resettled, Raine staggered upright, catching sight of Cheveyo releasing Tala a little ways away. The fog was denser now, creeping toward the partially open door. Cheveyo pushed Tala to the opening, then moved to Gavin's side. Tala wisped through the narrow space.

Raine looked back to find the two men merging their magic with incredible speed. Deep in her chest, she could feel the energy working. Caught up, she failed to notice the tendril of fog wrapping around her ankle.

Agony seared as hundreds of sharp teeth sank vicious fangs into her bones. Unable to separate her magic from Gavin and Cheveyo's, instinct had her nails thickening into curved claws as her leopard joined the fight. Slashing down, she tore the fog to tatters of smoke. Once free, she wasted no time moving to the open doorway.

Keeping one hand on the doorframe, she stepped through, relying on Tala's golden magic as an anchor. Not really understanding how, Raine used Tala's power to bind the lightning storm of magic—hers, Gavin's and Cheveyo's. Weaving the magics together, she was relieved to see there was no telltale change in its appearance. Point to the home team.

She turned to call Gavin, only to be slammed to the

ground with enough force to knock the air from her chest. Razor sharp claws slashed across the arm she threw up to protect her face. Another claw whipped down her thigh. Enraged, Raine freed her leopard.

The burn of shifting bones and muscles was lost in the speed of her transformation. In her animal form, she used her retractable claws to dig deep gashes down the sides of the misty monster trying to pin her down. Her leopard's scream echoed through the watercolor forest. Twisting her supple spine, she threw her attacker off. Snarling, she let the cat's instincts take control. She needed this thing back on the other side before Gavin came through, or she and Tala wouldn't make it.

As with every time she let her leopard out, she felt the blending of her intellect with her cat's instincts. Her cat lowered its head, and with slow, deliberate steps paced back and forth between Tala and the Soul Stealer. Deep inside, Raine tried to make some recognizable shape out of the writhing tendrils of smoke they faced.

The Stealer wasn't solid, but the smoke created a moving shadow—vaguely animalistic. There were four legs, the two hind muscled and powerful, while heavy shoulders supported the front legs. It appeared larger than her leopard. Was probably faster than her leopard too.

A twisted combination of images made up the head. From one angle, Raine swore it was a snarling, rabid wolf. Yet, when she turned to pace back, she caught a glimpse of ferociously bared teeth of some mountain cat.

Freezing in front of Tala, she watched the Stealer's skull change again, tendrils of smoke reshaping until a skeletal head with massive jaws, filled with ragged-edged teeth, sat below the sunken pits of empty eye sockets. The dense coldness emanating from the Stealer ate at Raine. Trying to ignore the spreading numbness, she concentrated on keeping it back from Tala and herding it through the door.

Low growls rumbled as she padded forward. She made it two steps before those empty eye sockets filled with golden flames. The Stealer leapt, claws extended. Relying on her cat's instincts, she reared back, swiping out at the Stealer's unprotected belly. Its claws changed into grasping human hands, which passed through Raine's leopard to the woman inside. They clawed and tore, causing both woman and cat to scream at the agonizing invasion.

The invading hands dug under her ribs, grasping for her magic. Raine fought back, reaching for the bony wrist delineated in gray smoke. She connected and silver sparked against the shadows. The monster screeched. She poured more power into her magic, even as an annoying voice in the back of her mind chanted, *'Wrong move!'*

The Stealer's raking movements slowed. The smoky wrist seemed to gain substance, sending another wave of icy shards through her torso. Golden flames set deep inside the monstrous skull dominated her entire field of vision. Fetid breath misted her face, bringing the smell of rotten meat. Her eyes watered. She couldn't catch her breath. She could feel her and her leopard's grip slipping, their struggles slowing.

Suddenly the Soul Stealer ripped its empty hand out of Raine and swung its other arm in her direction even as golden fire began to lick around its smoky edges.

She barely ducked out of the way, her leopard retreating deep inside. Raine crashed to the ground and curled into a ball, her shaking hands covering what felt like a gaping hole under her ribs. Behind her Tala stood burning brightly.

The unearthly shrieks of the Stealer filled the air, almost drowning out Tala's chants.

Raine pushed her aching body to her knees, her groan lost under the increasing volume of Tala's voice. Struggling to her feet, Raine stood between the blazing witch and the snarling, mist-shrouded Soul Stealer. Tala's power forced the monster back, one reluctant step at a time. Behind the Stealer, Raine could just make out the doorway. A few more steps, then she should be able to close the door.

Inside the ghoulish skull, the gold flames flickered, fixing on the two women. Like a series of still pictures, Raine watched Tala's glow flickered like a candle caught in a wind gust and her chanting faltered. Focused on Raine, the thing crouched, preparing to leap. From behind it, a dark–haired, silver-eyed woman let loose a harsh battle cry.

In stunned disbelief, Raine watched what looked like her twin slash the Stealer with a black-bladed sword. Slicing diagonally, it cut from shoulder through the barrel shaped torso. The creature gave an ear-splitting howl of fury, mixed with pain. It turned to face its newest attacker. Mesmerized by the combative dance, Raine wondered if she somehow manage to split herself by accident.

From under her bruised rib cage, a metaphysical punch shoved reality back to normal speed. Gasping, she dragged her attention away from the battle in front of her as Gavin pulled on her magic. On the other side of the door at the edge stood the faint images of Cheveyo and Gavin. It took her a few precious moments to realize why the two men seemed blurred. Gavin was distracting the Soul Stealer with his illusion of her twin and hiding the doorway.

Strangely, it was working. The monster remained totally focused on the woman it thought real. The Stealer stalked her image, closer and closer to the hidden doorway. Raine kept her inner barriers down and didn't dare move, worried she would break the link between her and Gavin and shatter the disorienting tableau in front of her.

Without warning, the monster sprang forward, and Raine's doppelganger stumbled back through the doorway. As both combatants tumbled through, Gavin's faint form slipped through the entrance. Relief bloomed and she didn't wait for his mental shout of "Now!" Grabbing the spiked wheel of the door, she shoved it closed, even as Cheveyo pulled from his side.

Before the door snuffed shut, she met his dark gaze. "You hold on. We're coming."

His answer was a grim smile.

CHAPTER 15

RAINE BLINKED AT THE FLICKERING LIGHT OF A CANDLE, SITTING IN a pool of wax, as Tala's living room came into focus. Breathing in the soothing bite of sage mixed with melted wax, she unfolded her legs. Waves of pins and needles danced through her limbs, causing a soft groan.

That quiet sound deepened into a moan as the aches and pains delivered on the spiritual plain manifested into actual physical suffering. Just once she'd like to regain consciousness without feeling as if she'd been run over by a semi.

The alternate memory of waking in Gavin's arms at the alpha's house sent heat spiraling through her bloodstream, adding a frustrating level of arousal to the weariness of battle. Tunneling her hands through her hair, she pulled sharply in an attempt to dull her mental schizophrenia.

The startling brush of fingers against her chin brought her attention to Gavin's rugged features and strangely intimate study. Shoving her emotional discomfort aside, she put her normal "deal with it later" philosophy to work.

"You okay?" His question was quiet.

Breathing through the combined battering rams of emotional and physical reaction, she unclenched her teeth and nodded.

He held her chin a fraction longer, before letting go and turning away. "Xander?"

The blonde snapped, "Give me a minute."

Raine turned to see Xander crouched protectively in front of them, facing down a very pissed-off Ash.

"What happened?" Using Gavin's offered hand, Raine rose to her feet.

Gavin kept his attention on the wolf. "Tala's unconscious."

Not good. Raine caught a glimpse of Tala slumped on the other side of the waning candle. She moved toward the witch.

Ash snarled, his canines flashing in warning.

"I'd stay still, Raine," Xander cautioned.

Heeding her warning, Raine addressed Tala's protector. "I don't mean any harm." Considering his continuous growls, the wolf obviously didn't believe her.

Raine lifted her hands. "I just want to check on her, make sure she's okay."

Moving slowly, she lowered her head. Hanging with shifters gave her some clues in how to appear non-threatening, but taking her eyes from Ash was a test in itself. Here's hoping he wouldn't get past Xander.

The threatening growls slowed then stopped. Ash took a stiff step back, staying in front of Tala, but obviously giving permission for Raine to advance.

Gavin and Xander held still. Taking care not to make any sharp movements, Raine approached Tala. Ignoring her protesting aches, she dropped to her knees.

Tala didn't look good—her dusky skin ashen, but more

worrisome was the obvious lack of life. Raine pressed her fingers to Tala's neck and the minute she touched the witch, Tala's chest rose in a sharp inhale and her lashes fluttered.

Raine waited while awareness of their surroundings filtered through Tala's hazy confusion. She stared at Raine, her brow furrowed as she pushed upright and leaned against Ash.

Aware any offer of help would be rejected, Raine sat back on her heels, giving the quietly murmuring witch and her pet a minute. The tension in the room eased as early morning light danced across the window. Startled, Raine realized their little foray had taken hours.

"You still have a hold of Cheveyo?" Tala's rough question brought Raine's head around.

Instead of automatically answering, Raine focused inward. Finding Cheveyo's magic wrapped inside a cocoon of silver and blue, relief hit. His earth tones appeared to be brighter, giving the impression he might be gaining strength. Even her magic seemed stable. Somehow, she and Gavin were enough to keep Cheveyo going. For now at least.

Realizing Tala still waited for her answer, Raine nodded. "We just need to piece together his location." Easier said than done.

As they cleared Tala's circle, they discussed their too few clues—the hazy images picked up when she first entered Cheveyo's body. Rough stone and a fire didn't equal GPS coordinates.

Exasperated by the seeming dead ends, Raine crouched to sweep up the last of the salt. "What about following his signature?"

Busy wrapping her tools in a velvet cloth, Tala stilled.

"Until we're closer it won't help." At Raine's questioning look, she explained, "It's like a game of hot and cold. If you're near him, his magic should burn brighter. Farther away, it fades."

Gavin shoved the last of the furniture into place. "It's fairly bright now, so we know he's in town somewhere."

Startled, Raine asked, "How do you—"

"I can see it—same as you." Keeping his back to her, he gave the couch a final nudge. "We're still bound."

Comprehension slammed home and the dustpan tumbled from numb fingers. Holy shit, she forgot to ask one very important question about his shadowing her. She rose and he turned to watch her approach. "How long are we tied together?" Nerves made her voice hoarse.

Determination and something else tightened his jaw. "As long as we need to be."

Uncertain if his answer was a threat or promise, her stomach quivered. "How long is that?"

He folded his arms over his chest and held her gaze, letting his silence speak for him. Gavin was clearly staking his claim. A soft growl of feminine frustration escaped as she turned on her heel, snatched up the dustpan, and headed for the kitchen.

Stupid, thick-headed male ass. She banged the dustpan against the side of the garbage can with unnecessary force. Salt and flecks of melted wax drifted into the garbage as she continued to silently fume. He thought he had the upper hand, but he'd soon learn differently. She tossed the dustpan into the utility closet as the shrill summons of someone's cell phone cut through her internal tirade.

As she came back into the living room, she heard Xander's hello. Leaning against the wall, she waited.

Weariness threatened to pull her under, but there were things to do, monsters to kill.

"Yes, sir. She's right here." Xander held her phone out to Raine.

Straightening, Raine reached for the cell phone, knowing the list of people Xander would be so polite to was small. "Hello?"

"McCord, what the hell is going on?"

The irritated voice almost brought a smile to her face. "Hello, Mulcahy. How's it going?"

His answering snarl made her lips twitch. Tormenting her captain was one of life's little delights. Knowing where the line was—now, that was trickier.

"I swear I haven't killed anyone." She left the *yet* unspoken.

"That may be," Mulcahy bit out. "But you've sure managed to piss them off."

"Not on purpose." She sighed. Really, it wasn't like she tried. It was just a gift.

A snort of what might have been laughter—or exasperation—sounded down the line. "Tomás Chavez called me this morning."

"That was fast," she muttered. Checking the clock, she saw it was barely after six in the morning, which made it just past five in Portland. Anger flared as the pointless, petty politics being played. Static burst over the line, causing her to hold the phone away until it died down. Electronics and her magic never played well together. Keeping her voice and emotions level, she went back to the conversation. "The Southwest Alpha was under the impression our first priority was to find his men's killer."

There was a pause, then Mulcahy's ice-shrouded voice replied, "You clarified your position, I assume?"

"We were very clear, sir."

She could easily picture her chief sitting in his office chair, sable hair brushing his narrow shoulders, his long fingers drumming on the desktop, while his coffee-colored gaze studied the early morning darkness outside his window.

The faint creak of chair springs confirmed her visual accuracy.

"Update me on the latest." Mulcahy's voice thawed slightly.

She quickly brought him up to speed. Very aware of Tala listening in, she kept her report as unbiased as possible, reciting the bits and pieces shared. Mulcahy was a master at reading between the lines, and this time proved no exception.

"Magi Whiteriver is there, listening," Mulcahy guessed, not expecting an answer. "So we have some ancient Native American spirit picking off Kyn, accompanied by some angry ghosts. Common consensus says Cheveyo is being held by this entity." He sighed. "You think the deaths are linked to the divisions between the Houses?"

"Right now it's all we have," she confirmed.

Mulcahy was quiet for a moment. "Ask Whiteriver who else knew Cheveyo was coming in to town."

The obviousness of the question slapped her. Damn, she must be beyond tired to miss that one. She turned to the other woman. "Tala, who else knew Cheveyo was heading in to help you?"

Gavin and Xander stopped what they were doing and came to attention. Everyone waited for the witch's response.

"Tomás and Rio." Tala's voice was even.

"Rio?" Who the hell was Rio?

Surprisingly, Mulcahy was the one who answered. "Rio Castle is the head of the Southwest Amanusa House."

"Guess we need to have a chat with Rio, then," she said as she watched Tala's jaw tighten.

"They aren't all like Natasha," Mulcahy warned. "So be careful."

Raine's thoughts flashed to Natasha Bertoi, the treacherous beauty who was the head of the Northwest Demon House. She and Raine tended to mix like oil and water. Unlike Raine, Natasha used her stylish business suits and her delicate femininity to hide her more lethal aspects —ones Raine heard whispers of, but never witnessed. However, Mulcahy had been dealing with the demon queen much longer than Raine, so if he felt the need to warn her, best heed his advice.

"Understood, chief."

"One more thing," he said. "During the last Council, there was some talk about the Southwest Houses facing a land fight with a human developer."

The Council occurred twice a year and was attended by the various Heads of House scattered through out the world. She never attended one, and had no desire to thanks to the stories she heard. With that many powerful egos under one roof, it was a guarantee Raine would say something to cause an international incident. Besides, some Heads of House, especially the European ones, were so old they teetered on the edge of crazy.

Picking at Mulcahy's answer, she asked, "How big of a fight?"

"Big enough to warrant a discussion of the pros and cons of sending a small group of Wraiths to address it."

The lack of inflexion in his answer sparked a sixth sense. If the Council considered sending the Wraiths in, the threat must have been pretty damn strong. "They chose not to?"

"In the end it was decided that it would create too much of a risk for the Kyn."

Mentally she translated—the Council decided it would bring too much human attention to them if they took out the developer causing the problem. "Do you have a name?"

"Ransom Developments, based in Phoenix. The CEO is Doug Ransom."

"Got it. We'll check it out."

"McCord?"

"Yes?"

"Don't leave me a mess."

She felt a cold smile stretch across her face. "I don't leave messes, sir."

His disbelieving snort was replaced by the drone of a dial tone.

She tossed the cell to Xander. "Catch."

Xander snagged the small device out of mid-air and pocketed it. "So, we have another name?"

"Actually, two." Raine leaned against the wall and watched Tala put the last of her witchy supplies away. "Rio Castle and Doug Ransom."

The purple candle in Tala's hand slipped to the floor. She raised her head to look at Raine. "Ransom? Why him?"

Raine shrugged. "Not my place to question my captain."

Gavin was caught in a sudden coughing fit.

Tala scowled. "Fine, whatever." She retrieved her candle. "I'll set up the meeting with Rio. As for Ransom, you're on your own."

Gavin stepped away from the couch. "You don't like Ransom?"

Tala gathered her things and moved toward Raine. "Not many around here do."

Raine waited until Tala brushed past her. "Didn't like the Council's decision, huh?"

Tala stopped short and turned, her expression stony. "Not my place to question the Council."

The subtle menace in her tone sent shivers coursing down Raine's spine. Tala continued into the kitchen leaving an unsettled silence behind her.

Xander broke it. "You just have to push?" Weary exasperation laced her question.

Raine shrugged, a little uncomfortable at Xander's reprimand. "Sorry, habit."

"Yeah, well," the shifter said. "It's going to come back to bite you in the ass, you know?"

"Yeah, I do," Raine muttered, as a wave of exhaustion hit her all at once.

Something gave her away, because Gavin took over. "All right, we need sleep. We'll catch a few hours and then decide who's talking to whom."

Xander nodded and headed to her room. Gavin waved Raine on ahead of him. She was moving toward the bedrooms when she realized he wasn't behind her. She turned to find him standing in front of a hall closet. The open door blocked her view of him. She took a deep breath. "Gavin?"

His muffled, "Yeah?" came back.

Nerves shimmered under her skin. "Where are you sleeping?"

He pushed the closet door closed and leaned his shoulder against the hall wall, arms filled with a pillow and a blanket. His gaze was steady, watchful. "You issuing an invitation?"

The damn, inconvenient blush was back. She shrugged, feeling awkward. It was all she could do to hold his gaze. "Maybe."

His slow smile was devastating to her nervous system. Her body might be exhausted, but the frustrated arousal from earlier was making a speedy comeback.

He pushed away from the wall and stalked forward. "Be very certain, Raine." Stopping inches away, he leaned forward and brushed his lips across her forehead. "I won't be stopping this time."

Nerves rioting, she told her fears and uncertainty to shut the hell up. This once she would dare to reach for what she wanted. Tilting her head back, she rose on tiptoes and caught his lips in a teasing kiss. "Good."

Arousal lit his eyes with answering passion.

She stopped thinking. Letting her emotions lead, she turned and headed to her room. The soft click of the door closing followed her in. She skirted the foot of the bed as the butterflies in her stomach became frantic.

She set her blades on the nightstand. Unarmed, she turned to face him. She was surprised to find her hand shaking when she grasped the hem of her shirt.

Before she could drag it up, he stopped her. "I want to do it."

His warm hands burrowed under the material to skim over her bare waist. Pulling her closer, he captured her lips. His tongue's light, teasing strokes eased her mouth open as she followed him down the path of wicked sensations.

She laid her hands carefully against his jaw, as if he was a dream her touch would shatter. The hair roughened skin rasped against her palms. Sliding one hand around to bury it in his silken hair, she stepped in, pressing herself tightly against him.

The hard angles and planes against her softer curves stoked the fire higher. Her gentle kiss turned hungry and demanding. Her hands scrambled to remove the cloth barrier of his T-shirt in an attempt to reach his skin. She grasped his shoulders, needing the anchor as her world went supernova.

Lost in his touch, she felt the room spin. Only when her spine met the bed did she realized he was laying her down. The heat of his mouth left her lips and trailed down her neck, sending chills over her skin.

He delved under her T-shirt and pushed it up, baring her to his touch. As soon as the cotton cleared her head, his hands retraced their path over her exposed flesh.

Her breath caught as he simply looked at her. The intensity in his dark green gaze stripped her of all defenses. Feeling vulnerable, she dropped her arms in a futile attempt to shield her body.

With a soft growl, he gently captured her wrists. Without taking his gaze from hers, he turned her hands over and placed a gentle kiss in the palm of first, one hand, then the other. The tenderness in his caress broke the dam holding back her rioting emotions.

He leaned forward to capture her lips. His kiss was full of gentler emotions now—and so at odds with the wildfire raging between them. Leaving a trail of wet heat, he burned his way down her neck with light nips. His wicked hands teased a path over her ribs and belly. Those same tormenting fingers danced over her stomach and brushed tantalizing strokes under the waistband of her jeans. While his fingers continued their erotic play, his mouth traced the edges of her bra. His beguiling touch left her nipples aching.

She arched, wanting more. Gasping, she tunneled her

hands into his silken hair, trying to hold on as her body began to melt into pure sensations.

He made quick work of removing her bra before flicking her nipple with his tongue. Desire punched low and fierce as he drew her supple flesh deeper into the heated cavern of his mouth.

A soft wail of need escaped her and she gave into the knowledge she had resisted for so long—this was the one man she could count on to hold her, protect her. Even as he set her world on fire.

She struggled for air as desire burned bright, searing her senses until all that was left was an endless need for his touch and the powerful sensations it evoked. As inescapable ecstasy washed through her. He pushed her pants over her hips and down her legs. Restless, she kicked them off. With one bare leg free, she hooked it around his jean-clad hip, drawing him relentlessly closer. She needed him to fill the aching emptiness consuming her from the inside out.

When he finally settled his hardness against her, their groans mingled. Somewhere along the line, he lost his shirt, leaving her a veritable playground of bare skin. Never one to back down from a challenge, she took extreme advantage. Leaning up, she nibbled and kissed her way down his neck until she could explore his chest. She dragged her nails lightly down his ribs and then wrestled with the stubborn button on his jeans. When it refused to cooperate, she gave a frustrated growl. Letting her nails sharpen, she ripped the material open. Her satisfied purr was drowned out by his dark moan as she wrapped her now less-lethal fingers around his steely length.

She was so intent on the newfound sensations, that the

sharp jerk as he tore away her underwear was soon lost under the erotic shock of his fingers delving into her wet heat, wringing a short scream from her. Her body curved into his touch. His wicked fingers teased her higher while he continued to lick and suck her nipples. The volatile combination drove the flames into an inferno. Lost in the maelstrom, she dug her nails into his shoulders.

"Please," she begged as he shuddered against her.

He lifted his head, lust and something she feared to name riding hot on his face. "Please what?"

"Take me," she whispered, too raw to use the word trembling on her heart.

His mouth came back, fierce and predatory as his tongue tangled with hers. His taste was dark and addicting, drawing her deeper into the abyss. She clung to him, rubbing against his muscled chest. The need to feel the rasp of his skin against hers stoked the flames higher. Spiraling sensations sent sparks sizzling through her veins, leaving her damp and needy. His erection pressed hot and heavy against her aching mound. She rolled her hips, trying to trap the delicious pressure where she wanted it most.

With a hungry sound, he ripped his mouth from hers to scorch a trail down her writhing body. The rough material of his jeans rasped over her sensitive clit, sending lightning streaking through her core. Her body arched, her eyes fluttering closed as desire consumed her.

He growled his explicit commands. Her body burning out of control as his rough voice teased and tempted. His destructive seduction reduced her to gasping sobs. Frantically, she reached for him and found only air. Her eyes snapped open.

Gavin stood at the end of the bed. Once he had her

attention, he began to push his jeans down. The striptease revealed long, muscled legs, and provided prominent evidence he was as ready as she was. Before she could react, he grasped her ankles, and drew her toward the end of the bed until her legs hung over the edge. His hands slipped up her calves then her thighs, caressing and stroking.

Her breath stilled as he dropped to his knees and with a slow possessive look lowered his head to her damp heat. Unable to look away, she could only give a strangled cry as he licked her. His treacherous tongue rasped against her sensitive flesh. Her body coiled tighter and tighter as his mouth worked its dark magic. Just before she broke, he stopped, pulling away.

"Please, Gavin!" Her voice was hoarse with desperation.

He didn't make her ask again but crawled up her body to reclaim her lips. The combined taste of them almost overwhelmed the feel of his body sliding over hers. He murmured against her mouth, his voice harsh with need, and her body rioted wildly.

Then she felt him, broad and thick, pressing against her entrance and time stopped. Sound was lost, leaving only spiraling sensation in its wake. As his shaft teased her, white lightning pierced her with exquisite pain.

"More!" Desperate for all of him, she dug her nails in to his shoulders to drag him closer.

He gave into her demands and trapped her hips in his hands as he draped her legs over his arms so he could glide over her sensitive nub. Drawing back, he stopped. For an endless moment she thought she would scream. Then he plunged deep, setting up a harsh rhythm, strong and fast.

It was everything she craved, needed. He stabbed so deep there was no telling where she ended and he began. He kept up his sensual assault, demanding her body follow his. Sensation built upon itself, burning her from the inside, until she was a mindless, writhing thing beneath his pounding strokes. Her breath came in wild gasps. Her nails raked his back as she fought for a non-existent anchor in the sensual assault.

Under her tempestuous emotions, terror stirred. Through their newly formed mental bond, she was losing herself to this man. The emotional threads tying them together tightened. Panicked, she tried to fight the overwhelming feeling, but it was useless. Her body was so lost in the storm she could only hang on.

"It's too late, Raine. You're mine," he growled as he claimed her on every level.

His words pierced her soul as she exploded into a white-hot blaze around him, her body and soul shattering into a million pieces. His hoarse cry echoed hers as their climaxes hit simultaneously.

When the dust settled, there was no denying he was irrevocably bound to her and her to him. As their bodies began to drift, she sent her own ultimatum through their bond. *"And you're mine."*

Sometime later, Raine jerked awake in the moonlit bedroom. Fear was a bitter taste in her mouth and her pulse raced from some half-remembered dream. The unfamiliar sensation of being held in strong arms deepened her sense of unreality. Gavin's deep even breaths feathered over her neck. He cradled her close, his arm lying across her waist. Not wanting to wake him, she lay still, taking in the enormity of her actions.

Old fears began pecking at her mind. She failed to save

her mother from the horrors of Talbot's experiments. Even Gavin's trauma at Lawson's hands could be placed at her feet. She failed him once. Who was to say it wouldn't happen again? Hell, her current situation boiled down to her being unable to save Cheveyo. Pissed off spirits or not, her job was to protect both Kyn and human from the monsters and their deviant wet dreams.

She waited for her internal voice to start yammering away about how this relationship was such a bad idea. Yet if she was honest, this stolen moment in time felt...right.

She worked beside Gavin for too long not to understand what tonight meant. He staked his claim and so had she. There was no backing out—for either of them. The thought of sharing her life with this man scared her, but not in the way she expected. There was no denying he was demanding, but he had proven he would stand beside her —not on top of her. Plus, he was okay with her being...her.

Nerves eased and she gently traced the back of his hand where it lay below her breasts. Relaxing into his warm body, she let her mind drift in hazy peace as she continued her light exploration of his arm. Her mind sank behind her shields and a soft glow flickered to life. As she focused, it strengthened, pulsing in soft waves, until she could distinguish the threads weaving between her and Gavin.

They appeared thicker and brighter than before. Squashing the habitual alarm struggling to rise, she lightly skimmed the glowing bond. Answers lay within this. Curiosity urged her to delve deep, but she held back. Did she really want to follow this through? Could she handle whatever answers she found?

A faint regret flittered at the back of her mind. It was futile to wish she could be the type of woman to believe someone could love her. She wasn't. Making her choice, she nudged the niggling worm of guilt aside. As far as she was concerned, curiosity never would have killed the cat, if the cat knew what it hid.

She studied the colors flowing under her psychic hand. Silver and blue intertwined in a mesmerizing light show. Steeling herself before she could change her mind, she grabbed hold.

Power ripped her into a rushing river of magic giving her no time to brace. She flailed as fear of losing herself in the roiling wave washed over her, bringing a flood of memories in its wake. She caught images, flashes of people and places that held no meaning for her. Emotions not belonging to her clashed, grasping and tearing at her mind until she wanted to scream. Her shields, already weakened from so many hits, crumbled and the wave rushed in.

She was standing in her bedroom in Portland. It took her a second to realize she was looking at herself, huddled in a ball in the middle of the bed, whimpering. A large, male hand gently stroked over her hair. A soft murmur of comfort followed. The need to protect rose, vicious in its intensity. It was then, she realized she was in Gavin's memories. Shock held her still as she played voyeur.

She remembered that night. She had taken him home, left him in the guest room and gone to bed. Nightmares had plagued her—brutal and soul destroying. He had been in her room, watching her, comforting her, and she hadn't known it.

Her house in Portland disappeared. Desire, bright and demanding, sent her heartbeat skyrocketing. She watched herself slowly rock in a porch swing overlooking the Willamette River. She recognized Gavin's house before the urge to draw the small female form closer mounted. The porch swing faded to be replaced by his front door. She could feel his arousal and need spike when she kissed him that first time. Her daring had sparked tenderness and pride. Shock rocketed through her as she understood that he knew how much courage it had taken for her to make that first move.

Their bond dragged her through the edges of his soul and the scene shifted. Magic held her fast, and now she was Gavin in a dark room, feeling the panic clawing at his soul. She lay on a bed, broken and bleeding. He was trying to hold her to him, physically and mentally—desperate to bring her back. His iron will focused solely on her. It was disconcerting, even as the fragile ember in her heart began to burn.

Suddenly a sharp physical pain wrenched her back. She sucked in a gasping breath. Like a swimmer breaking the surface, she broke out of Gavin's memories, only to discover him looming above her, his green eyes blazing.

"Found what you were looking for, Raine?" His voice was a low growl above her.

Tied so close to him, she couldn't separate their emotions. Anger, frustration, love, need, a fragile trust—all of it melding into a strange morass.

He nipped her shoulder, the small sting bringing her fully back to the present. Listening to his steady heartbeat, she struggled to focus. The sound of his heart was so similar to Tala's drumbeats.

Raine was able to slowly shut out her awareness of everything around her and concentrate on the repetitive pulses. Little by little, she pulled herself together, until her sense of self was re-established.

Gavin was curled around her back, holding her in a cage

of flesh and warmth. The crown of her head was tucked under his chin, and her fingers were clenched around his arm wrapped about her waist. Forcing her hands to relax, she felt his tension drain away as well. A whisper soft kiss brushed the top of her head. Dragging in a deep breath, she found her emotions were once again her own.

She tried to turn around and apologize. Before she could release the "sorry" on the tip of her tongue, he stopped her. "Don't do that again. Not alone. It isn't safe."

She didn't hear any traces of anger, just worry and frustration. He loosened his grip and let her turn toward him so she could see his face.

"I just needed..." She trailed off, her voice ragged.

His gaze was steady. "To what? Understand?" His voice sharpened. "Or were you looking for a reason to run again?"

Heat filled her face and she shook her head. She wasn't looking for an excuse. But reassurance? Yeah, she needed to know he really wanted her. This bond was getting tighter by the minute. It scared her.

"I don't know how to do this." Her heart was still reeling under the revelations her little journey had produced.

"Maybe." He tucked a strand of hair behind her ear. "But the real question is do you want to do this?"

There was no hesitation when she nodded. If she hadn't been so very up close and personal with the inner Gavin, she'd be freaking out about now. He'd taken chance after chance with her, and she could do no less. She was bound to mess this up, but if she was lucky, the reward would be well worth it.

Even without their connection, he left his fingerprint on her soul and she was determined to fight for what she wanted and damn the consequences.

"Then we'll figure it out as we go." He gently ran a finger along her jaw.

She smiled.

He settled in behind her once more and she let the strangely comfortable embrace anchor her as sleep claimed her.

CHAPTER 16

Several hours later, Raine was roused by a sharp knock. She pried open her eyes, squinting at the early afternoon sunlight filtered through the blinds. She was alone. Disappointment fought with a strange sense of relief. The knock sounded again. This time it was followed by the door opening.

Xander's distinctive visage came into view. "Hey."

Raine pushed herself up to a sitting position, raking back her tangled hair. "Hey."

Xander closed the door behind her and came over to perch on the end of the rumpled bed. The smaller woman watched Raine steadily with too-knowing eyes. "So, the rental company has delivered a new car for us."

"And the old one?"

A small smile appeared. "Tala and Gavin managed to convince them you had a run in with a deer. It seems deer qualify as 'acts of god' under the insurance coverage."

"Seriously?"

Xander nodded.

Raine gave a soft snort. “Go figure. Well, at least we don’t have to depend on Tala for rides.”

“I spoke to Warrick this morning,” Xander said with studied casualness.

“Your head’s still attached and I don’t see any claw marks.”

A grimace made the inked lines on Xander’s face twist like delicate vines. “Not where they’re visible at least.”

Something in her voice sent a twinge of concern through Raine. She was well aware of Xander’s tumultuous relationship with Warrick Vidis, the Northwest Alpha, and one fourth of the ruling body of the Northwest Kyn. “Everything okay?”

Xander skated her gaze over her before focusing out the window. “As much as can be expected, I guess.”

“Do you want me to talk to Vidis?”

“Oh hell no.” Xander’s head snapped around, and she actually paled before a sharp laugh escaped. “I appreciate the offer, but no—don’t talk to him. Please.”

In their line of work, women were rare. Even more, at the level she and Xander existed, they were unique. Both she and Xander were strong, deadly females who had earned a healthy measure of respect from their male counterparts. Yet, every now and then, some of those males would conveniently forget exactly what they were capable of.

“C’mon, Xander,” she said, frustration rife. “If Vidis is listening to the crap Chavez is spouting, someone should set him straight.”

Xander’s hand came up, halting her tirade. “Stop. Vidis is my alpha. He was within his rights to read me the riot act.”

“Maybe.” There was something else here. Raine could

see the woman's banked anger, but there was more to it. "But you're an important member of his pack. I'd think he'd listen to your side before making any decisions."

Worrying a loose thread in the quilt, Xander dropped her gaze. But not before Raine caught the flicker of hurt quickly hidden. "When it comes to pack politics, questioning any alpha is not exactly the smartest move you can make."

"So the fact that you questioned Chavez in the course of doing your job gets you bawled out by your alpha?" Raine wasn't sure where this conversation was going, but she struggled to follow along. "How's that fair?"

Xander gave her a bitter smile, gold-flecked eyes mirroring the chiding note of her voice, "Nothing's ever fair. You know that." Sighing, she rubbed her hands down her thighs. "Look, it's nothing new. Warrick and I will be fine."

Raine wondered if Xander could hear the question in that last statement. Throwing the blanket from her legs, she got out of the bed and went to the dresser. Using a brush on the wild mass of her hair, she considered how confusing and frustrating Gavin could be. Seeing Xander's slumped shoulders in the mirror, she stepped out on to shaky ground. "Um...you and Vidis have these disagreements a lot?" She winced. *Argh, what the hell was she doing?*

Xander turned to look at her.

Raine focused on carefully braiding her hair so she wouldn't have to meet Xander's eyes.

"As much as anyone else, I guess."

Raine was startled when Xander's voice sounded as uncomfortable as Raine felt.

Xander paused then continued, "Trying to keep the line between personal and professional has its challenges."

Finishing off her braid, Raine's voice was very quiet, "Is it worth it?"

The silence filling the room was deafening. She turned to tell Xander...what? Something...anything so she wouldn't have to hear the answer.

Yet as she faced the other woman, the flash of some undefined emotion was replaced by Xander's soft smile. "Yeah it is."

Discomfited by the unusual burst of female bonding, Raine searched for a change of topic to get them back on safe ground. "Who's going to see Ransom and who's going to see Castle?"

"Not sure." Pushing off the bed, Xander moved toward the bedroom door. "Gavin's waiting for us in the kitchen."

Raine toyed with an image of a bare-chested Gavin in nothing but jeans and bare feet. Her mouth watered. "Food?"

Opening the door, Xander laughed. "Yeah, with food." Shooting a mischievous look at Raine, she added, "You know, most women don't get that look for food."

Fighting back her sheepish grin was futile. "Who said it was for the food?"

Xander's laughter echoed down the hall.

After lunch, Raine and a fully clothed Gavin stood outside Rio Castle's residence waiting for the man to answer his door. Xander was with Carlos, visiting the families they missed the day before. Hopefully the duo would get more information on Jeremiah's disappearance. Since Phoenix was a three-hour drive from Flagstaff, Gavin scheduled the meet with Doug Ransom for tomorrow afternoon.

The air was cool and crisp, though nowhere near as chilly as what Raine was used to in Portland. As Gavin raised his hand to knock on the door again, she asked, "You sure this is the right address?"

He shot her an exasperated look and rapped on the door.

With her hands stuffed in her jacket pockets, she shrugged. "Just saying, this is not where I'd expect the head honcho to live."

"And what exactly do you expect my house to look like?" The caustic question had Gavin and Raine turning to the man coming up behind them.

The distinguished looking gentleman was bundled into a blue pea coat and wearing wire rimmed glasses. He climbed the stairs to the second floor condo with his arms full of groceries. Switch to a tweed jacket and add a pipe, he have the stereotypical college professor look down pat.

The man, who had to be Rio Castle, joined them and shoved the bags of groceries into Raine's hands. "Hold these while I get my keys out."

Stunned, she juggled the bags while Gavin watched with a small smile of amusement. The rattling of the keychain was quickly followed by the small snick of the locks opening.

Pushing the door wide, the older man walked through. "If you're waiting for a personal invitation, you'll be waiting a good long time."

Raine corrected her image from typical-college-professor to crotchety-old-man. Gavin mockingly waved her in ahead of him. Snorting, she stepped inside.

Gavin closed the door and followed her down the

narrow hallway. Tracking the old guy's mutterings, she entered an open living space. On her left was the living room lined with floor to ceiling bookcases, crammed to the seams with books and knickknacks. A huge sectional couch took up most of the floor. One corner held a desk. At least she thought it was a desk. Hard to tell with the leaning towers of papers creating their own cityscape across the top.

"Go out for groceries and get ambushed outside my own doorstep." The petulant tone had her turning to the small kitchen separated from the living room by a pass-through. The grocery bags slipped, so she adjusted her grip. An open refrigerator door of gleaming stainless steel reflected muted light. "Set the bags on the counter, young lady."

She did as she was told. "Rio Castle?" Better make sure they had the right individual.

White hair appeared from behind the refrigerator door, the kitchen's fluorescent light shining off the round lenses. "What? You expecting someone else to live here?" Not waiting for her answer, he began unpacking his groceries. "What do you want McCord?"

She shot Gavin a look. Neither one gave introductions or called beforehand. Standing in the open hallway, Gavin gave a slow shake of his head.

"Who called you?" Maybe Tala had forewarned Rio? Raine didn't think the witch would, considering how the Amanusa were viewed.

Rio stilled, a package of cheese in one hand. "What a stupid question." The hair on the back of her neck stood at attention as the temperature seemed to develop a sudden cold edge. "I hadn't heard you were stupid." He cocked his head in a strangely reptilian move and mocking smile appeared as he turned to put his dairy product away. "Perhaps the stories are a bit exaggerated?"

"Depends on the story you heard," Gavin's voice cut through the strange atmosphere.

Rio's answer was a wickedly dry chuckle. Folding the now empty bag, he watched them both. "Stories, good stories, are rare. Ever been to a Council gathering, son?"

Gavin shook his head. Unpacking the second bag, Rio shrugged his shoulders. "Too bad. I think you two would make great conversation pieces." Closing a cupboard, he folded the last bag and tucked it away beneath the counter. "No one called me. However, whether the precious witches and puppy dogs want to include me or not, I'm still very much aware of what is happening in my territory."

"Then you know why we're here?" Raine warily studied the man. Goose bumps still pebbled her skin. No matter how harmless he appeared, something deadly lay behind those spectacles and white hair.

"Sit." Rio waved them toward the oversize sectional. "You may want to stand and loom, but I'm perfectly happy to sit my tired bones down." He took a seat in the armchair nestled between the sectional and the desk.

Gavin folded his long frame onto the couch, his booted feet crossed, his arms stretched across the couch's back. Giving a soft sigh of resignation, Raine perched on the flat arm of the sectional.

Rio removed his glasses, wiping them with his shirt. Laying them on the table next to him, he met Raine's stare as he leaned back. "Neither I, nor my people, have anything to do with the missing Kyn." His voice was almost indifferent. Yet the cold calculation tempered with rage deep in his gaze gave lie to his tone.

"Yet you hold no love for the Lycos or Magi Houses?" Gavin cut in with a lazy drawl.

The red ring, common to all Amanusa, bled into Rio's brown eyes, igniting an inhuman light and sending Raine's pulse into overdrive. If she hadn't been familiar with the same angry reaction from Natasha, Raine would have released the blade at her wrist. Humans had definitely gotten the whole glowing-red-eyes thing for demons right.

"There is no love lost between my House and the pack."

"And the magi?" she pressed.

Rio leaned back, his fingers slowly tapping. "They're tolerable." He held one finger up before either of them could ask. "Don't misunderstand me. Old beliefs die hard, but the younger generations tend to understand not everything is defined by black and white."

Gavin quirked an eyebrow. "Shades of gray?"

The smile twisting Rio's lips was closer to feral than amused. "Gray is such a beautiful mixture of black and white, isn't it?" When neither of them answered, he continued. "My House welcomes inquisitive minds. An individual's search for answers can take them across many barriers."

Raine frowned. "Including the barriers of right and wrong?"

Gavin didn't move, but a stinging smack on her thigh left her hissing out a breath. She shot him a glance, surreptitiously rubbing the ache. This new talent of his was getting old real quick.

"Who defines those barriers?" Rio's voice deepened slightly, drawing her attention. His expression hadn't changed in the slightest. "How does one individual get to define what is right or wrong? What makes them the better judge?"

Listening to his questions, she almost missed the sly edge creeping into his voice.

"At what point do the needs of the many began to outweigh the needs of the one?" he continued. "And who determines when the many are more important than the one?"

The temptation to follow the old man's path down their inevitable rabbit hole was strong. His questions eerily echoed many of the ones she asked herself during dark nights when her decisions haunted her. It was a slippery slope, one she teetered on even as Rio whispered in her ear. One little push and down she'd go.

"So the belief of the other Houses doesn't worry you?" Gavin's voice broke through Rio's treacherous web.

Turning those disconcerting eyes toward Gavin, Rio asked, "Which belief are you referring to?"

Fighting her way free of the remnants of Rio's questions, Raine kept her voice bland. "The one where demons exists outside the natural world order."

An animalistic snarl echoed through the room. The deep rumble sent a renewed race of chills over her. Rio hadn't so much as twitched, but the threat riding the air increased. Gavin shot her a look. She shrugged. Okay, so she hit a sore spot. Rio should be old enough to hold it together, right?

The old man's head turned back toward her. It was odd to watch. The white hair and old professor image moved like a mirage, but there was a sense of something else, something other. That other was a lot larger than the frail human form sitting in his high backed chair. Larger and more monstrous. Something huge with teeth and horns. The image wavered and the only thing keeping it connected to the image of the man known as Rio was the red glow of his eyes.

The room's temperature dropped and she battled back the need to shiver. Her bloodless fingers clenched around a knife she didn't remember drawing. Next to her, Gavin tensed. She felt energy being sucked in and held steady. Gavin may not have a weapon visible, but a spell would work just as well. As a witch, he knew what would work against a demon more so than Raine.

Poised on the knife's edge of tension, they watched Rio and waited. It was never good to go against the top dog in the Amanusa House.

"The natural order," snarled Rio, "exists because the Amanusa exists. In every culture, in every ancient tale of creation, there is the light and there is dark. They balance each other." Watching them, he sniffed once, as if taking in their scents. The smile blooming on his face was far from comforting.

As he continued, the chill air in the room began to lessen. "For every living thing—human, Kyn, or what have you—there is balance. Opposites, if you will. Good and evil, light and dark, witch and wizard, life and death, Lycos and magi, right and wrong, fey and Amanusa. When you upset that balance you have chaos."

"The Amanusa thrive in chaos," Raine stated softly. It wasn't that she wanted to piss this demon off, but she was trying to feel her way through what he was sharing. She could sense the teasing thread of understanding lurking just out of reach.

Rio gave an unexpected laugh. It was a true sound, containing a dark joy as if she had said something truly spectacular. "Perhaps, McCord. We don't thrive so much as enjoy what emerges from the chaos. If the natural law is balance, then out of chaos something must emerge that balances the two forces. Sometimes it's worse than we can imagine, others it's better." His laughter faded but he still watched her closely. "And sometimes we have no idea what it is until it's too late."

Something in his tone made her flinch. His cryptic messages were pointless, a waste of their time. They needed answers and he was engaging in a philosophical debate. It wouldn't surprise her if Rio really was a professor, a theological professor. He'd get a kick out of that job. Talk about chaos.

Gavin's let his magic disperse, the tight knot of power slowly unraveling as if he decided Rio was no longer a threat. "What would be gained by taking out the shifters and witches?"

Rio shrugged, the persona of a crotchety college professor firmly back in place. "For me, nothing." At Gavin's look, he continued, "Granted, I find some amusement in watching the squabbles between the Lycos and the magi. However the tensions between the two Houses have been in place longer than dead bodies have been popping up."

Considering how closed lipped Tala and Chavez had been, Raine was unsurprised by that little tidbit. "How much longer?"

Rio pushed up from the chair. "I need a drink. Would you like anything?" He didn't wait for their answers and headed into the kitchen.

Through the pass-through, Raine watched as Rio stuck his head in the refrigerator, before answering her question. "Going on six or seven years now." Brown bottle in hand, he closed the door and pulled down a glass. "It's an old story, one even Shakespeare told." Pouring the bottle's content into the glass, he ambled back to his chair. "Teenage girl meets teenage boy. They fall in love, but their families don't approve."

Raine caught the faint scent of root beer. Uh, she figured him for the real thing.

Settling into his chair, Rio took a sip before continuing. "I don't know the details, just bits and pieces. Mainly from rumors and hearsay as I wasn't inclined to get involved."

He carefully set his glass down on the nearby side table. "The girl was from a family on the reservation. Witches I believe. I don't know her name, but I think it was just her and her mother. The boy was Chavez's son. They two met at some rodeo, hit it off, and dated for quite some time. The story goes the boy was thrown from a spooked horse while riding fences miles from home. By the time anyone realized he might be in trouble, it was too late. His family was devastated to lose their only son."

"And the girl?" she asked.

He took another sip. "I'm not sure who told her, but there were rumors she and the boy's mother got into it at his funeral. Words were exchanged, and the girl left in tears. The boy's mother was furious, looking for someone to blame, and the little girl was a good target."

"Where is she now?" Gavin broke in.

Rio shrugged one shoulder. "No one knows. She and her mother disappeared about a week later. No one knows why. Some say she couldn't stay where the memories lived, others say the boy's mother bought them off. Stories abound, some more believable than others."

But he had a theory, Raine could tell. "What do you think happened?"

Rio tapped his fingers against the arm of his chair, his gaze shuttered. "I think prejudices lie thick and deep around here. Regardless if you're human or Kyn, there are some who think the two should never mix. Others still who think even within the Kyn, you shouldn't mix bloodlines."

Recognizing his non-answer, Raine tried to fit the pieces together. "Where does Tala fit into this story?"

Rio studied her for a long moment. "For all her faults, Tala is a worthy Head of House. Her family has been in this land for a very long time. Not all of them were Kyn, and occasionally a human would marry into the family. If the rumors are true, this little girl and her family were relatives of Tala's. The witch takes familial ties very seriously."

Okay, so Tala had a personal stake in this mess. "So this fatal teenage romance created some new divisions between the magi and the pack?"

"Not between the alpha and the magi," Rio clarified.

"Between the alpha's mate and the magi," Raine said softly, remembering the subtle undercurrents in Tala and Lizbeth's interactions.

Rio gave an approving smile and a short nod.

Gavin leaned forward, his arms on his knees. "Lizbeth is Lycos, correct?"

"As far as I know, yes," the demon lord answered.

One of Rio's earlier statements had Raine asking, "Was she ever one of those inquisitive minds?"

His answer wasn't really an answer at all. "You need to be careful in your dealings with whoever is holding your magi. This land is old. Some of those who walk it hold to beliefs older still—and gray is the only shade they see."

CHAPTER 17

Caught in her thoughts, Raine sat quietly beside Gavin as they drove back to Tala's. Rio's story kept tugging at her. Something didn't fit. Thinking aloud, she worked it through. "Rio said Chavez's son was thrown by a spooked horse, but I thought other animals were naturally skittish around shifters?"

"I'm not sure." Gavin didn't take his gaze off the road, occasionally using the windshield wipers to clear the hazy slush thrown up by passing vehicles. "But we can ask Xander when we get back."

Grimacing, she realized most of her questions would have to wait. "Yeah, definitely need to run some things by her. Shifters are damn closemouthed about things."

He gave a short snort. "And the Fey and witches are open books right?"

"Point." Leaning her elbow on the edge of the window, she let her aching head rest on her hand. "Sometimes I think we need a Kyn For Dummies manual."

"Why?" he drawled. "You have such a diplomatic touch with everyone."

She didn't stop the small smile his sarcasm brought out. "Well, what can I say? When you're good, you're good."

Closing her eyes, she let the motion of the car lull her into the stage where she walked the line between awareness and sleep. The scrape of the blades against the windshield blended with the muted sounds of the other cars on the road. There was a soft whooshing sound as the heater fought back the cold. When she felt Gavin's hand gently still her fingers, she realized she had been rubbing the spot on her thigh where he had smacked her earlier.

Lifting her lashes, she studied him. He wasn't looking at her, just holding her hand. Such an innocent touch, but it felt like so much more. She dropped her gaze to their hands. His nails were short and his honey colored skin was marked with a few scraps and nicks. Her skin was noticeably lighter and her nails were longer, a few more ragged than the others. Both hands held similarities—old scars from past battles, calluses from years of weapons training—and each was deadly in their own right. Needing the newly intimate connection they shared, she turned her hand so their palms met and their fingers tangled.

"Does it hurt?" His question was quiet, but there was a touch of something akin to remorse threading through it.

Puzzled, she glanced up. "Huh?" Wow, that sounded intelligent.

He glanced at her then, without letting go of her hand, and used one finger to touch the spot on her thigh. "Did I hurt you?"

"I'm crippled for life." She rolled her eyes. "Don't be an ass, I'm fine."

There was a small twitch at the corner of his mouth, but it disappeared as quickly as it appeared. He gave her hand a small squeeze and happiness made itself at home. It was unsettling. How long had it been since she felt like this? Sadly, she couldn't remember.

Absently rubbing her thumb over the back of his hand, she studied the man she was now irrevocably tied to. No one would ever mistake him for other than what he was, a warrior. It was there in the way he carried himself, the quiet self-assurance and constant watchfulness. Add in his latent strength lying under a layer of discipline, and it created a very tempting combination.

How had he done it? Her small edge of jealously was petty, but she couldn't quash it. She was still dealing with the consequences of having her magic, her sense of self, altered so drastically years ago. Yet here it was, three months after he had his own magic blasted wide open, and he didn't seem much different than before. Granted, he had a darker edge, but overall, he was the same man who walked into her house in October and made a place for himself in her life.

"How do you do it?" As soon as she uttered the question, she could feel the heat stealing up her cheeks. The sad wistfulness tingeing her voice made her uncomfortable.

He tightened his grip until she stopped trying to pull her hand free. "Do what?"

Sighing, she gave an uncomfortable shrug. When would she learn to keep her mouth shut? "You're so normal." Maybe normal wasn't the right word, but she couldn't find a better one.

"Normal? Is that what you call it?" He shook his head. "I'm pretty far from normal."

"You seem to have your magic under control." Oh gods, that did not come out whiny!

"Ever hear the term 'fake it till you make it'?"

Right! A spike of hurt flashed. If he didn't want to share, so be it. She yanked her hand away, suddenly disappointed—but uncertain with whom. The car made a quick exit. "Where are you going?"

He didn't answer, but the grim look on his face set off her warning bells. Pulling into a parking lot of a strip mall, he brought the car to a stop. Throwing it in park, he left the engine running, but turned in the driver's seat to face her.

"You think I have it all figured out?" Strangely enough, his growling voice sent warmth spiraling through her.

She was one sick puppy if his yelling turned her on.

"You think I would ask if I hurt you, if I had this under control?"

Amazement rose. Gone was the calmly controlled man she was used to seeing. Unable to formulate an answer, she could only mutter, "You didn't hurt me."

"Maybe not this time. But what about the next time, or the one after that? What good am I if I can't control my own magic? I can't ignore it. It's always there, this roiling mass of energy screaming to be used."

His jaw locked, anger and frustration leaking from him. The quick flash of fear she discovered nestled deep inside him during her morning explorations started to make sense. Control was as vital to him as it was to her. Losing that control, even a little bit, was a frightening proposition, because the results could be disastrous.

Seeing this strong warrior begin to doubt himself left her heart aching. But as his last statement sank in, she wondered what she missed. "Used how?"

The look he shot her sent a slice of dread through her soul. "However I can. I've learned to use it before it builds up too much. The more it builds the less control I have over it."

Unable to stop, she reached out to gently touch his

clenched jaw. Just under the anger in his voice was the one emotion she never thought she would hear from him, fear. "You have to be one of the most disciplined men I know, Gavin."

"It may not be enough this time." His voice was quiet, eerily empty.

She narrowed her eyes. "Bullshit." The word was a whip. "I don't believe that. It's magic, no matter how it was created. You are Kyn. Not only are you Kyn, but you are a Wraith. You have fought worse things and walked away."

"Yeah but those monsters didn't live inside me."

"Seriously?" Her short laugh was sharp. "Think about it. As Wraiths we're the bogeymen to all bad little Kyn. You think that monster came from Lawson's little drug cocktail?" She leaned forward. "I hate to break it to you, but it was already there. It's why you're a Wraith. Don't you understand? We were picked to be Wraiths because to hunt the monsters, you don't send out hunters, you send out other monsters."

The bitterness in her own voice rang through the car's interior. Defiantly she held his narrow-eyed stare and folded her arms across her chest as the windows around them began to fog over. Obviously, Rio's little digs about judges and jury had gotten under her skin more than she realized.

"I'm not a teenager." He watched her. "I'm older and have a hell of a lot of practice with shields. You spent months at the mercy of twisted men. I spent a few hours. Granted, it was enough. I've spent the last three months trying to come to terms with what's been unlocked."

He shifted in his seat. "Some days are easier than others. For the first couple of weeks, it was all I could do to keep sane. If it wasn't for you and Cassandra, I'm not sure I would have made it back."

She looked away, fighting back shame. "I didn't do anything." She wanted to see him, but her guilt at putting him in Lawson's line of fire kept her back.

He grabbed her chin. "You survived, and I couldn't do anything less."

The intensity in his eyes had her tongue nervously wetting her lips. His thumb rasped against her lower lip, following the moist trail. The simple caress made her breath catch, and when his head lowered, she met him halfway.

The minute his lips touched hers, heat engulfed her. The whispers of doubt fled under the fire, and she gave in to the inevitable. He made her want things she never thought she'd get, and he made her believe. In him. In her. In them.

Her tongue teased his, and his groan turned her blood to molten lava. Their rising passion sucked her under. Tunneling her fingers through his hair, she reveled in the feel of the silky strands, using them to hold him close so she could plunder the heated depths of his mouth. The seatbelt was a minor inconvenience, holding her back from crawling closer.

His hands stayed as busy as his talented mouth. They stroked over her neck and caressed downward until he could fill his palms with her breasts. Her shirt was a flimsy barrier to his sensual assault. Ripping his mouth away, he flicked his tongue to trace the cord in her throat. Her head fell back, giving him better access. He gently nipped her skin where neck and shoulder met, his stinging bite lost in her rising passion. Those clever fingers forged a fiery trail that left her breasts feeling full and heavy, causing a small whimper of need to escape her. Constrained by the seatbelt, she could do nothing but surrender to his touch.

With a wicked chuckle, he bent down and drew one tight nipple into his mouth, shirt and all. She was lost as her body rocked under his touch. His tongue curled over her, tugging her deeper into his mouth, as his hand plucked and teased her other breast. The feel of being restrained as he tormented her was almost more than she could take.

The blast of a car horn shattered her haze of passion. "Gavin," she breathed, her voice hoarse with need. Awareness of their surroundings flooded back.

He nuzzled her one last time, before giving her a quick, hard kiss. His grimace as he shifted back into his seat drew her gaze downward. His hard-on was obvious, and her body didn't care where they were—it wanted. She closed her eyes, trying to get her breathing back under control. If she couldn't see him, maybe she could bank this fire. Instead, the heady scent of him wound its way deep inside.

"You're a dangerous woman, Raine McCord." His voice rough, he shifted uncomfortably.

She blinked. "I didn't start it this time." Was that husky voice hers? Damn him. She cleared her throat.

He gave a deep chuckle and leaned forward to wipe the fogged glass clear. She did the same on her side, trying to ignore her body's pleas. Windshield cleared, he clicked his seatbelt and put the car in gear.

Trying to diffuse the lingering sexual tension, she asked the one question wanted to ask for a while. "What did Lawson unlock?"

Yep, the tension definitely changed. She could actually feel him pull back emotionally. It hurt. Rubbing the phantom pain in her chest, she frowned.

Just when she thought he wouldn't answer, he did. "So far, I can make an individual believe an illusion is real."

Looking for clarification, she asked, "You alter what they think?"

His fingers tightened on the steering wheel. "Not exactly."

This was like pulling teeth. "So, what exactly?"

"Do you remember what happened when you were fighting with the Soul Stealer?"

"You mean when my long lost twin made her appearance?"

He gave a short nod. "I don't understand the details, but I know I was able to create an image of you, make it real enough to inflict damage on the Stealer."

She remembered how startled she was when the doppelganger popped up. The image moved like her, fought like her, and if she hadn't been on the ground on the other side of the Stealer, even she would have believed it was her. It was complex magic and hurt her brain to think about. "Could the Stealer see me? The real me, I mean?"

His answer was slow in coming. "I'm not sure. I don't think so. Cassandra explained it to me like this—if someone expects something or someone to act in a particular way, and if I can create a realistic illusion, their belief that it's real, makes it so."

"Really?" Magical philosophy always gave her a headache, and it was no different now. "Okay, so because it expected me to fight it, it reinforced your illusion until the real me disappeared from its view?"

"Something like that."

His response sparked another question. "Were you able to do this because we were walking between worlds?" The space where the colorful tapestry existed, where they traveled to track Cheveyo, existed on a plane between the mortal, or waking world, and the otherworld of magic. It was an alternate plane of reality, one most humans had no access to, but the Kyn, because of their nature, had no problems navigating.

He shrugged. "Probably."

She narrowed her eyes. "Have you tried doing the same thing in the waking world?"

He nodded

"That smack at Rio's and the other time at the Chavez's, that's how it manifests on this plane, right?"

He slid her a look. "You tend to speak before you think. It seemed the easiest way to get you to stop before you said too much."

Right, or not, she didn't have to like it. "I'm not a child." The feel of phantom fingers stroking over her sensitive breasts, made her breath catch.

"Trust me, Raine. I'm highly aware of that."

And that fast, the heat was back. Damn, maybe his newfound abilities had some positive benefits. An erotic shiver worked its way over her. "I'm not the only dangerous one here," she said softly.

His answer was a very male smile.

Ignoring the wild fantasies traipsing through her mind, she focused on the conversation at hand. "Is that all of it?"

"No." The single word was harsh.

"What else?"

Instead of answering, he switched lanes taking the turn to Tala's house. Finally he asked, "What did you see when we were tracking Cheveyo?"

Uncertain what he was looking for, she thought back. "Your magic is like mine. There are small flecks of black in your color."

"I'm not surprised." His tone was so matter-of-fact she couldn't help but stare. "What do you think it means?"

"It's a sign of the magic the scientists twisted in me, and whatever was in that injection you were given." *Wasn't it?*

"Maybe.

"What do you mean, 'maybe'? What else could it be?" Frustrated nerves made her voice harsh.

"I have my own theories."

"Like?"

"What if what happened to us didn't twist our magic, but unlocked something else?"

"Again. Like what?"

Obviously, he could hear the panic she was trying to keep at bay, because his tone gentled. "You and I aren't purebloods. We're both a mixture of Kyn bloodlines. Purebloods are few and far between. Each younger generation is mixed more and more. What if the mingling of the bloodlines created new forms of magic?"

"We would've had signs of it earlier," she argued.

"Would we? Maybe the trauma of having our natural shields ripped away triggered it. Kyn have depended on their natural shields for centuries. It's what helps us function in the mortal world. Without them, our magic is wild, unpredictable."

It made a terrifying sort of sense. "Evolution of magic."

His voice was grim. "Every living thing evolves. Magic isn't exempt." He pulled the car into Tala's driveway. Shutting the engine off, he turned to her. "I think we're the next step in the chain."

Her mind raced, and the clicking of the engine filled the silence. If what he said was true, what did it mean? She and Gavin were comparatively young by Kyn standards. Their magic had years left to develop. There were Kyn out there who'd lived hundreds of years, Mulcahy being one of them. Why hadn't any of the older Kyn come to this conclusion before?

Maybe paranoia was just raising its ugly head, but she couldn't shake the feeling she and Gavin were on the edge of something much bigger than even she could guess at. If so, it meant their career as lab rats may be far from over, and it wasn't just the humans they'd have to be wary of.

Her throat was dry. "How far have you gone with your magic?"

His green eyes were steady. She wished she could be as calm. "Not too far. I need someplace quiet and safe." He paused. "How far have you gone?"

She dropped her gaze and focused on her hands fisted in her lap. "Obviously not far enough."

Taking a deep breath, she stared unseeingly at the empty drive outside Tala's cabin, thinking. If he was right and they were the next step in the Kyn evolutionary chain, she'd be an idiot not to see how far she could stretch her magic. He kept quiet, letting her work it through, which made her strangely grateful.

The heat of his hand as he laid it over her clenched fists broke through her spinning thoughts. "We may not be able to wait until we're home," he warned.

His words made her breath stutter in her chest. She unclenched her hand and turned it until his palm pressed against hers. "I know." She took a deep breath. "I think we need to go back to where Jeremiah disappeared."

His brow furrowed and his grasp tightened. "You think that's wise, considering what happened to you last time?"

She shrugged. "We're missing something. If we go back, maybe I can find some trace of Jeremiah, even if I need to push a little deeper." He opened his mouth and she cut him off. "You'll be there to keep me from going too deep, but we need to know."

His searched her face. Letting go of her, he turned the key in the ignition and put the car in reverse. "You're scared," he muttered without looking at her.

Her normal flare of anger didn't come at his words. There was no denying the truth of them. Attempting to track Jeremiah's magic could just as easily kill them as work. "Yeah, I am," she admitted. "So if you can come up with something better, let me know."

He gave her a small, tight smile. As he steered the car to the clearing, the sense of standing on the edge of some great cliff came back in a gut-clenching wave. Her only solace was this time she wouldn't fall alone.

CHAPTER 18

Back at the spot where Jeremiah had disappeared, Raine tried to ignore the chill of the winter air. It joined forces with her nerves, causing a rash of goosebumps to erupt. Even with her barriers in place, there was something creepy about this spot.

The sunlight filtering through the bare branches did little to erase the gray shadows twisting in between the dormant trees. Strange, she never really thought of forests in Arizona. They weren't as thick, or as old, as the ones back home in Portland, but she could feel the thrum of natural magic lying in sluggish trails under the frost encrusted ground. Uncertain of what she would be facing, she reached for her magic.

She spun a delicate tendril out into the forest, a cautious greeting to the slumbering power. For a moment there was no answer. Then like a shy child, the natural magic reacted, weaving gold strands over and around her silver light. The sleepy forest choose to share its winter wonderland with her and her sense of self began to blur as she was drawn into the primitive magic.

She tumbled with the wind across the pristine beauty of a fresh carpet of snow. The quiet murmurings of frost filled her ears, as it laid its delicate lace patterns across branches and stone. The sharp sting of the air caressed her as it wound its way down the mountain, while the ever-changing, bell-like tones rang from the streams of snowmelt.

Under the onslaught, she let the natural magic share what it wanted, taking a brief respite from the outside world and the fears and worries that existed there. This wild peace was difficult to find, and she wasn't about to offend the ones so graciously sharing their bounty with her.

All too soon, the shy magic slowed and awareness of her surroundings fell back into place. With the added benefit of the wild magic, she could make out the ragged edges of dark shadows lurking farther back in the trees. She took a step toward the unsettling gloom, only to feel the psychic tug as the natural magic unwound and curled away, leaving her bereft.

Turning she reached out and a hand grasped hers. The brief ache faded under the light of the silver and blue bond she shared with Gavin. Keeping him close, she watched the natural magic recede, leaving the surrounding forest a little less bright, a little more ragged than before.

Blinking, she looked at him. "Even the magic doesn't want to mess with whatever this is," she whispered and waved a hand where the shadows gathered, their darkness more pronounced than when she had first arrived.

With a small tug, Gavin pulled her closer. "It has a choice, we don't."

"True." She took a deep breath. "Let's get this done."

He gave her hand a firm squeeze before letting go. Curious after their earlier conversation, she allowed her vision to split. An ever-changing play of light wreathed the real world as magic rode the air around them, blurring the forest and glade into watercolor-like scenery.

The minute Gavin lowered his barriers between the real world and his magic, Raine felt it. It started in the center of his body, a glow like a far off campfire. As he began to raise a protective circle, the campfire grew in strength.

Never would she tire of seeing the world stripped of its protective shell. When she was small, her mother shared tales of how the Fey existed in a world where the magic ran free and wild before the coming of iron and man.

Watching Gavin's magic burn as he wove the steel blue through nature's golden glow gave her a glimpse of those far away days. Even tied as close as she was to him, she could barely make out the murmur of his deep voice. He brought both magics together in a silent flash of light.

When her vision cleared, she was standing inside an undulating wall of blue and silver, interspersed with gold. No longer shrouded in the bright flares of magic, Gavin appeared more defined, sharper to her psychic eye.

Her lips curl in appreciation. She may not know much about how witches drew their power, but she knew enough. It took a great deal of strength to raise such a solid circle of protection without the benefit of a grounded power source. The fact he had done so effortlessly meant whatever power had been unlocked a force to be reckoned with.

There wasn't much room in the circle, just enough so they could step around each other without bumping. A movement outside the protective barrier caught her eye. Snagging his wrist, she pulled him back the circle's edges.

With her blade in hand, she stood between him and whatever lurked on the other side. Through the translucent wall she watched shadows snake over the forest floor. Narrowing her eyes, she stepped closer. Something was in those shadows, something she couldn't make out. If she was just a little closer—

"Stop." Gavin's low command was reinforced when his arm wrapped around her waist, pulling her back. "You can't cross the circle. You'll bring down the barrier."

His words cut through the strange compulsion. "There's something in those shadows." Her voice came out on a low growl. Startled, she turned her attention inward. Her cat was riding uncomfortably close under her skin.

"What?" He must have picked up her suddenly racing pulse.

"Something's messing with me." Pressing back into his solid form, she hoped the touch of his body would help ground her. Maybe stop the strange urges pushing at her.

His arm tightened and his magic poured over her in a warm wave. The unknown tension lessened. "Better?"

Doing an internal check, she found her leopard had slowed its pacing and was finally settling. The threat of a sudden shift receded. She uncurled her nails from Gavin's arm and relaxed, lowering the blade in her other hand. She gave the half-moon marks in his skin a stroke of apology. "Thanks."

"Be careful when you're under." His chest vibrated against her back.

Tilting her head back, she pressed a quick kiss to the underside of his jaw, touched by the concern in his voice. "I always am."

He looked down at her and an unfamiliar gentleness softened the lines around his mouth as he cupped the side of her face. Leaning down, he took her lips in a warm kiss. When he was done, he chided, "Try harder this time."

She stuck her tongue out in answer. As if she went looking for trouble. More like trouble found her.

He let her go and stepped back, giving her space.

She studied the weirdly dancing shadows outside their barrier. Time to get to work. "Ready?"

He nodded, his face grim.

Taking a breath, she made sure she anchored herself with their shared bond then dropped behind her barriers until the undulating magic filled her vision. Blue and silver hit the protective wall of power, causing small sparks of iridescent flames, which bled into the overall color.

She considered the circle's magic. The key would be to get past the protective edge without tipping off whatever it was lurking in the trees. Somewhere in this glade were traces of Jeremiah. She just had to find them and follow.

First, she would have to mute her psychic presence. Watching the rippling power, she began to recognize a usable pattern. Inspiration struck. She reached through their bond. *"Gavin?"*

"Yeah?"

"Can you resurrect my twin?"

His surprise echoed through their bond and he took a moment to answer. *"I can, but if you get into trouble I won't be able to hold it."*

She got that. *"Okay. Will you be able to shadow me and hold the image at the same time?"*

"Probably, but not for long."

"Hopefully I won't need much time."

He didn't answer. Instead, her identical twin stepped toward the edge of the circle, luring the seething shadows close.

Praying his illusion would hold, she slipped into their bond and made her way to the point where their combined magic met the protective barrier. Letting her presence flow into the power, she concentrated on riding above the wave. She held her breath. Here was where she would be the most vulnerable. Shifting from the protective circle into the existing web of the forest's magic, she risked exposing not just herself but Gavin as well.

"Move!" His mental push sent her scrambling into the uncertain web.

Trusting him to watch her back, she began searching for Jeremiah's trail. Relying on her memory of her first attempt, she glided closer to a group of young ash trees. She snuck a glance back and noted the sentient shadows stayed focused on her doppelganger. Her twin was busy sending psychic probes at various points of the barrier. Raine turned to the task at hand, resuming her search.

Something flickered at the end of her vision. Yet when she looked at the fluctuating magic, it remained unchanged. She held still, hoping to catch the anomaly once more. Within moments, it flickered again. Slowly she brought it into focus. There, in the magical web, a small inky blot winked along the threads. There was only one way to follow.

She snagged one of the marred threads. Ice-cold flame set her world afire. Unprepared she was sucked under so fast she couldn't react. Those searing flames licked over her, hungry and voracious, using her as dry tinder. With no choice, she could only hold on to herself as the chilling menace took shape and plunged her mind into a morass of confusing memories.

She wasn't Raine, but a wolf fighting for his life. Yet no matter how hard the wolf fought, he couldn't stop the agony roaring through his body. As the frigid fire etched into his bones, the man's spirit who lived deep within the wolf screamed.

As if that was the signal they were waiting for, the seething shadows swarmed him.

They clawed and ripped bits and pieces of his life into shreds. He couldn't find anything to fight, nothing to hurt, to rend or tear. There was only the never-ending freezing fire and the malevolent shadows engulfing him. His struggles weakened, as the mighty wolf failed to find the strength to continue the fight.

Despair rose. There was no way to escape alive. Man and wolf pushed the despair back by pure force of will. They were Red Thunder Pack and nothing could shatter their need to protect, not even death. They had to warn their alpha they were being hunted.

Raine felt the moment the wolf gave the man control, even as unearthly flames set their blood boiling. Trapped inside Jeremiah's memories, she watched as he lay on the forest floor the shadows pressing closer, morphing into ghosts of the familiar dead.

Chindis—the ghostly remnants of those taken before their time. The identification whispered through his fading conscience. No one mentioned how terrifying it was to be torn limb from limb, your spirit shredded by those you once knew.

Man and wolf were in agreement. They would be nobody's servant, not even in death. Hard as it was to block out the barrage of agony, and the futile attempts of his dying body to escape, Jeremiah and his wolf took refuge in one last piece of magic. If they were lucky, they might take a few of the chindis with them.

Raine was buried so deep in Jeremiah's memory she couldn't escape. The shifter's magic gathered and held until the end was imminent. Like a flash bomb, the magic exploded. Ghostly shrieks raked at her ears as the magic scoured over her soul and burnt the wolf and man to nothing, leaving her spirit trapped in the past.

Unfortunately, Jeremiah's last act didn't wipe out all the ghosts. Those remaining remnants found her.

Layer by layer, the chindis burrowed into her magic and peeled it back with greedy claws. Her ties with Gavin and Cheveyo begin to fray. The unnerving sensation sliced through her, arrowing deep where her wild magic roiled in fury.

Unable to think through the nerve-splicing pain, she released her iron control and let her magic loose. Flames, edged in black, roared to life, searing the sticky tendrils holding her to Jeremiah's memories and driving the chindis back.

Then the hellish flames surrounded her.

Outside the fiery walls, the angry wails of the chindis rose into a deafening crescendo, only to fall into startling silence. In that unexpected well, a black leopard with silver eyes appeared and paced protectively in front of her. As the cat brushed by, bumping against her crouched form, she reached out and curled her trembling fingers deep into its fur. The cat's message was clear—get up.

Straightening, she cautiously made her way to the edge of the flickering light. The chindis were gone. Behind the fire something huge and dark prowled. The Soul Stealer was back. It turned its head and Raine caught the impression of gold fire burning in empty eye sockets. The protective ring of flames sputtered and it lunged forward. She stumbled back even as the burning edge held.

As she and her leopard retreated, she did a quick check. They were safely tucked in position—two at her wrists, one at her back, and the two nestled in her boots. Here's hoping they'd work as well in the spirit world as the real one. Otherwise, she was in a shit-load of trouble.

The reminder of back-up had her mentally reaching for Gavin. Magic washed over her psychic fingers like water, leaving her with nothing to hold. Her stomach iced with dread.

The wall of hellish flames shrank again, allowing the Stealer to stalk closer. Breathing through her panic, Raine ruthlessly demanded her magic to answer. Cold sweat ran down her spine and her teeth clenched with the effort. The weight of her leopard curling around her legs broke her concentration. She looked down, unnerved to see the cat crawl inside her as predatory animal and the woman became one. The last of her leopard disappeared under her skin and her magic woke with a painful snap.

The momentary distraction cost her. The Stealer charged through the fading flames, slamming against her. Her mental protections shuddered under the hit and her tenuous hold on the fragile strand tying her to Gavin threatened to break. Channeling her waning power, she sent a surge of power along their bond, praying it would be enough for him to find her. She was out of time.

The Stealer swiped out with monstrous claws, shredding through the remaining black-edged flames. It gave a triumphant scream as the fire stuttered again. Left with only her blades as protection, Raine braced.

She needed to stay on her feet until Gavin arrived. And he would arrive. It was just a question of would it be in time? Her magic was draining fast and her leopard had nothing more to offer.

Lips curled into a snarl, teeth bared, she set her feet,

gripped her wrist blades, and let the last of the protective flames blink out, leaving her exposed.

The Stealer threw back its head, a long triumphant howl emerging from its throat. Lowering its head, the creature watched her with unholy glee.

"Bring it, asshole," she taunted.

It stalked forward. Instead of the smoke and shadow form from previous encounters, it now sported a massive wolf-like body. The head was still a Dali inspired nightmare of sharp, pointy teeth animals. Grateful the chindis decided to bow out, Raine left her back unprotected to keep an eye on the approaching monster.

Like the opening sequence in a dance, they matched steps. Without warning, the Stealer sprang forward, lashing out with unsheathed claws. Ducking, Raine rolled right, blade extended, aiming for a gut swipe.

The monster managed to twist its spine so her first cut merely scored its skin, leaving black ichor oozing in its wake. Unfazed, the Stealer spun with lightning speed and its sharp claws scored bloody furrows into her lower back. Ignoring the tug of pain, she stumbled to her feet, and waited for the next opening.

The Stealer lunged, knocking her down. Along her ribs and hips her skin shredded under its lethal nails. It snarled and snapped, trying to get to her jugular, but she kept it back with her left arm. Using the blade in her right hand, she stabbed blindly, her world narrowing to pure survival.

"Damn it, Gavin, where are you?"

Silence answered.

She jammed her booted feet into the Stealer's stomach. Muscles straining, she heaved the crushing mass off. Curved claws tore at her skin as the Stealer went airborne before tumbling across the ground.

Rolling to her hands and knees, Raine sucked in air, her vision obscured by the tangled screen of her hair. Blood coated her hands, leaving scarlet handprints on the ground. Surprisingly, she managed to hold on to both blades. Using a forearm to push the matted hair out of her face, she got her feet under her just as a deadly snarl filled the air.

She jerked her gaze up to find the Stealer scrambling back to its feet, its hind right leg held high in pain and a dozen wounds leaking the disconcerting black blood.

Halle-fucking-luja, she managed to do some damage. Unfortunately, it wasn't enough. Upright but unsteady, she watched the damn monster barrel toward her and knew another wrestling match would not end well. Ignoring her body's battered cries, she let her first blade fly.

The black-matted, silver tumbled end over end scoring a direct hit, sinking deep into the left eye socket, extinguishing the flames nestled inside. The Stealer jerked back, a tortured, angered howl ripping through the air.

Drawing another knife from her back, she grimly set her feet and held her ground.

The Stealer decided to stand upright on its hind legs, revealing fur matted with black blood. *Why wouldn't it just die already?* The various wounds she inflicted were definitely slowing it down—unfortunately, she could say the same about her injuries.

The Stealer charged. She stayed out of its reach, turning her blades into a lethal whirlwind. Back and forth they danced, each inflicting non-lethal hits. Then the Stealer managed to nail her with a brutal blow, weakening her already damaged leg. She stumbled. The Stealer took a vicious swipe, leaving its side unprotected. Raine lunged, punching her blade deep. Wrenching her wrist, she twisted the knife's edge before ripping it free, causing as much damage as possible.

The Stealer's shriek raked across her eardrums. Warm blood seeped from her damaged ears. The annoying voice in her head was back—*Too slow, too slow*. Off balance, she staggered forward, knowing she was in trouble but unable to stop what happened next. The Stealer's paw slamming into her, sending her crashing across the floor. White flare of pain seared across her senses and her blades fell like silver stars.

Desperate and determined, she rolled to her back, pushing up on her elbows even as her vision wavered. Still, she make out the Stealer stalking her with deadly purpose. She tried to get her legs to move, but her body refused to respond. After seemingly endless seconds, she finally flopped onto her side, grabbed her unresponsive leg, and dragged it up. Her fingers found the hilt of her boot blade.

The Stealer loomed closer, its uninjured eye full of malevolence.

Her blood coated fingers slipped on the hilt. She gritted her teeth and pulled it free. This bastard was going down if it was the last thing she did. Unfortunately, that might be just what the Fates had in store.

A sudden blinding explosion ripped through the air and a wall of blue flames edged in black roared to life between her and the Stealer. The monster screamed in frustration, lunging forward to rake at the newly raised protective barrier. For a moment, time blurred, slipped sideways, then steadied.

Armed with an elegant sword, Gavin forced the Stealer back, allowing the strengthening flames to rise into position.

Intelligent enough to recognize the shifting odds, the

monster screamed in fury and began to retreat. Gavin's magic forced the beast into the shadows outside the barrier, until the Stealer's presence began to fade and the real world began to bleed through the web of magic.

Relief left Raine shaky as the world dipped and spun around her. Slowly, she lowered herself to the ground and closed her eyes hoping to stave off the nauseating sensation. Instead of helping, the spinning rose to dizzying new heights. Prying her eyes open, she stared into Gavin's worried face. His jaw tightened as his gentle touch uncovered each injury.

"If you keep doing that, your jaw will break." Her voice was so rough it was almost unrecognizable. She wanted to touch him, to let him know she was okay, but couldn't get her hand to move.

"I told you to be careful," he growled.

She managed to curl her lips into a small smile. "I was. I just had to hold him off until you came."

He stilled, watching her closely. Frustration was rife in his tone. "Damn it, woman."

"Damn it, man," she chided. "What took you so long?"

He picked her up.

The sudden change in position left her stifling a moan. "That frickin' hurts!"

Ignoring her, he demanded, "Do you have any idea how deep you went?"

She shook her head once before giving up and leaving it on his shoulder.

"Too damn deep for my comfort. If it hadn't been for the flare you sent out, I'm not sure I would have found you. What happened?"

"Found Jeremiah," she mumbled. "But he sacrificed

himself, hoping to take some of the chindis with him. They weren't too happy about it. Then the Stealer came."

"Rest," he said. "Let's get you out of here."

She was more than happy to let him take care of things. Her eyes drifted closed. The heat of his magic twining with hers sent a small surge of needed strength through their fragile bond. It wasn't as strong as before, but better. So much better.

"Missed you," she whispered.

"Missed you, too, baby." His gentle words followed her into the darkness.

Sometime later Raine lay in the back seat of the rental car while the heater ran full blast. She woke when Gavin set her in the passenger seat and her body decided to see if it could shake itself apart. Before it could succeed, he dragged her into the back and wrapped his long frame around her, adding his own version of a thermal blanket to the mix.

Pressed between the slowly heating leather interior and his warm body, her muscles slowly relaxed. Bone deep aches and sharp pains clamored for attention. Considering how much damage she endured on the other plane, she wasn't surprised. No doubt she would soon be the proud owner of a few, new black and blue badges. As the minutes passed, she managed to unlock her jaw without worrying her chattering teeth would amputate her tongue.

She pulled the sharp intoxicating scent unique to Gavin into her lungs, unable to muffle her soft moan when her ribs protested. He shifted his weight, giving her enough room to slip her hands under the soft material of his T-shirt. Pressing her palms against the firm heat of his chest, she took comfort in the small touch. She left her head on the comfortable pillow of his shoulder.

"How bad?" His chest vibrated under her hands.

"Bruised ribs, my thigh burns like hell, and my back isn't any picnic." Her physical complaints could have been worse.

"Better than I expected." His casual statement caught her off guard.

Forcing her head up, she studied his face. "Excuse me?"

Dark green eyes burned out of a remote mask, making her heart stutter. This wasn't the Gavin she was discovering, the one who could hold her with such gentleness and strength. This was the warrior. Remote, cold, and calculating. The creeping chill slipping into the newly reclaimed warmth had nothing to do with the winter temperatures. Against his chest, her hands curled into fists.

He shackled her wrists, stopping her. "Don't." He stroked a thumb over her pulse. "I spent some time repairing the damage to our bond."

Only because they were face to face did she catch the glint of fear he quickly squashed. That peek sent worry spiraling, knotting her stomach. Determined to see for herself, she closed her eyes and slipped between worlds. The transition was becoming easier and only took a moment for her to bring the expected light show into focus.

Finding the unique tie she and Gavin shared, she discovered the reason behind his worry. Normally, her magic was a bright metallic silver with flecks of obsidian. Not now. Instead, it was a lifeless, pitted gray. Even more startling was the change in their bond.

Initially, their blue and silver had wrapped around each other to create one thick thread. Now she could see where he delicately combined his magic with hers, weaving a protective layer over her obviously fragile one.

Shocked and dismayed, she blinked back to the waking world. She reached for her magic and the slumbering cat residing inside only to feel...nothing. No wall, no answer, just an empty void. Panicked, she stiffened in Gavin's arms, trying to push free.

"Stop." His hold didn't relent, his arm becoming steel bands holding her flailing body tight. "It's not permanent."

"You don't know that." She stared into his face, trying to counter her rising desperation. "Let me up."

His lips thinned, but his arms loosened. Carefully, she braced her back between the seat and the window so she could glare at him.

Facing her with his back lodged in the corner of the backseat and one knee on the leather seat, Gavin laid his arm along the headrest. When she continued her silent condemnation, he flexed his mental muscles and those phantom fingers gave a sharp tug on her braid.

"Ouch!" She yanked her head back. "Knock it off."

"You ready to listen now?" he drawled.

Swear to gods, he drove her nuts. "I'm listening."

"Your magic isn't gone."

She narrowed her eyes. "There's nothing there when I reach for it. Sure seems gone to me."

He shook his head. "Think about it. Your magic is like any other muscle. You use it, it burns energy. Train it and it becomes stronger. You use it too much, you'll strain it." Catching her disbelief, he frowned. "Didn't Cheveyo teach you anything about how magic works?"

Defensive, she crossed her arms in front of her. "Yeah, some."

Gavin waited.

She ground her teeth. "Mainly we've been working on figuring out what, exactly, mine does."

Tapping his fingers on his knee he said, "Magic is part of you, but just like any other skill, it has limits. You draw on it too much in one go, you risk draining it. Then you have to refill your reservoir."

"And to refill?"

"Takes time." His answer made a strange sort of sense. He leaned forward and caught her chin. "Do you have any idea how much you used today?"

Unable to look away, she shook her head. He let go of her chin, but not before she caught a peek behind his mask, where worry and concern battled for supremacy. Her defensive anger drained away because leaking at the corners was a disconcerting fear. For her.

"You went under so fast, I couldn't follow." Impotent fury darkened his face. "I'd catch a glimmer of you and then the shadows would suck you back under. I knew you were in trouble, but I couldn't find you." His remembered frustration at being unable to reach her was evident in those dark green eyes.

"The shadows, those were ghosts," she said.

His head jerked at her statement. "Explain that."

She sighed. "We're not just dealing with the Soul Stealer. He has little ghostly carnivorous friends."

"Chindis." His voice was hard as steel.

She nodded and continued before he could interrupt. "Jeremiah's memories pulled me under before I realized what was happening." She kept her voice low, trying to calm the raging storm in the man sharing her space. "I couldn't get out of his head until—"

"Until he killed himself and almost took you with him," Gavin snapped.

She leaned forward and cupped his jaw. "He didn't, but it was enough to kick me back into my own head." She watched him carefully. "I knew my magic had taken a hit, but I held on to what I could. You obviously got my message."

"You scared the shit out of me, Raine." He leaned in to her touch briefly. "I don't like it."

Her laugh was rusty. "Yeah, I wasn't having much fun either."

"I told you to be careful."

She bit her lip not wanting to grin at the unusual grumpiness of his tone. "I tried." Her humor died as the ache in her head returned. "How long before it's back?"

He tucked her close. "The Stealer, the chindis, or your magic?"

She rested against his shoulder, taking what comfort she could. "Any."

"If you'd stop poking at them, the Stealer and chindis might leave you alone for a bit. As for your magic, you need to rest and eat." She felt him brush a kiss on the top of her head. "Back at Tala's I should be able to do a healing spell. It may boost your recovery time."

She remained silent, trying to find comfort in the fact at least their bond worked on some level.

"It's still there, promise," Gavin's voice was soft but sure. "We just need to let it recover."

She held his promise close, her throat tight as she tried to ignore the empty spot deep inside.

CHAPTER 19

Gavin pulled into Tala's graveled driveway as a sun-faded, blue pick-up followed close behind. Raine pushed her door open, while Gavin walked around the front of the car to meet Xander, who hopped down from the pick-up. Carlos, one of Chavez's men, gave a short nod then put the truck in reverse and drove off.

Gavin, Raine, and Xander trudged up the gravel path to Tala's cabin. Ash lay in the yard, basking in the brief wintry warmth of the late afternoon sunlight. He watched them approach, not bothering to move. When they were a few feet from the door, it swung open.

"Guess we don't need to knock," Raine muttered.

Xander shot a look at the wolf in the yard. "Better than a doorbell."

Ash's tongue lolled out in a silent laugh as he got to his feet and trotted through the door.

Coming in behind Gavin, Raine waited as he checked out the empty living room before moving to the kitchen. She shuffled over to the sofa, her unhappy ribs convinced she'd be better off sitting than standing.

Gavin reappeared, shaking his head. "I can't find Tala."

Getting comfortable, Raine said, "She's around, or we wouldn't have been let in." She waved a hand at Ash who was on his second circle of the same spot in front of the fireplace. "Ask him."

Ignoring them, the wolf sank into a curled position, his tail over his nose. Obviously, he wasn't concerned about Tala's nonappearance.

Gavin leaned his shoulder against the entryway, one dark eyebrow arching at Ash's unconcern. Xander settled at the other end of Raine's couch.

For the first time, Raine saw signs of strain in-between the delicate tattooed lines on Xander's face. "Rough day?"

Xander grimaced. "That's one way to put it."

"Chavez's boys marking their territory?" Gavin scratched his shoulder.

"Not so much marking it as protecting it." She leaned her head back against the couch and closed her eyes.

Sharing a concerned look with Gavin, who shrugged, Raine turned back to the shifter, careful to keep her tone low, just in case Tala was within hearing distance. "You okay, Xander?"

A small, mirthless smile crossed Xander's face. Her voice was just as low. "Yeah. It's nothing I haven't dealt with before." She opened her eyes to meet Raine's gaze before addressing them both. "They're hiding something. However, as long as Chavez's puppies are trotting beside me, I'm not going to get a straight answer."

Gavin shot a look over his shoulder to the still empty kitchen then moved to a chair next to Raine. He sat down, stretching out his long legs. "Chavez may be the Southwest Alpha, but aren't there others we can talk to? Someone who can give us a better picture of what's really happening here."

Xander sighed. "I was thinking of calling the alpha in Phoenix."

Gavin frowned. "I thought Chavez was the alpha."

"Chief Alpha of the Southwest," Xander clarified.

"How many alphas answer to him?" Raine hadn't paid attention to the lines of power in the other Houses. Considering her and Gavin's earlier conversation on the evolution of magic, maybe it was time to start.

Xander ran a hand through over her hair. "Chavez is the top dog, but there are four leaders under him. As the Southwest Alpha, he is the final authority for all packs located within Arizona, New Mexico, Colorado, Utah, Nevada, Texas, and Southern California. Chavez's personal territory covers northern Arizona, all of Utah and a small part of Nevada."

"What about Mexico?" Raine asked.

"Different alpha, Jorge Rodriquez. You don't want to mess with him." Xander's lip curled with obvious distaste. "He makes a caveman look liberated."

"So under Chavez is?" Gavin prompted.

"Under Chavez, you have the heads of territories. There's one other alpha in Arizona, Tobias 'Toby' Greene. His pack covers Southern California, Phoenix, and Tucson, along with the area south to the Arizona/Mexico border. Ryan Riordan holds a large pack in Santa Fe and his territory covers New Mexico and Colorado. Texas is covered by another large pack who answers to Jake Blackwood."

"So we have Arizona, Southern California, Colorado, New Mexico, Texas, and Utah all covered. So that leaves the rest of Nevada," Gavin said.

Xander nodded. “Right. Nevada has a very small pack and their alpha is Jeanette Claison.”

“A female alpha?” Raine broke in. “I thought alphas were all male.”

Something unreadable flashed across Xander’s face, too fast for Raine to catch. “Yeah, well, her pack is too small to be viewed as a threat so they let her claim stand.”

Uncertain how to interpret Xander’s tone, Raine decided to ignore it. “Guess we need to call Toby Greene.”

Xander shook her head. “No, I’ll call Toby.” Raine opened her mouth to argue but stopped when Xander raised her hand. “Look, you and Gavin have your meeting with Doug Ransom tomorrow afternoon. I’m breaking enough rules just placing a call to Toby without running it by Chavez first. This is going to be difficult enough as is. If all three of us go in asking questions, it will be viewed as a threat. Word will get to Chavez, who’ll call Warrick. I’ve already gone one round with my alpha. I’m really not up to another one.”

Raine wasn’t comfortable letting Xander field this lead solo, but understood Xander’s reasoning. “Politics suck,” she muttered.

Xander’s choked laugh agreed.

“When you were out with Carlos, did you find anything?” Gavin changed the conversation’s direction abruptly.

A grumbling sound answered, and Xander’s cheeks turned red at her stomach’s vocal response.

Raine gave a short laugh, and carefully got up from the couch to make her way to the kitchen. “Food first.”

All serious conversation was shelved as they prepared a simple dinner of soup and sandwiches. Realizing Xander’s metabolism would need more than a turkey sandwich,

Raine found a steak in Tala's freezer. It didn't take long before they gathered around a small table nestled in the kitchen.

After taking a few bites, Raine restarted the conversation. "So Rio Castle told us a story about Tomás's son, Brett."

Xander meticulously cut up the very rare steak dominating her plate. She brought a piece to her mouth. "Is it the one where he hooked up with a human girl and Mommy didn't approve?"

Her own mouth full, Raine nodded.

"Yeah, heard that one," Xander said before taking her bite.

"Did you hear how the son died?" Gavin asked, blowing on his soup. Xander shook her head while she chewed. "He fell from a spooked horse."

Xander choked. Raine set her sandwich aside, rising from her chair so she could pound the smaller woman's back. "Damn, Xander, you okay?"

After a few more coughs, Xander managed to clear the obstruction. She took her drink, and sipped slowly. "Yeah, went down the wrong way." She waved Raine back to her chair, her hazel eyes studying Gavin. "Tell me exactly what you heard."

"We were told the son was out checking fences. His horse got spooked and threw him."

Setting her glass aside, Xander narrowed her eyes. "Do you know how long he had this horse?"

"Didn't ask," Gavin answered.

"Should have." Xander took another bite as she gazed unseeingly out the patio door, her brow furrowed. For a few moments silence reigned. "If the horse wasn't used to his presence, it would have been difficult to control from the get go."

"If the horse was familiar with him?" Raine prompted.

"Then it would take something pretty big to spook it," the other woman answered.

"So the story has holes?" Gavin pressed.

Xander nodded. "Yeah. There's got to be more to it." She turned back Gavin and Raine. "I'll see what I can find out from Toby. Maybe we can get few more details."

Raine cocked her head. "You going to call him soon?"

"After dinner." Xander shot Raine a piercing look. "You look like hell. Who'd you run across?"

The flimsy hold on memories slipped, and Raine's sandwich turned to dust in her mouth. Setting it down, she pushed her plate away. "The friendly neighborhood Soul Stealer."

Xander paused with her fork half way to her mouth. Even the tattoos couldn't hide her surprise. "What happened?"

"She found traces of Jeremiah," Gavin answered darkly.

Xander put her fork down, food apparently forgotten. She looked from Gavin to Raine. "And?"

"He was being torn apart by the Chindis." Raine tried not to relive the horror of the tracker's last moments. "He didn't want to end up anyone's slave, so he cast some sort of death spell."

The shifter's face went stony. "Did he take some of them with him?"

Raine nodded.

"Good." Xander's voice was reduced to a growl.

Raine finished the rest of her dinner while the clinking of utensils punctuated the quiet. When they finished,

Xander went to her room to call Toby, leaving Raine to help Gavin with the dishes.

With the last dish put away, she leaned against the counter's edge, exhaustion leaving her drained. Drying her hands, she watched Gavin rinse the suds from the sink. "Gavin?"

He half-turned toward her. "Hmm?"

She rose up on her tiptoes and softly brushed his lips with hers. She drew back enjoying the surprised, pleased look lighting his face.

"What was that for?" he asked.

A little uncomfortable, she shrugged. "Just 'cause."

A wicked smile curled his lips at her answer. He deliberately dried his hands on the towel she clutched. Then his fingers wrapped around her hips, somehow avoiding the sore spots, and drew her close.

She met him halfway. As their lips met, she melted. Strength tempered with gentleness seduced her. Heat and desire flared, chasing the aches and pains away. Her hands went to his shoulders, needing an anchor. The hand-towel fell to the floor unnoticed as they kissed. The front door slammed and Tala's greeting to Ash quickly followed. Raine was the first to break free, but Gavin kept his hands at her waist as she turned toward the kitchen entrance.

Tala appeared in the doorway and shot them an unreadable look before heading to the cupboard next to the refrigerator. Taking down a glass, she kept her back to them as she opened the freezer door. "How was your conversation with Rio?"

Gavin found his voice first. "Enlightening."

Ice cubes tinkled against glass, then Tala closed the freezer. She turned and stepped forward, forcing Gavin and Raine to break apart, so she could get to the sink for water.

They waited as she filled her glass, took a sip, and stared out the window above the sink at the winter-shadowed backyard.

Early evening had come and darkness was making its way across the landscape. Neither Raine nor Gavin wanted to break Tala's strange silence. She finally came to some internal decision and turned to Raine. "I need to ask you for a favor." Her voice was calm, but the whitened fingers on the glass made it a lie.

Somewhat unnerved, Raine shot Gavin a look. Standing behind Tala, he shook his head, indicating he was mystified by Tala's behavior as well.

Determination clear in every word, Tala didn't wait for Raine's response. "Tomás shared the two theories you all discussed yesterday."

"The Soul Stealer and the chindis?" Gavin clarified.

Since he didn't elaborate, Raine guessed they weren't sharing that the theory was now fact.

Without taking her uncomfortable attention from Raine, Tala nodded. "Today I visited those who I thought could harness the power needed to summon either of those beings."

Unable to look away from the witch's dark gaze, Raine asked, "What did you find?"

"Nothing." Frustration washed over Tala's face. "Not one damn thing."

Knowing what it was like to be blindsided by those you thought you knew, a strange sense of empathy hit Raine. Her failure to see the madness in her best friend almost cost her the man she loved. That single word reverberated through her mind and soul, making her heart stutter.

Oh gods! Her panicked gaze latched on to Gavin. He frowned, but she gave a sharp shake of her head, which thankfully Tala apparently missed. Mustering a shaky smile, Raine tried to reassure both herself and the man who now owned a piece of her soul that she was okay. *'Fake it, till you make it.'* The reminder did little to ease the rocking of Raine's world.

This was not the time to dwell on emotional self-discoveries. "Are you sure?" She aimed the question to Tala, Raine's tone much more gentle than even she expected.

Tala set her empty glass down, her shoulders slumping. "As sure as I can be." The mantle of the Magi of the Southwest House flowed like a cloak over Tala, straightening her spine. "I want you to go back under and find out where Cheveyo is. I have a horrible feeling we're running out of time."

Raine blinked, but allowed no other expression to emerge. "You know what happened last time."

Tala stood unbending in front of Raine. "I do."

Gavin opened his mouth, but Raine raised a hand to stop him, never taking her gaze off the woman in front of her. "Then you have some plan to make sure that the Stealer guarding him won't be a problem?"

Tala's lips tightened. "I can't guarantee anything, but I think if you go in alone you can sneak past the Stealer."

Raine wanted to ask about the chindis, but didn't get a chance.

"She's not going anywhere alone," Impatience lent Gavin's voice a lethal edge.

Raine didn't dare let the smile inside show at his protective streak. "If I go in, I take Gavin with me. There's no way I go in alone. If he hadn't been there last time, I wouldn't be standing here now." No need to tell the witch what "last time" she actually meant.

Tala's gaze narrowed. "Fine, but I want you to go in now."

"Why the urgency?" Raine was curious as to the witch's change of heart.

Tala turned away, but not before Raine caught the subtle sheen of tears in her dark eyes. "I can't explain it." Her hands balled into fists at her side. "Something doesn't feel right. Like there's a storm coming."

Raine decided now was a good time as any to test her rebuilt ties with Gavin. Dropping behind her shields, she felt relief pour through her when she found their bond was slowly rebuilding. It took her a moment longer to locate her tie to Cheveyo. Alarm spread through her—the damage to that tie was unmistakable. The washed out earth tones were almost translucent. This time, she kept her touch light as she reached out. *"Gavin?"*

His gaze switched from Tala to her. *"I don't like it."*

His mental voice sent shivers down Raine's spine, touching spots she couldn't afford to acknowledge. *"Neither do I, but we talked about seeing how far we could go with our magic."*

"Not like this," he snarled. *"Not so soon."*

"I think she's right." She shared the image of Cheveyo's energy and actually felt the wariness bloom as Gavin took note.

"Can you reach him?"

"Not sure. I should have thought to check." She tried to bury her nerves. Suddenly, the warmth of strong arms engulfed her and sent her blood racing. It was tempting to sink into the offered protection, but they needed to save their magi.

"You aren't going without me," he stated.

"I know." She felt another wall around her heart

collapse into dust, and let him see how much his support meant. Gently, she pulled back, until she was once more in the kitchen with Tala. "I can try, Tala, but no promises."

Tala met her gaze, saying nothing about the extended silence. "Thank you."

It was obvious the words were offered grudgingly. To Raine's shock, Tala added in a small whisper, "I can't lose him again."

The depth of the witch's hidden emotions left no doubt how Tala felt about Cheveyo. This woman was desperate and willing to do whatever it took to save the man she loved.

Raine looked at Gavin, understanding completely. She took a deep breath, even as her stomach dropped. Stepping out into the unknown with only Gavin for an anchor was terrifying, but it looked as if they would be figuring this out a little earlier than planned. May the gods help them both.

CHAPTER 20

Gavin thwarted Tala's impatience to get started by digging his heels in and convincing her to wait. During their argument, Raine took a chair at the table, the aches and pains of her latest trip between worlds taking their toll. Laying her head on her folded arms, she let the rise and fall of Tala and Gavin's voices fade into the background. She wanted to ask Tala what the difference was between a chindi and a Soul Stealer, but didn't want to get dragged into their discussion. Instead, she sent the question to Gavin, letting him ask for her. She fought back her exhaustion, and tried to keep her eyes open.

The sensation of a hand brushing over her hair dragged her back from her semi-conscious state. Sitting up slowly, she rubbed a hand over her face and leaned into the familiar touch. "Did you win?" Her question came out mumbled.

A small chuckle echoed next to her. "Yeah, I bought us a few hours."

"Good."

Gavin led her to the bedroom. Her groan of relief

escaped as her body became reacquainted with the mattress. Gavin undid her boots, but she couldn't muster enough energy to help. Even the faint sounds of her blades being laid on the nearby dresser couldn't lure her back from the rolling waves of beckoning sleep. The weight of her boots disappeared. Her jeans soon followed.

She wasn't sure how much time passed before the slight weight of the comforter drifted across the bare skin of her legs. Warmth crawled in behind her. She curled her spine into the comfort offered and snuggled into Gavin's strong body.

Sleep tried to capture her, but she struggled free only to hear Gavin's quiet command, "Sleep, Raine."

"Have to find Cheveyo," she mumbled, a reminder for them both.

"We will. Just let me heal you a bit, okay?"

"Do I have to do anything?" *Please say no.*

"No."

She wasn't sure if he spoke aloud or in her head. Then she didn't care as her body succumbed to sleep.

Raine woke with a scream locked in her throat, her heart pounding and her body shaking. The ghostly cries of Jeremiah and his wolf rang in her ears. Struggling to sit up, it took her a moment to realize she was fighting both blankets and man.

Gavin's quiet reassurances broke through her panic. She stilled, allowing him to unwrap the twisted sheets so she could put her back against the headboard. Drawing her legs up, she curled her arms around them and let her head rest on her knees. The cold sweat along her spine dried as warm air blew over her from the vent in the ceiling.

Gavin lay next to her, saying nothing. One comforting hand wrapped around her ankle, giving her a physical anchor as she regained control.

The last moments of Jeremiah's life would haunt her for a good long time. Why was it hitting her so hard? She wasn't a stranger to pain. She had been a Wraith way too long for death to frighten her. So what about this situation was different?

She understood Jeremiah's revulsion at the thought of being under someone else's control for eternity. Hell, she faced things much more frightening than ephemeral mists bent on revenge, or a macabre collection of nightmares who wanted to shred her to pieces. So that wasn't it. Even the sadness and rage the tracker felt when he recognized the ghostly faces couldn't compare to some of her constant mental companions. *What was different?*

Needing to understand, she focused on Jeremiah's final few minutes. Peeling back his emotions and fears, she set aside the terrifying images of the chindis and replayed his last thoughts. There was his fierce independence, his loyalty to his pack, and his devotion to his alpha. Under it all, lay his need to take out as much of the threat facing him as possible. Then she found it, barely acknowledged, but there.

The ghosts managed to uncover the bond between Jeremiah and his wolf. The binding resembled a Gordian knot of light. Which made sense, considering how intertwined the wolf and man were. When the first of the ghosts reached that light, Jeremiah and his wolf felt the first tear in their binding. Gut clenching fear fueled their determination. They were so deeply connected that one would not exist without the other. Therefore, they would ensure nothing would separate them.

She couldn't follow the spell they wove or how it worked, but she understood the results. The shifter made sure no trace of either him or his wolf would remain behind for the ghosts to feast upon. Nothing for the chindis to use against his pack, because such a breach would leave his pack vulnerable. Being a soldier, Jeremiah's need to protect was an overriding force. He cauterized his ties, killing both himself and his wolf, but leaving his pack and alpha safe.

Just she did when she realized she might not make it back to Gavin.

The realization struck with crystal clarity. The damage to her magic wasn't the result of the Soul Stealer and its minions, but an act of self-defense on her part. The threat of losing Gavin, the fear of living without him, was more frightening than facing her own death. The last time she stared into this abyss, she was fifteen, and the human scientists were discussing how her mother died on their table. Back then, she fell head first into the pit. Now, she stood on the crumbling edge.

A tug on her ankle jerked her back from her dark thoughts and the morass of old nightmares. "You okay?"

Loosening her hold on her knees, she focused on Gavin lying next to her. "I will be." She paused. "I think I owe you an apology."

One dark eyebrow quirked. "Should I ask why?"

The darkness made it easier to confess her sins. "I think the damage to our thread was more my fault than the Soul Stealer's."

His fingers gently stroked over the top of her foot, making her toes twitch. "How do you figure?"

"When I realized what Jeremiah was going to do, I didn't want it to touch you."

The stroking movements stopped. "So you broke the strands?"

"I don't know." She shrugged uncomfortably. "Maybe."

"I can't ask you not to protect me, because I know you won't listen." He was silent for a moment. "Next time, try to have a little faith. I'm not in any hurry to lose you either."

She smiled to herself, understanding what he didn't say, and luxuriated in the intimate quiet. She took a chance and snuck a peek at their bond. Tension drained from her shoulders. The magic was healing, just as he had promised. Probing, she found her cat curled in a sleepy ball deep inside. She resettled next to Gavin.

A long while later, he finally broke the quiet. "You ready to check on Cheveyo?"

Instead of rushing to answer, she thought it over. The aches and pains from earlier were twinges now, a good indicator his healing session was doing its job. Her magic might not be up to full strength, but it was stronger. Considering it was the dead of morning, Cheveyo's captors may not be all that alert, leaving surprise on their side. "Not sure what it'll accomplish, but we can try." A thought hit her. "Shouldn't we wait for Tala?"

"No. Told her we'd do it on our own schedule."

She twisted around to look at him. "And she agreed?"

He shrugged. "Didn't give her much choice."

"You're playing a dangerous game. She's still the head magi here. They don't just hand out those jobs, you know."

"I'm aware of that," he muttered, "but it's never stopped you." His answer left her speechless, and he took advantage of the unintentional opening. "Let's get started. Maybe we'll get lucky and get some sleep tonight."

She felt her lips twitch at his snippy tone. “You have an urgent appointment I don’t know about?”

His chest vibrated against her back with his low chuckle. “Funny girl.” He settled back on the bed, drawing her with him, his humor fading. “Maybe your paranoia is contagious, but I’m concerned about this tie you have with Cheveyo.”

She frowned, toying with the hairs dusting his arm at her waist. “I explained about the door between us. You’ve seen it.”

She could almost hear the whirring as his thoughts churned. The subtle tension in his body hinted he was debating sharing those thoughts with her. Needing to see his face, she turned and her legs tangled with his. Folding her arms on his chest, she rested her chin on her hands and stared him down.

Sighing, he gave in. “Remember our conversation about the evolution of magic?” He played with a strand of her hair, letting the dark ribbon slide through his fingers. She was amused to notice how much attention he paid that small movement. He seemed reluctant to look at her, as he continued. “I’m starting to wonder how altruistic Cheveyo really was to bind you together all those months ago.”

For a moment, she wondered if he was jealous. Then the obviousness of his observation hit, sending her mentally reeling. It was so logical. Why hadn’t she thought of it?

Thinking back to when Cheveyo revealed how he tied them together, she searched for some clue but couldn’t find it. When she questioned the witch after his little bomb, he seemed as perplexed as she at his actions. If anything, he seemed uncomfortable, not as if he was plotting to use her.

The small hitch in Gavin’s breathing let her know he

was snared in her rush of memories. More proof that their bond was growing stronger. Neither one had put up any barriers, so there were times, like now, when they unconsciously merged. A small worm of worry poked its head up. Would she be able to maintain her sense of self if this continued to grow? She took comfort in the fact she was stubborn enough to make sure her hard earned independence survived.

She watched Gavin carefully. "You saw?"

He nodded.

"If you can see my memories, did you catch anything?" Here's hoping he hadn't caught her latest vow.

He stared into space, thinking as she waited. After a few moments, he spoke, weighing each word carefully. "If we trust your impressions, I'd say Cheveyo had no ulterior motives." He met her gaze. "However, I'd rather be safe than sorry."

A wry smile twisted her lips. "Guess you and I are going to go up against the top dogs of the Kyn, huh?"

"Not unless they come after us first."

At his dry tone, she raised her eyebrows. He met her gaze without flinching. That unbreakable confidence turned her on.

Focus! "Right, let's do this then." She turned and settled in, dropping behind her shields.

His arm came around her waist and held her close. This newfound need for his touch was disconcerting, but she didn't let go of his anchoring arm. Scanning the magical tapestry, she found Cheveyo's psychic trail. Concentrating, she reached out, only to stop short. She felt for Gavin behind her. "Ready?"

"Ready."

Taking a deep breath, she grabbed hold. This time,

instead of the magic dragging her under, she was able to ride above it. With Gavin shadowing her, she surfed along the lines of light.

The trip to the psychic door was quick and thankfully uneventful. Standing before it, she could make out Cheveyo's earth tones sluggishly snaking their way under the door. Kneeling, she gathered the delicate ties in her hands and sent a small pulse of power down the bond. Not enough to alert whoever held him, but enough to make Cheveyo pay attention.

Studying the ribbons of energy, worry gnawed at her. Based on how thin and stretched it appeared, Tala's assumption that Cheveyo was still somewhere near Flagstaff might be wrong. With Raine and Gavin heading to Phoenix tomorrow, she feared the added distance could snap their connection. A brief pulse in the earth tones cut her thoughts short. Cheveyo's answering flare dissolved some of her tension. He was still hanging on.

Knowing time was running short, she slipped further into the magic, only to run into a psychic wall. Undeterred, she pushed, adding her magical weight. The answering shove sent her reeling back. She tried again, only to snarl at the resulting slap. *Damn stubborn witch!* Cheveyo wouldn't let her in.

She studied the door and considered her options. She could force it open, but didn't dare. No way in hell did she want the Soul Stealer to tear through her shields again. Besides, between her, Gavin, and Cheveyo, mental space was becoming a premium. A low, sleepy growl rumbled, and she added one more to the psychic party, her leopard.

Resigned to taking the difficult road, she began to feed the combination of her and Gavin's power down the link. Gods only knew what Cheveyo was facing, but until they had more information, the possibilities were endless and daunting. Since he refused to open the door, she was left with only one option—send enough power to help him endure.

Worry coalesced with dark memories, but unwilling to trigger alarms on the other side, she concentrated on keeping her touch light. Letting her sense of self fade away, her world narrowed to strengthening the ties.

The brief brush of Gavin's mind had her opening eyes she hadn't realized she'd shut. Her knees ached as she knelt by the steel door. Cheveyo's thread lay in her lap, her hands petting it gently. She was relieved to find the bond appeared thicker than before. Here's hoping it would hold. She let it go and rose to her feet, her head spinning at the sudden position change. Either she used too much power, or something was interfering with her connection to the captive witch.

She followed Gavin's psychic trail, stumbling a bit. A nudge at her hip announced her leopard's arrival. She glanced down to find it padding alongside. Taking the offer, she buried her hand in the ruff behind its ears and found her balance.

CHAPTER 21

Raine hung back while Gavin dealt with the pencil thin brunette manning the desk at Ransom Developments in Phoenix. Most females tripped over themselves to give him whatever he wanted and then some. This time was proving to be no exception, for the most part.

Gavin leaned against the high counter with a lone, elegant orchid standing guard over the discreet nameplate reading, "Carrie Hernandez". "We have an eleven o'clock appointment with Mr. Ransom."

Although Carrie managed to pull off the sophisticated receptionist role upon their arrival, it wasn't long before she fell under Gavin's charm. "I'm sorry, Mr. Durand." A blush rode high under her skin. "Unfortunately, Mr. Ransom had to cancel all his afternoon appointments."

Carrie's poker face was horrible, but Raine managed to keep her disbelieving snort silent.

"Ms. Hernandez?" Gavin's voice dropped, "Carrie? We drove down from Flagstaff. We're only in town for the day. I'm sure Mr. Ransom could squeeze us in."

"I'm so sorry, Mr. Durand," the flustered woman answered. "I did leave a message on your cell."

"My reception must be spotty, because I never got that message."

Neither Raine nor Gavin intended to leave until they got a chance to speak with Ransom. A nervous receptionist wouldn't be much of a challenge.

"Why don't you just slip back to his office and double check for me?" Gavin cajoled. "We'll be just a few minutes and I know Mr. Ransom was looking forward to our meeting."

Carrie gave him a jerky nod, flicked a wary glance at Raine, and walked quickly into the hall behind her desk.

Gavin gave Raine a very smug, male look. Damn man knew his effect on females. Hell, he exploited it shamelessly. Laughter bubbled inside her, but she kept her expression neutral. It wasn't safe to encourage him.

Carrie returned her blush higher and more pronounced, wearing a look Raine recognized. Someone had been royally chewed out. At least it answered one question, Ransom was in.

Carrie stepped up to the desk, her jaw set. "I'm sorry, Mr. Durand, but Mr. Ransom is not available for any appointments at this time."

Charm disappeared and Gavin stared her down. She paled.

Pity rose, and Raine decided it was time to intervene. She tapped Gavin on the arm.

He switched his stare from the secretary to her, but moved aside.

Ignoring his glare, Raine leaned over the counter and flashed a smile that was all teeth. "I don't think you understand, Carrie." A small curl of dark glee unfurled as a tremor visibly raced over Carrie's arm as she gripped the back of her chair. "We did not just drive three hours to be blown off by Mr. Ransom. So if you'll excuse us, we'll let Mr. Ransom know how hard you tried to keep us away." Without waiting for her response, she stalked into the hall, Gavin close behind.

By the time the receptionist regained her composure and managed to teeter after them, Raine pinpointed Ransom's corner office. Not all that hard considering his name was etched on the half-open, blind-covered, side window. Without bothering to knock, she stepped into the office.

To her right, tinted windows lined the wall, letting winter sunlight filter in. Fluorescent lights chased the dim shadows back and an icy blast of air cut through her sweater. Raine's magical shields snapped into place as the blurry, unnatural shadows swam at the edge of her vision, surrounding the man who rose to his feet at her rude entrance. She slid a wrist blade into her hand as the hair at the nape of her neck rose at the unseen threat.

Gavin closed the door firmly on the chasing secretary before moving to Raine's right. His shields locked into place with a faint reverberating psychic echo.

Holding her blade along her wrist, she set her body at an angle. "Doug Ransom. I believe we had an appointment."

Training became her only tether as those flickering shadows taunted her. She didn't dare drop her shields to take a closer look. Unfortunately, she was fairly certain of what they faced. Despite their respective shields, she shared her hunch with Gavin, and received a small answering vibration in return.

Standing behind the large desk, Doug Ransom wavered

between anger and fear. Sweat dotted his forehead, the damp sheen darkening the graying edges of his thinning hair. He had to be in his forties, but with his skin currently taking on an unhealthy pallor and his eyes ringed by dark circles, she put his age closer to fifty.

He sported some excess weight around his middle at some point, but now his suit hung on him. She bet that the not-quite-there shadows milling behind him were a great dietary tool.

"Ms. McCord, Mr. Durand." Ransom remained standing, his hands braced on his desk. "This is really not a good time."

Gavin shifted, coming forward. "We only need a few minutes."

Ransom's gaze flicked beyond Gavin and he waved his hand, probably sending Carrie away. He settled back into his chair with a dark frown of displeasure. He motioned to the two cushioned chairs arranged in front of his desk. "Take a seat."

Gavin removed his jacket and laid it over the arm of the chair before making himself comfortable.

Raine hesitated. The quivering shadows began to quiet, but instead of expected relief, she felt edgy. Moving cautiously to the front of the chair, she sat. Using the edge of Ransom's desk for cover, she slipped her wrist blade back into its sheath. Her shoulders were tight, but until they were out of this office, all she could do was wait, and watch.

"We have a couple of questions for you," Gavin said.

"About?" The CEO set his elbows on the desk and folded his hands.

The unnatural shadows shifted. Raine sucked in a breath, waiting.

Gavin kept his focus on the man behind the desk. "Your role in a situation up north."

The shadows darkened and began to twine about Ransom. A swell of malicious intent washed over Raine, causing her to gasp. The small sound was drowned out by Ransom's quickly smothered moan of pain. Wiping a shaking hand over his face, his eyes were a tad wild. "I don't know what you're talking about."

"We were given your name by the Chavezes." Raine watched him closely. "We were told you were interested in purchasing land up near Flagstaff."

The phantom shadows paused and held still, as if listening.

"Is that a question?" Ransom grabbed the handkerchief from his suit pocket to dab at the sheen of sweat on his forehead.

"Is it true?" she pushed, splitting her attention between him and the unmoving mist.

"Currently, yes." His pudgy hands shook slightly as he meticulously folded the handkerchief into a neat square. "Ransom Developments is considering purchasing some land near Flagstaff."

"Why that land?" asked Gavin.

"Why would a Security Agent from Taliesin Security in Oregon be interested in a land deal in Arizona?" Ransom shot back, eyes narrowed.

"We aren't," she cut in. "We're following leads in a disappearance."

The phantom shadows eddied then quieted again.

She didn't think he could pale any farther, but she was wrong. Lines of pain bloomed at the corners of his mouth and his voice sounded breathy. "What are you talking about?"

Gavin took over. "An outside consultant was called in by both the Chavezes and the tribe whose land you're looking at purchasing. Unfortunately, he's gone missing."

An unhealthy red color started at Ransom's neck and worked its way up his face. "I run a legitimate business. We don't go around kidnapping people."

Raine never saw the shadows move. Ransom's body jerked and went stiff. He clawed at his throat, as his face went from red to pale to purple in a matter of moments. The man was silently being choked to death in his leather office chair.

Jumping up, Raine cleared the far end of the desk as Gavin rounded the other side.

Ransom's heels drummed on the floor.

She grabbed his hands, forcing them away from his neck and locking them to the chair arms. She was surprised by how much strength she needed to use to subdue a mere human. The force of their struggles rolled the chair back until it hit the wall and stopped. Meeting Gavin's gaze over the gasping man, she saw a matching grim realization. They needed to see what they were fighting. She dropped her shields and her blood iced over. "Chindis."

Gavin flicked his hand, and magic rolled through the room. The blinds in the hall window snapped shut, giving them the illusion of privacy. The last thing they needed was Carrie waltzing in while they tried to save her boss from some truly pissed off ghosts.

Raine tightened her grip on Ransom's jerking arms. "Shit, Gavin. If we don't do something they're going to rip him apart."

"At least we know he's linked," he muttered, adjusting his shield to merge with hers. Together they drew the magical protection around the dying human. When it clicked into place, an unearthly howl ripped through the psychic plane as the lurking ghosts were denied their feast. Instead of turning on her and Gavin, they disappeared, winking out as if some large rubber band had snapped them back into the ether.

She sent her magic out in pursuit, but ran smack into a silver blue wall. "What the hell?" Blinking, she found Gavin glaring at her over Ransom's twitching body.

"Don't even think about it," he snarled. "I don't have time to go riding to your rescue."

His comment stung, but he was right. No matter how much she wanted to hunt the ghosts down, they couldn't follow the chindis and save Ransom at the same time.

Switching her attention to the more immediate situation, she winced at the gaping holes dotting Ransom's aura like vicious wounds. "Holy hell," she muttered.

Gavin shot her a grim look even as he tried to undo the damage the Chindis had wrought. Since Gavin was the one with healing magic, she opened her side of their bond, lending what strength she could.

Cassandra, a healer witch who saved both Raine and Gavin at separate times, once explained that human auras served as the simplest forms of psychic protection, similar to the shields Kyn utilized in their everyday existence. Raine found it ironic that magic protected even those who didn't believe it existed. Yet in this case, she could clearly see what Cassandra meant.

Gavin frantically patched the numerous holes in Ransom's aura, but it was like trying to hold a dam back with a colander. There were leaks everywhere. She laid a light touch on Gavin's arm.

His head jerked up. "What?"

"You won't make it." Her voice was quiet, but sure. He

was fighting a losing battle. "Can you shrink a protection circle around him? Like this." She showed him an image of a protection circle warping to the outline of Ransom's body, like a shrink-wrapped spell.

He narrowed his gaze, thinking. "It's worth a shot, but..."

"But?" she prodded.

"I'm not sure how long it will hold. It may keep his body alive, but it only gives us a few moments to question him before it snaps into place."

The cold logic that served her as a Wraith woke. Ransom's survival wasn't important, the information he held, was. Whether he was working with another Kyn, or simply a stupid human who managed to trigger this entire mess on his own, he was involved. If Gavin set the protections in place, Ransom would appear to have slipped into a coma. However, there was a slim chance they could get some answers before he did. Eventually the spell would fade and Ransom would be dead. Either they let him die now, where they would be the last ones seen with him, leaving a lot of questions they didn't have time for, or set the spell and try to get some answers. The choice was easy.

"Do it," she said. "We need to see what he knows."

Gavin gave a short nod and began to weave the spell into place. She kept a careful eye on Ransom. When his eyelids flickered open, she made sure her face was the only thing he saw.

"Ransom," she called. His panicked gaze flittered then latched on to her. "You need to tell me who set those ghosts on you."

"Know you," his voice was a hoarse whisper. His gaze kept sliding away from hers as his body twitched.

"Ransom, focus," she hissed. "Why are you being haunted?"

"Land wasn't theirs. It belongs to humans, not the monsters."

"Monsters?"

"K—Kyn. They call themselves Kyn." His eyes flicked back and forth. She heard his heartbeat began to race. "Made a deal—take out the witch, get the land."

"Not much longer," Gavin growled between clenched teeth. He was trying to give her time, but it was running out.

She tightened her hold as Ransom began to struggle in earnest. "Who'd you make a deal with?" He writhed under her hands. "Who? Give me a damn name!"

"Noooo!" His raspy cry was a harsh whisper of air as the protection circle locked into place. He sagged into a boneless heap.

There would be no more answers. She cursed and met Gavin's steely gaze.

"I have to call for medical assistance," he said. "It'll give you a few minutes to check his desk."

She rose to her feet, as Gavin pulled a still breathing Ransom out of his chair. He laid him on the floor, loosened the CEO's tie, and unbuttoned his shirt.

"What the hell, Gavin?"

He didn't bother looking at her. "Have to make it look like we tried CPR."

She turned away, shaking her head. Let him set the scene. A computer screen dominated the massive desk, but very few papers were visible.

Gavin grabbed her wrist. "Leave the computer alone. It won't do you any good." He handed her the phone. "Call 911." He slipped out of the office, calling Carrie's name.

Holding the phone to her ear, a screech of static filled the line. Damn it. She consciously dampened her magic. Finally, a dial tone emerged. She dialed 911.

Call complete, she went back to the desk knowing Gavin would keep Carrie away. She hit a lock on the bottom drawer. Flexing her wrist, she snapped the flimsy device and yanked the drawer open. Inside, under a cardboard tube, lay a pile of folders.

Pulling the tube free, she cast a quick eye to the door, and listened carefully. Carrie's sobs were answered by Gavin's voice, but no sound of the EMTs.

She flipped through the files. It took a few moments to understand what she was looking at—mineral right reports and property deeds. She didn't have the luxury of time, nor could she risk taking the files with her. Eyeing the tube, inspiration struck. She popped the top off the cardboard tube and pulled out the rolled paper. She began to unroll it when the muffled sounds of the arriving emergency crew filtered through. Re-rolling it into a tighter tube, she tucked it under the spine sheath strapped between her shoulder blades. Shaking her head to settle her hair along her back, she replaced the now empty tube in the drawer and closed it. When the office door swung open she was hovering over Ransom.

"Over here," she pushed frantic desperation into her voice. "I've been doing CPR, but I don't know if it's working."

"Let us take over." A young EMT gently nudged her out of the way and took over.

She fell back and slowly got to her feet, watching the EMTs work. Making her way to the office door, she snagged Gavin's jacket from the chair, moved past an incoming EMT, and strode down the hall, slipping the jacket on.

She reached the front office to find Gavin with an armful of sobbing brunette. Barely squelching the momentary urge to jerk the woman out of his arms, she ignored his questioning look when he saw his jacket. Stalking by them, she threw herself onto the couch lining one wall of the reception area and glared at the clinging weeping willow.

Even knowing she was being petty didn't stop the possessive feelings reeling through her. She passed time with some pleasant images of ripping the little human out of Gavin's arms and tossing her through the glass doors. Or maybe she should toss them both through the doors. A serious consideration when she remembered his scathing comment in Ransom's office. *Ride to her rescue? One stupid situation and suddenly she was the damsel in distress?*

A pair of scuffed black shoes interrupted her daydreams of saving Gavin's ass. Blinking, she lifted her head, taking note that the shoes' owner wore a pair of tan chinos and a tan belt where a badge rested. A soft summer blue button-down shirt complete with tie and dark jacket ended at bronze skin with short, dark wavy hair and dark eyes.

"Ms. McCord?" The voice was a pleasant tenor.

"Yes?" she answered cautiously.

"Detective Montiel, do you mind if I ask you a few questions?"

Giving the detective a nod, she set aside her thoughts of Gavin's payback to concentrate on answering the nice detective's questions.

He motioned to the couch she sat on. "Is it okay if I sit next to you?"

"Go ahead." She scooted closer to the armrest, giving him room.

Montiel sat down, pulling out a pad of paper and a pen. "Your name is Raine McCord, correct?"

She nodded even as she split her attention between answering the detective and sending Gavin a telepathic question. *"What's our story?"*

"You reside in Portland, Oregon?" Montiel asked.

"Yes." Short and simple, the easiest way to answer.

Gavin's steady voice broke into her thoughts. *"We were hired by Whiteriver as consultants on the land deal with Ransom."* She glanced over to see him answering an older detective's questions.

"Why were you here?" Montiel continued, eyes sharp.

"Mr. Durand and I are security consultants for Taliesin Security. We were asked by Ms. Whiteriver to come in and advise her on a business deal Mr. Ransom was pursuing."

"Had you every met Mr. Ransom before today?"

She shook her head.

"So you don't know if he was acting out of character or not?" Montiel pushed.

She sighed, letting a look of concern filter over her face. "I have no idea, Detective. We arrived for our scheduled meeting and his secretary told us he was unavailable."

Montiel narrowed his eyes. "Why didn't you leave?"

She met his shrewd look. "Because we had driven three hours to make this meeting on a limited schedule. We weren't sure we'd be able to make another appointment. Plus, it struck us as curious that the appointment which had been set the day before was suddenly canceled."

Montiel consulted the pad in his hand. "The secretary says you two bullied your way in."

She raised an eyebrow. "Bullied?" She let a small smile curve her lips as she looked at the sniffling woman talking to another officer. "Seriously, Detective, I think that's a bit strong."

"Really?" Montiel's face and tone were neutral, but watchful.

"The poor woman shouldn't play poker," she murmured, turning her attention back to the man in front of her. "It was obvious she was lying when we arrived. We weren't in the mood to play games." She shrugged. "So we announced ourselves to Mr. Ransom."

"And his reaction?"

"He was understandably upset."

"Did you threaten him in any way?"

"No, sir." She paused. "He seemed ill."

"How so?" Montiel pushed.

"He was pale, shaky, and sweating."

Her description settled something in the detective's mind. "And in regards to your conversation with Mr. Ransom?"

She crossed her arms. "It was limited and non-productive."

His mouth tightened. Obviously, not liking her evasive answer. "What happened while you were talking?"

There was no way to say, *Well, you see detective, there were these pissed off ghosts who weren't really happy with the man so they decided to choke him to death.*

Instead of letting her dark humor free, she tried to look appropriately somber. "He starting choking and grabbing his chest." She tightened her arms, feigning distress. "Then he collapsed. Mr. Durand and I started doing CPR." She gave a helpless shrug, "We weren't sure what else to do."

The young detective asked a few more questions and took down her contact information while Ransom was wheeled into a waiting ambulance.

CHAPTER 22

RAINE OPENED THE PASSENGER DOOR ON THE RENTAL SEDAN AND paused before getting in. The feeling of being watched left the spot between her shoulder blades itching. Resting one arm on the car's roof, she took a moment to scan their surroundings. The parking lot at Ransom Developments was half-full and the early afternoon traffic on a nearby street was a dull, persistent buzz.

A slight breeze twisted through the maze of steel and glass reaching into a shockingly blue sky. Unlike downtown Portland—where trees blocked out as much sky as the tall buildings—here in Phoenix, the towering structures etched their sharp edges against the expanse of blue. Squinting against the twinkling glare of sunlight on the myriad of window glass, she felt exposed.

"You okay?" Gavin drew her attention back to earth.

"It's too open here." She ducked into the car.

While he settled behind the wheel, she shrugged off his jacket and handed it to him. He tossed it in the back, shooting her a piercing glance. "What do you mean?"

"It felt like I was being watched." She twisted her hair so it lay over one shoulder. Reaching around, she pulled the rolled up paper from under her spine sheath and set it in her lap. Over the rumble of the car's engine, she continued, "Maybe because it's too exposed. It's all structures and pavement. At least in Portland, buildings and nature tend to blend a bit."

He stretched one arm along her seat, his attention on backing out of the parking space. "It's why Portland has one of the largest populations of the Fey. However, due to the large spans of desert, the Southwest holds the highest shifter and magi populations."

"Makes sense." She watched the cityscape flow by as he navigated the streets. "So, if Ransom Developments is threatening to take some of that space, it would really put a crimp in Chavez and Whiteriver's style."

"Yeah," he answered. "We both know territories are zealously guarded. From what little I've seen with the shifters, there are a few things you don't mess with. Pack and territory are at the top."

"What about the magi?" She turned to him. "What's their priority?"

"That's easy." A small, bitter smile appeared. "Power." He gave a stiff shrug. "For magi, whether witch or wizard, power defines who and what you are."

She chewed her lower lip, thinking. "For the Amanusa, power is key as well."

"That's different," he said. "Power for the magi is what you wield and how you use it. For the demons, it is how you use someone's power against them and what you can make them do for you."

"Manipulation versus ability. It makes a sort of twisted sense. What better way to ensure chaos than manipulating those around you," she mused. "Kind of like siccing a bunch of vengeance hungry ghosts on someone who's threatening to take your territory."

"It's a possibility." He slowed for a red light. "So what do the Fey value?"

She hadn't really given it much thought. Considering what they suspected, it was probably time she did. She thought of her uncle and his CEO position at Taliesin Security, the business front for the Northwest Kyn. Once focused on something, very little could sway him. Even being a blood relation couldn't warm his personal logic. She was testament to that. "Power, territory, and politics. Not necessarily in that order."

"So, which House is the biggest threat?" Gavin muttered as the light changed.

Her answer was very certain. "All of them." She tapped her fingers absently on the document on her lap.

Slanting a look at the movement, he asked, "What did you find?"

She wasn't surprised at his change of subject since it was hard to argue with the truth. "Something helpful, I hope." She began unrolling the document. "It looks like a map of some sort."

It was a struggle to get the paper to lie flat, not only because it was damn big, but because the stupid ends kept curling inward. Muttering a curse at the stubborn object, she glanced up. "Is there any place we can pull over and lay this thing out?"

"There's some sort of coliseum at the next exit." He merged to his right. "Should have a parking lot."

"That works." She let the map re-roll itself.

He followed the signs to Phoenix Coliseum. In a few minutes, a large round building appeared on the left side, complete with large, empty parking lots. Driving around the grayish white building, he found a spot.

She released her seatbelt and snagged his jacket from the back seat. At his raised eyebrow, she said, "Need something to hold the edges down."

Hopping out of the car, she met him at the hood. Together they laid out the map. Using the jacket, Gavin's wallet and the car keys, they anchored down three of the corners. Gavin held the fourth.

The document was a stylized map. Red lines moved across the paper in waves, while dotted lines and various squares and triangles created a crisscross pattern. The only recognizable parts were the block-lettered captions.

"This may be Flagstaff but it's not looking like any map I'm familiar with," she said.

"Topographical map." He traced a finger along the dotted line framed by a solid border that branched into a Y before snaking across the map in the bottom left quarter. "I think this is I-17 as it heads into Flagstaff from Phoenix."

"Only one way to find out." Leaving the map to Gavin, she rounded the open passenger door and slipped into her seat. She popped open the glove compartment and pulled out the traditional road map they had been using.

When the rental's GPS system had shown some psychopathic tendencies to send them careening off the side of steep mountain roads, they decided to use the less technologically advanced version. Unfolding the road map, she set it just above and off to the side of the one taken from Ransom's office.

"Yeah," Gavin muttered, studying both maps. "That's the freeway all right."

"Okay so if we follow I-17, it turns into that main road, right?" She skimmed the route with her finger. "That means this weird little mark over here is—" She double-checked against the road map. "—Lowell Observatory?"

"Right." He sketched farther north. "This is roughly where Tala's property is." The area was marked with a red square.

Checking between the two maps, she pointed to another spot farther up and to the left marked by another red square. "And that's the Chavez's," she said. "Check it out. This red square just north of the University, that's Rio's place."

"He's got each of the Kyn leader's homes marked." Gavin's voice was neutral. "That's not good."

She wasn't surprised. "He admitted to knowing about us. The only humans who have that information either belong to, or work with, the government."

More and more humans were starting to realize they weren't alone in their world. It always surprised her that the thin curtain of secrecy over the Kyn's existence had lasted so long. Based on human history and their need to share every little bit of information, she never thought the Kyn would have kept their existence a secret this long. The time for them to step forward was creeping closer.

"If Ransom marked each of these spots, then who does this belong to?" Gavin brought her back to the discussion at hand, pointing to a lone black square sitting roughly in-between two blue areas.

Her instincts perked up. She compared the two maps. The location was remote. "I don't know. The two blue areas have to be these lakes." She showed him the clearly labeled road map. "There aren't any roads out there."

"What?" he asked absently, still absorbed in his study of the maps.

She nudged his shoulder. "Pay attention." Laying the

road map over Ransom's, she pointed, "Look, the only way out there is forest service access roads."

"Those will be closed this time of the year," he muttered.

"He's got to be hiding something out there." The more she thought about the little black dot and its remote location, the louder her instincts hummed. "You don't lock a map in a drawer unless it means something."

"Maybe it's a someone, not a something," Gavin said.

"You up for a hike?" Raine's mind spun with possibilities as they refolded their maps. "We'll need to call Xander and see if she can meet up with us."

For once, they had a solid lead. If they were lucky, they might find Cheveyo. Then she could concentrate on hunting down the chindis and the Soul Stealer.

She dug out her cell as Gavin drove. Thankfully, the signal was strong and there was no sign of the static from her interfering magic. Punching in Xander's number, she frowned as the call went to voice mail. Once the annoying beep screeched across the line, she left her message. "Xander, call me. We need to meet up. There's something we need to check out." She hung up.

Impatience beat at her. Unable to sit still, she drummed her fingers against her thigh. Ransom made a deal with someone to take out a witch. Assuming Cheveyo was the witch in question, the only Kyn who knew Cheveyo was heading down was Chavez, Rio, and Tala. As much as she disliked the Southwest Magi, she didn't think the woman was faking her feelings for Cheveyo.

Chavez's main priority was his pack and his territory. Which meant if he felt threatened by Ransom's inquiries, he would have taken Ransom out, not partnered with the human land developer. Plus, she couldn't understand how such a partnership would benefit Chavez.

Rio was a different story. Amanusa were as likely to partner with an enemy—just to mess with everyone else around them—as they would be to take out a potential threat. Here in the Southwest, the relationships between the Houses was so screwed up, Rio could jump either way.

None of which answered the question of who raised the chindis or the Soul Stealer. Which reminded her. "Hey, did you ever get a chance to ask Tala what the difference between a chindi and the Soul Stealer is?"

"I did." Considering how fast his shoulders tensed the answer was not good.

"The conversation didn't go well?"

"She wouldn't give me a straight answer."

Some note in his voice left a small ball of dread in the pit of her stomach. She wasn't stupid, he might come across as charming and laid back, but piss him off and you'd best duck for cover. Especially lately. "What did you do?"

He shot her a disgruntled look. "Not whatever horrible thing you're thinking of." He shook his head and visibly forced himself to relax. "She argued that no one would be stupid enough as to raise both. I told her it didn't matter how smart her people were, but some dumbass had managed to do just that."

She choked back a shocked laugh and laid her hand on his thigh. A quick flash of Tala's enraged face popped into her mind before a stinging sensation burst along her cheekbone. Her burst of humor disappeared and a low growl rumbled through the car's interior. "She hit you."

His hand covered hers as her nails dug into his jean-clad thigh. "I deserved it."

She caught the small, satisfied smile lurking around his lips. "Maybe."

He chuckled. "No maybe about it, but it did get her to answer the question." He turned serious. "Tala agreed with Andrew's explanation that chindis were soul remnants, however she gave a different reason for their existence."

"Really?"

He nodded. "According to her, these ghosts are raised as tools but they don't have enough magic or power to exist on their own. Which is why they have to obey whoever raised them."

Raine thought it through. "Which means it's not the chindis picking who to haunt, but the one who raises them?"

"Right."

"How do they manage to stick around then?"

"The chindis?" He released her hand to maneuver around a dilapidated old van puttering up the freeway.

She tried not to cringe at how fast the rusted bumper approached her side of the windshield.

"Whoever raises them, fuels them with a bit of their life force." He whipped past the van and semi in front of it. "It's what holds them here until they finish whatever job the summoner gave them."

Okay, that made a sick kind of sense. "And witches are still our best bet for being the summoner?"

He shook his head. "Actually, that would be Andrew's personal bias peeking out. Tala said this type of magic is ritual based. Therefore, anyone who can harness magic could do the spell."

"Well, shit. That widens the suspect pool," she muttered. They were back to square one. Frustration gnawed at her and she rubbed her forehead. "Okay back to the main topic. When these chindis are done doing whatever it is they are commanded to do, they what? Disappear? Go back to being dead?"

He nodded. "It's what makes them such good tools. You raise them, lock a metaphysical collar and leash around them, point them in the direction you want them to go, and let them do their thing. And they have to come back to you. You take your collar and leash off and the ghosts fade away."

She drummed her fingers on her thigh. "A Soul Stealer is a different animal altogether, right?"

"Right. A Stealer is more of an independent thinker and is more tightly bound to its summoner."

"How so?"

"Chindis are ritual magic." A grim note entered Gavin's voice. "The magic needed to raise a Stealer is much more involved. It requires a great deal of will on the part of the summoner."

"So we're hunting one very pissed off, determined castor." She frowned. "Soul Stealers grow in strength with each soul they consume." A dark thought hit her. "Does that mean the person holding its leash grows in strength, too?"

He slanted her an unhappy look. "The stronger they grow the hungrier they get, and the more they'll fight their ties to the master."

"If those ties break?" She had an unsettling feeling that she knew the answer before he gave it.

"You have a very angry, very violent ghost whose only goal is to hunt down anyone standing in its way. Its strength will increase with each death. As long as it's bound, it follows its master's orders. If it breaks the bindings..."

The ice reappeared in the pit of her stomach. When his fingers tightened on her hand, she realized she had once again reached out. Relaxing, she put the pieces together.

"A rogue Soul Stealer." Gods help them. Yet remembering the Stealer's attacks, something didn't ring true. "Wait, it doesn't make sense."

He shot her a look. "Which part?"

She took a moment to order her thoughts. "The death that brought Cheveyo down here. Daniel, I think."

"The boy who was skinned alive?"

"Right." She pushed on. "The Stealer isn't sentient enough to perform the dark magic needed to keep a person alive through that kind of pain."

He frowned. "What are you thinking?"

"I think our Stealer is still leashed." She bit her lower lip, trying to move the facts around. "When Cheveyo and I were attacked in that clearing, there was someone else there, laughing." She pulled her hand free and rubbed her head, trying to get past the haunting memories. "It was like what Jeremiah endured."

"You think you were attacked by chindis?" Gavin's voice was quiet as he tried to follow along.

"Not the first couple of times."

"You're losing me."

"The initial attack, there were no chindis, just the Stealer. It did whatever the person standing in the shadows wanted."

"It beat the hell out of you," he growled.

"It did, but when I went after Cheveyo, it wasn't as strong. It acted like a guard dog, attacking because I made contact with Cheveyo."

"That last go around, it almost took you out." Anger laced his voice, and this time, knowing where that anger came from, a curl of warmth unfurled in her heart.

"The last time, it wasn't just the Stealer," she stated softly. "The chindis helped."

He shot her a confused look.

Since he deserved a full explanation, she elaborated. "When I first breached the protection circle, it was the chindis who dragged me into Jeremiah's memories, not the Stealer."

"They let you go."

She thought about it, really thought about it. "No, not exactly. They couldn't make it past the circle of flames."

"But the Stealer did?"

"Yeah, it broke through." A shiver of remembered fear walked down her spine.

His gaze narrowed. "But the chindis didn't follow it through?"

She shook her head.

His frown deepened. "Where did they go?"

"They disappeared."

"Why?"

Frustration boiled and she snapped, "I don't know." Yanking on the seatbelt, she shifted until she could turn enough to face him. "A better question is who's the one raising all of them?"

Gavin's hands flexed on the steering wheel. "What about Ransom?"

"What about him?" She might sound like a petulant child, but this conversation serve to raise more unanswerable questions. Catching sight of the contemplative expression on his face, she sighed. "You can't possibly think he had something to do with this mess."

"Why not?" He shot back.

"He's human. There's no way he would know how to bind a Stealer." She shook her head. "He was being haunted by the Chindis, which means he couldn't be the one controlling them."

"But the one he made a deal with could," he said.

She opened her mouth, but shock stilled her voice. In some twisted way, it made sense. If raising chindis was simply a matter of knowing how to perform a ritual, what was to stop a human from performing it? If he raised them and then someone, perhaps a Kyn, decided to take advantage of the situation, it wouldn't take much to wrest control of the chindis away from Ransom. "Oh dear gods," she breathed. "That means someone figured out how to bind both."

His face darkened and his fingers tightened on the steering wheel. "That's not good."

"Tell me about it." Staring unseeingly out the window, she winced as the implications washed over her. "If this Stealer wasn't on a leash, shouldn't we have more than four bodies on our hands?"

"Five."

"Huh?"

"Jeremiah makes it five," he corrected.

She disagreed. "No, you aren't listening. Jeremiah was torn apart by the chindis, not the Stealer. Someone has their hands full, controlling the chindis and the Stealer."

"Which brings us right back to the beginning." Clearly frustrated, Gavin's statement came out just shy of an accusation.

"And there's no way we can ask Ransom." Caught in a coma, the developer's chances of survival were pretty damn slim. "Maybe we'll find something at wherever it is we're going." Not that she believed in the power of positive thinking, but at this point she'd take what she could.

"Here's hoping you're right," he muttered.

CHAPTER 23

Raine tried calling Xander twice more before she and Gavin reached the exit leading to the forest access road. The second time she was shuttled to voicemail, she uttered a soft curse.

"Nothing?" Gavin asked.

She shook her head, worry seeping to the surface. "Something's wrong."

"There's nothing we can do from here." Grim resignation hung heavy in his voice as the car bumped over the dirt road clearly marked "Forest Personnel Only, Access Restricted." A pad locked chain strung between two posts ended their trip.

Bracing her hands on the dash, she leaned forward. "Got a key?"

"Don't need one." He left the car idling and walked up to the heavy-duty lock. A heartbeat, maybe two, then he turned around with a very open padlock dangling from his hand.

Grinning, she applauded. She chuckled when he bent at the waist, one hand tipping an imaginary hat. Scooting over to the driver's seat, she drove the car forward, bumping over the chain lying like a discarded jump rope. She twisted in her seat to watch him reattached the lock. She slid back into her seat and moments later when he opened the door and got behind the wheel, said, "Nice trick."

He grinned. "A newly discovered one, actually." He deftly maneuvered the car over the pitted road. It was slow going, but faster than hiking in.

It took a solid hour before they were forced to admit that taking the rental car any further was futile. They pulled into a small, relatively flat area. The winter-colored trees provided some camouflage for the gray sedan. Although anyone driving by would see it, the lack of any other vehicles and the remoteness of their location encouraged their hopes of finding it undisturbed when they returned.

Outside, the temperature difference between Phoenix and Flagstaff was obvious. Despite Raine's sweater, the cold still cut its way to her skin. A shiver wracked her as she turned to grab the well-worn travel map from the car.

Gavin shrugged into his jacket. "You have everything?"

She held up the folded map. "I'm good."

He gave a short nod and they set off down the road. They hiked in, rechecking their position often. By the time afternoon started to fade into early evening, they found what they were looking for.

Back in the trees, resting on the ridge was a small shack. The surrounding forest hid it from casual view. The combination of stone and boards composing the frame helped it blend with the landscape. Although the hunter's shelter seemed deserted, Gavin and Raine didn't want to take a chance on altering any residents of their presence.

There wasn't much to see from their hidden vantage point. The roof offered an attempt at protection from the elements, and under it, a window sat high and to the right of the wooden door. Three warped boards created the stairs spanned the gap between the rough ground and the actual porch.

Using the early evening shadows, Gavin moved closer to test for wards. He approached from the back, only to draw up short about a stone's throw away from the shelter.

Worried she would miss something, Raine straddled the thin line between the mortal world and the other world of the Kyn. The quiet scene gained depth as reality was stripped away, leaving only the luminous magical scenery behind.

Gavin's questing magic hit the warded boundary, sparking colors into brilliant life. She scanned for the murky blotches, which would indicate a return of the chindis, or the pits of emptiness revealing the presence of the Soul Stealer. She found neither. Instead, the shack was wreathed with a dull, flat magic.

Gavin's power wove around the drab hues, webbing the perimeter. The bright lines of his energy pushed its way into the openings of existing wards. Wonder held Raine still, her awe growing as his magic absorbed and altered the old wards in mesmerizing display. When the last section of the cabin's wards flowed into new paths, there was a silent flare of light, followed by a pop as if the air pressure suddenly adjusted.

Blinking to adjust her sight, she noted the altered warding now tuned itself to Gavin. She gave a silent whistle. He manage to replace the entire warding without setting off any alarms. Granted she could set decent wards, but she leaned toward the smash-and-burn theory. This level of magical manipulation was damn impressive, but way out of her league.

The evening light began to retreat before the coming night, deepening the shadows around the ramshackle structure. Gavin disappeared around the back of the shack, only to reappear on the far side a few moments later. His mental voice cut through her thoughts. *"We're clear."*

Raine had to admit that the intimate tie they shared was coming in handy. Even if it occasionally gave rise to distractions in the form of some unexpected fantasies. Tuning out her wayward thoughts, she broke cover, careful to keep her footsteps light, as she made her way to him. *"Anyone inside?"*

"Not sure." He stared at the seemingly empty cabin, his brow furrowed. *"Something or someone is in there. Just can't get a read on it."*

She stopped next to him as they stayed in the shadowed depths crowding the side of the cabin. *"What's the plan?"*

"You take the far side of the door, and I'll get the lock."

She nodded and went to step forward, only to stop when he grabbed her arm. She shot him a questioning look.

"Be ready," he cautioned.

Thrilling at the male concern he didn't bother to hide, she found it amusing that he, of all people, would worry about her. Turning a little more, she pressed a quick kiss to his unsmiling lips then hid her small grin as she left. Like the Wraiths they were, they flowed silently into position.

She called on her inner cat's night vision. Her surroundings morphed into shades of yellow, red, and green. Keeping her back flat against the rough boards next to the door, she dropped her wrist blade into her palm while Gavin worked the lock. In moments, the quick snick of the lock releasing sounded. He pushed the door open and she glided inside.

Crouching beside the door, she scanned the room. Although her night vision allowed her a more detailed picture of her surroundings, it was just enough to know that nothing resembling prey lingered here. *"Clear."*

As he moved inside, she kept an eye on the sparsely furnished room even as she straightened, tucking one wrist blade back into its sheath. Cupping her palm she uttered, "*Tachair.*"

A ball of soft white light blinked to life, and her vision adjusted to normal. Setting it to hover behind her shoulder, she surveyed the interior. In a rough kitchen, a rickety table sat near a small sink and what looked like a two-burner camping stove. A black, pot-bellied stove, and its matching pile of chopped wood, took up one corner. Shoved against the far wall was a cot with a ratty-looking blanket.

Striding over to the cot, she used her blade to draw back the blanket, uncovering an abandoned animal nest. She turned to Gavin. "I don't think anyone's been here for quite some time."

Shutting the door behind him, he prowled the room, his frustration mounting. "Something or someone is here," he growled.

Not wanting to crush his fragile male ego, she wisely refrained from pointing out the obvious lack of anything living, except maybe the bugs. As he completed another circuit of the one room shack, she re-sheathed her other blade.

He stopped in front of the stove and dropped into a squat. His fist clenched, and a tingling rush brushed over her as his magic scoured the area. When his eyes narrowed and a predatory grin crossed his face, she perked up. He motioned her over. "Check it out."

He pulled her in until she stood directly in front of him. The line of warmth curling along her spine fractured her focus. It would be so easy to lean back into that tempting heat, but she crammed her heightened awareness of him down. She needed to concentrate on what he was trying to show her. Lowering her protective shields, she slipped into their bond and found what caught his attention.

Anticipation coursed through her, setting her instincts on point. Barely discernible under the woodpile was a small warp in the way his magic flowed, as if it hit some sort of barrier. She took a step forward, only to be stopped by his arm at her waist. Leaning forward she tried to bring the warped image into clearer focus. "What is that?"

"A keyed ward." His voice rumbled behind her. "It's meant to only work for whoever set it."

Straightening, she studied the strange weave. "Can you get through it?"

He hesitated. "It wouldn't take long." He let her go and crouched next to the woodpile. "Do you see anything else?" His question was carefully neutral.

She looked at him, wondering at his tone, but couldn't read anything in his face. "Like?"

"Cheveyo?"

The obviousness of his question made her wince. Turning back to the woodpile she concentrated on the lines tracing though the shack. This time she narrowed her focus to Cheveyo's earth tone hues, allowing her shields to drop a bit more. When her magic didn't surge to the forefront, a tremor of nerves sprung to life. She took a deep breath. Now was not the time, nor the place, to doubt herself or her ability. Her magic was just strained, not crippled.

Working carefully, she finally unearthed the tie linking her and Cheveyo, hidden under the overlying power of the ward. Excitement stirred. Gavin was right, someone was here, and she was betting it was Cheveyo.

This time, the weakened tie didn't startle her. Not wanting to endure another attack by the chindis or whatever the hell else might be lying in wait, she reached for Gavin. Their connection sparked and strengthened. Together they sent a gentle push down the line, keeping in mind the fragile nature of the magic stretching between them and the witch.

Trying to follow its path, she wasn't surprised when she couldn't get beyond the strange warp of the keyed ward. Blinking, she found herself on her haunches before the woodpile with Gavin behind her. "We have to get this wood moved."

They cleared the wood in a matter of minutes and revealed a trap door nestled in the floor. She reached to pull it up, but Gavin's quick reflexes stopped her hand inches away from the handle.

"Ward!" he snapped.

She fought the color stealing up her neck at his reprimand but kept her mouth shut, realizing her careless impulse could have caused irreparable damage. Jerking to her feet, she stalked away to lean against the far wall, her arms crossed across her chest. Gavin stayed in front of the trap door as she studied the boards between her boots. Impatience beat at her, but she accepted that his caution was a necessary evil at this stage.

It took longer than she expected before he rose to his feet.

Straightening from her slouch, she caught sight of his pale face as he turned to her. Setting her earlier annoyance set aside, concern rose and she moved to him. "Gavin?"

"I'm fine." His voice was rough.

She gently snagged his chin, forcing him to meet her gaze, and let her silence speak for her.

He leaned into her touch. "I'm fine." This time his voice was a bit stronger.

Smart enough to know when arguing with his indomitable male ego was a lost cause, she sighed. She'd just have to keep an eye on him. She peeked around her shields and noted that the strange warping was gone. In its place were the now familiar traces of Gavin's magic and deep in their midst, she saw Cheveyo's telltale color.

She moved back to the trapdoor, her hand hovering above the grip. She looked at Gavin. "Ready?"

At his nod she pulled the door open. The damp smell of wet earth and cold underground air wafted through the opening. Directing her globe of light down into the dark maw, she rubbed at the aching mix of anticipation and trepidation clawing at her stomach. The steady light illuminated the dirt floor and dug out walls of crumbling dirt.

Seemingly undaunted, Gavin braced his hand on the floorboards next to the opening and leapt down. He landed on the balls of his feet, his knees bending to take the brunt of the impact. When he rose to his full height, she realized the tunnel was taller than she had first thought. He looked up. "You coming?"

Her feet hit the dirt and even with bent knees, the impact jarred her. Rising, she noticed that the sphere of light hovering near them didn't make much of a dent in the darkness stretching down the tunnel. Uneasiness crept over her.

Some long dormant instinct began buzzing under her skin, chittering along her spine. The darkness could hide so much, and you never knew what was coming at you, until it tried to rip your face off.

Under normal circumstances, the idea of walking into the foreboding tunnel might give her a reason to pause, but she could do it. Unfortunately, the last few days had been anything but normal. Her magic was iffy at best, and her confidence in her ability to defend herself and those around her was seriously undermined. Her safety net of anger was riddled with huge gaping holes. Perhaps moving forward was not such a wise idea.

The shocking unnaturalness of her last thought pulled her up short.

Her sharp intake of breath brought Gavin around to face her. "What's wrong?"

Unable to figure out what was triggering her internal alarms, she ignored him. Instead, she set her back against the dirt wall directly under the trap door. Instinct dropped her wrist blades into place. The feel of leather wrapped metal against her palm helped stem the rising uneasiness. She was under some sort of attack. The paralyzing self-doubts didn't belong to her. Since she couldn't see any physical manifestations of an attack, she let her shields drop and the magical world snapped into view.

Gavin's bright form blocked her line of sight. Hissing in frustration, she sidestepped him, aware on some level that she and her leopard were both staring out at the psychic light show.

A hand wrapped around her wrist and, caught in the strange spell, she twisted, yanking free. She spun around, her blade poised to slice through the threat, but found herself trapped in steel bands. The sudden sense of being forcibly restrained separated the woman and cat. The sundering of her two halves fractured the cloying web of the spell. Her face was pressed into a firm chest while her blade hand was locked behind her back, her wrist held immobile just below her shoulder blades.

Reality returned.

"You back?" His gentle voice was a heady contrast to the controlling grip on her wrist. The tension in her body dissipated, only to be replaced by an erotic heat. His hold caused her to arch into him, spiking her blood pressure. Her head fell back and she tried to breathe through the sudden, sharp arousal.

In the flickering light, his gaze darkened and focused on her parted lips. Lust left his body hardening against hers. Held as she was, she felt the low rumble of a distinctly male growl reverberate against her chest before he claimed her lips with a power that stole her breath.

He took control, allowing her only to respond. His tongue delved deep, demanding she follow. Heat and fire rushed in, burning away her will. There was no teasing, no gentleness in his possession. It was a claiming, a male dominating his female. There was no option but to give in to what he demanded, no space for second thoughts or muddied emotions. Pure sensation dragged her under as the raging desire consumed her.

Lost in the heat of his kiss, she forgot her surroundings, wanting only to quench the wildfire spreading through her. His ravaging mouth moved down her neck, the sensation so primal, she could only moan. He released her wrist. The sound of her blade tumbling to the ground couldn't stop her from using her new found freedom to tangle her hands in his hair.

When his lips covered hers again, he teased and

tempted until she became the aggressor, forcing him back against the wall of the tunnel. She ravaged his mouth with the sole goal of driving him mindless. Freeing one hand from the silky strands of his hair, she ran her nails down his T-shirt-clad chest. A sense of feminine triumph rose as she wrestled another low growl from this alpha male. Nipping at his lips, she stroked him, moving down until his hardness filled her palm. Her low groan was drowned out by his.

He moved liked lightning, capturing both hands and spinning her until her back hit the wall. His forehead pressed against hers, his wide chest heaving as his eyes burned into hers. "Damn, you tempt me."

Between her primitive mind wailing in frustrated need, and the strident voice of reason reminding her of where she was, it took a moment to find her voice. "You started it." There was no hiding the painful ache in the words.

The devilish grin he gave her didn't help. "I promise to finish. Later." The dark vow made her tremble in a purely feminine reaction.

They stared at each other, both fighting to get their flash-fire lust under control. Slowly, he stepped back. She was perversely glad to see him wince and adjust his jeans. She dropped her gaze, hoping a change in scenery would allow her to regain her sanity.

Her blade glinted from the dirt floor. Sighing, she bent down to retrieve it. Dear gods, if the heat between the two of them kept rising, she was in serious trouble. Hysterical humor had her lips twisting as she considered the wisdom of taking a vacation purely so they could spend some quality time in bed and possibly burn this fire out.

"As much as I enjoyed that," he said, watching her, "are you okay?"

Keeping as much careful distance as she could within the confines of the tunnel, she nodded. "I am now. It was just..." She trailed off, uncertain how to continue.

"What?" he prompted.

"I got down here, and suddenly the thought of going through that tunnel scared the shit out of me." She didn't hide the defensive anger in her voice. She didn't like being scared, something he was highly aware of.

He looked into the heavy darkness stretching in front of them. "Maybe it was part of the warding."

She raised an eyebrow, feigning mock disbelief. "You missed something?"

He didn't bother to respond to her taunt. Instead, he sent his magic to probe around them. She cursed at the sudden sensation of ants biting her skin.

"Hold still," he said. "I've got to make sure it's gone."

Pure force of will kept her motionless, trusting whatever he was doing was necessary. Within moments, the uncomfortable stinging feeling faded away.

"Remnants of a spell," he explained.

"A human can't ward or set a spell like that." She followed him into the tunnel's darkness.

The small orb of light glided ahead of them nudging the inkiness back a few feet at a time. "Adds weight to Ransom not pulling this off on his own."

There was some relief in validating one of their theories.

"Yeah, but we still need to figure out who was pulling his strings." Gavin's voice was muffled as he forged through the dugout passageway.

"I know." She picked her way over the rough ground while keeping pace. Since she hadn't fared so well in her previous encounters with the Soul Stealer and the damn chindis, the thought did not inspire confidence.

As the tunnel made a sharp right, a cold breeze caught them unawares. He jerked to a stop while she quenched the small fey light with a thought. Shadows seeped around them. The breeze came again. Peering down to the far end of the tunnel, she noticed a faint difference in the darkness.

"Can you see anything?" His question filtered through their bond.

Moving up beside him, she dropped her shields. There was a moment of anxious anticipation before both her magic and her leopard surged forward. Gently, she urged her cat into the background, not trusting its more instinctive responses. Especially now, when caution was key.

Gathering her magic, she sent it out to search. The world spun. Faster than expected, she stood before the door leading to Cheveyo. He was so close. Fighting the urge to let him know they were just on the other side, she took a moment to center herself.

A delicate touch was needed if she wanted to accomplish this without alerting the Soul Stealer. Double-checking her anchor to Gavin, she drew on his strength and control. Slowly, she began to send her magic through, using the mental equivalent of scratching at the door.

Dear gods, please let Cheveyo hear her. Nerves stuttered beneath her forced calm. Minutes ticked by with no answer. If she didn't get something soon, she'd be forced to open the door regardless of what was waiting on the other side.

Just when she began to give up, she felt a faint responding pulse. Worry spiked. It was so weak. This was not good. This close, Cheveyo's response should be stronger.

Possible scenarios ran through her mind, filling her with dread. She kept a light level of energy flowing and slowly backed away from the door. She and Gavin needed a plan because she was damn certain Cheveyo was out of time.

Back in the tunnel, her shields in place, she felt Gavin's stillness as he considered the situation. She marveled at how fast he weighed and discarded various scenarios as she studied the plan forming in his mind.

Together, they moved forward, each taking a side of the tunnel. Her blades were in her hands, while his remained sheathed along his spine. He began amassing his magic, the surrounding earth making it both faster and easier. Without their small light, her night vision was back in full force.

The tunnel ended in a roughhewn opening. Letting him watch her back, she stepped to the opening and hugged the rock edge as she surveyed the chamber. The slight lightening of the dark wasn't due to any light source, but the empty space framed by a massive rock dome. Gazing up, she made out a small opening letting the air circulate. The night sky seemed tiny, dwarfed by the darkness of the cavern.

Scanning the massive room, she found a faint tone of orange huddled near the far wall where something warm blooded clung to life. She had a horrible feeling she knew who it was. Dread echoed down the magical tether to Gavin.

The hair at the base of her neck rose as her night vision crumbled under the psychic onslaught of Gavin's magic. His power ripped through the shadowed web shrouding the underground cavern. Blue fire began devouring the strands spanning the entire cavern.

As difficult as it was, she left her end of the bond wide

open, trusting his ability to shield them both. He continued to battle the writhing strands as her doppelganger made a reappearance. Leaving this part of the battle to him, Raine used the distraction to swiftly cross the dirt floor.

Dropping to her knees in front of Cheveyo's still form, she dragged in a shuddering breath and placed her hand on his dirt-encrusted hair. The lightning storm of the battling magic around her faded, replaced by the steel door connecting her and Cheveyo.

Back on the psychic plane, she pounded on the door. "Cheveyo!" she yelled. "Open the damn door!"

She sent a strong surge through the weakening tie snaking under the barrier. Nothing. Panic clawed at her. Her mind worked furiously. There wasn't time to coax the door open. There had to be a way to force it.

Stepping back, she narrowed her concentration on the immovable object in front of her. Gathering every bit of magic she could find, she created a ball of burning bright flames in between her cupped palms. She was about to drag the stubborn-ass witch back into the land of the living whether he liked it or not. With a fierce effort of will, she forced the burning orb into the fragile threads, feeling them stretch and warp.

Sacrificing skill for speed, she shoved ruthlessly, sending the speedball of painful energy through. When it found Cheveyo, it would detonate, shocking the witch into a response. She felt it hit and the resulting explosion shattered the vault door into thousands of shards of colorful glass. The agony reverberating through the bond sent her to her knees.

She had just enough presence of mind to shut down the tie between her and Gavin before it could drag him under. Then there was no time to worry about the repercussions of her actions. Her vision whited out under the rising tide of pain as her unruly magic looped between her and Cheveyo.

The maelstrom of power swept over her in a crushing tide. She struggled to the surface, fighting to break through the cresting waves. They continued to suck her under. The lull between waves became longer and she was wrenched back, as if snagged on a hook. The sharp sting was lost amid the numerous other pains. A wave began to crest and she felt the tug, deeper this time. She grasped the phantom hook only to find herself holding her connection to Cheveyo. Clumsily, she wove her magic with his, strengthening the tie and, finally, she broke through the surface of her rampaging magic.

Dragging her tired body out of the whirlpool of power, she collapsed next to a very pale, worn-looking Cheveyo.

"You have got to be the most stubborn, pigheaded woman I've ever met!"

"Screw you," she gasped. "You're welcome." She looked at him, fighting not to let her shock show. The reason behind the weakening bond became obvious. Instead of the rugged warrior, she found a fragile-looking old man. "What the hell, Cheveyo?" Her voice was soft.

"*Nomâhtsé'héõò Adanata.*" Soul Stealer. His short answer and the way his gaze seemed to focus on something only he could see sent ice careening through her veins.

Ignoring her body's whimpers, she scrambled to her feet. "Come on." She offered her hand to the unnerving image of her mentor. "We're getting you out of here this time." When he continued to look at her blankly, a sick feeling spiraled through her. Lowering into a crouch until she was eye level, she waved a hand in front of his face. "Cheveyo? You in there?"

There was a flicker of recognition, there and gone.

"Damn it," she muttered. "Fine, we'll do this the hard way then." Leaning down, she wrapped one arm around his waist and lifted. Hauling him to his feet, she slung his arm around her neck, and held his wrist to steady him.

Stuck on the psychic plane, she would need Gavin's help to pull the weakened Cheveyo back. Reaching for their bond, she tore down her hastily erected barrier, flinching as the sharp pull on her already-stressed magic almost dropped her to her knees.

She gritted her teeth, knowing if Gavin was drawing this much, things were not going according to plan on the other side. Stumbling, she made her way back to the metaphysical doorway, or what was left of it. Between trying to keep Cheveyo on his feet and the draining of her magical strength as Gavin continued to reinforce his own magic, the journey took forever.

She almost didn't recognize the remains of the mental door. Twisted and torn metal lay like discarded shrapnel, and she could see the other side. She tried to figure out how to bring the battered spirit of Cheveyo back to his physical body. Frustrated tears sprang to her eyes as exhaustion and pain waged a seemingly never-ending war.

"Raine." Her name was spoken so quietly she thought she imagined it.

It came again and she realized it was Cheveyo. It was awkward but she managed to look at his face. Awareness fought for supremacy as he tried to focus on her.

"Watch..." His cracked lips moved, the word escaping on a breath.

Scattered images seared through her mind. Even forewarned, it took effort not to let her natural defenses rise as he pushed his memories into her consciousness. She remembered what he told her when they had first discussed their newly formed tie. If either one needed knowledge the other held, all they had to do was ask.

She was definitely asking now.

The answer came. To reunite his spirit and body completely she would have to break the tie the Soul Stealer had erected. To do that required undoing the magical weave of the Stealer's bonds to Cheveyo's spirit. Considering how interwoven that was, it wouldn't be easy.

As his memories and lucidity faded, she gently set him down. Calling her leopard forward, she let it curl around her mentor's spirit. It was the best protection she could offer. She had to go back and face the Stealer.

Touching her anchor with Gavin, she let her mind go back to the physical plane. She opened her eyes to find she was still crouched over Cheveyo's motionless body in the dark cave.

Uncertain how much time had passed, she turned. Gavin was standing between her and the mouth of the cavern, wielding both magic and blade against the stalking monster of the now physical Soul Stealer. Her doppelganger was nowhere to be found. Getting to her feet, she gritted her teeth against her body's protests. Her wrist blades were in both hands as she stood beside Gavin.

Never taking his eyes off from the threat in front of him, he snapped, "Did you get him?"

"Yeah." Utilizing their telepathic connection, she shared her plan.

His spark of concern was quickly squashed. "Let's do this," he growled and went on the offensive. Using the distraction of his sudden attack, she dropped her psychic barrier.

The dark weave—of what she now knew were consumed souls which gave the Soul Stealer its power—

filled her sight. Every inch of her spirit cringed from touching the fouled magic, but she had no choice. Using the information Cheveyo shared, she lunged.

She expected pain. She hadn't expected the sadistic, twisting pleasure flooding her mind. Every monstrous urge she fought to conquer, every dark desire haunting her nightmares, and every lethal temptation she walked away from, slammed into her, sending her into a huddled ball of agony. Everything she locked away, broke free into a howling mass of vicious joy.

The Soul Stealer's essence found her, rejoicing as it began to suck the meat of her soul from her bones. As each mental lock shattered under the attack, her spirit shuddered under the blows. No matter how hard she tried, she couldn't rise above it. The whirlwind of darkness was winning.

She was going to fail Cheveyo.

She was going to fail Gavin.

Again.

The soul tearing agony of that realization seared through her mind. Fear and despair disappeared under a fatalistic determination. Failing him was not an option. She loved Gavin. Never again would someone she loved suffer because of her actions. Least of all him.

Deep inside—where she never looked—the determination to win grew, fueled by rage and an even older anger that something so twisted and dark took joy in her suffering. Buried deep in her magic, where the Stealer couldn't sense it, pulsed the silver blue bond securing her soul to Gavin's. Strength flooded into her, bringing her to her feet, blades in her hands.

Baring her teeth, she waded in. On some distant level, she was aware she was mimicking Gavin's attack in the physical world. Between the two of them, they began to shred the Stealer apart.

Unable to defend against their joint attack, the monster began to pull back from the physical world, focusing on what it perceived as the weaker threat. Raine. As its physical body began to dissipate in the real world, the one on the magical plane became stronger.

It was the moment she had been waiting for. She had one chance to cut the connection between the Stealer and Cheveyo's fading spirit—when the Stealer fully manifested on the magical plane. Gavin would use the spell she shared, retying Cheveyo's body and spirit together, leaving her alone to face a very pissed off Stealer.

She waited, baiting the Stealer with sneak attacks, drawing it back to the psychic plane. There was a flash-bang of an earth-toned flare deep within the Stealer. With a roar of undiluted fury, the monster pulled itself completely into the magical realm.

She threw her blade. Not waiting to see if it struck its mark, she sliced out with her magic, cutting the tie between the Stealer and Cheveyo. The monster screamed, the unnatural sound making her ears bleed.

Unfortunately, she was directly in the path of its massive claws. The pain of the impact was lost with the others as she went airborne. She hit the wall but stubbornly clung to consciousness as she fell. Until Gavin was done, she had to stay on her feet or they risked losing Cheveyo. She tried to stand but failed miserably. Her breath sawed through her aching chest, and she had trouble focusing.

"Get up! Get up!" She knew that mumbled command was her own voice, but her body wasn't listening.

"Damn it!" she screamed hoarsely. "Move!"

Somehow, she made it to her feet, swaying, but upright.

Something warm dripped into her eyes, but she wiped it away. When her vision cleared, she looked up to find the evil creature bearing down on her.

Her blades were gone, so she reached for her magic. Her desperate prayer was answered as white flames burst into life. She threw the first volley. The white flame hit the Stealer in the face, bringing it to an abrupt stop. It began clawing at the silent, ghostly flames, letting out a high-pitched squeal of agony that echoed off the walls. Through her shock, she focused on the flames writhing over the creature, making them burn faster and deeper.

The squeals turned into howls. The cacophony was deafening. Then, just when she was sure her eardrums would shatter under the barrage, the Soul Stealer disappeared.

Dumfounded, she stood in the vast magical tapestry, staring at the rips and tears giving mute testimony to the battle waged. Her knees weakened and she dropped to the ground. Debilitating fear rose in her. Gavin! What if the Stealer had gone back to the physical world? Her spirit shuddered, but she reached out to their binding and dragged herself back.

This time when her spirit dropped back into her body, the jolt was excruciating. She curled into a ball as every muscle seemed to spasm at once, stealing her breath. A weak whimper made it past her clenched jaw. Even worse were the tears she felt escaping her tightly closed eyes.

She breathed through the worst of it and—when she was sure she wasn't going to scream—unlocked her jaw. Prying her eyes open, she was met with the sight of Gavin's back. He was crouched over something. Her natural barriers were back in place and the thought of lowering them to see what was happening was too daunting.

Slowly, like an old woman, she pushed to her hands and knees. Although the space between them wasn't more than a few feet, it felt much longer as she crawled over to him. When she was within touching distance, she reached out and brushed his back weakly.

He half rose and spun, his green eyes glowing with magic. If everything hadn't hurt so bad, she might have faltered under his coldly distant gaze. Instead, she stared up at him mutely.

His jaw softened and he knelt, gently gathering her sore body into his arms. He settled back on the ground, cradling her. Together they faced Cheveyo's still form.

"Did it work?" she whispered. Even with her barriers up, the skin-tingling sensation of Gavin's magic flowed over her.

"Yeah." His voice was rough and his jaw tight.

"But?"

He looked down at her, the magic that swirled in his gaze slowing. "We may have reunited the spirit and the body, but I'm not sure if it's enough."

She wanted to ignore the warning in his words, but she understood. She studied the unconscious witch in front of them. "The rest is up to him."

CHAPTER 24

Gavin held Raine as he worked over Cheveyo. She could feel him drawing on her magic as he continued to weave another piece of the spell Cheveyo had given them. The tingling sensation of his power dulled the sharper complaints from her aching body and she fell into a semi-conscious state.

Sometime later, she jostled awake when Gavin adjusted his hold. Leaving her head on his shoulder, she pried her eyes open. Her night vision flickered with the familiar hues of yellow, green, and red in the lightless black of the cavern.

Gavin rested his chin against the top of her head. His shoulders relaxed under her cheek as exhaustion replaced his body's earlier tension. She let her lids drift down, cherishing this small respite with him. Silent moments passed.

"We need to get moving." His low voice blended into the surrounding darkness.

Licking her dry lips, she coughed. "How long have we been here?"

"An hour and a half. Maybe two."

She didn't want to move, but they were racing the clock. There was no way to tell what damage their fight with the Soul Stealer had done to it, or to the one holding its leash. If they were lucky, they managed to score enough hits to make the hellish duo hole up somewhere and lick their wounds. *Please gods, just a little break would be nice.* Just long enough to get Cheveyo out of here and back to Tala's. Thinking of which...

"How are we going to get him out?" Considering the shape they both were in, hauling out the deadweight of a six-foot-six male was going to be a challenge.

"The passageway is narrow, but I think we can use a travois to transport him." He rubbed his chin against her head. "Finding a couple of long branches shouldn't be too hard."

Remembering the ratty blanket on the cot in the cabin, she added, "We could use that blanket up there as well. I'm just not sure how long it will hold."

"My jacket's down here somewhere," he muttered. "Think you could get us a little light?"

Checking, she was unsurprised to find her magical reserves precariously low. But she'd worked with less. A soft word and the fey light winked into being. She squinted against the barrage of white spots dancing in her vision. When they cleared, she stared into Gavin's drawn face. Worry plagued her. His skin held an unhealthy pallor making his eyes appear sunken and his cheekbones sharper. "You okay?"

He shrugged. "I've been better." He studied the prone witch in front of him. "The spell was a bit more difficult than I anticipated."

She struggled out of his lap, trying not to moan as her movements increased the complaints of her battered body.

Once on her feet, she took a mental inventory, knowing their night was far from over. Her magic was sluggish, but there. Reaching a little farther, she met the eerie silver gaze of her cat. It was curled up, the tip of its tail twitching.

Using Gavin's shoulder for support, Raine stretched a bit farther, this time focusing on their bond. The worry in her belly unclenched as she confirmed he wasn't lying. He was drained, more so than expected, but he'd be okay.

There was one last metaphysical tie to check, then she could concentrate on getting out of here. She searched for her tether to Cheveyo and found...nothing. Startled, she tried again. Unable to find the familiar earth tones of the witch, she sent a questing spark and received a weak answer. Mentally turning until she faced the direction of the dim pulse, she discovered a new addition to the tapestry.

At first, what she saw didn't make sense, but as she studied it, pieces fell into place. Cheveyo's magic was unrecognizable because it was no longer just his. Instead, his translucent signature was nestled inside a silver-blue cocoon. Looking closer, she found delicate tendrils weaving through his damaged magic. She and Gavin were providing the only psychic protection the witch had. No pressure, she thought darkly, bringing her physical surroundings back into focus.

Gavin found his dust-covered jacket, balled it up, and tucked it under Cheveyo's head. Rising stiffly to his feet, he said, "I'll head up and get the branches."

He was about to disappear through the stone archway when she called, "Gavin? You want some light?" She sent the little floating orb toward him with a small, mental push.

"Sure, thanks." He vanished down the passageway, the

glow from the fey light eaten up by the shadows in the tunnel.

Without the comforting light, her night vision kicked back in. Sighing, she settled next to Cheveyo. With nothing to do but think, she turned the situation over in her mind.

Considering how damaged Cheveyo's magic appeared, it was a wonder he was still breathing. There was no doubt much of his strength had gone into fighting the Soul Stealer. Even though she had severed the parasitic ties, it didn't mean he was out of the proverbial woods.

If she believed Gavin's magic-muscle theory, then Cheveyo was going to have a damn long road to travel before his magical strength returned to anything near normal.

What would that mean for the Northwest Magi House? Would there be witches and wizards waiting to challenge him for leadership when he got home? Or, would they allow him the time he was going to need to recover?

She snorted. Knowing that crowd, there was no way they were going to cut the wounded Cheveyo any slack. Until recently, she never paid attention to the political games the Kyn leaders played, believing the bigger threat existed with the humans and their inability to accept what they couldn't understand. Thanks to Gavin's questions, she needed to reassess where possible threats would come from.

If they really were being studied by the Kyn leaders, would those same leaders find the metaphysical tethers she and Gavin had woven between them and the most powerful magi in the Northwest a threat?

Hell yes, they would.

In the months she had spent under Cheveyo's tutoring, she got the impression even he was uncertain of how deep their "little" connection really went. Sprinkle in her unpredictable magic, and the witch had created a volatile stew. Now that it had been altered with the addition of Gavin's magic, she'd bet good money Cheveyo would start considering his options.

If their positions were reversed, and it was her in the witch's position, she'd be seriously contemplating how to use her new tools to increase her power base. 'Use your tools, don't let them use you.' Her uncle had said that more than once.

You can remove the threat, cold practicality whispered. It was just her, the weakened witch, and the dark shadows. She wasn't a fool. Embracing the unemotional assessment, she recognized the valid point. Getting rid of Cheveyo would ensure she and Gavin would remain safe from the other Kyn. Letting him live meant he could turn this link around on her and Gavin.

She looked at the man lying on the ground. He could be a threat. She lifted her hand to his face, letting her palm cup gently over his mouth and nose. The soft brush of his breath against her skin gave her pause.

'Use your tools.' Her uncle's voice echoed through her mind. Killing was not always the answer. Tied as he was to her and Gavin, he could become a very powerful ally, especially since his existence hinged on theirs. She took her hand away.

Besides, there was a time when their positions had been reversed, and she was the one dying at his feet. Instead of removing a possible threat, he bound them together, pulling her back to the land of the living. Could she return the favor with a blade to the heart? More importantly, after the soul-shredding light the Soul Stealer had shed on her blackest aspects, could she afford the cost?

The answer was a quiet but resounding, No.

For the first time in forever she held something precious in her clumsy grasp—her burgeoning relationship with Gavin. It was something she thought she'd never find. Granted, she already made so many mistakes, but compared to what she was considering, those were fixable. If she took this step, she would lose not just Gavin, but the last remaining aspect of the woman she fought so hard to save.

Light danced in the shadows and the sound of wood dragging against dirt preceded Gavin's approach. Getting to her feet, she met him at the stone archway. He carried two sturdy branches and the ratty blanket from the cabin. She was happy to see his face was a little less pale. They worked in companionable silence, constructing the travois. Once both the blanket and jacket were tied between the wooden branches, they loaded Cheveyo.

"Ready?" Gavin grasped the wooden handles.

Nodding, she led the way back through the tunnel with the light bobbing along. It was slow going. The narrow passageway and rough dirt floor made it nearly impossible not to jar the injured man. Lugging the deadweight took its toll on Gavin as well, and she insisted on stopping a few times, ignoring his protests.

One benefit of the tight tunnel was her ability to stand in front of him. Short of bowling her over, he didn't have much of a choice on whether or not to stop. The second time she did that, he growled at her. Frustrated with his pigheadedness, she growled back. Then the silliness of their actions struck them both and they shared a smile.

Reaching the trapdoor, they found a new challenge.

She pushed her tangled hair out of her face. "Well, damn."

Gavin stopped, laid the travois down, and joined her as she frowned at the square pale opening sitting above them.

Hands on her hips, she transferred her glare from the opening to the prone form of Cheveyo. "How are we supposed to get him up there?"

"We need to get him on his feet."

She cocked an eyebrow. "Okay, and how do you propose we accomplish that? If bouncing along the dirt for the last twenty minutes hasn't even produced a moan, how do we get him upright?"

He shot her a wicked grin. "I got it covered."

She so didn't want to know. "Fine. Once he's up then what?"

"I'll go up first, while you keep him upright. I pull and you push."

Since the upcoming trip through the forest was daunting enough, she thought he was being overly optimistic. But they really didn't have any other choice. "If he falls, I'm blaming you," she muttered.

His only answer was a low chuckle. He crouched over the witch and placed his hands on either side of Cheveyo's temples. She wasn't sure what he was doing until his magic sent ants crawling over her skin.

When the first faint moan surfaced, she thought she imagined it. But it was quickly followed by another and then Cheveyo's eyes snapped open.

She peered over Gavin's shoulder. Tension crawled up her spine as she caught the cloudy confusion in the Cheveyo's dark eyes. The disturbing vagueness only added to Gavin's earlier warning of how much may have survived the rejoining.

Gavin worked an arm under Cheveyo's shoulders. "Come on, man. On your feet."

With none of his usual grace, Cheveyo pushed to his feet. Instead, each movement seemed to belong to a painfully old man. There was nothing for Raine to do but stand to the side until Gavin propped him against the wall near the opening. Taking Gavin's place at Cheveyo's side, she shouldered his weight.

Gavin jumped and grabbed the edge of the trapdoor. His shoulders and arms coiled and bunched, as he dragged his body up. He reappeared and leaned most of his upper body through the hole.

Raine strained under Cheveyo's full weight. Somehow, she stayed on her feet and got the witch positioned under Gavin's outstretched arms. "Cheveyo." She sharpened her voice into a command. "Arms up!"

He blinked vacantly and his weight settled more firmly against her. Frustration spiked as she adjusted her hold.

"Damn it," she hissed.

Staring angrily into his slack face, her volatile emotions had her cat padding closer to the surface. It was a bit of shock to feel her nails alter into the thicker, curved points of her cat's claws. She flexed her hands, digging the sharp points into his ribs. Finally, she got a spark of the man buried deep inside. Arrogant anger suffused his face. Before any scathing remark could be made, she snapped, "Raise your damn arms and help Gavin get you up, or I'm leaving your sorry ass here."

When he did exactly what she asked, she didn't dare let her relief show. Silently, she thanked the gods for the height of both men as Gavin grasped Cheveyo's forearms and pulled. Squatting, she did what she could to help by wrapping her arms around Cheveyo's legs and lifting. Together she and Gavin got him out of the thrice-damned tunnel.

Bent over, Raine rested her arms on the top of her thighs. Her head hung low and her hair was a matted, sweaty mess.

"You ready?" Gavin's voice brought her head up.

Straightening, she passed the folded travois to him. When he reappeared a few minutes later, she leapt and grabbed his wrists. He pulled her out. Lying next to each other on the wooden floor of the cabin, they took a moment to catch their breath. Cheveyo was once again unconscious in the travois.

"I've got a suggestion," she croaked.

Gavin didn't even turn his head. "I'm listening."

"You dragging that thing is going to take forever." She began laying her blades between them.

He turned toward her. "And?"

Instead of answering, she reached for her cat and let her magic shift body and bones. Gavin rolled over into a low crouch, one of her blades in his fist as he faced the black leopard. His eyes narrowed. "A little warning next time."

Deep in the cat, she smiled at the disgruntled comment. The cat twitched its tail. Uncertain if their bond would still work with the cat in charge, she sent, *"Tie the travois to the cat. We'll make better time."*

"Fine." He lifted a hand then paused with it in midair, eyeing her. She held still until he finally stroked over her head and down her back. She and the cat purred at his touch. "If it gets too much, change back and we'll continue on foot." He collected the rest of her weapons.

The leopard huffed at him. Shaking his head, he began cutting strips off the blanket to create a primitive harness. Soon they were heading into the night.

The trip back was draining but uneventful. Inside the big cat, Raine almost cried in relief when they stumbled upon the car. Her shoulders were burning and exhaustion wore at both her and Gavin.

Stopping, the cat swayed, limbs trembling as abused muscles spasmed. Even Gavin's approach couldn't raise a reaction. At least not until he lifted the makeshift litter from its shoulders. Then it gave a low mewl. It walked to the far side of the car, stopped, and then arched its spine.

Tugging on her waning magic, Raine felt her heart skip a beat when the power didn't immediately respond. She and the cat both stilled before trying again. Her magic sluggishly answered. The shift from cat to woman left her a shaking mess—a cold, naked shivering mess, actually. One day she would figure out the whole shift-with-clothes-on process.

The chilly night air ruffled over her exposed skin. Shivers blossomed—hardly surprising, considering how much was on display. Something heavy and warm settled over her back. As the supple leather hit her sore shoulders, she winced and pulled Gavin's jacket closer letting his woodsy scent envelope her. A minute later, the man himself was back.

Kneeling next to her, he added a rough blanket around her shivering body as he drew her closer. "Where are your clothes?" His question was a vibrating rumble under her ear.

"Still trying to figure that part out," she answered, burrowing into his tempting heat. "Are you complaining?" she teased weakly.

"Nope. I was about to suggest helping you practice, actually."

With her head against his chest, she let the silly smile escape. "Practice makes perfect."

His sexy chuckle did more to chase away the cold than the layers covering her. When the worst of the tremors calmed, he helped her to her feet. Wrapping the blanket around her sarong style, she zipped up his jacket to help hold it in place. Together they got Cheveyo into the back seat of the sedan.

Collapsing into the passenger seat, she caught sight of the clock in the dashboard. Lord and Lady, just after midnight? She would've sworn it was a hell of a lot later.

Warm air gusted from the vents, chasing the last of her chills away. Gavin pulled back on to the rutted road. As the miles passed under the crunch and snap of gravel, Raine sank into her mind-numbing exhaustion.

Frigid air snaked through Raine's hazy awareness. The vibration of a door being closed was followed by the murmur of hushed voices—one deeply male, the other female—that teased her awareness. There were a few surreal moments of quiet, and then she was wrapped in familiar arms. One lone shiver managed to make itself known before she was pulled tight to a hard chest. Something warm fell over her blocking out the cold.

Burrowing closer, she tried to obey her body's pleas for more rest, but her mind nudged her closer and closer to awareness. She fought her heavy lids to blink owlishly in the spill of light falling over Gavin's shoulder.

When he straightened, she looped an arm around his

neck. As the cold air snapped at her, she buried her face into his neck to avoid the chill. "Where are we?" she mumbled.

"Tala's." He bumped the car door closed with his hip before turning toward the house.

"She needs to set some protections in place." No telling if the Stealer would be able to refocus on Cheveyo. Or her, for that matter.

"Already done," he said. "I called ahead."

The combination of skin-ruffling magic and the bittersweet musk of sage hit her as he crossed the threshold. The cloying scents left her nose wrinkling. As he set her on the couch, the sharp, biting scent of wintergreen cut through the barrage. Once again, the furniture had been pushed to the edges of the living room.

The familiar lines of a protection circle stood starkly against the wooden floor. Inside knelt Tala, Ash next to her. Her entire focus was on the bare-chested, battered body of Cheveyo lying on a pallet of blankets.

Gavin locked the front door then sprawled next to Raine on the couch. Slouching, he rested his head against the back of the couch, his hands laced over his stomach. The glint of jade under his half-closed eyelids meant he was watching Tala work.

Raine scooted over until she could rest her head against his shoulder and curl up next to him. A strange quiet fell over them as they studied the woman. Even though most of her power stayed within the circle, soft waves of her healing magic lapped at Raine's shields.

"Gavin?"

"Yeah?' Even his mental voice sounded tired.

"Do we trust her?"

She could actually feel him start at her question, then

muddled confusion colored their connection. *"What do you mean?"*

She ignored the whispers of caution emanating from the merciless psychopath that dwelled inside her. *"When you left me alone with Cheveyo in the cavern..."*

Muscles tightened under her cheek, the only sign he was bracing himself for something unpleasant. *"Yeah?"*

"I noticed the changes you made to the tie with Cheveyo."

He stayed silent, waiting for her to continue.

"Did you mean to do that?"

"Do what?" he asked.

"Tie him to both of us?" She felt him pause, as if considering how to answer her. *"Don't."* She didn't want him to hide. If he demanded unvarnished truth from her, she would accept no less from him.

The predatory stillness rippling through their connection was followed by a simple, *"Yes."*

A small smile rose to her lips. *"Good."*

It was reassuring to know the softer feelings she shared with this male weren't impacting either of their abilities to assess the threats around them. Until tonight, she hadn't even been aware of her deep worry that, by allowing Gavin into her heart, it would somehow negate her ability to be the warrior she needed to be.

"I almost killed him." Her barely thought words were a deadly offering of understanding.

He pressed his lips against her hair. *"So did I."*

She continued to watch the woman in front of them. *"Will she?"*

"No," he answered decisively, *"but it may not matter."*

Needing to see for herself, she dropped her shields. Tala's magic burst into vivid, Technicolor life. The swirling white-edged gold energy was a clear indicator there was no malicious intent in the spells she was weaving over Cheveyo's still form. Under the radiant glow of Tala's magic, Raine could barely make out the paler earth tones of Cheveyo's unique signature. Puzzled, she leaned forward. Why couldn't she see the silver blue layer? She sent a wordless question to Gavin.

"Illusion."

Nice to know she wasn't the only one worried about how the reformed ties would be viewed by those more powerful. She gave him credit. It was brilliantly sneaky. She loved it.

Tala drew more and more magic to her and began weaving it tightly around Cheveyo. When he was wreathed from head to toe, she did something Raine couldn't follow, but considering the sharpening of Gavin's attention it had to be important. *"What?"*

"Tell me what's different about her spell."

It took a minute to finally see what caught his attention. What appeared to be a blanket of magic began to fray. The loose threads tried to latch on to Cheveyo's body, but they stopped just short of actually touching the witch's energy.

"Damn it." Gavin snarled in frustration as the problem crystallized.

"We have to let it through," she said. *"If we don't, he's dead."*

"I'm not sure I can."

She studied the struggling energy. The way the tendrils tried to burrow past the invisible barrier reminded her of something. The jumbled memory of how the Stealer had siphoned Cheveyo's magic fell into place.

"I can." Pushing away from him, she fell to her knees

outside Tala's circle. She ignored the warning growl from Ash as he rose to his feet.

"Tala." Her voice seemed unnaturally loud.

Protected by the circle Tala raised her head. Raine fought not to flinch as she met the milky blind eyes staring back.

"What do you want?" Tala's voice was deeper, as if a group of voices spoke in synchronicity. The unearthly sound sent shivers over Raine's skin.

"Let me in."

The witch's head tilted, combined with the eerie blind look, the simple movement retained an alien quality. "There is no breaking the protection circle until the ritual is complete."

She buried her impatience, answering the cold intelligence with logic. "The tie between Cheveyo and me is holding your magic back. If you don't let me in, I can't open it."

"You can't break the lines," the strange multi-tonal voice responded.

"I won't. I just need to reach the tie between us."

"Raine, I can't follow you." Gavin's voice was a soft murmur in her head.

"Will our bond hold?"

"I think so."

"Then that will have to do."

The swirling energy slowed and then settled. "Would you enter this circle of your own free will without intent to harm those held within?"

The ritualistic words were weighted with power, making even the air heavy with expectancy. There was no room for deception. Good thing at this point her sole purpose was to help save the man between them. "I so swear."

"Enter, Raine McCord."

Although her body stayed kneeling on the outside of Tala's circle, her spirit stepped over and glided toward Cheveyo. Settling on her metaphysical heels, she reached out to the line they shared. Even as Raine slipped along the power, Tala and her pet watched every move she made. The knowledge added a layer of tension to her dangerous game of sleight of hand.

She was going to press her advantage at being the only one who could see the unique energy signatures of the amassing magic. The theory was familiar. Let your prey think you were a weaker target, while your backup lay hidden from sight. Problem was, she never attempted such delicate manipulation of magic. She would need to create openings to Cheveyo, while using her magic to provide a thin barrier between Gavin and Tala.

She prayed Gavin's illusion held as she began to work. If she let either Tala or Gavin's power touch at any point, the gig would be up. She began creating openings in the protective silver blue shell so Tala's healing magic could tunnel to Cheveyo.

It was a good thing Tala tended to trust her supposed allies. Sadly, her honorable tendencies allowed Raine the necessary cover in keeping the Southwest Magi clueless. Ironically, if Tala ever discovered how intrinsically tied Cheveyo was to the two Wraiths, Raine had no doubt her reaction would be swiftly lethal. Honorable didn't mean forgiving.

Keeping her focus sharp, Raine continued to create small holes up and down the protective barrier. When the healing magic began to pause before arrowing downward, her nerves sharpened. Tala was sensing the changes. A litany of silent prayers ran through Raine's mind. *Please don't let the illusion falter.*

When nearly a half a dozen tunnels were completed, she stopped. The strain on her magic left her feeling thin. The urge to reach for Gavin's support grew, but she couldn't chance it, not yet. Not until there was no other choice.

Tala continued to funnel her power through the openings, and Cheveyo's earth tones began to darken. Time passed with excruciating slowness. The first warning tremor in Raine's magic signaled Cheveyo's returning strength. She was about to be caught between two very powerful witches. Not a good place to be—ever.

Hoping Tala's concentration was solely focused on Cheveyo, she reached out psychically to Gavin. As if he'd been waiting, she felt a lessening in the magical load as he added his strength to hers. Her shaky tunnels steadied enough so she could get Tala's attention. Raine's spirit was held inside the protection circle. "Tala."

The witch didn't respond.

"Tala Whiteriver."

The use of her full name worked and the weirdly inhuman gaze locked on to her.

"I can't hold it open much longer," Raine said.

"You will hold until I release you."

Anger sparked but she clamped it down. "You don't understand. I can't hold the energy between you and him much longer." It was a viable excuse. "My magic is too drained by freeing him from the Soul Stealer. If you don't let me stop, my power will falter. It'll damage him."

A frown tugged the corners of Tala's mouth down. She

studied Cheveyo, her eyes flickering between milky white and deep brown. With a strangely gentle move, she brushed Cheveyo's hair back. "No, I don't want him hurt anymore." That was Tala's voice, not the multi-tonal alien one.

Raine didn't release her sigh of relief. "Thank you." It cost her nothing to offer the small courtesy.

Tala's magic receded and Raine ensured Gavin's protections remained intact. A weary sense of satisfaction coursed through her as she withdrew her magic. Cheveyo's energy appeared stronger. It wasn't anywhere near the same deep tones she was used to, but better. Time, she reminded herself. It would take time.

When the last of the tunnels flowed close, Raine drifted out of the circle and into her body. Her battered magic was depleted and her physical body was once again singing a chorus of various aches and pains. Gavin was now kneeling beside her on the floor.

"Tomorrow," Tala stated, staring at the two of them. "We begin again." The strange alien presence was gone, leaving only the Southwest Magi behind.

Feeling the rejection rising in Gavin, Raine covered his hand, urging caution. "It took the Soul Stealer days to drain him to this point." She was proud at how...polite she managed to sound.

"And it will take days to bring him back." Tala began releasing the protection circle, walking counter clockwise.

"We don't have days." Raine's flat statement sent emotions too quick to be read crashing over Tala's face. "Will he hold his own?"

Stopping near her and Gavin, Tala dragged an afghan off the corner of the couch. Raine felt Gavin stiffen in readiness, neither of them certain of the witch's intent.

She shot them an unreadable look before turning to drape the blanket over Cheveyo. Her face softened. "He'll hold."

"Then if you'll excuse us," Gavin said. "We need to rest."

He helped Raine to her feet. Upright, she swayed as a soul deep weariness crashed through her. They crossed the room to the deserted hallway.

Pulling Gavin to a stop, she turned back slightly to Tala. "Where's Xander?"

In the midst of collecting her ritual items, the witch paused. She kept her back to them. "Until you arrived, I thought she was safe with you."

Her evasive answer left both Wraiths stilling with deadly intensity.

"Excuse me?" The cold question shot from Gavin before Raine could even open her mouth.

Ash stood stiff-legged between them and his companion, a low growl rumbling in his chest. Not sparing the protective wolf a glance, Gavin's entire focus remained on Tala. She took her time facing them.

Raine wasn't certain if it was a deliberate jab or if the woman was trying to decide what she could tell them without setting them off. Either way, the tension in the room spiked.

Stepping in front of Cheveyo's prone form, she laid a hand on the ruff of Ash's neck. The low growl cut off, leaving a strained silence. "Earlier I received a phone call from Toby Greene."

It took Raine a moment to place the name. When she did, she got a bad feeling. "The other alpha of Arizona. She went to see him today."

Tala gave a sharp nod, her lips tightening. "Whatever they discussed left him on edge. He said she had just left his place. He wanted to make sure you all knew what you were stepping into. His message was short and concise." She dropped her hand from Ash, her eyes wary and her voice careful, as she relayed Greene's message. "Watch your backs."

CHAPTER 25

Raine was sure sleep wouldn't find her. After receiving Greene's ominous message, Gavin took her to the room they now shared, ushered her into the bathroom, and pretty much bullied her into a hot shower.

He helped her peel off the odd combination of blanket and jacket, before making quick work of his own clothes. When they were both naked, he drew her in to the steamy enclosure. As the water fell over them, she let her forehead rest against his broad chest. Closing her eyes, she luxuriated in the feel of his hands as they began to stroke over her damp skin. Desire rose and deepened under the heat of his touch, chasing away the chills that had settled into her bones.

He said nothing as he gently washed away the remnants of the day. Drifting in a languorous haze where need washed over her in a warm wave, she let her body take the lead.

When his fingers massaged her neck, she moaned softly. Tilting her head back, she blinked against the misting water, snared by his mesmerizing green eyes.

Passion tightened the skin along his cheekbones, adding a dangerous edge to his slumberous perusal. Using his chest for balance, she took his mouth with slow precision.

He let her tempt and tease with small nips and wild forays. She deepened the kiss as her body flared into a voracious wildfire. His hands locked on her hips, dragging her tight against him.

As if that was the cue she had been waiting for, she began to explore his body. Her hands drifted to his shoulders, only to stroke down to other, more tempting targets. Her fingers closed over his velvet length and she tore her lips from his. Letting her head fall back, she sucked in desperately needed air.

Steam and their combined body heat made the air heavy. Taking advantage of her exposed neck, his wicked lips blazed a trail of fire down the sensitive column of skin. Her moan was shaky and she almost forgot the treasure she held in her hand when he found her breasts. He drew on one turgid tip. Her fingers tightened reflexively as she caressed him. She continued to stroke, and his deep male groan was all about pleasure.

Her head spun when he turned her to face the tile wall. The heavy curtain of her wet hair was brushed aside so he could rain heated, open-mouthed kisses over her neck and shoulders. His delectable body pressed demandingly behind her. His hand cupped her breasts and began to torment her nipples with exquisite tugs. Whimpers fell in unconscious pleas.

"Like that, kitty cat?" His rough question demanded an answer.

"Yesss," she hissed. "More!" She shoved back against his hold, offering herself.

With a low growl, he took her. She muffled her cry

against her forearm as he slid deep inside her damp heat. Slowly, he drew back, dragging his length against her most sensitive spot. She tried to push back, but he held her still, controlling the speed and depth of their erotic dance. His deliberate pace had her begging.

"Damn it, Gavin!"

His raw chuckle was her only warning as he jerked her hips back, showing her no mercy. The now familiar wildfire raged. Her fractured cries filled the small room as he took her higher than she'd ever been. Just when her body threatened to implode with the near-violent sensations, he pulled back.

Her wail was full of anger and frustrated desire. She was so close. The desperate sound was cut short when he spun her around and took her mouth, delving deep.

Clawing at him, she let her kiss turn feral, nipping and biting. She wanted him to finish what he started. It was a toss-up whether she wanted to kill him or fuck him. Only he could make her so wild, so crazy.

He freed her lips as he captured her wrists and locked them above her head against the slick tile. "I need to feel you burn." His voice was thick with heat and need. "Let me in."

Her frantic movements slowed and she met his eyes, revealing all that raged inside. As she acknowledged the love she held for this man, their bond ignited. She hid nothing, and gave him everything.

Desire darkened his face as he held her gaze and slid in deep. Sensations coalesced into each other when he moved inside her. Each movement drew her higher, sending the heat deeper until the explosion ripped through them both. Their mingled cries echoed throughout the bathroom.

Limp and sated, she didn't argue when he rinsed them

off and picked her up. Exhaustion left her limp until all she could do was hold on to him. Outside the shower, he set her on her feet and used a fluffy towel to wipe away the water beading her skin. She wallowed in his careful touch. A quiet expectancy rode the silence between them.

He knelt, running the towel down her legs. She reached out a shaky hand and gently drew it through his hair. The damp strands ensnared her fingers. Looking at him, the reality of how close she had come to losing him, losing this, hit her. Even their future was up for debate, but right now, they had each other. This might be her only chance to offer the one thing she could.

She gave a soft tug on his hair until he raised his face to hers. She let her legs fold until she was eye-level with him and, cupping his jaw, laid a chaste kiss on his lips. Pulling back, she let the truth of her feelings echo through their connection and whispered the words she hoarded for so long. "I love you, Gavin."

The answering emotional flood he sent back left shock rocketing through her. Love, need, pride, respect—all she held for him given back in spades.

Then he gathered her close and held her tight to his heart. "I love you, too, Raine."

Hours later, Raine lay curled next to Gavin in the darkened room. She wanted the oblivion of sleep, but it slipped through her fingers. Worry twisted through her mind. Gavin had gone down earlier to get what information he could from Tala.

Xander had disappeared somewhere between Tucson and Flagstaff. There was no sign of the car she rented, and she wasn't answering her phone. Chances were high, whoever was holding her was the same person holding the Soul Stealer's leash. Something in the questions Xander asked Toby set off warning bells. For now, Raine and Gavin could only wait until morning.

Problem was, they were running against the clock. The one bright spot was that if they had wounded the Stealer, maybe they had wounded its handler. She prayed it was enough to spare Xander during the brief hours until daylight. Old memories taunted as they mixed with Xander's situation, creating new nightmares. Sleep was an exercise in futility.

Tala and Ash were staying with Cheveyo in the living room. There would be no help forthcoming from that direction. Not only was Tala reluctant to leave the unconscious man's side, but it was too dangerous to rely on her. At this point, Raine was reluctant to rely on any of the Southwest Kyn leaders.

When she had shared her concerns with Gavin, he was quick to agree. They were in unfamiliar territory, he pointed out, and too many personal agendas made navigating the political quagmire treacherous. So for now, they had to play things close to their chest.

Even Cheveyo's improvement was tempered with caution. The consequences of Gavin switching the power base from Cheveyo to him and Raine was still left to play out. On one hand, the added strength the two of them could offer Cheveyo would help him hold his position as head of the Northwest Magi. At least until his magic got a chance to rebuild. On the other hand, there was no predicting what the magi's reaction would be when he realized what they had done. Plus, there was the question of what shape he'd be in, if he even woke.

"Stop thinking so loud," Gavin said, his voice cutting through her "doom and gloom" meanderings. He propped himself up on his arms, the dark outline of his head and shoulders rising in the dark. "You need to rest."

"So do you." She twisted around until she could face him, her head pillowed on her bent arm. Here under the cover of night, she stroked her fingers over his bare chest.

"Tomorrow we'll get some answers from Toby," he assured her.

She frowned. "Actually I've been thinking about that. Maybe it's not Toby we need to talk to."

"What are you thinking?"

"Xander was going to Toby to get the real story behind the rumors floating around up here."

"So?"

Her fingers stilled. "So who would have the most to lose if the truth portrays the pack in an unflattering light to an outside party?"

He grasped her hand and gently pressed a kiss to her palm. "Chavez."

She curled her hand into his. "Bingo."

"Confronting the Southwest Alpha comes with a shit-load of problems, especially if we have no concrete evidence."

"I know." She tugged her hand free. As her abused muscles groaned in protest, she turned over and scooted back until she was cradled against his warm body. When he wrapped an arm around her waist, she wove her fingers with his. All her physical aches and pains quieted down under the comfort of his surrounding presence. It gave her a haven where she could think.

"Maybe it's time to call Mulcahy." The deliberate lack of emotion in his voice revealed how little he liked the idea.

Angling her head, she glared into his night-shrouded face. "And what will that accomplish?"

"Down, girl." There was a flash of white as he smiled before leaning down to gently nip her lips. "We need to let him know Cheveyo's back and update him on what's going on down here."

"And what do we tell him? Everything we have is theory, nothing's solid yet," she argued, ignoring the small fire his kiss sparked. "You know as well as I do, he's going to want proof. All we've got is Ransom in a hospital, Cheveyo unconscious, and one missing Wraith." Tightening her hold on his hand, she turned back to the room. "It's not like we have any good news to share."

He tucked her head under his chin and whispered softly, "Maybe not. But what we do have is a solid tie between Ransom and a very powerful Kyn. Right now, those who qualify are Chavez, Rio, and Whiteriver. Do you really think kidnapping one of Mulcahy's Wraiths and Vidis's Tracker, is going to sit well back home?"

"How stupid can they be?" she muttered. "Mulcahy's going to be furious. He'll see this as a personal attack." A dreadful thought hit her. "Oh damn! Do you have any idea what Vidis will do?"

"He'll be beyond furious." Gavin's quiet answer confirmed she wasn't the only one to notice the close bond between the Northwest Alpha and their friend.

"They have no idea what they've unleashed." Her few interactions with the Northwest's Lycos leader left a definite impression. Warrick Vidis was a man who knew his strengths and weaknesses, an unusual trait in Kyn leaders. The most reclusive of the four Northwest Heads of House, he normally steered clear of the political power plays. The rumor was, he had taken the alpha position only because the Lycos House wanted someone who could hold their own against the other three leaders. Yet, it was well known if you threatened what was his, your best bet was to start digging your own grave.

Frustration and exhaustion left Raine's thoughts muddy. "This isn't making sense."

"Which part?"

"All of it. It can't be Tala, because she called Cheveyo down here to help her figure out who was hunting her people. Since Cheveyo and I ran into the Soul Stealer before we even made it to her house, logic says she wouldn't be behind the attack." She paused. "She told Rio and Chavez she was bringing in outside help.

"So maybe Rio or Chavez are linked to the Soul Stealer?" Thinking it over, he stroked over her shoulder and down to her hip with slow movements. "I don't think it's Rio."

"Why?"

"He's the obvious choice. It's too straightforward for a demon."

"Yeah, they tend to be a lot more devious." The whole chaos thing was like crack to the Amanusa. The more confusion and disorder they could cause, the more they got off on it. This would be too easy, too direct.

The warm weight of his hand stilled on her hip. "That leaves us Chavez."

She wasn't so sure. "I don't know. What does Chavez gain by raising a Soul Stealer?"

"That's the question, isn't it?" He traced light circles on her shoulder. "Whether it's Chavez or another unidentified player, they're going to be linked to Ransom through the chindis."

"And we know Ransom struck a deal with a Kyn to get

rid of Cheveyo. Which means our next questions should be who would raise a Soul Stealer and why?"

"The why is easy," he answered, his voice contemplative. "To cause dissension between Houses."

She gave a soft snort. "They were doing pretty good all on their own, don't you think? All that crap about how the shamans think the Amanusas and wizards aren't part of the natural world because of where their magic comes from. I agree that most of the demon-born are pains in the ass and wizards have some serious personality issues, but really?"

"Don't forget, part of the pack believes the same thing. They tend not to trust witches in general."

Considering how hard it was to get a straight answer from Cheveyo, she could understand the pack's distrust. Hell, getting a straight answer out of the very sexy man behind her had its own challenges. Probably not something she should mention, though.

He nipped her shoulder.

The darkness hid her rueful smile. "Caught that, huh?"

He kissed the abused spot. "Yeah, I did."

"Okay, so we have one unknown Kyn linked to Ransom, who's linked to the chindis. Ransom knows about the Kyn. It stands to reason he would do his research, discover the divisions between the Houses, and then capitalize on it. If Kyn are busy fighting amongst themselves, they'd never see him coming and it leaves the Kyn community vulnerable. Especially if, say, a savvy human land developer decides the Kyn have something he wants."

"Right. Remember the pressure of this land deal was enough to make it a topic of conversation at the Council meeting."

She fought back a threatening yawn. "Mulcahy said they considered sending some Wraiths to address it." The yawn won and it was a moment before she could continue. "You saw Tala's reaction. I bet none of the Southwest leaders liked that their business was under discussion."

"I'm sure it went over like a lead balloon."

She gave a halfhearted grin at the dry observation. "Ransom said the land belonged to the humans, not the monsters."

Something tugged at the edges of her mind. Some snippet of conversation. She reached for it, only for it to float out of reach. "Let's say Ransom decides to split the existing Kyn division wide open. Not completely stupid, he needs a way to do it that won't point directly back to him." A flash of Jeremiah's last memory surfaced. "He wanted to warn his alpha that they were being hunted."

Confused by her half-muttered comment, Gavin frowned. "What?"

Excitement stirred. Ignoring her body's protests, she rolled onto her stomach and propped herself up on her arms to face Gavin. "One of Jeremiah's last thoughts was to warn his alpha they were being hunted."

All the information on chindis began to coalesce and a phantom of an idea began to emerge.

"Okay—" he began.

Knowing she was on to something, she cut him off. "What if we're right? Tala said it only took ritual magic to raise the ghosts. What if Ransom found the spell and raised the chindis on his own? What if he sent them to the wrong Kyn?"

"Say a Head of House?" Gavin's voice sharpened as he followed her logic.

"Right. So Ransom sends them after Chavez and Tala because they hold the land he wants and their biases are strong enough to give him the opening he needs. Using the chindis as elimination tools, he sends them after the witches first. The chinidis only turn on a shifter after Jeremiah went sniffing around the last death scene. Wouldn't it make more sense to attack both the shifters and the witches at the same time?"

He shook his head. "Not necessarily. Think about it. If you attack just one House, especially the House with a contingent of members who are barely tolerated, wouldn't it come across as the shifters against the magi?"

"It would cause some serious in-fighting," she admitted.

"But something happened to change that." Lost in his thoughts, he absently curled a strand of her hair around his finger. "Because at his office, he wasn't the one in control, someone else was."

"Maybe the same someone who raised the Soul Stealer." No matter how she arranged the pieces, she couldn't line them up. "Still doesn't answer why that same someone raised a Stealer."

Gavin's absent movements stilled, and his jade gaze locked onto her. "What if Xander found out?"

Raine blinked.

He gripped her shoulders and gave her a light shake. "Think about it."

Pieces shifted, rearranging into a fuzzy picture. Feeling her way, Raine said, "She went to Toby to find out the story on the local situation and the truth behind Brett Chavez's death."

Saying it aloud, the missing piece fell into place with a quiet snick. Tala's comments on the amount of dedication needed to raise a Soul Stealer circled and landed. "Lord and Lady, that's it."

A rush of adrenaline washed her aches and pains away, and she scrambled out of bed.

Gavin flicked on the table lamp, light flooding the room in a warm off-white glow. Finding her pants, Raine dug through the pockets until she came up with her cell phone.

"Who are you calling?"

"Rio."

Gavin raised an eyebrow in question but she ignored him, listening to the phone ring on the other end. When static began to streak across the line, she took a deep breath and tamped her emotions down. Sitting with her back against the bed, she made some headway as the static faded. On the fourth ring, it was picked up.

"Do you have any idea what time it is, McCord?" The growl coming through the phone had her flinching.

"My apologies, Mr. Castle, but I need to ask you a question."

"It had better be damn important, woman, or I swear I'll make your life hell."

"You said inquisitive minds went to you if they had questions."

His only answer was a grunt.

Taking it as agreement, she pushed on. "Has anyone ever asked you how to raise the dead?"

"Anyone who loses someone close to them asks that question at one time or another. Any particular dead you're looking at?" An anticipatory glee crept in to his question.

"Brett Chavez."

The rough chuckles coming over the phone sent shivers over her skin, and she tightened her grip on the phone. "That boy was well loved, McCord."

"So someone asked."

"Two someones actually."

Holding her breath, she waited for her suspicions to be confirmed.

"Lizbeth Chavez and Jenny Walker."

"Jenny Walker, the girlfriend?"

"The one and only." A loud sigh came over the line. "Can I go back to sleep now, girl? This old body doesn't do well on limited sleep."

"Thank you, Mr. Castle."

The drone of the dial tone filled the line. Sitting cross-legged on the floor, she held her cell phone as Gavin leaned across the bed until his head appeared over the edge next to her.

She looked at him from mere inches away. "Now you can call Mulcahy and give him three names."

"Tomás Chavez, Jenny Walker..."

"And Lizbeth Chavez."

CHAPTER 26

Dawn still slept when Gavin and Raine finally reached Mulcahy in Portland. Their boss was en route to his office, and Raine let Gavin do the reporting. Wrapped in a blanket, a cup of hot tea in hand, she leaned back against the porch railing to watch Gavin pace in the cool morning air. Only getting one side of the conversation was enough to confirm her decision.

Occasionally she caught the buzz of her boss's voice as Gavin laid out their suspicions. Impressed at how well he parried Mulcahy's rapid-fire questions, she took a sip of her tea and scanned the empty kitchen through the sliding glass door. Standing outside in the freakin' cold wasn't her top choice, but it ensured their conversation stayed private. She missed the first part of the conversation while she made her tea and peeked in on the two witches and wolf in the front room. The only one awake was Ash, and he watched her warily from his protective spot next to his slumbering companions.

An icy breeze wafted over the deck, sending sneaky fingers under her blanket and burrowing under the thin barrier of sweats and T-shirt. The tea helped, but she was still cold. And uneasy.

Giving Gavin her back, she surveyed the surrounding shadows of the forest standing sentinel around Tala's yard. Was the uneasiness just her imagination, fueled by the fact that every time she was near a bunch of trees down here something tried to eat her? Or was it an early warning system? Either way, she was jumpy.

"I understand the position it puts you in, sir." The carefully controlled tone of Gavin's voice pushed her unsettled instincts aside and she paid attention to the conversation. "However, the game changed last night. We got Cheveyo, but now Xander's missing."

Even she caught the dangerous silence his comment evoked. Gavin took a deep breath, met her questioning look, and continued. "The last person to see her was Toby Greene. She disappeared somewhere between his place and Tala's."

Mulcahy's response left Gavin stifling a small wince as he lowered the phone until it was in-between the two of them. He pressed the speaker button.

"Why was she going to Greene's?"

The snap of Mulcahy's question made Raine start. Tea spilled down the front of her blanket.

Her quiet curse hung on the morning air, seemingly louder for the quiet. Brushing at the rapidly cooling drops, she answered, "Because we needed to find out what the hell is going on up here."

"And you let her go on her own?" The small phone's speaker was no deterrent to the resonating intensity of Mulcahy's too level question.

She stopped fussing with her blanket to glare at the phone. "Xander is a highly trained Wraith and, as such, I trust her assessment of any given situation. She felt if we went in together, it would be viewed as a threat. Considering how evasive Chavez's people have been, she thought she'd get a more honest opinion of what was up if it was just her and Greene."

"And because the three of you felt whatever Greene had to say may not reflect positively on Chavez, she did this without Chavez's permission?"

Even the soft static crackling across the line couldn't disguise the censure in his voice. It scraped like nails over a chalkboard and she struggled to remember who she was talking to. "They called us in. If they didn't want their dirty laundry hung out on the line, then maybe they should have thought of that first. There was no way Chavez was going to let any of us, including Xander, talk to someone he couldn't control. So no, she didn't ask his permission. Sir." She tacked on the last with a snap of her teeth.

"Where is Cheveyo now?" The question was etched in ice.

"With Tala," Gavin answered before she could. She curled her lip and he gave her a short shake of his head. She took the minute he was giving her to rein in her frustration before it fell out of her mouth and got her in trouble.

"Awake?"

"No. He's still unconscious."

"Can he be moved?"

Gavin stared at the phone, his brow furrowed. "I'd have to check, but probably."

"Good, because after I update Vidis, you're not going to have much time before he's down in Chavez's yard. If you're right, and either of the Chavezes are involved, there's no way this will end well."

"You don't think it's Jenny Walker?" Raine asked.

"No." There was no hesitation in his answer.

"Why?"

For a moment silence echoed down the line, then their boss answered, his voice flat, "Because the loss of a child will take more of a soul than the loss of a lover. Grief will lead to desperate decisions and grave actions. One basic tenet of magic is that a spell's strength is dependent on the user's will. To raise a Soul Stealer, you have to be walking the edge of madness. That speaks more to a parent's grief, than a girlfriend's."

Studying Gavin, she had to silently disagree with her uncle. It was too easy to remember facing the Stealer as she realized she'd fail Gavin again, and the resulting wave of choking horror sucking her into a bottomless well of despair.

"Go talk to Tala." The sound of Mulcahy's voice cut through her dark thoughts. "See what she can give you on the Walker girl."

Her grip tightened on the blanket and she moved toward the patio door. As she drew even with Gavin, he snagged her close. She leaned into him briefly. The faint brush of his lips against her hair helped to chase away the lingering shadows, settling her. She left him to finish the conversation.

Sliding the patio door open, the cabin's warmth wrapped around her, battling back the early morning chill and leaving pebbled skin behind. She set her teacup in the sink before heading to the living room. Time to go wake the witch.

Ash's quiet warning snarl as she stepped just inside the living room made her pause. Crouching until they were eye level, she met the amber gaze and flared teeth of the guarding wolf. "I just need to talk to her, and I'm really not in the mood for you this morning."

Another snarl rolled forth.

Taking a page from Tala's book, Raine leaned forward and nipped Ash's nose. His startled yip and disgruntled look left her smiling.

"Ash." At the quiet command, the wolf turned to look at his mistress. He swung back to Raine, huffed, then with careful dignity, made his way to Tala.

Raine settled on the floor tailor fashion. Tala's blonde hair was a tangled mess, the typical braid a long forgotten memory. Sleep erased the drawn look from the night before, but the bruised circles under her eyes stood out starkly against her pale skin.

Raine watched Tala scratch Ash absently behind one ear then turn her attention to Cheveyo. The soft mutterings of the fire smoldering behind the couple broke the quiet. Skin-ruffling magic tripped across Raine's flesh as Tala examined Cheveyo on every level.

Mentally, Raine held her breath as the minutes ticked by. She wasn't as convinced as Gavin that his illusions would hold. When he asked her why, she explained how—if she knew to look for it—she could see the subtle differences in his magic. It didn't make sense that someone as powerful as Tala, or Cheveyo, for that matter, could miss it. Even Gavin's assurance that she was the only one to "see" magic hadn't helped.

The unsettling feeling of Tala's power faded away. The blonde rubbed her eyes and arched her spine, a low moan escaping at the soft pop when her vertebrae realigned.

"How's he doing?" Raine asked.

Tala looked at her, and Raine was relieved there was no

freaky white in those dark eyes. “The same,” she said, her answer quiet.

Raine frowned. “Shouldn’t he be getting stronger now that we’ve broken his connection to the Stealer?”

Tala cocked her head. “Have we?”

Confused, Raine stared. “Have we what?”

“Cut the ties between him and the Stealer.”

Too much lay under that question and Raine fought to keep her pulse level and her body relaxed. “What do you mean?”

Tala watched her closely as the tension in the room began to rise. “What do you see?”

Raine felt herself getting lost in this conversation and that was not a good thing. She looked at the unconscious man between them. “He’s too thin, starved. He looks like he’s been a prisoner for months instead of days.”

“No!” The word snapped out like a slap, jerking Raine’s attention back to Tala. Red rode high on the witch’s cheekbones. “What do you see, McCord?”

Choking back her automatic need to retaliate, Raine paused and realized what Tala was really asking. Taking a breath, she lowered her psychic barriers until the scene in front of her burst forth, its light and colors painting a surreal picture. “What am I looking for?”

Tala’s aura shimmered as she leaned forward. “What do you see when you look at Cheveyo?”

Tricky question. Raine chose her words with care. “His magic is still weak, but better than before. It’s wrapped in your magic.”

“And yours?” Tala’s question was sharp.

Examining the connection between her and Cheveyo, Raine could make out the delicate warp of Gavin’s as it merged with hers. “It’s still connected to him.”

"Are there others?"

Raine switched her attention from Cheveyo to Tala. The witch's glow pulsed, the gold darkening as if agitated. "Others?"

"Yes." Tala's tone was impatient. "Other magic, something that doesn't look right."

Besides the newly formed bond between her and Gavin and the sleeping witch? She studied Cheveyo's magic, trying to skim the psychic waves. She didn't want to go too deep, not without Gavin next to her and he was still outside talking with Mulcahy. Nor did she want to disrupt the delicate weave of Tala's healing magic. With her luck, she'd end up bound to another damn witch.

"Everything seems as it was last night," she answered, still trying to figure out what she was looking for. "I don't know what you want me to see."

Cool fingers snagged her chin and yanked her head up. Tala's face was inches from her and the unsettling white was bleeding over her pupils. The spooky multi-tonal voice was back. "You will look, Weaver, and you will find the damaged bonds. Find them and fix them."

Raine slammed her mental barriers back up so fast, sharp needles of pain reverberated through her skull. Raising her hands, she shoved the witch back. The steely fingers on her chin left gouges in her skin as she scrambled backwards in an awkward crab-crawl, leaving the blanket behind. "What the fuck?"

Her shove sent Tala back a few feet. "Find the threads," the spine tingling alien voice commanded.

Pressing her back into the wall, Raine warily watched the crouching witch. Tala's neck was bent as she visibly fought for control. When she threw her head back, her mouth twisted into a grimace. Raine saw the swirling fight of white and black in her eyes.

Wiping the back of her hand against her stinging chin, Raine smeared blood over her skin. *Damn witch!* Using the wall for leverage, she got her legs under her and, balancing on the balls of her feet, waited to see if Tala would rush her again.

Instead, Tala's head fell forward and she inched back until she could touch Cheveyo's hand. She stilled, hair veiling her face, shoulders heaving as she drew in air. When she looked up, Raine flinched. Tala wasn't in there. Creepy choir was back in control.

"He is not healing." The eerie voices made her bones ache. "You must find the damaged bonds, repair them, or nothing we do will help."

Not about to argue with whatever entity or entities had taken up residence in Tala, Raine wasn't sure she could do what they were asking. "Fine. I'll look again, but you need to move to Cheveyo's other side." She wanted space between her and whatever hijacked Tala.

"Why should we do as you ask?" Arrogance bled through skin and voice.

"Do you want me to do what you ask?"

The strange birdlike nod was short.

"Then move on the other side of him."

"You don't trust us?"

She swore the entity was laughing at her, but she didn't care. "Not one damn bit."

A small, condescending smile twisted Tala's lips.

Raine kept an eye on the other woman as she moved to Cheveyo's other side. Only when Tala was situated did Raine let out a disgusted breath. "Right, then."

She scooted away from the wall until only a few feet

separated her and Cheveyo. It took a bit longer to drop her barriers. Between the dull ache of slamming them closed and the tension of his psycho girlfriend's stare, it was like trying to walk a tightrope and not disturb the cobra coiled on the rope in front of you.

As her magic flared, Raine kept her gaze on Tala. The witch's gold aura now held an array of swirling colors deep inside. Like a faint, opalescent rainbow.

Tearing her attention away from the mesmerizing show, Raine focused on Cheveyo. "What do you want me to look for?"

"Broken magic."

"That's helpful," she mumbled.

Narrowing her concentration, she systematically scanned Cheveyo's earth tones, following them as far as she could. Bright healing magic wrapped protectively around the pale tones of Cheveyo's damaged magic. Braided between Tala and Cheveyo's signatures, was Raine's magic. She hoped the small warps of Gavin's power were visible to only her.

It didn't look as if it had changed since last night. "Nothing's broken." She waved a hand over Cheveyo's inert body. "Look for yourself."

Tala's opalescence rainbow bled around the edges of Raine's vision as the witch drew closer. "Don't mock us, Weaver."

Who knew a choir could hiss in harmonic chords? Raising her hands in surrender, Raine tempered her response. "I'm not. Can't you see the magic?"

Those unnerving eyes focused on her and it was all she could do not to flinch under that piercing stare. "We do not see the loom as you do, Weaver."

Okay, what was with the "weaver" thing? Raine opened

her mouth to ask then thought better of it as some instinctive warning system blared its little heart out.

The weird choir wasn't done. "The fabric of magic reveals itself only to those who understand the warp and weave of its many threads. It has chosen to share itself with you. Since we cannot view the pattern of his magic, you must find it and correct it."

Yeah, that was terrifyingly vague and ominous. "What I see looks the same as last night."

"What do you see?"

Since Tala and company seem to be listening to her, she fought down the frustration of explaining things yet again. "Colors, energy. There is no real pattern. Each person has a unique signature...umm...color. Their magic's strength reflects as dim or bright." She looked back to the man between them. "Right now he's holding his own, but he's not as bright as normal. The healing magic Tala spun last night is a protective layer over his magic." As she spoke the shimmery gold flashed softly and wrapped a bit tighter around the pale earth tones.

"You need to go deeper." The unnerving voices gentled. The spill of inky color over the white was back in Tala's eyes, indicating she was trying to regain control.

Raine found it disconcerting, so she focused on Cheveyo, silently praying Tala would make it back into the driver's seat. Dealing with the witch was so much more preferable than dealing with whoever those voices belonged to.

A few moments later, Tala's voice emerged carrying a noticeably slur. "They're right."

Raine looked up to find the strange opalescent rainbow gone, leaving only the gold behind. Tension eased and her shoulders slumped as she raised her mental walls, the world reclaiming its normal appearance. "Thank the gods." Her earlier headache came back with reinforcements. Rubbing a trembling hand over her face she said, "Promise me, you won't invite those friends back?"

The choked laugh from the witch was strangely reassuring. "I'll try."

"Who are they anyway?"

"Ancestors."

Raine made a rolling motion with her hand inviting more details.

Tala sighed and fiddled absently with edge of Cheveyo's blanket. "The damage was so great, I invoked the tribe's Ancestors. I've never dealt with a *Nomâhtsé'héōò Adanata's* victim." Those nervous fingers paused. "At least not one who still lived. Nothing I tried worked. He needed something more than I could give."

"So Creepy Chorus is..."

Panicked surprise flicked across the witch's face. "Creepy Chorus? Dear gods, Raine, tell me you didn't call them that?"

Feeling weirdly connected to Tala, Raine shook her head. "Not out loud, but the multitude of voices was downright eerie." Time to get the conversation back on track. "So who are these Ancestors?"

"They are the collection of knowledge gathered from all the past magis."

Raine let out a low whistle. The thought of having access to that much knowledge was...well...mind blowing. And scary.

Tala gave a grim nod. "They're a last resort."

"He's still holding on, so that's something." Raine offered gently, watching the play of raw emotions on Tala's face.

"I hope it's enough." Tala pushed to her feet, her movements stiff. Beside her, Ash rose, staying protectively close to his mistress. Considering how pale and exhausted she appeared, Raine understood his concern. She wondered how much of Tala's magic was being siphoned off to help Cheveyo.

The woman gathered an empty bowl and other supplies and turned to the kitchen.

Raine's quiet, "Tala" had the other woman turning back to her. Raine didn't want to ask the question hovering on her tongue, but the fact that the witch went to such extreme lengths to save her mentor, meant Raine could do no less. "What did you mean when you said they were right?"

Puzzlement clouded Tala's face, but as the moments ticked by it cleared. "He's not healing because something's not right. If we can't figure out what's going on, we're going to lose him."

Her stomach clenched at the defeat underlying Tala's voice. Frustrated, Raine clenched her fist. "Maybe they don't know what they're doing. Like I told them, I don't see anything broken."

"They know."

"Are you sure? They kept calling me 'Weaver,' whatever the hell that means."

Tala's mouth dropped open and the items in her hands rattled. "What?" The question came out on a choked gasp.

Her dramatic reaction forced Raine to her feet. Before she could respond, Gavin came up behind Tala.

"Something wrong?" His question caused Tala to start violently. He managed to rescue the bowl that slipped from her grasp.

"You need a bell." Tala ignored his question as she studied Raine. "Tell me what they said to you."

Folding her arms across her chest, Raine countered, "Don't you know? You were in there too, right?"

Tala growled, spun, and dumped the items she held into Gavin's arms. "Could you please put those in the kitchen?" She pushed him back out.

He sent a questioning look to Raine. When she shrugged, he did as the witch asked.

Tala turned to Raine, hands on her hips. "I'm there. I just don't catch all of the conversations. It's too chaotic."

Considering how impressive the Ancestors were from Raine's perspective that made sense. Sort of. "They said something about magic choosing who saw it, and since they couldn't see it and I could, I needed to fix it."

"But you can't see anything to fix?"

"Right."

Looking away, Tala's jaw tightened and a rush of emotions passed so quick Raine wasn't sure what she saw.

"There are individuals who can see magic," Tala explained. "Then there are those very rare individuals who can not only see magic, but change it."

Raine's confusion was rapidly replaced by a horrible sense of understanding. "I can't change magic."

"Have you tried?" Tala's question was sharp.

"Hell no. Why would I?" She lifted her chin. "If it was something I could do, don't you think Cheveyo would have mentioned it?"

Tala didn't answer.

That annoying small whisper was back, this time repeating the conversation between Raine and Gavin on the possibility of being manipulated by their leaders. She fought to ignore it. Now wasn't the time for doubts.

Paranoia was a wonderful edge to have, but sometimes it was a pain in the ass.

Keeping her thoughts from her face, Raine waited while Tala watched her. She must have succeeded, because after a moment, Tala waved Raine over to the couch.

"If the Ancestors think you can find the damage and fix it, then you can." Tala sunk into a chair. Ash trotted over and curled at her feet. "Gods know I've tried everything."

Gavin came back to the living room and Raine scooted over, her invitation obvious. He settled next to her, stretching an arm along the back of the sofa. *"I can't leave you alone for five minutes without you baiting for trouble."*

"I didn't start it." She shared her encounter with Tala's multiple personalities. Although he gave no outward reaction, she felt the tension thrumming through him.

"I don't like this."

"Yeah, welcome to the club." She was pulled from the internal conversation by Tala's voice. Raine blinked. "Sorry?"

Exasperation deepened the lines bracketing Tala's compressed lips. "I asked what they told you to do."

"They said I had to go deeper."

"So why won't you?"

"Because I'm still trying to recover from the Stealer's tender ministrations. Every time I touch Cheveyo's magic, it sucks me under. I'd be lucky if I made it back."

"Use Gavin as an anchor then."

The absolute flat tone, a clear indicator the witch had no qualms of using whatever or whoever to get Cheveyo back, erased any softer feelings Raine harbored. She might understand the sentiment, but it didn't mean she liked it.

"Just because Raine can go in, doesn't mean she'll find whatever it is you think she will." Gavin's tone was as hard as his face, proof that Tala's casual disregard had well and truly pissed him off.

The witch sent a pointed look at Cheveyo. "I think it's worth a shot." She paused. "I'm sure Mr. Mulcahy would agree."

Raine dug her nails into her thighs at Tala's very correct assumption. "If—" Raine stressed, "—I go in, what am I supposed to look for? Broken magic doesn't seem to cut it." As if she had a choice here. She knew she was going back in and so did the witch sitting across from her.

Satisfaction lightened Tala's eyes. "When you're in there, you need to look for weaknesses. Breaks, frays, gaps, anything that disrupts the normal flow."

Gavin's fingers drummed on the edge of the couch behind Raine's head. "You think the Stealer has pieces of him." It wasn't a question.

Tala's sharp nod confirmed his statement. "If I'm right, you're going to find pieces of Cheveyo's magic are still missing. You may have broken the immediate ties, but you didn't replace what was stolen."

Comprehension bloomed and Raine's stomach pitched, nerves leaving her cold. "When we destroy the Stealer, will Cheveyo's magic return to him?"

"Probably."

Gavin's fingers stilled. "Probably?"

Tala shot him an unfriendly look. "Magic is energy, and if you destroy the Soul Stealer, you destroy the bindings holding all the consumed energy that created it."

"Which means if Cheveyo's magic still exists, it should come back," Raine followed along. "And the souls? Will they be freed?" She wasn't sure 'free' was the right term, considering the psychotic joy the Stealer felt tearing Raine apart. Gods only knew what state the spirits would be in after their horrific time with the monster.

Grief washed over Tala's face, softening her voice. "There may not be anything left to be freed."

Gavin's fingers stilled. "We do this for you, you'll owe us." The gravity of his statement hung heavy in the room. Raine brushed a light mental touch to his thoughts, needing to know what was at stake.

Tala studied him. "What are you asking for?"

"Honesty."

She raised an eyebrow. "Regarding?"

"Jenny Walker," Raine answered.

Tala blinked, confusion furrowing her brow. "Done." Her answer was hesitant as if she was looking for an unseen trap.

Gavin gave her a solemn nod.

Raine pushed up from the couch. Stretching her spine, she took a huge breath and let it out. "Fine. Let's get this show on the road."

She moved back to her initial spot by Cheveyo and felt Gavin settle in behind her. Lowering her barriers, a surrealistic vision of reality took form around her. Looking over her shoulder, she found Gavin behind her. Turning back to the undulating streams of magic, she took a breath and dove in.

Energy swirled and sucked her under. This time she focused on the waves tossing her around, riding them until they finally deposited her on solid ground. As the energy receded, she crawled up dull brown sand and got to her feet. Dull browns, faded greens, and sickly yellows danced around her, letting her know she stood in the midst of Cheveyo's magic. Scanning the scene, she felt the weight of

Gavin's hands settle on her shoulders and relief nudge some of her worry aside.

Keeping her attention on the magic, she asked, "Where do I start?"

"Up."

His answer had her twisting around. "Excuse me?"

He cocked a half-grin and pointed straight up. "You're in too far, you need to draw back a bit."

Navigating this magic sucked. "And we do that, how?"

There was a sudden shift, a sharp tug and then she was pulled straight up. The sickening sensation of the ground falling away washed a wave of nausea through her gut. She scrunched her eyes closed. Before she could do more than gulp, she jerked to a stop. Gavin's hands at her waist kept her on her feet.

"Never again," she gasped, trying to slow her pulse.

His only response was a soft chuckle.

Prying her lids apart, she studied the flow of Cheveyo's magic running like river of light below. Just above it, like a faint mist, rested Tala's healing magic. In a barely discernible layer between them, pulsed the silver blue of her and Gavin's power. Tala's energy seeped through, but, at this level, it was obvious the slow trickle of healing power wasn't enough to keep Cheveyo alive.

Leaning over, Raine peered closer—realizing Tala was right. Pieces were missing. Some of the bands of light remained unbroken, while others were marred with nicks and cuts. Just below Tala's light was Cheveyo's sluggish band, peppered with tiny holes that left his innate magic stretched to dangerously thin levels.

Cheveyo's magic resembled a colander, unable to hold enough of Tala's healing magic to repair the gaps. The added binding of Raine and Gavin's magic simply slowed the inevitable.

"Damn it." She leaned back into Gavin's hold. "She was right."

"Now what?"

Staring at the brutal evidence of the Stealer's work, her stomach iced and dread gathered. "I don't want to do this." Here, where it was just them, she let the harsh truth free. His hold tightened. "If I go in there and start messing around with Cheveyo's magic, there's no telling what the end result will be," she continued. "It's too damn risky."

"Just because you can see this, doesn't mean you can fix it."

"I know, but we both know she's going to push." She studied the waves. "Can you do it?"

Silence answered her. Unable to see his face, she pulled to the side and looked back. He studied the motion below them, his face empty. It wasn't that he was avoiding her, more that he was thinking something through.

"You realize the only reason I can see this is because I'm shadowing you?"

She nodded.

"So why do you think I can do it?"

"You were able to switch the bond between Cheveyo and me, to all of us. I thought maybe you could do something similar." She resettled in front of him, careful to make sure he didn't lose his grasp on her. She so didn't want to experience another free fall through...whatever this was.

He tightened his grip on her waist. "That was altering part of Cheveyo's original spell. I don't think it would be smart for me to mess around with this."

Yeah, she got that. "Fine." She covered his hands with hers. "Let's get back and go hunt ourselves a Soul Stealer."

Tala ushered them into the kitchen, supposedly to let Cheveyo rest. Personally, Raine thought nothing short of an atomic bomb would bring that man around anytime soon. However, it made Tala happy, which meant a chance at straight answers for a change. Answers they needed to find Xander.

Gathered around the table with Tala between them, Raine started collecting on Tala's debt. "Tell me about Jenny Walker and Brett Chavez."

"They were dating for a while before Brett's death. They were young and in love." Ash's head lay in Tala's lap. She scratched his ears and leaned back in her chair. "What does Jenny have to do with any of this?"

Exactly how to answer that? Telling Tala they were going after the Chavezes was not a healthy move. "Rio mentioned her when we spoke to him."

Tala scowled. "Why?"

"She went to see him." Gavin sat across from Raine, his legs sprawled, his hands linked behind his head. Despite the deceptively lazy pose, his attention was focused on the witch.

Tala tucked her flash of confusion away, but not before Raine noted it. "Did Rio say why?"

"She wanted to know how to bring Brett back," Raine said.

This time Tala wasn't fast enough, her shock obvious. "Excuse me?"

Raine watched the witch closely. "Who was she to you?"

Tala's spine stiffened and if looks could kill, Raine would be a smoking pile of ash. "We share a grandfather a couple generations back, she's my second cousin, once removed."

Gavin dropped his hands. "Was she a strong witch?"

Tala shook her head and looked down at Ash. "That branch of the family never produced particularly strong magic users." She buried her fingers in the wolf's ruff.

Raine picked up on the tell. Every time Tala was uncomfortable she reached for her pet. "So you don't think she'd be able to raise a Soul Stealer?"

It was hard to see the woman's face. "No, I don't think Jenny could do that." Raising her head, she met Raine's gaze head on. "Most of the family members married humans."

Gavin sat a bit straighter in his chair. "But she was still a witch."

Tala flicked a wary glance his way. "Yes, she was."

Raine's fingers drummed an absent rhythm on the tabletop, as she stared unseeing out the patio door behind Gavin. A young witch with little power, grieving over her lost boyfriend, could try something desperate but, without the power behind the intent, it wouldn't happen.

"A witch and a shifter," she muttered to herself. Her fingers stilled. "That could not have been a welcome announcement to the Chavezes."

Tala's lips thinned and her arm tensed as she clutched at Ash, but she remained stubbornly silent.

Oh yeah, not welcomed at all. Time to push. Raine let her lips curl. "Considering how deep prejudices run down here, I can't think the alpha pair liked the thought of their only son dating a witch."

No matter how much Tala fought to keep her face blank, Raine knew she scored a hit. If Tala's spine stiffened any more she'd snap in half.

"The alpha felt his son was too young to be dating," Tala confessed. "But he was wise enough to let it run its course. He felt, given enough time, their relationship would go the way of most first crushes."

And from what Raine read between the lines, Tala agreed with him. "I'm guessing it didn't?"

Tala let go of Ash with a sigh. She wouldn't meet Raine's gaze as she played with her mug of tea. "Jenny came to me about a week before Brett was killed and told me they were considering eloping."

Only one reason for that event. "Was she pregnant?"

Tala shrugged. "She wouldn't say, but probably."

Gavin let out a low whistle.

Tala grimaced. "I asked if they were planning on telling their parents." She stopped.

"And?" Raine prompted.

Tala's restless movements stilled, and she raised her head. Sorrow and anger were etched into the skin around her mouth and eyes, aging her. "She said they would, after they were wed. That way no one could separate them."

"Poor kids." Gavin's quiet mutter turned both women to him. He frowned. "What? Every hormonal teenager thinks love will conquer all until reality cold-cocks them."

His words wrung a faint wry smile from Tala. Raine shook her head, ignoring the small ache of being left out of their little moment of understanding. Fighting for her sanity and training for revenge left little time for things like crushes. "So it wasn't just Brett's parents that didn't approve?"

Tala shrugged. "It was just Jenny and her mom. Her dad passed away when Jenny was little." Tala's shoulders slumped. "Erin, her mom, worked long hours so Jenny pretty much raised herself. I don't think Erin had any idea of what was going on in her daughter's life."

"If she had?" Raine asked.

"I don't think it would've mattered." Tala grabbed her cup, pushed up from the table, and took it to the sink. Ash stayed by her chair, but his attention solely on his mistress. "Jenny was a good girl, a great student, and her mom trusted her to keep a level head." She set the rinsed cup on the draining board and rested her hands on the counter, keeping her back to Raine and Gavin. "When she disappeared, it broke Erin's heart."

"Did anything happen before she disappeared?" Gavin asked. "Something that would trigger her to run away?"

Tala turned and leaned against the counter's edge. "I'm not sure." Folding her arms across her stomach, she frowned at the floor. "At Brett's funeral, when Jenny showed up, Lizbeth got angry. Said some pretty vicious things." She paused. "Brett was Lizbeth's pride and joy. That boy meant everything to her. She had big plans for her son, and Jenny wasn't a part of them." She shook her head. "Grief can make strangers of those you know, and grief had a tight fist on Lizbeth."

"What did Jenny do?" Raine did her best to keep her question non-confrontational, needing Tala to keep talking.

"Nothing." Tala straightened. "There was nothing she could do. She took the verbal beating Lizbeth gave her and when Tomás dragged his wife away, Jenny stayed." She dragged a hand over the back of her neck and rubbed. "I tried to talk to Jenny afterwards, but she...she wasn't really there."

"What do you mean?"

"It was as if she had shut down. I knew this girl and if anyone went after her the way Lizbeth had, she would've given as good as she got. Instead, she just stood there and took it." Frustration and confusion shimmered in Tala's voice. "There were no tears, no anger, nothing, and it was heartbreaking. It was as if Brett's death had broken her spirit. A week later, she was gone."

Gavin leaned forward, bracing his arms on his knees. "Does anyone know where she went?"

"No. Her mom tried to report her missing, but the police said Jenny was eighteen and if she wanted to leave, she could."

"No body, no worries," Raine muttered under breath. It was an attitude she'd run across more than she'd wanted to over the years. Gavin must have caught her words as he sent her a pointed look. 'What?' she silently mouthed back.

Turning away, Gavin shot Tala a new question. "Do you think Jenny is alive?"

Tala's restless movements halted and she stared at Gavin. Her mouth opened but nothing came out. Her eyes narrowed as grim resignation turned her expression from shocked to mutinous. Raine watched Tala pull her Magi-mask in place. "I have no proof."

"But you have no proof she's dead, either," Raine countered, pushing her chair back. She didn't want to sit anymore. It was time to move things along.

"Do you have proof of her death?" Tala's question was hard enough to make Raine reconsider the words sitting on the tip of her tongue.

"You said you used a necromancer before you called

Cheveyo down," Gavin said. His response clearly indicating he didn't share Raine's concerns.

Tala pressed her lips together so tightly they became thin, pale lines under her flared nose. She gave a short jerk of her head and nothing else.

He stood, and something in his movement had Ash scrambling to his feet. "We need to go see your necromancer."

"Why?"

It was Raine's turn to antagonize the witch. "Two reasons," she started. Standing, she took her time pushing her chair back in place. "One, we'd like to make sure your necromancer isn't the one behind the Soul Stealer." She leaned a hip against the chair back and propped a hand on her hip. "Two, we think it might be worthwhile to see if we can reach Jenny. She might be able to give us a little insight into what's going on around here."

CHAPTER 27

Mulcahy's phone call to Gavin delayed their trip to the necromancer's house. After changing into something more practical than sweats and a blanket, Raine moved down the hall tucking her knives into place as Gavin's cell rung. She stepped into the kitchen and leaned against the entryway, waiting for him to finish his conversation.

"I understand." Gavin's phone was pressed between his ear and shoulder as he shrugged into his battered leather jacket. "No, we're just getting ready to head out and check in with Tala's necromancer, Nati Alcaina." He moved the small phone to his other ear, listening. Catching sight of Raine, he mouthed, "Mulcahy," and pulled out a set of keys from his front pocket. The soft jangle of metal on metal was cut off as they disappeared into his fist. "So she's alive?"

At his terse question, renewed tension sang through Raine. She moved closer, needing both sides of the conversation. She gave him a mental nudge.

He flicked her a frown and lowered the phone.

"According to Vidis." Mulcahy's explanation sounded tinny as it emerged from the small phone. "He can feel her through the pack link, but something, or someone, is making it so she can't respond."

"Can he tell where she is?" Gavin tucked his keys back into a pocket.

"No. Whoever, or whatever, has her did something to weaken the bond she shares with Vidis and the pack. He did what he could to strengthen it before he left."

A sick feeling churned in Raine's gut as she stared at the phone in Gavin's hand. "How much time does she have?"

There was a pause, filled only by the quiet static, then, "Vidis is on his way down. He'll be arriving in a couple of hours. He already called Chavez and demanded the Southwest Alpha be there to meet him."

"You're ignoring my question, Mulcahy."

His sigh was slight but audible. "Because I don't have an answer."

His response left her gritting her teeth in frustration. Xander was tough. She had to be. You couldn't make it to Xander's level without being one tough bitch, but still... Flashes of the Stealer's attacks ran like some badly wound film reel. The thought of Xander being picked apart, piece by piece, made Raine want to rend something limb from limb, with as much pain as possible. Preferably the Stealer.

"Maybe we should skip the necromancer." Her hands curled into fists, driving her nails into her palms. "We should go to the Chavez's ranch and tear it apart."

"No!" Mulcahy's sharp reprimand pulled her up short. "You and Durand go find out what Ms. Alcaina knows. Vidis will keep Chavez occupied. If either Alcaina or Chavez have Xander, they won't be able to do anything more without being caught. The last thing I need is for you to try to take out the Southwest Alpha based on suppositions. We're going to have enough explaining to do if Vidis slips his leash and takes the fool out."

Frustration and worry coalesced into a simmering brew, stringing Raine's nerves taunt, but she kept her mouth shut. Fine. She'd go talk to the necromancer. No one said she had to be nice about it. She spun around to stalk out, but Gavin's hand locked around her wrist, holding her captive. She twisted, trying to escape, but he didn't budge. She gave him a silent snarl, which he returned with a raised eyebrow. Damn him!

"Where are Chavez and Vidis meeting?" There was no sign of their silent argument in the question he directed at Mulcahy.

"A private airfield just north of Chavez's ranch."

"Is he coming alone?"

"Yes."

Gavin frowned at Mulcahy's answer. "That's not wise."

"He has no choice. He's invading another alpha's territory without permission. If he brought in reinforcements, Chavez would be within his right to forcibly keep Vidis out."

"Coming in by himself isn't safe if Chavez is in league with the Soul Stealer," Gavin said. "What's to stop Chavez from doing whatever he did to Xander to Vidis?"

"Vidis will eat him alive," Raine snapped.

Mulcahy's short bark of grim laughter came through the phone. "She's right. I wouldn't worry about Vidis. Chavez will have his paws full if he picks that fight." The muffled sounds of movement filled the airwaves. "Go see the necromancer. If it's not her, make sure you're at the ranch when Vidis and Chavez return." He didn't wait for their terse, "Yes, sirs," before the line went dead.

Gavin slipped his phone into his pocket and finally

released Raine's wrist. She shook her hand out. Not that his grip hurt, but she was trying to ignore the tingling of her skin from his touch.

"You lied to me."

The words whipped through the kitchen. Raine turned to face Tala who stood in the entryway. To say the witch wasn't happy, was a vicious understatement.

"No, we didn't."

Raine was impressed at the calm, unruffled tone of Gavin's voice.

The fury riding Tala was a living thing and Raine didn't trust her in this mood. Since Raine was ignoring Gavin's subtle touch to move, he stepped to her side. When she kept her body between him and Tala, she got a sharp smack on her butt. She lovingly stomped on his foot in response.

Oblivious to the by-play, Tala charged, "I heard you. You're going after Tomás."

"No," Raine corrected, commandeering Tala's attention. "We're going to pay Nati a visit, then we're going to the ranch to meet up with our alpha."

"Cheveyo doesn't have the luxury of waiting while you two go chasing after the wolves," Tala sneered, color staining her skin a dusky red. Her eyes narrowed, and even though Raine could see the underlying exhaustion and worry, it didn't lessen the impact of Tala's next verbal assault. "Your job is to protect your magi, Raine McCord. Have you forgotten your duty or are the rumors true? Are you really nothing more than Mulcahy's pet weapon? He aims and lets you loose on his enemies."

She didn't give Raine a chance to respond, her temper fierce. "I'm not letting Cheveyo be his next victim. You promised me you'd find the Stealer and get Cheveyo's magic back. You're going to keep your promise." She brought her hands up, and Raine could feel the magic amassing around her. Before she could react, Tala's hands opened, releasing her spell to wrap around Raine.

It didn't hurt. That realization penetrated Raine's momentary shock at the unexpected attack. The next was that she recognized the spell. A geas. Tala had just linked Raine's life with the return of Cheveyo's magic. Unfortunately, thanks to her tie with Gavin, if Raine failed, she wasn't the only one paying the price.

A tidal wave of rage and resentment washed through Raine, scouring her soul. She was so tired of being used by those around her. She may have given her life into Mulcahy's service, but she wasn't a mindless weapon. Threats aimed only at her were allowed, but to include Gavin? Oh hell no.

"Pet weapon?" She stalked forward, backing a stunned Tala through the door. When Ash darted between the two women with growl, Raine didn't even stop. Flicking a predatory glance to the snarling wolf, she hissed a warning as her leopard surged to the surface. Ash's ears flattened and he backed away, keeping his body between Raine and Tala.

"I am no one's weapon, Magi." Raine forced herself not to reach out and shred Tala's skin until it was nothing more than bloody ribbons over bone. "It wasn't me who called the man I loved into a situation without telling him all the facts. It wasn't me who put Cheveyo in danger in the first place. I wasn't the one who too scared of looking weak to be honest when I went looking for help. I'm not the one unable to protect my people."

Blind with rage, she had the witch pressed up against the wall now. She was careful to make sure she didn't touch Tala because one touch would break the fragile chains holding her back. She leaned in until only a breath separated them. “I have never forgotten where my duty lies. That honor is all yours.”

“You promised,” Tala whispered, chest heaving as she pressed her spine against the wall, keeping what distance she could manage from the fury facing her.

Raine snapped her teeth in Tala’s face, causing the witch to flinch. “Take it off.”

“I can’t. It’s done.”

The urge to obliterate Tala surged until Raine’s pulse pounded in her ears. Violent tremors wracked her straining body leaving her afraid to move for fear her tenuous control would snap with devastating consequences. Strong arms caged her, pulling her back and she broke.

Throwing back her head she screamed, giving voice to the fury, anger, and fear, as wave after wave of violence tore through her. She struggled against that which held her from her prey, and when those proved useless, she focused inward, shattering the locks holding that wild, twisted magic deep inside.

Her magic rose like a silent hurricane, dragging her along even as it gained strength from her chaotic emotions. The now-familiar light show of the magical world flared into existence. For a timeless moment her world held its breath and everything turned crystal clear.

The geas was a limited binding that tied together two magics until the given purpose was completed within the set timeframe. She could see the exact pattern Tala used to set the spell, but if she changed the weave like so, a dark whisper taunted, she could turn it back on the witch. Savage satisfaction roared as she re-worked the magic.

Vaguely she could hear someone shouting at her, but their voice was too far away to understand. She didn’t stop, couldn't stop until the change was complete. She couldn't negate the impact on her and Cheveyo, but she'd be damned if Gavin was going to get sucked into Tala's little tantrum. Raine set the last of the magic in place triggering a silent explosion. Her surroundings snapped back in a flood of sound and frenetic movements. When her vision cleared she realized she was no longer in the kitchen. Where was she?

"Raine! Damn it, stop it!" Gavin's voice came from above her and sounded hoarse.

She blinked until his face came into focus, only then recognizing she was on the ground with something heavy lying over her. She went to move her arms, but they didn't budge. At her wrists a pressure tightened and the heavy blanket moved. Her body recognized Gavin's, and the instinctive struggles stopped, her muscles relaxing as he held her still.

In the sudden quiet, only the harsh sound of heavy breathing filled her ears. The fierce angles of his face closed in as he leaned forward until all she saw was the jade green of his eyes. "Are you done?"

His question feathered across her lips, sparking the ever-present burn. She couldn't stop instinctive arch as the feel of him, hard and heavy, sent desire spiraling through her nerve endings.

His eyes burned with an answering hunger as he settled deeper into her. "Not the right time."

She stifled her inappropriate moan, shocked at how fast the situation changed. Closing her eyes didn't help, it only sharpened the feel of him. She fought her body's responses reaching for the clarity needed to analyze what happened. Heartbeats passed, but she managed to lock her reactions into familiar prisons so logic could filter through. An instinctive dread made her stomach pitch, but she lowered her shields to face what she created.

The geas Tala laid was still there. There was no breaking the binding requirement of Cheveyo's health for her life. The geas' tendrils that once latched onto her bond with Gavin were gone. She followed the energy, and her relief sputtered and died.

Oh shit! Stunned, she stared at the signatures now trailing from Cheveyo, to her and back into Tala's healing magic.

Her eyes snapped open as her blood congealed in her veins, leaving her shaky and cold. She managed to turn a magi's magic back on itself. Something only another magi should be able to do.

"There are those individuals who can see magic, and then there are those very rare individuals that can not only see magic, but change it." Tala's earlier words came back with a vengeance, and panic clawed under Raine's skin.

No, no, no—she couldn't change magic. It wasn't possible. But the inescapable reality stared grimly back.

A soft whimper escaped and Gavin pulled back, a frown turning his lips down. *"What is it?"* His question filtered through their mental connection.

She scrambled to conceal what she had done, and the need to hide translated into a frantic twist of her hips, a desperate attempt to dislodge him. Tugging against his hold on her wrists proved equally futile.

He was having none of it. Before she could get her mental blocks in place he was inside and she cringed as he studied the undulating magic.

What had she done? This wasn't natural. She knew better than to let her darker urges free. When the geas locked onto the connection between her and the man she loved, unreasonable fear broke her normal steely control. It didn't matter that it shouldn't be possible to do—the driving need to stop the threat from dragging Gavin into the madness surrounding her dominated.

She couldn't feel Gavin's reactions, and she didn't dare reach out. He demanded honesty in all things from her, and right now, he wasn't giving her much of a choice. So she waited. Waited for him to put as much distance between them as he could. Because once Tala realized what Raine had done, Raine would become the hunted.

Raine had been a Wraith too long not to understand what would happen next. Tala would identify Raine as a threat, rightly so, since this would prove that Raine could manipulate magic and turn it back on the caster. It wouldn't matter that Raine couldn't repeat her actions. Once Tala shared the news, there would be no protection from the Kyn leaders.

Raine had no intentions of dragging Gavin down with her. Desperation beat through her as she reached out to the bonds she shared with Gavin. It didn't matter if her heart was shattering under the knowledge that she'd be alone once again. She should've known better than to try to claim someone as hers. Monsters didn't get happily-ever-afters.

Before she could touch the magic, a hand snatched her metaphoric wrist and jerked her around. Gavin's jaw was tight as he glowered at her. *"What the hell do you think you're doing?"*

"Keeping you safe."

"For the gods' sake, Raine, dramatic much?" Exasperation echoed through their link. *"Snap out of it."*

His harsh words held her still. *"I'm not letting them hunt you down."*

He gave her a short shake. *"Stop being so melodramatic.*

No one's hunting anyone down." He spun her back to the magic and what she saw left her knees weak. *"Did you forget what I can do?"* His magic overlay the geas, the small telling irregularities visible only to her. It edged through the spell, erasing the visual line to Tala. Illusion.

"But—"

"You are the only one who can see magic. Think about it." His mental voice was hard. *"If they can't see it, they can't prove it."* He spun her around to face him, and she held onto his upper arms. *"We're going to kill the Stealer and get Cheveyo's magic back. The geas will be broken and she'll never know it was tied back to her."*

"Unless we fail."

"We won't."

She thought about it, really thought it about. It might work. The geas would demand she fulfill the spell's requirements, but the link to Cheveyo and Tala wouldn't be felt unless the Stealer killed her. In which case, it wouldn't really matter would it? Cautious relief flowed through her.

"Okay, okay—" Her words were cut short when he kissed her. She expected a fierce demanding hunger to compliment his frustration, instead he took his time with a gentle exploration. He sipped from her lips, his hands framing her face with an exquisite tenderness she didn't understand. His touch soothed the ragged edges of panic, and replaced it with desire and love.

She dragged him closer with one hand fisted in his T-shirt, the other tangled in his silky hair. Wanting to crawl inside the haven he offered, she pressed against him, opening to him, his tongue stroking along hers in a gentle enticement. She let her fears and worry dissipate as her body began to burn in earnest.

He drew back and nipped along her chin. *"We have to go back or Tala's going to wonder what were up to."*

She gave a small nod and let him pull them both back into the waking world.

Lifting her lashes, she brushed her hand lightly along the side of his face. He turned and pressed a kiss into her palm. Her fingers curled around the small piece of heat.

"You ready to get up?" The rumble of his voice vibrated against her chest.

She gave a slow blink as their surroundings penetrated the haze of desire—the firm press of the floor into her spine, Ash's low resonating growls from above, and the harsh breathing of someone else. Yep, they were back in the real world.

Gavin released her wrists and pushed himself up.

She lay there for a moment trying to regain her equilibrium. Taking a deep breath, she rolled over and got to her hands and knees. Her head protested the movement and she choked back her groan. Ash's continuing warnings were getting on her nerves, adding to her rising resentment. She knew better than to trust someone like Tala. Lifting her head she let her leopard lead and sent a savage growl at Ash. His rumbles stopped, but she didn't drop her gaze from the amber-eyed wolf. Tension sang through the silence.

Tala tucked her hand into Ash's ruff, breaking the staring contest. Raine pushed to her feet. They didn't have time for this crap. Once upright, she met Tala's gaze. The witch's chin lifted in defiance, arrogance drawn close like a cloak.

Raine gave her a cold smile. When Tala couldn't completely hide her flinch, Raine's smile widened.

"We're leaving." Gavin's announcement cut through

the room. His hand latched on to Raine's arm and steered her to the door.

Tala didn't say a word.

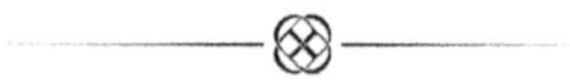

Sunlight warmed the edges of the winter-chilled air as Gavin and Raine pulled into the dirt drive of Nati Alcaina's house, one of a handful of manufactured homes scattered among the pines lining the back road located north of town. They parked behind a battered compact sitting off to the side. The echo of their car doors reverberated through the quiet morning. Considering the scenery, Raine expected the inevitable greeting of barking dogs or, gods forbid, chickens, to round the corner of the house. Instead, only the song of the breeze dancing over leaves could be heard. The underlying scent of wood-smoke accompanied the crunch of gravel under their feet.

Reaching the cement steps leading to the screen door, she slowed and stopped. Something skittered along her spine in an undecipherable warning.

Gavin stopped short. "What?"

"I'm not sure." She scanned her surroundings.

He touched her hand. "Your blade is out."

She looked down, frowning. Sure enough whatever triggered her internal alarms was strong enough to have her unconsciously dropping a wrist blade into her palm. Her hand tightened on the blade as she looked around.

Through the winter-bare trees a thin wisp of smoke trailed up from another home. Nothing lurked in the early morning shadows. Sunlight sparkled across the light layer of snow lying farther back from Nati's home.

"I can't put my finger on it," she muttered.

Gavin sent his magic questing out. Like the heat of a warm summer afternoon, his power flowed over her, rolling over the area in a silent wave. It took only moments before he drew it back, his magic's warmth replaced by winter's breath leaving goosebumps rushing over her skin. "Wards."

She tilted her head. "Those are some damn weird wards. Creepy."

A grin flashed before he turned and headed up the stairs. "What did you expect for a necromancer?" He rapped his knuckles on the doorframe, making the screen door rattle. "At least she's not using ghosts."

She stopped in mid-step. "Ghosts?"

As they waited for Nati to answer, he gave her a casual shrug. "Some necromancers like using ghosts as their personal warning systems."

She came up beside him on the small porch. Thinking of the chindis, she could see the appeal of using ghosts as your own personal security system. "Gives a whole new meaning to silent alarms."

He laughed. As they waited, she put away her blade. There was no sound of movement from inside. She shifted her weight. "No one seems to be home."

"Car's here," he noted before rapping on the doorframe, He followed that with ringing the doorbell. The monotone bell echoed through the house.

Her earlier uneasiness crawled back. "Something's not right."

Instead of answering, he grasped the screen door's handle. It swung open on squeaky hinges.

The sense of disquiet rose until it raked its nails over her internal chalkboard, drawing her nerves taunt. Once again, a blade slipped into her palm.

Picking up on her uneasiness, he put the screen door to his back, holding it open. She stayed to the side and moved forward. Her hand hovered over the doorknob. Watching him, she caught the dull glint of a blade in his hand. He gave her a short nod. She wrenched the knob, breaking the flimsy locking mechanism, and pushed it open.

As the morning breeze flitted through the ominously silent opening, the smell hit first—a coppery scent of blood. The heavy odor was so thick it lay like a metallic film in her mouth leaving her fighting not to gag. She tried to make out details in the dim interior, but there wasn't enough light. She didn't want to go in and see what was behind the sickening stench. Ignoring her body's reluctance, she forced herself to step forward, only to be jerked to a stop by Gavin's grip on her arm.

"Stop," he hissed. "Don't forget the damn wards."

Right, because the last thing they needed was another surprise attack. Switching places, she held the screen door open while he crouched at the threshold. The warmth of his magic played along the edge of her awareness as she kept an eye on their surroundings.

The edgy prickle of the wards dissolved in minutes, lending evidence to his warding expertise. He straightened and stepped cautiously inside the small house.

Using one hand to keep the squeaky screen door from slamming shut, she followed him in. His tall shadow moved through the dimness as he picked his way through the disaster that was the living room. Overturned and broken furniture littered the space.

Something was piled in the center. She had a sinking

suspicion of what, or more accurately, who it was. Unfortunately they needed to clear the rest of the house before confirming her suspicions. She'd be surprised if whatever was behind this destruction was still around, but better safe than sorry.

It didn't take them long—the house was small. The fight was contained to the living room, the rest of the home eerily untouched by the raging violence. When they were sure they were alone, Raine called up the soft fey light to hover over her shoulder.

Gavin crouched in the remains of the living room, studying the red ruin of what had once been a person.

Picking her way carefully through the blood stained mish-mash of splintered wood, gutted cushions, and shattered multi-colored glass, Raine's attention stayed on her feet instead of what waited when she stopped. "Is it Nati?"

"Yeah," he answered.

Her foot landed awkwardly on what use to be part of a leather couch and she stumbled. Only Gavin's quick reflexes and firm grip kept her from face planting into the gory mess of the necromancer. She tightened her hand on his, grateful for his support. Not letting him go, she folded into a crouch and processed what lay before her.

Under the fey light, the blood was almost black. It painted the remains of the furniture. She looked around and found it on the walls and ceiling, as if a mad artist had flung his paintbrush in some wild arc. Dragging her gaze away from the horrific canvas, she studied the body. At first she thought Nati had been pierced through by the broken wood of the furniture. Yet the more she studied the corpse, the more she realized that what she was seeing was bone—

Nati's bones—snapped like fragile sticks, the edges ragged and splintered.

Pity spiked but she pushed it ruthlessly down. Now was not the time for emotions. First, they needed to figure out what happened. Nati had been young, maybe early thirties or so. Her hair short, the color hard to determine as her blood left it dyed in a dark, sticky mess. She had been crawling away from whatever tore her apart when she died.

"It played with her," Raine muttered, taking in the deep gouges running from shoulder to mid-thigh. Deep enough to injure, but not to kill. There was something strange about the marks though. Something floating just outside her grasp. Using Gavin's grip for balance, she leaned forward and traced above the marks. "Claws?"

"I think so." He untangled his fingers, tilted his head and shuffled a little to the side, being careful to stay clear of the body and blood as he leaned forward, balancing on his fingertips. "That's not what killed her though."

From her angle, she couldn't see what he saw. "What do you mean?"

He rocked back on his heels, his eyes dark and serious. "If you look at the edges of these marks, they were made from the inside out."

"Lord and Lady," she breathed, seeing it now that he pointed it out. The flesh on the edges of Nati's wounds were turned the wrong way. When someone was gouged or clawed, the edges of their wounds curled in under the pressure of the claws. Nati's were curled away, as if what had made the marks had gouged its way out of her body.

Looking at the broken bones she found the same signs in the splintered edges of bone. They, too, had been snapped from the inside. Trepidation burst into ugly life. If the Stealer could do this to Nati, it meant Xander was in deep shit. "We injured the Stealer. How did it get this strong?"

"It wasn't the Stealer."

The absolute certainty in his voice pulled her up short. Crouched over the sickening remains of the necromancer, she stared at him.

"Think about it." His voice was harsh, rough. "Nati was a necromancer."

She dragged the mental pieces together. Necromancers raised and communed with ghosts. Really strong necro's could do one better. They could raise and commune with the actual spirits. Ghosts were the memories of an individual energy. Spirits contained some part of the actual person, making them much more...alive...for want of a better word, than ghosts. Raine was missing something, because she couldn't see where he was going and told him as much.

"Do you know how necromancers communicate with ghosts?" he asked.

She shook her head.

"They act as the conduit." Gavin watched her closely. "What if Nati was asked to raise a ghost that was stronger than she expected? Where would it be trapped?"

Sickening horror blossomed. "Inside her."

"Right." His jaw tightened. "Considering the prevailing prejudice toward the demons, who's to say that Jenny or Lizbeth didn't come to Nati first?"

"But why wait to kill her then? Why take her out first?"

"Because until we showed up, Nati wouldn't have been a threat."

The puzzle pieces fell into place. Until Tala brought in Cheveyo, the deaths were contained to the magi's House, and could easily be viewed as a personal vendetta against the witches and wizards. Ransom and his partner could then exploit the division between Houses, fracturing the Southwest Kyn. With Cheveyo's arrival, the partners panicked and attacked the Northwest Magi, never considering how such a threat would be answered.

Once Gavin and Xander entered the picture, their presence sent Ransom and his partner scrambling, trying to snip loose ends before the Wraiths could get to them. When Gavin and Raine called Ransom for the meeting, the more powerful partner set the chindis loose, guaranteeing Ransom wouldn't break under their questioning.

"How long has she been dead?"

"No more than a day."

Nati was another loose end. Only four people were even aware of Gavin, Raine, and Xander's investigation. Tala, Rio, Tomás, and Lizbeth. Whoever Ransom's partner was, they had power, which meant...

"Jenny's dead." Raine felt the truth of her words as she rose to her feet and stepped back from the pitiful remains. "It's not Rio. He gains nothing. Tala wouldn't destroy Cheveyo."

Putting his hands on his thighs, Gavin pushed to his feet and stepped out of the shambles to the edge of the room near her. "You certain?"

Hands on her hips, she gave a sharp nod. "She loves him enough to pull stupid shit like laying a geas on me, but I can't see her doing this." She turned away and headed for the front door. "I need some air."

She didn't stop until she reached the car. Leaning her arms on the hood, she laid her head on them. Slow, deep breaths cleared the coppery stench from her nose and replaced it with sharp winter air. The soft thud of the door closing and the squeak of the screen door cut through the morning. The grinding crunch of gravel heralded Gavin's approach. She didn't bother lifting her head, even as he ran a comforting hand down her spine.

"Damn them, Gavin." Her voice was rough. "Damn them both."

CHAPTER 28

WHILE GAVIN BROKE AS MANY SPEED LIMITS AS HE COULD, RAINE called Mulcahy to warn him about the Chavezes.

"You have to get a hold of Vidis." She pressed the phone to her ear and grabbed a hold of the chicken handle as Gavin careened around a sharp curve at a speed that left her stomach behind. "Make him stay away from the ranch."

"I don't know if I'll reach him in time. He's probably still in the air," Mulcahy answered, tension riding through the line. "You two get over there and finish this." Order given, he hung up, not giving her a chance to respond.

Her soft snarl turned into a sharp yip as Gavin took another turn on two wheels. "Gods' sake, Gavin, don't kill us before we get there."

"Mulcahy won't reach Vidis." His calm statement was so at odds with his hair-raising driving, she could only stare.

It took her a couple of tries to find enough moisture in her dry mouth to get the words out. "Maybe, but we have to get to that ranch before he does."

"And once we're there?" He took his eyes off the road.

When she paled and an undignified squeak escaped, he turned back. "That ranch covers a lot of land."

Maybe it would be better if she closed her eyes. That way, when they flew off the mountain road into a fiery metal ball of death, she wouldn't see it coming. She chanced a look out her window, but the plummeting drop speeding along had her scrunching her eyes closed. "Someone's going to be there. Either Carlos or Andrew."

"Not if Tomás took them with him to meet Vidis."

"He wouldn't take both and leave his mate undefended." Shifters tended to be a little possessive of their significant others.

"We could waste a lot of time trying to track someone down."

"We won't need to track anyone down." Since the car appeared to be staying on the road, she risked a look under her lashes. When a straight ribbon of asphalt greeted her, she let out a breath and pried her fingers from the handle above the door.

"We won't?" His question was sharp.

"Nope. We're going to trace them by their magic." She caught the clenching of his jaw. Oh, he was so not happy about that. He opened his mouth, but she cut him off. "Don't argue. You know it's our best chance."

His mouth snapped shut, his lips pressed into thin lines and his nostrils flared. "I don't like it."

She didn't like it either, but they were out of choices. They needed to get to the ranch, find the Stealer and Xander before the Chavezes harmed Vidis. The thought of the Northwest Alpha sparked a new worry. She bit her lip. "You have to protect Vidis."

Gavin shot her a puzzled look before going back to his kamikaze driving. "What do you mean?"

"Tala's geas means I have to return Cheveyo's magic. To do that, I have to destroy the Stealer." Banked anger began to peek through. "With the way the spell is laid, I don't think I'm going to be able to do anything but destroy the Stealer. Regardless of what's going on." Bitter resentment colored her voice. "The damn witch hobbled me."

The phantom brush of fingers along the back of her neck eased her tension. "We'll get through this." She held tight to the assurance in his voice as he shot her a grin. "Besides, I think you're underestimating Vidis. He's more than capable of defending himself."

Logically, she agreed, but based on her experiences with the Soul Stealer, she worried. Her magic was stretched thin. Cheveyo's was even more fragile. Gavin would need every bit of his own skills and magic to hold everyone off of her, even as he protected Vidis and Xander. She needed to find a way to destroy the Stealer without taking herself and Cheveyo with it.

The sedan bounced over the rough road winding its way to the Chavez's ranch. Neither Gavin nor Raine were interested in keeping their arrival quiet. They pulled into the crescent shape drive, got out of the car, and hurried to the front door. An oppressive stillness blanketed the ranch house. Raine would have preferred an angry furry welcoming committee. The edgy atmosphere left her leopard stalking under her skin, slowing her steps until she came to a stop. As Gavin passed her, she grabbed his arm.

He stilled under her touch. "What?"

She surveyed their surroundings. "I'm not sure."

Late morning sun cast shadows over the porch and

washed the front window in shades of gray. Heeding the animal prowling inside her, she gave her cat enough control to scent the air around them. Her mouth opened and she dragged air in to roll over her tongue.

The uniquely spicy scent of Gavin hit first, but it wasn't what she was looking for. She concentrated on the cold wetness of the winter air under laid with the dry, dustiness of hay. Her nose twitched and she sucked in more air.

From behind the house a heavy muskiness emanated, accompanied by the faint wickers and huffs of the horses housed in the stable. Working past her cat's consideration of the possible challenge of hunting the horses, she stretched her senses, closing her eyes to concentrate. On the very edge of her ability she caught it. The warm, metallic-copper taste she knew all too well. Blood.

"There." Pointing, she opened her eyes. At some point she stepped around Gavin and moved to the side of the house. Her finger was aimed at the faded barn standing beyond the metal, oval fence dominating the back yard. "Something's bleeding over there."

Together they crossed the hard-packed ground. As they drew closer, they could see the large doors pushed back. A shiver crawled down her spine. The morning light didn't pierce the gloom of that gaping hole where the muffled snorts and soft whinnies of the animals inside escaped. A hoof slammed into the wood, the sharp crack sent both Wraiths dropping into a protective crouch.

"What the hell?" she muttered under breath as her heartbeat began to level.

"Something has the horses spooked." Gavin's voice was soft as they continued forward.

The horses' discomfort got louder, and the disturbing

scent of blood became more pronounced. "You think whatever it is, is still in there?"

He shrugged. "I don't know."

"Great." She dropped a blade into her hand. Flexing her fingers around the familiar weight, she crept closer to the barn door. Taking a position to the side of the entrance, she caught the muted flash as Gavin held his weapon close to his body as he mirrored her on the other side.

His mental voice flowed over her. *"Give me a second."* If they hadn't been tied together, she would've missed the subtle wash of his magic as he sent it through the dim barn. *"I'm not sensing anyone, just horses."*

He slipped into the barn and she followed, her eyes taking a disorienting moment to adjust to the lack of light. Her night vision flickered but was useless considering it was neither light nor dark, but that strange in-between gloom. Some light filtered in from the windows set high on the edges, but down near the hay-covered floor, the shadows reigned.

The scent of blood was stronger, mixing in with sweat of the horses and the dry, scratchy smell of hay. The animals nickered and shuffled in agitation with only the occasional snap of iron against wood. She searched the dim interior for any hidden threats. A sharp whinny from behind a stall on the far end broke the tense atmosphere.

Gavin moved, leaving her to follow. Rounding the corner, she pulled up short as a wild-eyed horse pressed itself against the far wall of its stall, legs tap-dancing against the floor. Gavin's hands were empty and he held them out to his side. His voice was a soft croon as he inched his way closer to the nervous animal.

Raine held her breath, sure that at any moment the horse would bolt and tap-dance its way right over him.

The animal's nervous movements quieted until Gavin was finally able to snag the bridle hanging like loose hair ribbons.

Only then did Raine take in the empty saddle cinched to the animal's back. Not wanting to set the horse off, she stayed near the stall's opening, utilizing her mental link. *"Since when did you become the horse whisperer?"*

He kept his attention on the skittish horse. *"I am a man of many talents."*

She couldn't argue that one. *"Where did he come from?"*

Working his way back to the saddle, Gavin's hands moved in long comforting strokes. *"There's blood on the leather."*

"How much?"

Continuing his petting, he studied the saddle. *"Enough that whoever it came from can't be in good shape."*

He began to undo the countless straps and buckles holding the saddle in place. The horse's tail flicked back and forth. Although it kept a wide eye on him, it held still.

"What are you doing?" The urge to get out and move pulled at her. She didn't know if it was the need to find out where the blood came from, or Tala's damn geas starting to kick in. Either way, sticking around to play with the horse was not on her to-do list.

"I have to get this saddle off or the horses are going to go nuts." He managed to undo the last strap, the muscles in his shoulders and back flexing as he hefted the saddle loose. He threw it over the sidewall of the stall and went back to the horse, who appeared a little less psycho. *"Take it outside."*

"Excuse me?" Despite her irritation at his command, she tucked her blade away and reached for the blood stained saddle.

He moved to the far side of the horse and ran his hands over its back. *"Blood upsets the horses."*

It wasn't doing much for her either. Tugging, she pulled the saddle down, the weight heavier than expected. She took a step to regain her balance and noted the darker stains against the leather and streaking over the pommel. Blood.

Gavin's hissing intake of breath told her he found more. If the amount on the matching side of the saddle was any indicator, it wasn't just the rider who'd been injured.

"How bad?" She stepped outside and set the saddle on the ground.

Instead of answering, he shared the image of long gouges running from the horse's ribs to its rump. She winced. Damn, the stupid animal was lucky it made it back to the barn. Which meant its rider couldn't be too far away. She lowered her shields, hoping to catch some trace of the missing rider. Instead, the tugging from earlier came back, sharper than before. Turning in a slow circle she followed the insistent pull, sighting a dark flicker in the distance. Understanding dawned when the tug became an ache. The Stealer was out there. She wasn't going to be able to fight the summons for very long. *"Gavin?"*

"Hmm?" His answer was distracted.

"I have to go." The geas was done being polite. A sharp jerk and she was running toward whatever lurked out there. She fought, even knowing it was futile. Every time she forced her body to stop, a white wash of pain shattered her concentration and she was running again.

"Raine!" Gavin's frantic shout echoed behind her.

"Hurry!" The compulsion was so strong. The combination of her magic and Tala's geas kept her emotions distant. Under the inescapable urge, worry and

fear roiled. Even the familiar comfort of her anger was muted, buried under Tala's thrice-damned spell. A strange clarity emerged—find and destroy the Stealer. Faint worries darted like moths around a light, only to be burned to ash as the geas took over.

Her body came to an abrupt stop, leaving her weaving on her feet in the middle of a deserted grassy field. Air was a harsh burn in her abused lungs, but the need to move was gone. The geas and her magic were quiet.

Where was she? Even more important, where was Gavin? The edge of the forest spread in front of her. Turning in a circle, she could make out the faint outline of the barn in the distance.

She reached down their bond, strangely unsettled. *"Gavin?"*

An overwhelming sense of relief came back. *"Are you okay?"*

"I think so."

"Where are you?"

She sent him an image of how the barn looked to her.

"Don't move."

She gave a soft snort. *"If the geas wakes again, I'm not going to have much choice."*

"Two minutes, damn it," he snarled. *"Just give me two damn minutes."*

She couldn't make any promises.

A quiet moan broke the silence, and she froze in sudden wariness. Only her eyes moved, searching for the source of that pain-filled noise. It came again, a soft muffled sound as if whatever was making it didn't want to be heard. It was eerily similar to the sounds she made when crawling through the forest to escape the Stealer. Whatever dulled her fear disappeared. Terror flitted on the edges of her mind, causing her breath to stutter as she listened hard.

When the noise came again, she moved through the grassy plain, her steps light. The cool breeze weaved through the long blades of grass bringing the cloying scent of blood and terror. A couple more steps revealed a body to match the scent.

The gray-streaked brown hair was matted with blood. The scarred hand clawing at the earth was desperately trying to drag its wounded body across the ground. Kneeling, she reached out to the battered man, but stopped, hand in mid-air, rife with indecision. Considering the visible damage, no matter where she touched, she would hurt him.

His face was turned away, his soft whimpers a mere breath of sound. He was completely oblivious to her presence.

She crawled around him to see his face. It was a macabre mask of blood and torn tissue but the crooked nose prompted a memory. "Eric?"

Her soft question sent him scrambling away, those horrible fear noises rising in volume until they were shrieks.

"Shh—shh—I'm not going to hurt you." She tried to calm him, but nothing she said seemed to penetrate whatever hell tormented the Chavez's foreman. Keeping her distance, she grimly accepted there was nothing rational left inside the broken man. The Stealer had claimed another victim.

Long bloody gashes left his clothes in ribbons, the skin underneath in a similar condition. She was amazed he was still breathing. Pity rose. Even if Eric managed to heal his body, his mind was gone. Unfortunately, she wasn't the one with healing magic. That was Gavin, or better yet, Tala.

Eric's shrieks turned to airless screams, the sounds so filled with agony she would have given anything to make them stop. Sitting there watching him fight against the monster now firmly entrenched in his mind, ripped tiny tears in her soul. *"Please hurry, Gavin!"*

A soft touch on her hand opened eyes she hadn't realized she'd closed. Gavin knelt in front of her. He pulled her hands from her ears, and under his touch, they curled into fists. "Eric?"

"I put him under."

"Will he make it?"

Resignation carved deep grooves around his mouth and he gave a short shake of his head. She was unsurprised by his answer. Before she could ask anything more, he was ripped away from her.

Scrambling to her feet, she found him wrestling with a light colored wolf. The wolf was on top, but Gavin got his feet between them and heaved. The wolf flew to land in a pile a few feet away. Blades dropped into her hands as she dashed between the scrambling wolf and the man she loved. The wolf was bleeding, favoring a back leg, and blood streaked his light coat. Growls rumbled, his muzzle flaring to display a truly intimidating set of fangs.

Seems they found one of Tomás's bodyguards. Raine gave him fair warning. "Carlos, you better back down, or this won't end well."

He ignored her, taking a deliberate step forward. She braced, but he stopped, his amber eyes focused on Eric. The massive head swiveled back to them.

Gavin answered his unspoken question. "We found him like this, but he's not going to last."

A ripple of magic ran over the wolf and when it faded, a naked Carlos limped his way over to Eric. Ignoring Raine and Gavin, he knelt down.

"I think you can put the blades away." Gavin brushed his lips against her hair then stepped around her and moved to Eric's other side. Out loud he addressed the kneeling shifter. "What's going on, Carlos?"

"Just because he's naked doesn't mean he's not dangerous." She tucked away one of her blades, but the other would stay out until Carlos was gone. He was Tomás's third, and right now anyone connected to the Chavezes was under suspicion.

"Stupid bitch has gone *loco*." Carlos's words were growled, evidence that his wolf was too close to the surface for comfort.

Standing behind him, Raine didn't miss the deep claw marks that left his back a gory patchwork. Serious bite marks dotted his skin and along one side of his ribs, the edge of a dark bruise was forming.

Carlos turned his head to her. "If you're going to stab me in the back, *chica*, you'd better make it count."

She curled her lip. "If I'm going to kill you, it wouldn't be from the back."

"Nice to know." He dismissed her. "Move to your man, then. You're making my skin itch."

She moved next to Gavin. "Who tore into you?"

"Lizbeth." The anger in his one word vibrated in the air.

"What happened?"

Carlos ignored her and reached down to pick up Eric. Gavin grabbed his wrist, stopping him. "What do you think you're doing?"

Grief, anger, and helpless fury washed over the shifter's face. "Taking him home."

"No."

Carlos leaned over Eric to snarl in Gavin's face. "You can't stop me."

Nothing changed in the way Gavin held himself, but Raine felt his readiness. It wouldn't take much to send them both back to wrestling in the dirt. They didn't have time for a pissing contest. They needed answers and the geas was making a comeback, like an annoying flea, snipping at her skin, each bite digging deeper.

Crouching, she snagged Carlos's chin and dragged his fierce face to her. "Why did Lizbeth attack you?"

"There was a phone call this morning for the alpha. When he got off, he was furious. He told Lizbeth to stay at the ranch and ordered me to watch her. He took Andrew to meet with your alpha. Before he left, Tomás and Lizbeth argued. She wanted him to take both of us. He refused."

"Smart man," Gavin commented.

Since Raine still held his face, Carlos rolled his eyes to Gavin. "How do you figure?"

"Our alpha is coming to discuss the kidnapping of his Tracker," Gavin explained. "If Tomás brought more than one person to stand with him, it would considered a challenge."

Carlos ripped his face free of Raine's grip, leaving the red marks of her fingers behind. Anger and arrogance warred over his bruised countenance. "We have nothing to do with your missing wolf. Your alpha shouldn't even be here."

"We're not here to argue with you," Raine cut in. "Tomás left, Andrew went with him. What did Lizbeth do?"

Carlos narrowed his eyes, something flickering across his face. "She was restless. Unable to settle, on edge."

"Why?"

His answer was slow in coming. "I don't know. Perhaps she was still upset with her mate. She wanted to go for walk."

"A walk?" That made no sense to her. Carlos gave a sharp nod. "Why?"

For the first time, he dropped his gaze, trying to hide the movement as he touched Eric's still shoulder. "I don't know."

"Liar." Gavin's accusation rang through the quiet.

Carlos pressed his lips together, grimacing. "When she gets upset, she goes to visit Brett."

Raine frowned. "Brett's dead."

"She loved her son a great deal." The wolf raised his head, grim acceptance pushing his shoulders down. "He's buried on the ranch."

Mulcahy's earlier statement echoed through her mind, *"To raise a Soul Stealer, you have to be walking the edge of madness. That speaks more to a parent's grief, than a girlfriend's."*

"You called her crazy," she accused softly.

Carlos flinched. "We were almost to the grave when we ran across Eric. He was out riding fences and got spooked. Said something was haunting Brett's grave, that we needed to get someone out to bless the ground." He paused and visibly swallowed. "Lizbeth went real quiet. She just stared at him. Then she gave him the creepiest smile I've ever seen." A shudder worked its way over him, leaving visible goosebumps in its wake. "She said, 'It's just hungry, Eric. Why don't you feed it?'"

Carlos stared at Eric's broken body. "*Lo siento, hermano.* I didn't know." A lone tear wove its way down his face. He took a deep breath and raised his head, cold practicality carving his face into harsh angles. “She sent that abomination after Eric. You must stop her.”

Raine felt her fists clench as Carlos provided the final confirmation of who held the Stealer’s leash. “Is Xander with her?”

“I never saw her. The Stealer went after Eric and Lizbeth attacked me. I had a choice to go after her or Eric.” Painful misery clouded his face. “I lost track of Eric and the Stealer. Lizbeth was running in the other direction when I left.” This time neither Raine nor Gavin tried to stop him as he gathered the dying man into his arms. He pushed to his feet, and they rose with him.

“Where would she go?” Gavin asked.

“There’s an old shack out on the edge of the ranch about three miles out. She might go there.” Carlos turned to head back.

Raine touched his arm. He stopped, but didn’t look at her. “Does your alpha know about his mate?”

“No.” His voice was resigned. “He would not believe it.” He looked at the man in his arms. “Even I am having trouble understanding what has happened.” He shrugged off her touch and began his trek back to the ranch.

CHAPTER 29

Gavin tried to reach Vidis once more as they started after Lizbeth. When he got the alpha's voicemail, his explanation was short and to the point. "Lizbeth has Xander. She raised the Stealer. Tomás doesn't know. We're going after her. Ask Carlos for directions."

The geas's insistent tugging was back, and now the aching pull of Raine's tracking magic was getting tougher to ignore.

"You okay?" Gavin stood behind her.

She shook her head. "It's getting stronger."

"It knows we're coming."

"I don't think so." She rubbed her palm over her chest, trying to alleviate the sharp pull of the magic. "The draw is coming from me."

He raised an eyebrow.

Unable to explain it, she gave him the image burning behind her eyes. The world was a hazy, light-filled landscape of washed-out colors. One distinct band wove through the surreal surroundings, no end in sight. Even as they watched, it brightened briefly and the resulting painful tug dragged her forward a step. Something solid and heavy wrapped around her wrist, holding her still. The watercolor world slid away to be replaced by a broad chest. Tilting her head back, she read the worry and frustration in Gavin's clenched jaw and furrowed brow.

"We can't run into this blindly," he said, his words sharp.

"I realize that," she snapped. "If you have a suggestion, share, before I do my track-and-field impression."

"Let me shadow you."

"No." The rejection was out before she could stop it. The last time she faced the Stealer, it almost won, taking her and Gavin with it. If she lost Gavin....a soul-chilling fear rose.

His eyes narrowed and his grip became a steel vise, but before he could say anything, the confusing morass of emotions pushed the words out of her mouth. "I can't risk that." She wanted to say, *You, I can't risk you.* "If you shadow me, then the Stealer will have access to you. I can't accept that. You save the others."

He gave her a small shake. "Do you have so little faith in me? I've been facing down scarier shit than this for years." He leaned down until his face was inches from hers, his gaze dominating her world. "Do you think I'm weak?"

There was no warning, no time to prepare as his magic slammed into her, tearing through every shield she possessed, laying her bare. Her initial reaction was to strike back, to destroy this threat, but a simple truth held her in check. This was Gavin. The man she loved. She never considered him weak. A weak man couldn't capture her soul, couldn't understand the darkness that made her who she was, could never stand beside her.

As he tore his way to the very heart of her, the warrior in

her watched in awe. For the first time, she saw the full measure of the man she had tied her soul to. His magic was a cleaner, more defined version of hers. Where he faced the changes wrought in him by Lawson's injection, she spent her life fighting and hiding from them. He took those changes and created something beautiful and deadly. She created something deadly, but fractured—not as deeply as it once was, but those fissures still existed.

His furious determination to prove he wasn't weak burned through her. Her lack of confidence hurt him, and his pain scraped at her, but she knew better. Of the two of them, she was the weak one. Losing him would break the chain holding the monster clawing for dominance sending Raine crashing into a fathomless pit of nightmares. She would cease to exist.

His magic bore down and unable to hide the depth of her emotions, her words were torn from her soul, a plea from one heart to another. "I can't lose you. Don't ask that of me, please." She showed him what she would become without him, exposing her weakness, giving him the power to destroy her. The ugliness of the lurking monster inside shimmered like a dream on the cusp of reality.

His choice. Stay or leave. Because she would never be able to walk away.

The emotional storm changed, the fury riding the edge gentled, then wrapped around her, filling in the holes, until nothing separated what was Gavin and what was Raine. The feather light touch tracing down her jaw anchored her spirit to her body. She stared into his rough-hewn face as his gaze roamed over her.

"Don't you understand?" He captured her chin and rasped his thumb over her lower lip.

She let her tongue follow his path, and he repeated the

caress. The resulting curl of warmth had her pulse speeding.

"You can't lose me." His head swooped down and his lips captured hers.

With a gentle swipe of his tongue he coaxed her mouth open. She held nothing back. All her fear, her love, she poured into her response. Desire flared and the kiss deepened.

She dragged his head closer as she angled her mouth. The need to breathe became secondary. When he tore his lips away, she struggled to recapture them, only to find herself held captive as he rained small nips down her jaw. She arched her neck as he tugged sharply on her hair, leaving a clear path for his destructive caress.

There was no stopping her low moan as her body went pliant, melting against his dominant strength. His teeth raked lightly over the sensitive spot where her neck and shoulder met and her breathing stilled. She waited in almost painful anticipation, keenly aware of his tongue laving the area then the sharp sting as he bit down. Her body liquefied under that primitive press of teeth. Never in her life had she ever given anyone such a submissive response. Only him. Only Gavin.

He raised his head. Her eyes fluttered open and met the burning intensity of his gaze. Desire carved a ruthless beauty on his face. She rested her palm against the strong line of his jaw, the rasp of his stubble causing her stomach to quiver in delight.

He pressed a kiss against her hand. "I'm going to shadow you." It was a statement with no give in it.

She curled her hand, holding that brief touch tight, and gave a small nod. It was all she could manage as her roiling emotions seethed and her throat constricted. There was no way to win this argument. They were warriors, and in this battle there was no room for her personal insecurities. Together they would find Xander, protect Vidis and Cheveyo, and take down the Stealer. The nasty grip of her trepidation, anger, and resentment began to loosen.

Unfortunately, the sharp tug of the geas and her tracking magic came back with a vengeance. The compelling power was like a blood-sucking tick as it latched on to the magical traces of the Stealer, tugging painfully on her, urging her to follow—now!

A particularly fierce pull had her hissing in a sharp breath and drawing out of his embrace. She stumbled forward a couple of steps before wrestling her body back under control. He grabbed her hand, and she clutched his offered anchor.

The geas was relentless. The demanding magics slammed into her. Her feet flew over the ground, the binding using the faint magical trail of the Stealer as its map. She sent a quick prayer to whomever was listening that Gavin would keep up.

Scenery passed in a blur of watercolors, but the writhing shadows, she now knew belonged to the Stealer, twisted like some evil fog just ahead. The overcast sky grayed the light of the early afternoon, leaching the color from everything. Fighting through the compulsive haze, she struggled to make sense of where she was.

Winter-bare limbs left scratches on her exposed skin as she dodged through the trees. Her boots splashed through sludgy, half-melted snow dotting the ground in drab piles.

Without warning, her body stopped. The abrupt movement sent her to her hands and knees. Head hanging down, she started cursing, low and vicious, as the demanding magic disappeared, leaving her winded and lost. Now that she was back, she reached down the tie to Gavin. *"Where are you?"*

"Not too far behind."

She caught the sense of speed as he raced toward her. Relief loosened an unknown knot in her heart. *"Hurry the hell up."* The soul-numbing chill heralding the arrival of the Stealer swept over her. *"It's coming."*

She pushed to her feet. The shadows were deeper here. They felt alive and not in a good way. Settling both wrist blades into her palms, she set her emotional upheaval aside and let her calculating Wraith mind weigh her options.

Through the dimming light, she spotted the shack Carlos mentioned. The weathered wood blended in with the surrounding trees. Two small windows sat like empty sockets on either side of the warped door. There was no discernible movement. She crept closer even as a skittering warning crept along her spine. She was being hunted. Considering the ice spreading through her soul, she knew exactly who the hunter was.

Scanning her surroundings, she tried to determine where it would attack first. A sickening sense of déjà vu hit. The scene before her was replaced by the clearing where she and Cheveyo fought the Stealer. Phantom pain tore through her leg, while ghosts shredded her spirit. She wrestled the haunting memories back. Distractions were lethal.

Using the sparse coverage afforded by the surrounding foliage, she worked her way closer to the cabin. Crouching at the foot of a tree, somewhat camouflaged by an olive-gray bush, she took in the deceptively quiet scene. A whisper of touch on the mental plane heralded Gavin's arrival. She directed him to the other side so the two of them could approach the cabin from the front.

When he was in place, she sent out, *"Ready?"*

"Ready."

Taking a deep breath, she pulled the colorful tapestry of magic over the real world. The shack was caught in a living spider web of black tendrils. Through their shared bond Gavin's shock echoed hers. The web pulsated with evil, the magic a black living weave of flames. Melodramatic, but it was the only way to describe it. Somehow, she knew that to touch it would be lethal. As it undulated in a strangely hypnotic dance, she tried to determine the pattern of the corrupt energy.

"Raine!" Gavin's mental bark snapped her out of the mesmerizing spell.

Tearing her gaze away, she focused on the ground at her feet. Regaining control took precious moments. She needed to see beyond that web. She needed to know who stood in the center. Using the same formidable will that got her through the months at the lab, she concentrated on the cabin. This time, she kept her attention off the web, peering behind it.

Faint, dull tones of shifter magic in a dusky purple, similar to the evening sky right before a storm, flickered against the far side of the cabin. Xander. The faintness of color worried her.

If she could make a hole in the web large enough for Gavin to get physically through, he could pull Xander free. Problem was, there was no way Lizbeth had left Xander unguarded. So, where was the female wolf?

Raine scanned again, this time taking her time even though every nerve in her body screamed to hurry. She knew Lizbeth was in there. No way in hell was Raine sending Gavin in without knowing where the bitch was hiding. It took several vital minutes, but Raine finally caught a glimpse of something from the corner of her eye. She stilled and waited.

This time she caught the gleam of sickly orange heavily wrapped in shadows. The flashes of color making brief appearances. Lizbeth was pacing in front of the windows. Raine quelled her need to burst in and drag Xander out.

Gavin's quiet, *"Wait,"* was unnecessary.

Raine had one more threat to identify. The Stealer.

CHAPTER 30

Frustration mounted as Raine failed to sense the Stealer. Some sixth sense yelled it was close. Too close. *"I can't find it,"* she sent to Gavin.

"Can you get me in?" His reply was unruffled, calm.

His steadiness bolstered her. *"Maybe."*

On the psychic plane, she drifted closer to the spider-webbed cabin. The sensation of something oily and smothering inched over her, growing stronger, the closer she got. As hard as it was to ignore, she couldn't afford to get creeped out. Prowling around the magical web, she realized the ties flowed back into the shadow-covered presence of Lizbeth.

"It's warding magic," came Gavin's quiet observation.

Connected as they were, she drew on his understanding of wards and began to plan. Each strand of the spider web was a ward. Each ward was anchored to something. Tracing the strands of disturbing magic, Raine discovered why the magic contained to the cabin. Lizbeth tied the wards to herself. Which meant, to weaken a strand to let Gavin through, Raine would have to weaken Lizbeth.

Grim satisfaction rose. She knew exactly how to break through Lizbeth's wards. *"Can you create this image?"* She sent Gavin a picture of a young man with dark hair and laughing eyes. It was a wild plan and if Lizbeth was still sane, it would never work.

"Got it." He was silent for a moment then, *"Say when."*

Raine slipped back into her body and moved as close as she dared to the undulating wards. As she broke through the shaded protection of the trees. *"Now."*

The image of Lizbeth's son Brett formed in front of her. Standing behind and to the side of the eerily real image, she kept her blades visible. "Lizbeth Chavez," she called, shattering the early afternoon quiet.

A strange, deafening silence fell. Not even the wind dared to dance through the trees. Raine held her position, half-hidden behind the illusion of the boy. To Lizbeth, it would appear as if Raine held her son hostage, raising every protective instinct the shifter possessed, something Raine counted on.

The door swung open and the blood-spattered mate of the Southwest Alpha stood in the doorway. Gone was the gentle wife and grieving mother. Instead, her honey-brown hair was a rat's nest and her hazel eyes blazed with an insane fury. "Get away from my son!" She moved with smooth predatory grace to the edge of the rickety porch, only to pause at the first stair, the warding magic holding her in place.

"You took something of mine, so I took something of yours." Raine kept her voice cold. She needed Lizbeth to move away from the cabin, just a few more feet, far enough to stretch the ties of the ward.

The woman wasn't completely gone, though. She

teetered on the first stair. "Brett, come here." The demand was made in a tone mothers everywhere had perfected.

When the illusion made as if to move, Raine raised her blade until it rested against the boy's neck. She *tsked*.

Lizbeth snarled and crouched, her wolf swimming to the surface.

Come on, Raine urged silently. *You know you want to rip my throat out.*

Lizbeth trembled with the need to lunge.

The illusion whimpered.

The small sound broke Lizbeth's leash and she was airborne.

Raine's magic tore through the thinned thread of warding. *"Go, Gavin!"* Using her cat's inherent reflexes, she leapt out of the way of the raging she-wolf.

Landing in a crouch where Raine once stood, Lizbeth reached for the image of her son, only to have it disappear as the ward broke with a sharp snap. Her anguished howl rent through the clearing.

Gavin burst from his spot and sprinted up the stairs to the now unprotected cabin, leaving Raine with Lizbeth.

Feral madness robbed Lizbeth of any semblance of humanity. Only an insane beast remained. She began to circle Raine, forcing her away from the cabin and toward the woods.

Raine let her, needing to keep the woman away from Gavin and Xander. Besides, she could handle one crazy shifter.

Lizbeth lunged again, and Raine tried to spin out of the way. Instead, she slammed into a tree trunk. Her shoulder and back screamed at the impact. One of her knives fell from her numb fingers. Careening off the tree, she flew backward as Lizbeth barreled into her. Deadly claws now tipped Lizbeth's hands and the snarling mouth was filled with sharp teeth—teeth that were trying to rip out Raine's throat.

Raine got her arm under Lizbeth's chin. The slicing claws shredded her shirt and the skin along her ribs. Hot, fetid breath mixed with the low growls as Lizbeth ignored the choking pressure on her throat and continued to lunge for Raine.

Raine's remaining blade was clutched in the hand holding Lizbeth back, while feeling slowly returned to the other arm. Needing another weapon, Raine let her cat out to play. The shifting of hand to claw was quicker than usual, the pain of the shift lost in the numbness. Raine wasted no time in raking bloody furrows along Lizbeth's side.

The wolf's low growls turned into sharp howls of pain. The pressure of Lizbeth's body suddenly disappeared.

Using the momentary breather, Raine shoved to her feet, ignoring the streaks of fire along her ribs.

Lizbeth crouched in front of her, her wolf flowing over her human features, watching. Blood dripped from her shredded skin, but those hazel eyes were now a blazing gold. Her lips were pulled back in a snarl, but she made no move to charge. Instead, she just stood there.

Uneasy, Raine tried to figure out what the other woman was waiting for. The icy fingers of dread spreading over her soul clued her in. She didn't need the geas or her tracking magic to realize she had forgotten what else was tied to Lizbeth. The Stealer.

With no time to waste, Raine lunged for Lizbeth. The shifter met her half way, going in low, trying to take Raine's legs out from underneath her. With her leopard so close to the surface, Raine let the cat's instincts take over.

The muscles in her thighs curled and then she was airborne.

Lizbeth's claws missed by a hair's breath. Twisting in mid-air, Raine managed to land in a crouch and swiped out, her claws scoring Lizbeth's back.

The wolf managed to stop her forward momentum and executed a graceful spin. Without pausing, she leapt, teeth bared, claws curled. She may not have shifted completely to a wolf, but it was obvious her animal was in control. Normally, that would count in Raine's favor. Not this time. Lizbeth and her wolf both knew they had nothing left to lose. Desperation made her unpredictable. Add in the fact that the twisted evil of the Stealer was a constant wave of ice over Lizbeth's spirit, and Raine needed to end this quickly.

Dodging a wild swing by Lizbeth, Raine missed the furtive swipe that took her just under her ribs. The searing impact drove the breath from her lungs in a harsh rush. Doubled over Lizbeth's arm, Raine snapped her hands around the woman's wrist. Spinning herself into Lizbeth's body, she kept Lizbeth's arm extended with an unyielding grip.

With a savage growl, Raine straightened. Using her shoulder as a fulcrum point, she pulled down on Lizbeth's outstretched arm. Lizbeth's agonized howl accompanied the sharp snap of bone. Letting go of the now useless arm, Raine swung back with her left fist and scored a hit to Lizbeth's ribs. Continuing her spin, she delivered a short, but damaging strike just under Lizbeth's jaw.

Lizbeth crumpled to the ground in an unconscious heap.

There was no time for relief. A heavy weight slammed into Raine from the side, sending her over the heap that was Lizbeth. She met the forest floor with a sickening impact. Her vision grayed as her body fought to drag in much-needed air. Fetid breath curled around her face as her body clawed for freedom. Using the flexibility of her cat, she managed to twist her spine, throwing her opponent off balance. It gave her some room to move. Her booted heels dug into the spongy ground and she scraped her palms raw as she scrambled back, trying to get away.

The sharp bite of bark against her spine stopped her retreat. Using the tree for balance, she dragged herself upright. She pressed back against the tree and tried to focus on the ever-changing image of the Soul Stealer. Here in the physical world it was more a construct of writhing shadows, except for the gold eyes. Even with the shifting darkness, there was a sense of lethal muscles coiled in readiness. The constant roiling movement was difficult to watch, almost nauseating.

Right now the hellish gaze was focused on her.

In comparison, Raine's legs were shaky and the wounds Lizbeth inflicted were edged in fire. Shoving her body's complaints into a little compartment in her mind, she locked it closed and took a quick weapons inventory. Both wrist blades were gone, leaving only the blades tucked along the sides of her boots. Behind her back, her sharp claws dug into the bark, a sure sign her cat was barely leashed. And locked behind her shields, lay her magic. For the first time since arriving in this damn desert it was a pulsating mass, wanting—needing—to be freed.

In the space between her and the unconscious Lizbeth, the Stealer paced, its gaze never wavering.

The normal forest noises were preternaturally quiet.

Knowing she would need both her knives and her magic, Raine settled into a crouch. Her hands curled around the hidden hilts nestled in her boots as she thinned the shields holding her magic in check.

In front of her, the Stealer mimicked her crouch and shifted its weight to its haunches, head lowering, the demonic gaze focused with predatory precision.

Never breaking the lethal staring contest, Raine drew her blades free. At the same time, she drew on her magic, bringing forth the same white flames that managed to push the Stealer back in their previous encounter.

Tendrils of white fire crept over the crouching monster. Silent and lethal, they grew in speed and strength, seeming to burn through the shadows making up the Stealer. Its' shriek was like nails scraping over metal. Yet as Raine watched, the creature shook its monstrous head, flinging the white flames off like water. Fear bit Raine hard. It was obvious the unnatural fire was not as detrimental here as it was in the spirit realm.

Options. She needed options because her odds of surviving a physical fight were pretty damn low. Her mind cycled furiously even as she maintained the tense staring contest. Last time, she hurt it by tearing apart its bond to Cheveyo. Souls fed the Stealer. Gave it energy. Was there some way to rip apart its ties to the souls it had consumed?

The Stealer shifted, revealing the crumpled form behind. Lizbeth was the key.

A solution burst into blinding clarity. No matter how many souls the Stealer consumed for strength, at its core, it was created by the strength of the summoner. If she could draw it onto the magical playing field, maybe she could tear apart the bindings between monster and creator.

The Stealer lunged.

Her cat, who was crouched in readiness, took over. She dodged, animal instincts pushing the thinking woman aside. She ran, the Stealer close behind. Flying over downed logs and twisting through the winter-bare forest, the image of a cat fleeing a wolf flashed through her mind. It wasn't until the image changed and showed a cat dropping from the trees on to the unsuspecting wolf's back, that she understood. The leopard needed control.

Using the opportunity her animal half offered, Raine surrendered her body to the leopard and stepped into the magical landscape. The scene changed. Now, she and her leopard ran side by side while the ever-changing image of the Stealer chased. Trusting the cat to keep them both ahead of the pursuing monster, Raine used her bond with Gavin to share her half-formed plan.

She found him frantically trying to repair the damage Lizbeth and the Stealer had inflicted on Xander. Until Vidis arrived, Gavin wouldn't be able to physically help Raine.

"Stay," she urged. *"I can do this."* She felt his frustration and worry even as he gave her everything she asked for.

"You come back alive." It was nothing less than a command.

Instead, of setting her teeth on edge, it wrapped around her heart like a warm mantle. *"I will."*

She and her leopard scrambled up an incline and dropped over the side. Her twin popped into existence as soon as they were out of the Stealer's line-of-sight. Thankfully Gavin was able to give her that much. While the Stealer would see only Raine in the physical world, if it decided to move the hunt to the psychic plane, her twin was a necessary diversion.

Raine peeled off, leaving her leopard with her doppelganger. She worked her way through the dense underbrush to hide behind a particularly thick tree trunk as her twin and leopard disappeared into the trees. The cloying wrongness of the Stealer flowed over her a moment later as it chased its prey.

Raine followed, keeping to the shadows and muting her magic as much as she dared.

Raine's leopard stopped under a huge tree, crouched, and sprang. The shock of shared pain echoed in Raine's fingertips as claws dug into the bark and dragged the leopard's body up. The animal managed to pull its entire body into the tree just as the Stealer skidded to a halt underneath.

Raine crept forward, worry surfacing. Although the Stealer tended to act like a wolf, there was no reason it couldn't follow the cat. As it continued to snap and snarl underneath the branch where the hissing leopard padded, she prayed her luck would hold.

Blades in hand, she made her way around the tree, circling to the left of the Stealer. Letting the physical world slip a bit more beneath the magical one, she concentrated on the undulating mass of black belonging to the Stealer.

As before, the darkness called to her, tantalizing whispers of vicious needs and brutal desires. Her barely repaired barriers broke under the onslaught, but instead of fighting it, she let it drag her deeper into the writhing mass.

Oily slickness crept over her skin, weighing her down. Images coalesced, spiraling like a demon-infested montage of the twisted path that could still be hers. Her thoughts began to warp as she was drawn deeper into the miasma of the Stealer's evil influence.

Twisted visions swamped her—Lizbeth, bloodied and eviscerated, her body a red ruin in a ruby pool spreading over the white blanket of snow. Tala, mouth open in silent screams, as bits and pieces of her body and magic were torn asunder. Cheveyo's spirit in tatters, his earth-toned energy nothing more than mere shreds, his skin stretched like some macabre Saran Wrap over his bones.

The last image triggered a response—a sharp scrape over her soul as the geas kicked in. It left her clawing to the surface of the vile tide. The wave of deadly possibilities pulled back, and she struggled to find her honor and humanity in the strange pause. Into that instant of quiet came the lifeline of Gavin's iron will, determination, and love. She grabbed hold, even as the next stygian wave pushed her under.

This time the images weren't possible options, they were past truths. A red-haired woman in a lab coat, her mind fragmented under the influence of the drug Raine pushed into her veins. The soul-chilling joy as the woman was reduced to a screaming, mindless creature. Whips of burning flames, claws tearing through skin, raking bone aside to tear into the soft muscles of a beating heart, while the demon-rimmed eyes of her best friend stared into hers. Screams of a woman crouched over a fallen man, lips tinged in blue as he struggled to drag in one more elusive breathe only to find...nothing. Walking away as silent, sociopathic satisfaction of a job well done filled her.

"You are mine—blood, mistakes, and all." Gavin's voice sank through bone and blood, through her spirit, until the words scored themselves on her soul. Their bond seared, yanking her from the nightmares of her past.

The wave receded, leaving her spirit battered and torn, but still whole. Gritting her teeth, she focused on her surroundings. Thick, twisted, dark ropes tangled around her. She never realized how many different shades of black existed. Here, in the depths of depravity at the heart of the Stealer, the energy was so nefarious, it seemed to swallow all hints of life. Even as the Stealer focused its foul attention on shredding her spirit, Raine held on, Gavin's strength and love giving her a small space to think.

The core of the Stealer was a tight ball of evil. The consumed souls nothing more than threads of black magic. She considered hacking her way through, but quickly dismissed the idea. As soon as she cut through a bond, it would reform, stronger than before. There was no differentiating the energy of each thread, no way to tell which ones belonged to Lizbeth. Which meant she had to find a way to destroy the entire core so it had no chance of recouping. Hopefully, the mass destruction would also destroy its ties to Lizbeth.

The darkness deepened, cutting off all sensation. Her vision tunneled until the core was barely discernible. Light —she needed light. White flames burst into being and the strangling magic loosened. Some bonds burnt to nothing, others retreated. But the flames weren't enough. It would take her too long to burn through the thick mass.

As the pinprick of returning physical sensations raced over her, the feel of something solid in her palms reminded her of the other weapons she still possessed. If her fire could burn the Stealer, how much more damage could she do if she combined her blades with the fire? Would it be enough?

There was only one way to find out.

She sent her magic into her two blades until they glowed white, then began carving a path to the center of the Stealer where the inky shadows undulated in a sickening ball. The mass retaliated, hundreds of twisted threads lacerating her skin, leaving bloody cuts of varying degrees behind. But pain could be ignored. She had years of practice. She sliced her way forward, hearing the screams of the Stealer as it realized the biggest threat wasn't the woman pacing above it, but the one cutting a path to its heart.

Raine brutally slashed another tie, burning it to ash, only to come face to face with her goal.

On the physical plane, the Stealer struck out and her leopard screamed. Searing agony tore through Raine, freezing her in mid-motion. Between one breath and the next, the agony snapped off and her arm continued, severing another thread. Vicious triumph flared under the exhaustion and slicing pain of hundreds of small cuts.

She raised a glowing blade determined to jab it as deep as she could, only to be knocked aside as if rammed by a frickin' truck. Her spirit was dragged back from the Stealer's heart and hurled into a familiar arena. The Stealer had abandoned its physical body for the psychic plane and was now focused solely on Raine.

Oh goody.

Needing the leopard's strength and cunning, she reached for her cat. There was no answer. Whatever the Stealer had done, it was bad. Or—a small part of her whispered—she was too deep in the magic for the leopard to find her.

Either way, she was truly on her own.

Putrid breath fell over her face, and she gagged at the acrid smell of rotten flesh. Crouched over her, the Stealer's massive head darted close. Using her knives, Raine slashed out, her blades the only thing keeping it from ripping her face off. Each time she slashed the burning weapon across the creature, it screamed, but it didn't let up.

Her left arm was trapped between her body and the Stealer. So she fought the massive jaws and jagged teeth back with sharp, deadly stings of the blade in her right hand. Locking her jaws, she shoved the knife between the Stealer's ribs.

White flames ripped through the monster. It shrieked and twisted, desperate to get away from the fire eating its way through its vulnerable underside.

As it reared back, Raine rolled out from underneath it, scrambling to her feet, both blades still dancing with flames. The Stealer turned its wounded side farther out of reach as they circled each other, both looking for a vital opening.

There would be no leaving until the Stealer was destroyed. She could continue to slice and dice, trying to take the creature apart piece by piece, but it would return the favor. She needed to do something drastic.

"There are those individuals who can see magic, and then there are those very rare individuals that can not only see magic, but change it." The words of the creepy ancestors came back.

After what she did to Tala's geas, there was no denying she could re-weave magic. Which meant there was nothing stopping her from undoing the magical weave of the Stealer. *Except for the small question of retaining your sanity and soul.* The irritating, internal voice was back, snottier than ever. Even as reason and loyalty warred, the geas added its two cents leaving her no choice.

CHAPTER 31

The Stealer snarled, its focus fixed and lethal. Raine gritted her teeth and lunged forward. Her sudden attack took it by surprise and its awkward paw swipe was easily blocked. It did what she wanted and reared back. Taking advantage of the move, she rammed her blade to the hilt in the Stealer's chest.

Its agonized howl made her ears bleed and she was unable to avoid the slashing paw as it raked deep gouges from shoulder to hip. It was harder than she expected to think past the burning agony of the attack. Still, neither her will, nor the geas, would let her retreat. She pushed deeper into the magic.

The Stealer's ebony bonds closed around her. The perverted intentions shaping its magic joined the sickening sense of creeping darkness and spilled across her soul like a foul tide. Frantically, she grabbed hold of the bonds. Terrified, she watched them melt into her. Black veins began snaking under her skin.

"Like calls to like." The insidious words raked over her.

There was no holding back her panicked scream of

horror. Her breathing turned ragged and she could do nothing but watch the inky trails spread faster and faster. Every beat of her heart pumped the sickness farther along. The malignant energy swallowed the silvery light of her magic, the color eaten away.

Unable to slow the psychic assault, she was forced back by the encroaching darkness until she stood before the last remaining barrier protecting her soul and the two men tied to her.

Helpless fury bloomed. She had bled for Cheveyo, dragged him back even when he didn't want to return. And Gavin. He was hers. There was no way in hell she would give him up without a fight. The protective fury built until it became blinding rage, sweeping the useless terror under.

This time she funneled her fury into a single-minded focus. Her palms lit with white fire and when she grasped the Stealer's warped magic, it struggled to get free. The strands of evil flailed against her hold. Its frantic movements left specks of red where they cut through her skin. She wrapped the foul magic around her hands. Tearing some ties while burning others, she began to uncover the faint colored remnants of the Stealer's victims. As each bond broke, she let the newly freed energy float away.

There was no sense of time passing. Her movements became repetitive as she worked. Here in the heart of blackness, there was no Raine. All that existed was the tapestry under her hands. These dark threads weren't right and shouldn't exist.

The massive knot of ebony began to unravel, revealing something deep inside. Her hands slowed and the roiling magic swarmed to hide its prize. But this was her tapestry and she chose the pattern, not it. Digging her fingers in, she began to rip the twisted, psychic fabric apart.

Stinging slashes teased the edges of her mind, but her focus was complete. She had to uncover what it was trying to hide. Urgency pushed her hands faster. The white flames edging her hands began to flicker up her arms. Each piece she touched shriveled and dropped away until the prize was laid bare.

Shock snapped her out of the strange hypnotic state. Every gash, every cut inflicted by the Stealer's magic hit in one brutal wave, sending her to her knees. It wasn't enough to stop her from stretching one trembling hand to the thin, flickering spirit huddled in the inky remains.

"Brett?" His name was a whisper of sound. She drew her hand back before she could touch him.

He raised his head, endlessly dark eyes staring out of a pale face. "Why won't she let me go?" The words were soft, but traces of the long ago child remained.

The remnants of the concealing magic pulsed along the fragments covering her hands. Memories crowded her. Memories belonging to the boy. All she could do was watch. And feel.

A sunny afternoon, feeling the power of the horse beneath him. Thoughts of a shy smile filled with love. The overwhelming mixture of joy and nerves at the realization of impending fatherhood. Then, like a snake hidden in the grass, something slithered across his nerves. The horse stumbled to a stop, prancing in place. Brett looked around, trying to find the source of discomfort, turning his horse in a wide circle. There—at the edge of the tree line, something flickered.

Deep inside Brett's memories, Raine cried out knowing it would change nothing.

He urged the reluctant horse forward a few more steps before it became a battle of wills—his and the horse's. He started to dismount, knowing that to push the horse any more could break the beast's mind. The milling shadows changed and suddenly the screams of chinidis raked across his skin. Fear turned his mouth to cotton, but even worse, the chindis's cries pushed the horse over the edge. As they swarmed forward, the horse reared. Caught in that awkward dismount position, Brett was thrown.

Slamming into the ground, the pain of his spine snapping shot white agony searing through him. The chindis swarmed his broken body. The pain of his damaged spine was nothing compared to the excruciating sensations as they tore into him, ripping him and his wolf apart. The ghostly predators feasted, glutting on his pain and terror. Piece by piece he was taken and his last thought sliced through Raine. He'd never see his baby or his mate again, and that broke him.

Caught in the rush of memories, her heart bled as Brett's spirit was mauled, but a furtive movement caught her attention. Struggling against Brett's agony, she saw a man, hands over his mouth as he watched the scene with horror. Doug Ransom. The horse's loud whinnies snapped his trance. He muttered something and the chindis reluctantly pulled away from the now still body of the boy to gather round their master. He backed away, with a few steps, turned, and ran.

Dark, deadly intent rushed over Raine as she watched the coward flee. But these were not her memories. These belonged to Brett, so she couldn't follow, couldn't punish. Which meant, if these were Brett's memories and he was dead, why was she still here?

As a soft rattle of breath emerged from the fallen boy, a

sickening feeling turned Raine's blood to ice. The chindis hadn't finished their feast. A wisp of Brett's spirit was trying to hold on. The next few moments lasted an eternity as she was forced to watch him struggle to survive.

Images blurred and a woman's screams cut across Raine's pain. Lizbeth fell to her knees cradling her son as her keening cries tore into the sunny afternoon like jagged knives. "No, no, no."

The echoes of a mother's breaking heart looped endlessly. Finally, Brett bowed to death's demands.

Released from his memories, Raine swallowed, reaching for her voice. "She loves you." It was hard to get the words pass the ache in her throat.

The huddled spirit didn't respond. Instead the cloying magic flickered, dragging her back in. She watched Lizbeth tighten a rope on the unconscious young woman lying at her feet. Firelight flickered off the edge of a blade, and the stench of black magic filled the small cavern. There was a faint rush of pain, love, and terror. What little was left of Brett's spirit struggled against the spell his mother cast. Betrayal and fury mixed with devastating anguish as he watched, helpless to save the life of the woman he loved and their unborn child. His mother made the ultimate sacrifice, a life, and perverted magic enveloped Brett. His rage and need for vengeance twisted and spiraled until all that was left was a nightmare. A monster who craved the blood, pain, and essence of souls. *Nomâhtsé'héōò Adanata* rose from the ashes.

The memories stopped.

Cold dread spread through Raine's bones. The pale face across from her twisted into something dark and tainted then, just as fast, smoothed into recognizable features. "That isn't love."

"No," she agreed softly.

"I loved once." His voice was flat.

She nodded. "Jenny."

"Jenny," he repeated his face brightening with a beautiful serenity.

The faint echo of feminine laughter drifted to Raine.

Brett unwound his arms from his legs and between one blink and the next he was crouched in front of her. Those endlessly dark eyes were unnerving, but she didn't back away. Even when that other, darker presence peeked from behind the boyish face. "She killed my Jenny so she could keep me here. She taught me to kill." He leaned forward until mere inches separated them. "I like it." The words were a feral hiss.

"Why?"

He pulled back, emotion draining away as she watched. "It chases the cold away."

Pity seeped around the edges of her mind. In trying to bring back her son, Lizbeth had unknowingly tortured his soul. Raine was certain the woman had no clue who really killed her son. If the grieving mother knew, she would have never been able to handle working with her son's murderer. Unfortunately, Raine wasn't sure there was much of that mother left anymore.

She reached out and gently stroked her hand over Brett's hair, knowing what needed to be done. "I can keep you warm, Brett, if you want." The solution would cost her something, but she was willing to pay the price to give this boy peace.

He tilted his head toward her, leaning into her gentle touch, eyes closed. "Please," he whispered.

As soon as the heart-rending plea passed his lips, she let the white fire of her magic flare into brilliant life. Not wanting to hurt him, she pushed hard and fast. She ignored the flailing tendrils of black trying to breach her magic and wrap back around the boy in her arms. The flames washed over the bowed head under her fingers. Her hands and arms turned luminescent as the flames grew and spread, eating through the bonds connecting Brett's spirit to Lizbeth's spell.

Unable to handle the searing light, she let her eyes close. She felt her magic burn through the last tie. The resulting silent explosion threw her back.

Brett was gone.

Raine wasn't sure how long she remained sprawled on the ground, her eyes closed as she relished the simple act of breathing. Little by little her numerous injuries began clamoring for attention. She groaned. As if waiting for that small acknowledgement, her mind added its concerns to the mix.

She couldn't stay here—wherever here was. Rolling to her side, she curled into a ball. She was deep in the magical plane, deeper even than when Gavin had pulled her out. Forcing her eyes open was akin to lifting a three-ton elephant—with an eyelash.

No clues to her current whereabouts were forthcoming from her current prone position. Gritting her teeth, she began the arduous task of getting her body upright. Her bloody palms pressed into the ground, and the bite of gravel on her already lacerated skin blended with her body's choir of pain.

It took forever and then some, but she finally sat up. Breathing through the lead-lined blanket of exhaustion, she pushed to her feet, and turned to find a never-ending wall rising just above her head. She recognized this from her lessons with Cheveyo. He made her come here once, explaining how everyone protected their core spirit in their own unique way. Just beyond this psychic representation lay her soul.

She had an overwhelming urge to make sure that what lay behind it remained untouched.

Swaying slightly, she searched for a way in. Some people, Cheveyo said, used elaborate mazes laced with deadly traps. Others had impenetrable fortresses, which would give some of the castles of old a run for their money. Whatever image the individual used, it was unique to them.

Her never-ending stone wall was made of smooth river rock. It looked as if there were plenty of nooks and crannies for finger and toeholds, but this was magic and just because something looked easy, didn't mean it was. There were numerous deadly traps laid within the stonework and along the ledge sitting high above her—every single one meant to discourage visitors. Carefully craning her neck, she made out the heavy canopy of trees cresting behind the wall.

Walking along the wall, she let her palm drift across its surface. Under her hand, the stone was absolutely smooth, like a sheet of metal. She continued to check for any weak points, relieved to find it as solid as ever. A small vibration under her touch revealed the presence of a well-camouflaged door. The vibration grew in strength as her bloodied hand moved closer. When it settled over the lock, the combination of her magic and blood melted the image away.

Stepping through the small archway, she faced the massive forest. She moved forward, only to stop and turn, remembering to seal the wall closed. But there was no opening, only a solid rock. Sighing at magic's capricious nature, she headed into the dense foliage. A small hunting trail curved its way through the woods. She followed it. She stopped once to look back, only to find no path, no wall, just endless forest behind her.

If anyone else managed to breach her protection, they wouldn't be so lucky to have a path to follow. It was keyed to her blood. Everyone else got to enjoy the various denizens she created as welcoming committees.

It wasn't long before she broke through the edge of the forest and stopped at the bank of a bubbling creek. On the other side was a small clearing where a cabin sat among the trees. She used the stepping-stones to make her way across. Once on the other side, she stepped on to the wide porch and looked around.

The scene was straight out of some story book. Should an attacker ever get past the protecting wall, the impenetrable forest, and its denizens, they would face this. The soothing babble of the creek which could turn into a ravine filled with raging floodwaters, and the grassy clearing could transform into a writhing pit of venomous snakes. Then there was the cabin. It might look harmless, but Amityville had nothing on it. It was her most lethal and final protection.

She pushed open the door and stepped inside, stumbling over to the simple wooden table where a single flower sat in a vase. Weary, she collapsed into one of the sturdy chairs. Her body cried out for rest, but she couldn't stop. She needed to ensure everything was okay before making her way back to her leopard and Gavin. Slumped in her chair, her eyes drifting closed, she undid the last of her locks on her magic.

There was a noticeable shift as her power settled. When she opened her eyes, the interior of her cabin was gone. Instead, she sat on a soft rug on the stone floor of a well-lit room. A multi-paned window allowed light to filter through various colors of glass, sending a warm rainbow of light across her face. The walls on either side of the window were draped in tapestries of various sizes.

Rising to her feet, she moved to one wall, where the tapestries fluttered, the flashes of color drawing her closer. Carefully, she lifted the edge of a banner and realized there were layers underneath. She let the tapestry slide back into place and studied the scene woven into the cloth lying on top.

Her fingers shook as she traced the image of a dark-haired woman and child, their hands clasped as they danced. Their laughter whispered against her. A feminine voice sang a child's nursery rhyme, the notes clear and beautiful. Painful recognition hit her as the sound of her mother's voice and her own answering childish laughter dragged the buried memory to light.

Stumbling back, Raine spun and staggered across the floor, only to be faced with another tapestry on the opposite wall. This one was dominated by darker colors, the weave rougher as if its creator had forced the pattern into the cloth. The images seared across her brain—images she didn't need a tapestry to remember—lab tables, blood, skin, and screams. Backing up, she forced her body to still as she stood between the two cloth covered walls of memories.

She could feel the heat from the light coming through the rainbow window behind her. It was almost a physical presence, wrapping around her, giving her waning strength a boost. It seeped through her, blurring the two opposing walls and helping her focus. Taking a deep breath, she looked at the last wall. An unfinished tapestry stared back.

Unlike the others, this one was created of living threads. There were no hands directing movement, but the undulating strings were made of familiar colors. Silver was tightly interwoven with blue. Together they created their own piece of fabric. Earth tones, lined with gold, touched the cloth and then moved away, leaving small patches of the picture behind. In some areas thin, black threads hung in tatters. In others, the dark color edged the holes the material was trying to repair.

The Stealer managed to hurt her more than she realized.

The tapestry was a mesmerizing creation. Somehow she knew it wouldn't be finished until she took her last breath. Still, it was strangely terrifying to see a physical manifestation of her every decision.

A flash of silver drew her eyes to a patch that was slowly unraveling. A detailed image of a leopard was beginning to fade. The Stealer inflicted lethal damage there. Blue threads tried to wrap around silver, but the silver thinned, becoming fragile. Gavin was trying to add his strength but it wasn't enough. His blue was split by the storms belonging to Xander.

They were all running out of time.

Raine was in too far and her ties to Gavin and her leopard apparently weren't going to survive. She reached out and brushed her fingers across their fragile bonds.

As if that was what it had been waiting for, the world spun and colors streamed around her. Too tired to fight, she let the magic take her. As she was dragged through an ever-shifting landscape, she tried to reach for Gavin or her leopard. The connections stayed out of reach. She found it ironic that she had destroyed the Stealer, set a child's soul free, but would still die because she couldn't get out of her own damn mind.

The relentlessly dragging magic waned and then abruptly stopped. Fighting the roiling nausea of her rebelling stomach, she found herself on her hands and knees. Her lungs sucked in air with painful gulps. Blinking away the white starbursts threatening to gray out her vision, she struggled to pull herself together. It took a full minute to get to her feet. Even then, she swayed as the ground refused to level.

Where the hell was she now?

She staggered forward, her stomach dropping as she took a step and fell into a free-fall. Arms pin wheeling, she tumbled into nothingness.

Her battered instincts flailed and the bright flare of a familiar silver thread sprang to life. She grabbed hold with both hands. As her fingers touched it, her body was yanked up and back. Red-hot pokers gouged out her eyes and the taste of blood filled her mouth. Both her and her leopard's screams broke free. When the stomach churning journey finished, wet sandpaper was dragged along her face.

Groaning, she lifted her heavy hand and batted away the uncomfortable sensation, only to have it growl at her. Blinking, she turned her head until her cheek pressed against the ground. As her eyes began to refocus, silver cat eyes set in black fur dominated her vision. She didn't want to lift her head. It weighed too much. So she drew her hand over the muzzle lying mere inches from her face.

"Hey, you."

Relief swam through her as she and her leopard reconnected, their bond snapping into place. A streaking burn ate across her ribs and down her hip, echoing the mark the Stealer had left on her leopard. The brush of its fur along her body had the pain receding along with the debilitating fear of losing her inner cat. It hadn't hit her how much she relied on the animal who made up her other half until she was faced with the possibility of never seeing it again. Little by little, strength seeped back in. Rumbling purrs vibrated the skull under her hand. The sound brought a small smile to her face.

"Since you're here, we must be getting closer, uh?" The leopard stayed silent, but managed to set its muzzle between Raine's chin and shoulder, nudging her. "Yeah, yeah—I'm moving."

There was no stifling her groan as she pushed to her hands and knees a-freakin'-gain. Using the leopard for balance, she got to her feet, swaying slightly.

Looking around, she recognized the surreal clearing where she and her leopard had separated. They weren't too far in, but it was going to be a bitch to get back. Everything hurt. Between the injuries she and her leopard had collected, her body would've done better facing off with a Mac truck.

"Okay, kitty mine," she muttered, tightening her fingers in the thick fur. "We have to get back and take care of Gavin and Xander."

An image of Lizbeth's snarling face filled her mind.

"Yeah, and her, too." She took a deep breath and gathered the remnants of her exhausted magic. "Let's finish this."

CHAPTER 32

Raine shifted out of the psychic realm and came to in a pain-filled huddle on the chilly winter ground of the physical world. Blood from numerous wounds decorated the snow-dusted ground. Using the trunks of the trees around her and gritting her teeth against the unrelenting complaints of her battered body, she managed to get herself upright. As she re-traced her path to where she left Lizbeth, she searched for her bond with Gavin. The tight bands around her chest loosened when she found it. Muted, but there. As drained as she was, it wasn't enough to stop her from reaching down the tie and brushing her spirit against his. When they connected, her sense of urgency increased as she realized why their connection was so one sided.

Gavin was losing the fight for Xander.

A sick feeling weakened her already shaky knees and she caught herself against a tree. Panting, she pushed away and set off faster than before. She didn't have much to give him, but that didn't matter. She kept her side of their bond wide open, letting him pull whatever he needed. They had to save Xander. She couldn't think about losing another friend. Not again.

Bursting into the space where she left Lizbeth, she was actually surprised to see the unconscious woman still there. The glint of sunlight sparked off the blade Raine had lost in the fight. Not taking her eyes off the prone figure, she went and picked it up.

Approaching cautiously, she checked Lizbeth's pulse. Still there. Okay, so that meant she couldn't leave the crazy woman here. *Simpler if she was dead*, the cold, practical part of her mind reminded her. Growling, she shoved the temptation away and tucked her blade into a sheath. Tugging and pulling, she got the limp woman in a rough fireman's carry.

A string of curses accompanied each step she took. Damn shifter weighed a ton.

"If you even twitch, I'm breaking your neck," Raine muttered, sweat running down her face, despite the cold air.

Her knees shook precariously as she passed through the edge of the forest. If she was a lesser person, she would've collapsed in tears at the sight of the cabin. Instead, she trudged on. The three steps up to the door were the toughest, but she finally made it.

Using her shoulder, she pushed the door in and managed a couple of shuffling steps before her legs gave out and she dropped to the floor. Lizbeth's dead weight slid off and she let the shifter's body tumble to the floor. Too tired to even contemplate walking, she crawled toward the far side where Gavin sat, his back to the wall, eyes closed, and a fragile figure cradled in his arms. Even as she made her way across the room, she could feel the press of magic as he worked over Xander.

When she reached them, she stopped, unwilling to break his concentration. The strain of using so much magic had thinned his face, stretching his skin tight over his bones' sharp angles. It worried her, but she had faith he knew his own limits.

Xander looked bad. Although a petite woman, her personality always made her seem stronger than her physical appearance. Her time with the Stealer stole that from her. Now she looked as if a stiff wind would shatter her into a million pieces. The delicate tattoos on her face stood out starkly against the unnatural pallor of her skin. Cuts and bruises marred her face and arms. Her clothes were torn and shredded in places. Raine knew Xander would hate the analogy, but Raine thought she looked like a battered fairy.

Her heart clenched and she covered Gavin's hand curled around Xander's shoulder. As her skin touched his, his eyes snapped open to lock onto hers. Some small tension seemed to ease when he saw her.

"You look like hell, baby," he murmured, his voice low and rough.

"You're not doing much better," she shot back.

His attention dropped to Xander and lines around his mouth deepened. "I don't know how much longer I can hold her."

Before she could reply, the door to the cabin slammed open. Instinct sent her spinning around on her knees, knife in hand, as she came to a crouch in front of Gavin and Xander.

Framed in the doorway stood Warrick Vidis, Northwest Alpha of the Motoki Pack. Considering the absence of his normal calm demeanor, she had no intention of putting her weapon away. Standing six-feet tall, in jeans and a T-shirt, most people wouldn't understand why a seemingly average-looking guy could make them do whatever he wanted. Last time Raine saw him, she delivered a traitorous human scientist as payment for the death of his pack-mate and fellow Wraith, Chet. The scientist was later identified by dental records.

A rumbling growl filled the small room of the cabin. The volume increased as Vidis's gaze locked onto the woman in Gavin's arms. There was no mistaking the threat, even if you were blind to the burning gold stare of the wolf set in a human face. Or the fact that his body was poised to attack. No matter how possessive the alpha wolf was of Xander, Raine and her leopard were no less possessive of the man trying to heal her. Leopard and woman snarled in unison, their warning unmistakable.

Vidis stopped just out of reach, turning his inhuman gaze to her, his lips curled back from his human teeth in a distinctly canine expression. Worried that the man was lost under the wolf, she kept her blade up and made her voice sound like quiet steel. "Vidis, we need you here."

It took a breathless moment before the roiling energy of the shifter began to recede. His lips uncurled and some of the stiffness left his body. Slowly, he reined in his wolf.

Raine kept silent, not moving from her protective position. She wasn't a fool. Among the Northwest Kyn it was common knowledge that Vidis and his wolf walked a thinner line than most about who was in control. It was pretty obvious his legendary control was currently shot to hell.

"How bad?" The words were more growl than speech, but at least they were understandable.

"We aren't going to be able to hold her for long."

His fists clenched and his mouth thinned. "I'll take her."

He closed the distance to brush past Raine and kneel in front of Gavin. A visible shudder shook him as he pulled Xander into his arms. As the tingly sensation of shifter magic rose, Raine felt the increase of Gavin's pull on their bond. He and Vidis were combining their healing magic.

Pushing to her feet she half-turned toward Gavin and Vidis when a male's harsh cry broke through the room. "Lizbeth!"

Snapping back around, she brought her knife up as Tomás Chavez fell to his knees next to his wife. His cry changed to a howl. Things were about to go south fast. As his howls faded away and he cradled his mate, Raine didn't dare look away from him.

"What did you do?"

His wolf was so close to the surface Raine almost couldn't make out his words.

"She's alive."

He snarled, the animal surging forward under his skin as he gathered the limp form closer. "She's weak. Something's wrong."

"I broke her ties to the Stealer."

Tomás's eyes widened, fury twisting his features into an ugly mask. "You lie."

Not bothering to answer, she stayed focused on the enraged wolf, concentrating on the coiled body, watching for telltale muscle movements indicating an attack.

A sharp scrape against her magic left her dragging in air through gritted teeth. *"Damn it, Gavin that hurt!"* Even as she uttered the reprimand, she widened her side of their link, giving him unfettered access. The scrape morphed into a constant pull. Uncomfortable, but bearable.

Lizbeth's low groan heralded her return to the land of awareness and ratcheted Raine's tension up another level.

One weakened Wraith against two crazed werewolves was not good odds. Thanks to her earlier confrontation with the Stealer and Gavin's drain on her magic, she couldn't even bring her leopard out to play.

Lizbeth's lashes fluttered open. Tomás curled her closer, lowering his shoulders over her. He didn't take his attention from Raine. "Lizbeth?"

His only answer was another low moan. Even around Tomás' stocky body, Raine could see the stunned panic replacing the confusion clouding Lizbeth's face. She began to thrash in her mate's arms.

"Let me go! Where is he?" Even with one arm obviously broken, Lizbeth twisted and clawed her way free. She rolled to her knees, cradling her wounded arm. Seeing Raine, she gave a shriek of fury and hate. "Bitch! It's your fault!" Unmindful of her body's injuries, she hurled herself forward, her lethal intent obvious.

Raine stepped back, bracing for an impact that never came. Moving with the lightning speed of shifters, Tomás caught his wife in mid-leap. Even as she clawed his arms, leaving his skin in bloody strips, he held her captive, dragging her back.

"Where's my son?" There was nothing left of the composed woman Raine met days earlier. Her face was a warped mask of hate, her light tan replaced by a sickly pallor, while blood and mud mixed in a gory spatter across her torn clothes.

"Lizzy, love," crooned Tomás in a fruitless attempt to reach the woman in his arms. "Brett's dead."

"No! I brought him back!" She stilled, her bloody fingers digging into her husband's shredded arm wrapped around her waist. "He was here." The words were a hiss. "She took him!"

Tomás arms loosened with shock as Lizbeth's words sank in. It was all she needed. She sprang out of his arms and straight at Raine.

Not willing to let the crazy werewolf bitch near Gavin and Vidis as they worked to heal Xander, Raine lunged to meet her. She underestimated Lizbeth's ability to ignore her injuries, because at the last moment, the woman struck out and slammed a solid punch into Raine's collarbone just below her right shoulder. The flash of pain was swallowed under the wave of numbness that sent her knife tumbling to the floor.

Unarmed, she twisted away, but Lizbeth's hands curled around her throat, nails digging deep as she began to squeeze. Unable to use her right arm, Raine's left arm came up and swept over Lizbeth's arms, trapping them. Twisting her body, Raine bore down on Lizbeth's weak arm and yanked the enraged shifter off balance. The hands at her neck lost their grip, allowing her to suck in a lungful of air. Ignoring the screams from her abused ribs, she straightened her arm and wrapped her hand around the back of Lizbeth's head, pulling her down and forward. Lizbeth's skull met Raine's knee with a sickening crunch.

Tomás's, "Lizbeth!" and Gavin's, "Raine!" fell on top of each other. Raine stepped carefully around the now sobbing Lizbeth, pins and needles skating down her arm as the feeling crept back. The urge to kick the werewolf while she was down rode Raine hard, but Gavin's voice held her back. Sickening anger and resentment churned with pity as she kept her attention on Lizbeth.

Flashes of Brett's tortured memories wiped away the beginnings of any pity with a sheet of ice. Kneeling, she wrapped the matted hair in her fist and pulled Lizbeth's head back. She jerked the woman to her knees. "Why'd you do it?"

Hands clawed at Raine's skin. "Do what?"

"Why did you turn your son into a monster?"

Cunning intelligence peeked out behind the grieving mother. And something else, something twisted. "He was mine! Mine to protect!"

"Protect?" Raine didn't bother hiding her scathing disbelief. "Is that what you were doing when you killed Jenny? When you sacrificed the woman your son loved and the child she carried? When you fed their souls to the Stealer?" Leaning closer, she ignored Lizbeth's flinch. "Is that what you were doing when you teamed up with the man who killed your son?"

The urge to snap Lizbeth's neck sent tremors through Raine's body. Mothers were supposed to protect their children, not torture them. Her hand tightened.

For a moment, confusion stilled Lizbeth's clawing hands and smoothed out the twisted face. "What are you talking about?"

"Doug Ransom killed your son." Cold and cutting, Raine slashed Lizbeth with the truth. "He wanted the land you and the Magi House held. He was in the middle of raising his pack of chindis when Brett stumbled on to him. Ransom set his pets loose on your son after Brett's horse threw him." Leaning close, she let all her disgust and sick fury echo in her words. "And instead of protecting your son, you taught him to kill. You didn't avenge his death, instead you teamed up with his killer."

Lizbeth's anguished wail filled the small cabin.

Yanking her hand out of Lizbeth's hair, Raine stumbled back. She needed space or she would do something she wouldn't be able to take back. Spotting her blade she turned to pick it up. Before she could, two things happened simultaneously.

A sudden, sharp pull on her waning magic doubled her over. Then she found herself on the wrong end of a battering ram. Growls, fur, and shredding claws wiped the cabin and its occupants away in a brutal swipe.

Somehow her inner cat came to her rescue. Curving her body and bending it in a purely feline move, it wrenched vulnerable body parts out of the line of fire. Arms that had been fending off the sharp canines and thick claws of a maddened werewolf were now covered in dense black fur, tipped with deadly, curved nails. The pain of her shift was lost amidst the adrenaline and the accumulation of earlier wounds.

At Raine's change, Lizbeth's wolf lost its earlier advantage. The two animals, leopard and werewolf, circled each other. Threatening rumbles trickled from the wolf, while the cat remained eerily silent. Deep inside, Raine could still feel the steady drain on her magic, but using her bond with Gavin wasn't an option thanks to her fading magic and the pissed off bitch in front of her.

In wolf form, Lizbeth was larger than a normal wolf. Deep reddish-brown fur was flecked with black. The cunning human intelligence radiating in the wolf's eyes was strangely disconcerting. It didn't help that Lizbeth's grief and madness was etched through the amber orbs like cracked lightning. Unlike Raine and her leopard, who were still trying to figure out how to work as a unit, Lizbeth and her wolf faced no such problems.

Considering she was fighting a calculatingly insane werewolf, Raine knew her best bet lay with her cat. Pulling her rational mind back, she urged her leopard forward. The cat stopped moving, which skyrocketed Raine's pulse.

Stopping and waiting for Lizbeth to attack wasn't smart. Her cat disagreed. Gritting her mental teeth, she squashed her instinctive need to move.

The cat lowered on its haunches. Power built in the coiled muscles of its hindquarters. Claws curled deep into the wooden floor. Whiskers noted the minute changes in the air. The tip of its tail twitched. Once. Twice. Its lips curled back in a silent snarl. Its gaze locked onto the angry wolf, its focus lethal and complete.

A small shift of the wolf's stance, and some elemental signal only the cat understood snapped the deadly standoff into furious motion. As the leopard sprang forward, the wolf went in low, the intent to cripple obvious. The snapping jaws missed their mark by a fraction as the cat's flexible spine twisted the unprotected stomach out of reach.

Raine felt the heat of the wolf's breath ruffle her fur. Deep inside her cat, she shivered. Dear gods, Lizbeth may be nuts, but she was damn fast.

Lizbeth's claws scrambled for purchase against the wooden floor. Finding traction, she spun around.

Raine's cat drew in a lungful of air, dragging in the metallic bite of blood just before Lizbeth crashed into her. The cat's need to kill coated everything in a confusing kaleidoscope of fur, teeth, and claws leaving Raine holding on for the ride.

The bite of claws finding tender skin and muscles under fur blended into a continuous ache. She was distantly amazed at the singular focus her cat displayed. Numerous injuries piled up on both sides. The pain was ignored, but the blood loss became a different matter. Even her cat's indomitable will couldn't offset the weakness creeping in. They needed to finish this, quickly.

While the two animals fought, Raine studied her opponent's moves and the cat's responses. It was an instinctive practice that saved her hide more than once as a Wraith.

Much like her cat, she blocked out the shock of each new injury Lizbeth managed to score, looking for that one crucial opening. As Lizbeth's wolf slipped in a puddle of blood, she found it. Acting as one, she and her cat attacked. Using Lizbeth's momentary loss of balance and the cat's own body mass, it slammed into the wolf, sending Lizbeth onto her back. Ignoring the flailing claws tearing down the feline's sides and the hind claws desperately trying to find purchase in the cat's tender belly, the cat locked its teeth over the wolf's throat.

Lizbeth's frantic struggles began to fade. Both the leopard and Raine knew it was a matter of moments before their kill was assured. The maddened amber light began to flicker and fade.

Locked on her kill, a savage snarl and a man's shout snared both the cat and Raine's attention. Something darted past them. Not daring to release its prey, the cat kept its jaws locked and began dragging the heavy werewolf across the floor. Crouched over its kill, it took a minute for Raine to comprehend the scene in front of her.

Gavin partially blocked her view, but she could see a large black wolf standing stiff legged, teeth bared, deadly intent oh so clear, at the other end of Gavin's unwavering blade. As the last breath stuttered out of the wolf in the cat's jaws, it didn't drop its gaze from the one held at bay.

"Tomás, Lizbeth attacked first."

Raine couldn't see Gavin's face, but the utter ruthlessness in his tone was sharper than the gleaming edge of his weapon.

As Lizbeth's body went limp, Tomás lunged forward. Gavin must expected the move, because he lifted his blade before the Southwest Alpha could slit his throat, and instead body checked the animal. Both man and wolf hit the floor in a tangle of limbs.

Raine's leopard released Lizbeth's throat and lunged forward, the need to help and protect Gavin uppermost in the minds of both the woman and the cat. Thanks to their numerous injuries and the blood-strewn floor, her lunge turned into a pitiful tumble. It took precious seconds to find her footing.

"Stop!" There was only a few feet between her and the struggling duo when Vidis's order fell over the room like a weighted blanket, turning the air into a heavy mass. There was no escaping the pressure. Raine felt the cat's muscles tremble as she struggled to reach Gavin. Her need to protect raged against Vidis's edict. She managed another foot before her body collapsed to the floor under the weight of his command.

She wasn't the only one fighting against the press of Vidis's directive. Tomás's wolf was having more success than Raine's cat, but not by much. His movements slowed and there was no doubting Tomás was now fighting both the weight of Vidis's alpha command and still trying to get past Gavin. A flash of claw had Gavin spinning away. As he and Tomás slowly circled each other, the red ribbons etched along his cheek forced both Raine and her cat another foot closer.

"I said, 'Stop.'"

Her stiff progress came to a screeching halt as Vidis's low growl rumbled from behind her. She wasn't the only one. Tomás froze in place. If the increasing volume of his growls and the depth of retribution turning those eyes into pits of flaming gold was anything to go by, the Southwest Alpha was more than willing to tear through Gavin, Raine, and Vidis. In no particular order. There was no one rational behind the wheel.

The alpha's pressure was so strong, her cat couldn't even twitch its tail. It didn't silence the leopard's low, vibrating rumbles of displeasure, though. Neither she nor her cat were thrilled with Vidis right now. His command left her no way of protecting him or Gavin should Tomás manage to break through the order.

Since Tomás's attention was focused behind her, he must have finally figured out who was the bigger threat in the room. The sound of cloth rubbing against cloth and a quiet shush of something being carefully lowered to the floor, meant Vidis was setting Xander down. There was a change in the air. Raine hoped Vidis was only standing up and not shifting. She didn't want to be stuck like a frozen "dog treat" between two pissed off alpha werewolves.

As a pair of jeans-clad legs came into view at the edge of her vision, she felt a little of her tension fade. Vidis moved in front of her. Gavin took advantage of Tomás's inattention. He had the wolf down on the ground, using Tomás's spine to shield his own stomach and other vulnerable parts. The speed of his move was so quick it left Tomás no chance to react. Gavin managed to snake his arms around the wolf's neck in a chokehold, tucking his head down, covering Gavin's last weak point, his throat. Using his body weight and the pressure of his hold, he kept Tomás's snarling jaws and twisting body under control. A warm spark of pride bloomed inside Raine. This cunningly intelligent warrior was all hers. Inside the cat, she grinned.

Vidis stalked—there was no other word for it—toward the now immobile wolf and the warrior wrapped in a deadly embrace. When he slowly lowered into a crouch in front of Tomás, Raine realized Vidis didn't need to physically change to make his position clear. From the aura of dominance bleeding off of him to the ripple of the animal under the human skin, he was an alpha even in human form.

Ignoring both the cat plastered to the floor and the man wrapped around the wolf, Vidis pushed his face close. Too close, as far as Raine was concerned. One little slip in Gavin's hold and Tomás wouldn't have to go far to rip Vidis's face off.

"Your mate is dead." Vidis's words hit with destructive accuracy. The feral anger in Tomás's eyes flickered. "She meant to kill Raine. Unless you plan on challenging me, you better pull your wolf back."

The wolf's struggles stilled, but Raine was glad to see Gavin didn't relax his hold in any way. A tense moment passed. The burn of magic vibrated through the room. A shower of sparks and a minute later, Gavin was shifting his hold to accommodate the smaller neck of Tomás's human form.

"Let go, Gavin." Although the tone was gentle, there was no hiding the core of steel in Vidis's words.

Slowly, reluctantly, Gavin unwound from the now naked man. Each movement slow, testing Tomás's control and intentions. His arm was the last to go and as it dropped away, Tomás rolled to his feet keeping Gavin and Vidis in sight.

The restraining pressure of Vidis's earlier command lessened. As the weight dissipated, Raine and her cat didn't wait for an invitation but darted across the floor to Gavin. As he pushed his body up to a sitting position, she delicately bumped his chin so she could see his wounds. Getting a grumpy male look, she curled her lip. She wasn't backing down till he showed her. Grimacing he gave in, letting her see that the scratches were just that, scratches. They were already healing.

Mollified she put her body between Tomás and the other two males. There was no escaping the hatred directed toward her as she and Tomás faced off. She couldn't blame him. If it was Gavin's lifeless body on the floor, not even the gods themselves could have stopped her from tearing apart his killer.

"That bitch provoked my Lizbeth," Tomás snarled.

Behind her, she felt the displacement of the air as Vidis rose to his feet. "She only stated the truth." There was nothing confrontational in his tone. It was a simple statement of fact.

Raine's unblinking stare was broken when Vidis lightly pushed her out of his way. Twisting her head around to snap at him, she was startled by her cat's hissed warning to let it go.

"Lizbeth didn't kill our son." Denial, grief, anger, all that and more was wrapped up in those five words.

"No, she didn't," Gavin said. "But she did team up with the one who did."

"She wouldn't do that," he argued.

"She's a mother," Gavin stated. "She would do whatever she needed to avenge her son." There was no arguing the obvious truth.

Tomás dropped his gaze briefly and caught sight of Lizbeth's now human, but motionless body. Heartbreak and the beginnings of acceptance tightened the skin around his eyes as his lips pressed tightly together.

"It was so hard." His voice was soft, as if he were trying

to rationalize his wife's actions. He moved toward her body. "When we lost Brett, it almost broke her."

Raine was certain there was no "almost" about it. It had broken Lizbeth.

"For a while, I worried she wouldn't make it." He gathered Lizbeth into his arms and held her close to his chest. "She was so angry. You couldn't mention Jenny without setting her off. She needed someone to blame." Those workman hands smoothed Lizbeth's hair from her face. The love in the small action shot an ache through Raine's heart. "Then shortly after the funeral, she seemed to find her way back. Little by little, she became my Lizzy again."

"She's your mate, Tomás," Vidis said. "How did you miss this?"

A ruddy flush worked its way over Tomás's face. "We were mated, not bonded." He looked up at Vidis. "You and I both know how rare bonded couples are. We loved each other. It was enough."

Raine really wished she had enough energy to change back, because there were questions she wanted answered. Like what the hell was the difference between bonded and mated? She'd have to remember to ask Vidis about it later.

Vidis studied Tomás. "She used black magic. You had to have known."

"I didn't!" Tomás snarled.

There was a flicker of guilt quickly hidden under the angry denial. Raine would bet money he caught some hint but had chosen to ignore it.

Strangely, Vidis didn't push the point. Instead he cocked his head and asked, "Are we through or do you want to issue a challenge?"

Tomás's lips curled back from his teeth and his wolf

came dangerously close to breaking through. "No, we're through."

Rising with the fluidity inherent to shifters, he cradled Lizbeth's limp body in his arms.

As he moved forward, Vidis turned, allowing him to pass. Raine didn't need Gavin's brief touch on her head to step back. At the door, Tomás stopped. Without turning around, he said, "You have forty-eight hours to leave my territory, Warrick. If you're still here after that, I'll consider it a challenge to my authority."

He left without waiting for a response.

CHAPTER 33

WITH TOMÁS'S DEPARTURE THE TENSION IN THE CABIN DROPPED. Vidis didn't even seem fazed by the parting threat. Instead, he crossed the cabin and went to Xander's side.

"Change back." Vidis tossed the order at Raine as he gathered Xander in his arms.

She growled. If she could have, she would have changed back a hell of a lot earlier.

Rising to his feet, his arms full of unconscious woman, Vidis met her frustrated stare. He gave a small sigh and before she could brace herself, the agonizing wrench of bones realigning and skin replacing fur roared over her.

When the sickening pain lessened, she was huddled on the floor, hoarse curses tumbling from her lips. "Damn it, that fucking hurt!"

"Don't whine." Vidis stepped past her. "We need to get to Tala's. I can't do much more for Xander here." He headed out the door.

Beside her, Gavin pulled off his T-shirt. The unexpected move cut off her biting retort.

"Can you walk?" He crouched next to her. Up close she

could see the various scratches Tomás scored. She reached out to trace one of the worst curling from his upper chest and down along his ribs to his back.

"Are you okay?" she asked in a husky voice.

"I'm fine." He caught her hand and moved it away then coaxed her arms into his T-shirt. "Not that I don't enjoy the view, but let's get you dressed." As the soft material fell over her, the clean, woodsy scent belonging exclusively to him surrounded her, dulling the painful edges of her many injuries.

She rose to her feet and didn't argue with the arm wrapped around her waist, grateful for the added support. Together they gathered their weapons. She handed him her blades as she had nowhere to put them.

Stepping out on to the rickety porch she caught sight of Vidis making his way through the trees as he headed back to the ranch. The cold wood pressed against her feet. "Wish he had left me alone," she muttered.

Gavin cocked an eyebrow.

She wiggled her toes. "Bare feet, no fur, it's going to be a hell of a trip."

He chuckled. "Buck up, buttercup. You've survived worse."

There was no arguing that one. Together they trailed behind Vidis. It didn't take as long as she thought before they emerged onto Tomás's ranch. There was no sign of anyone. Even the horses in the barn were quiet. She gave a brief thought to Carlos, hoping he made it back. Which reminded her. "Where's Andrew?"

Gavin shrugged. But she'd forgotten about how sharp shifter hearing could be.

"At the airstrip," Vidis answered as he reached the car.

He opened the back door and carefully got in without dropping Xander.

Gavin opened the passenger door and helped Raine get settled, before coming around to the driver's side. A few moments later they were backing out of the gravel driveway. Once on the road to Tala's, Raine twisted in her seat until she could see Vidis and Xander.

Her friend's face was so pale, it was almost gray. "Is she going to be okay?" There was no way to hide the worry in her voice.

"She'll be fine," Vidis answered, as if his grim determination was all that the small woman in his arms needed.

Raine could still feel the dragging pull on her magic. Sighing, she turned back, sinking into the seat. Even the feel of warm fingers brushing delicately above her knee couldn't force her heavy lids open. She tangled her fingers with Gavin's.

The Stealer was gone, but things weren't finished. Worry about what would face her at Tala's gnawed at her. Raine didn't have the energy to even attempt opening the door between her and Cheveyo. Part of her hoped the missing pieces of his magic were back, but another, darker part, hoped not. If Cheveyo returned to full strength, would he be able to detect the change in their bond? Would he be able to sense what Gavin had done? If he did, what would it mean for her and Gavin? She stopped her paranoid thoughts before they dragged her too far down a dark road.

Instead, she focused on her bond with Gavin. It didn't take much to step out onto the magical plane and study their connection. The more she studied, the clearer the picture became. There was no doubt she and Gavin were now intrinsically joined. Their magic was so interwoven that trying to untangle one from the other would cause irreparable damage. Instead of the expected fear and resentment, she felt...complete and whole. Gavin knew her —warts and all—and he was still there.

A small, vile worm wiggled in her thoughts. Had he deliberately manipulated her into this bond? Before she could stop herself, it squirmed down their bond. The quiet chuckle that echoed back startled her.

"You think I didn't know you'd doubt me?"

"You did this on purpose?"

His fingers tightened on her knee. *"Would you have let me in otherwise?"* They both knew the answer. *"Do you want out?"* There was no inflection in his question, revealing how important her answer was to him.

She didn't hesitate. *"No,"* she said, reveling in his instant relief.

The remainder of the ride passed in silence. By the time they pulled into Tala's drive, most of Raine's lesser wounds were well on their way to healing. Yet a few more serious injuries still lurked. She'd have to deal with them later. First Xander, then Cheveyo. Dragging her eyes open, she watched Gavin cross in front of the car. The door to Tala's cabin flew open and the witch herself appeared in the doorway, her expression giving nothing away. Raine's tension returned.

Vidis got out of the car as Gavin came around to help her. As they climbed the steps to the door, Tala stepped to the side, allowing them entry. The front room hadn't changed since this morning. Furniture remained pushed against the walls. Cheveyo lay on a pallet on the floor. Next to him, Ash leapt to his feet, his focus on Vidis as the shifter set Xander on the couch.

Raine checked Cheveyo over, hoping to see a change. Maybe it was just her, but his color seemed better.

"You killed the Stealer." Tala's voice cut through her thoughts.

"Wouldn't be here if I hadn't." Her resentment sounded loud and clear. She wasn't about to forget the geas this witch set on her.

Keeping Gavin between them, Tala moved to Cheveyo's side. "Figured you're too damn stubborn to die."

Her careless disregard made Raine grit her teeth. Only Gavin's restraining grip on her wrist stopped her from lunging at the arrogant witch.

"Cheveyo?" Gavin's question cut through the angry tension between the two women.

Tala's face softened slightly. "Better." She lifted her chin and met Raine's mutinous glare. "Thank you."

The tightening of Gavin's fingers had Raine rethinking her response. Instead of egging the witch on, she muttered, "Welcome."

There was an awkward pause, then Tala asked, "Nati?"

"Dead," Gavin answered.

Tala's lips thinned. "She raised it?"

"No." This time it was Vidis who answered. "That would be Lizbeth Chavez."

Shock raced across Tala's face. "Lizbeth? But...but why?"

"She wanted her son back," Raine said. Tala blinked at her, confusion evident. Raine decided to explain. "Brett was thrown from his horse when he ran across Ransom and his pet Chindis. Seemed Ransom decided to use a different route to get your land. If he could play one House against the other, then he could turn the monsters against each other and get the land he wanted."

"Ransom raised the chindis?" Tala repeated, obviously trying to follow along.

"You don't need to be Kyn to make a spell work," Gavin cut in. "Ransom panicked when Brett stumbled into the middle of his little plan, so Ransom had his chindis tear the boy apart."

"But he stopped them before they could finish," Raine added.

Horror washed over Tala's face, as she collapsed next to Cheveyo.

"Unfortunately, Lizbeth needed someone to blame for her son's supposed accident," Raine kept going. "So she focused on the one person who dared to step between her and Brett."

"Jenny," Tala breathed.

Raine nodded. Using Gavin's arm, she slid to the floor. Her legs were shaking. Gavin settled beside her and they continued the story.

"Lizbeth studied under Rio at one time," Gavin said. "She approached him about raising a Soul Stealer. Just like Jenny did."

Tala shook her head, tears swimming in her eyes. "Jenny wouldn't do that. She wouldn't use black magic."

"She would if she thought it would bring Brett back," Raine countered. "Instead, Lizbeth did it first."

The fingers absently brushing Cheveyo's hair trembled as Tala dropped her gaze. "She used Jenny to fuel the spell?"

"And the unborn baby." Raine kept her voice gentle. It was apparent how much the truth was tearing Tala apart. Jenny had been her family. The Chavezes may not have been close friends, but the depth of their betrayal was leaving deep gouges. Only time would tell if the Southwest

Kyn would manage to come back from such a vicious division.

"Why would Lizbeth team up with Ransom?" Tala asked before comprehension dawned. "She didn't know."

Gavin nodded. "She had no idea Ransom killed Brett. Instead, she jumped at the chance to destroy your House. Jenny belonged to you, Brett belonged to her. Therefore, you had to pay. This way she could get her revenge, but everyone would suspect Ransom."

"Lizbeth didn't expect you to call in help," Raine said.

Tala's lips twisted into a grimace. "So it's my fault Cheveyo got hurt."

"No." Raine shook her head, strangely wanting to reassure the woman. "That's solely on Lizbeth."

"Where's Lizbeth now?" Tala asked.

"Dead." Vidis's answer turned all heads to him.

Tala's fingers stilled as she studied the man cradling Xander. "And Tomás?"

He shrugged. "Alive."

Her head tilted. "If his mate is dead, how is he still breathing?"

"They weren't bonded."

"Which reminds me," Raine interrupted. "What does that mean?"

Tala and Vidis continued their strange staring contest for a moment longer. Then Tala gave a short jerk of her head and looked away first. Apparently satisfied, Vidis turned to Raine.

"There are two kinds of joining for shifters," he explained. "A mating is the most common. It is a connection created by deep emotional ties between two shifters."

"So what?" Raine asked. "Instead of getting hitched, shifters mate?"

Vidis nodded. "The second is rare, but much more permanent. It's bonding. It is a connection on the soul level. When a bond manifests, the couple become one."

"One what?" Bonding sounded suspiciously close to what she and Gavin shared.

"One soul." Vidis's too-knowing gaze landed on her. "If one partner should die, the other follows."

Raine swallowed, trying to ignore the leaden pit in her stomach. "So why weren't Tomás and Lizbeth bonded?"

Vidis's smile was all teeth. "You don't choose to bond, it chooses you." Xander gave a soft groan, snagging his attention. "I need to finish healing her."

Tala was suddenly beside him. Magic rose in a ruffling wave and that fast Raine was swept back to the psychic plane. Unprepared, she reached for Gavin on both planes. As her hands wrapped around his, their tie flared to brilliant life and she held on. Huddled on the floor, she felt Gavin gather her into his lap. Letting her head fall against his chest, she focused on his steady heartbeat to help her stay above the magic.

It was tough keeping her mind in both realms at once. Tala's form became etched in gold as she began to work over Xander's spirit. The storm-colored magic waxed and waned under the witch's hands.

Raine could see the holes the Stealer left behind in Xander's aura. The gaping cavities were closing, but it was too slow. Xander was too weak to help and her grip was slipping. Panic crept in. *"Gavin, what can we do?"*

"I don't know."

Before Raine could react, Tala turned to her and, from

the white film over her eyes, Raine knew the multi-tonal chorus was back in the driver's seat. "Weaver, you must fix the tapestry."

Fear spiked. Raine didn't want to mess with Xander's tapestry. Every time she heeded the creepy chorus, things changed. And not for the better either. "I can't." The denial came out choked.

"You will." The steely strength of Vidis's command snapped her out of the blind panic. He was still connected to her and Gavin.

"I'm here." Gavin's quiet words allowed her to find her metaphysical feet.

Trying not to acknowledge the growing dread that they were fighting a losing battle, she blocked out the creepy chorus along with Vidis's expectations. Instead, she narrowed her focus to the magic wrapped around Xander's spirit.

She found Vidis, his unearthly amber fire curling around Xander's small body. As Xander's spirit flickered in his arms, he gave a low hair-raising growl. "Not a chance in hell, pixie girl."

The depth of feeling behind the alpha's snarled command made Raine hesitate. Distant warning bells pealed, but she ignored them. Clearing her mind, she began repairing the damage in Xander's energy. Again time lost its meaning as she delicately rewove the magic, closing the holes. As the gaps began to disappear, she noticed the color she used for the repairs was off. Xander's storm-ravaged purples now held flickering amber flames of lightning.

Her fingers stumbled to a stop. *What had she done?* Worry hit like a tsunami. She reached for Gavin, needing his reassurance. But before she could find him, a scorching torrent of energy tore through her. It whipped through the bond she and Gavin shared, the strength of the invasion bowing her back into an arch, her head thrown back, her mouth opened in a soundless scream. She was barely aware of Gavin's frantic struggle to keep her in his arms as his body jerked with the impact.

As power poured through them and down into Xander, a distant part of her knew Vidis was the source of the influx. Using his tie with Gavin and Raine, he directed the heat and fire toward Xander's spirit. His amber flames encircled Xander's purple storms. Flashes of lightning sparked then settled. There was a pause, followed by a flash bang of light so bright it left Raine's vision filled with shadows. Then as suddenly as it hit, the magic quieted.

Blinking her vision clear, Raine made sure her bond to Gavin had survived whatever Vidis had done. It was there, steady and strong. A shaky sigh of relief escaped. She turned to check on Xander and stared, not wanting to believe what she was seeing.

"It's like a firestorm," she breathed. "Vidis, what did you do?"

Grim determination settled over his pale features as he cradled Xander closer. "I kept her alive."

"You've triggered a bond." Tala's voice was shaky, but solely her own. "Your alpha just bonded your Tracker."

All Raine could think was, *oh, shit*. "How upset is Xander going to be?" She didn't want to sound accusatory, but thought she might have failed.

"I don't care," Vidis snarled. "She's alive and that's all that matters."

Gavin's embrace tightened in warning, so she choked her words down. Xander was a big girl, but damn, she didn't want to think about what this meant for her friend. Or, she thought as she caught a small flare of panic before Vidis wiped it away, what it meant for the alpha.

"They'll be okay," Gavin assured her.

Dear gods, please let him be right.

CHAPTER 34

Forty-six hours into Tomás's forty-eight-hour deadline, Raine and Gavin were trying hard to avoid the various arguments whirling around them. In the room they shared at Tala's, Raine was zipping up her suitcase as Gavin finished putting on his jacket. Both tensed as they heard Xander's door being yanked open.

"Don't you snarl at me! I'm perfectly capable of carrying my own damn suitcase, you flea bag!" The neighboring door slammed closed causing both of them to flinch as their door rattled in its frame.

"Yeah, they're going to be just fine," she drawled sarcastically.

Gavin's lips twitched as he settled his jacket. "At least you don't have to worry that Vidis will walk all over her."

"Maybe, but now I have to start setting aside bail money."

"She's a Wraith, love. She won't get caught."

His dry rejoinder made her laugh. Dragging her suitcase to the door, she stopped in front of him. As he looked at her, she rose to her tiptoes, curled an arm around his neck, and indulged. He didn't need much encouragement. Soon she was lost in the firestorm of their kiss.

As they broke apart, he traced his thumb across her lower lip. "What was that for?"

She nipped his finger and let a wicked smile spread across her face. "Luck."

She opened the door and his low chuckle trailed behind her. As they stepped out into the hall, Xander's door opened and an obviously frustrated Vidis stepped out.

"Morning." Raine's greeting got only a growl in response.

She tried to smother the snickers tickling her throat. The last few hours had been very revealing. As soon as Xander had regained consciousness and figured out what Vidis had done to the two of them, she'd been nothing but a snapping, snarling bitch.

If Raine hadn't caught those rare moments when Xander thought Vidis wasn't paying attention and the woman's heart-rending emotions flashing across her face under her delicate tattoos, Raine would've been more worried. As it was, she agreed with Gavin. It was best to leave the two of them alone to figure it out. For now, it was more entertaining to watch the diminutive shifter drive Vidis insane.

Vidis followed Xander out the front door. Raine and Gavin stepped into the living room. Tala was standing stiff-backed by the fireplace, glaring at Ash, who sat by Cheveyo's feet. Pale but upright, Cheveyo was slouched in a chair, his expression inscrutable. Raine didn't want to feel sympathy for Tala, but it still leaked through.

Sometime in the previous evening, Cheveyo had made

his way back to the living. There were no discernible differences in his behavior. He was a bit quieter, understandably so. Gavin and Raine had been wary, but as the hours passed and Cheveyo didn't say anything, they started to relax.

"I still think you should reconsider," Tala said, her voice stiff.

"There's nothing to reconsider," Cheveyo answered, his attention centered on Ash so he apparently missed the flash of hurt sweeping over Tala's face.

"You go back before you've fully recovered, and you're opening yourself to unnecessary challenges." The bite of her voice was like the flick of a whip. "I didn't piece you back together just so you could be ripped apart."

Her comment got a reaction. Cheveyo's lips firmed and his eyes narrowed as he pushed out of the chair. It took precious few steps before he invaded Tala's space.

Raine gave the female witch credit. She didn't back down an inch. Instead, she leaned forward, chin jutted forward.

"You and I both know what being a Head Magi means, Tala," he said. "If I thought I couldn't handle any challenges coming my way, I wouldn't be going home."

She laid her hand on Cheveyo's chest, just above his heart. "I worry."

He covered her hand with his. "I know, *tsu-na-da-da-tlu-gi*." He leaned down and pressed his lips briefly against hers. "We both have to see to our Houses."

"I will see you soon." It was nothing less than a command. Tala gently pulled her hand away and stepped back. "*Do na do'go hr iyu.*"

Cheveyo traced one finger down the side of her face

then turned and made his way out of the house. As his tall form disappeared, Tala's shoulders drooped. Ash trotted over to his mistress, and she tangled her fingers in his fur.

As much as the female witch pissed her off, Raine could relate. It was hard to let someone you loved stand on their own. From her spot at Gavin's side, she cleared her throat. "We'll watch out for him."

A flash of gratitude was there and gone as Tala nodded her head.

"Are you going to be okay?" Raine asked. True concern prompted her question. They were leaving a hell of a mess in Tala's lap.

Tala straightened and the haughty arrogance from their first meeting fell into place. "I'm Magi for the Southwest. I am always fine." A bitter smile curled her lips. "You best hurry. Wouldn't want you to miss your flight. Tomás might get upset."

With nothing left to say, Raine gave Tala a short, mocking bow, then turned and left the cabin. As she made her way down the steps, a tidal wave of relief washed over her. They were going home. All of them.

"Ready?" Gavin asked down their bond.

"So ready." She caught a speculative look from Cheveyo who was standing next to the car. The man's expression sent her pulse racing. *"Gavin?"*

He stepped close to her and wrapped his arm around her waist. Together they faced the Northwest Magi as a united front. *"Together, Raine. We'll face it together."*

For the first time in a long time, the thought brought her comfort and, strangely enough, hope.

Stalk through the shadows with Xander and Warrick as the line between instinct and intellect blurs in SHADOW'S MOON.

Now available at your favorite bookseller!

KYN APPENDIX

GLOSSARY

Amanusas:

One of four Kyn races, delight in chaos, half-demon and half-human or Kyn. Six bloodlines—War, Earth, Secrets, Enticement, Death and Inequity—referred to as 'Blood of'. For example: Natasha is Blood of Secrets.

Between:

The second realm between the mortal and magical worlds, accessible by the Kyn.

Bitten:

Humans transformed to shifters through vicious attack. Magic needs human to be on brink of death to complete conversion. They are lower in the pack's structure as the control of wolf is tenuous at best. Tend not to live long.

Biovita:

A biotech lab in Hillsboro, OR where Brant Sutler, a human geneticist worked creating drug to turn Kyn wolves feral.

Blood ward:
A magical construct based on a castor's blood to defend or protect a place or person.

Bonded:
Rare metaphysical tie between Kyn, generally shifters, that connects two individuals at soul level. A step above mated. Partners generally don't survive the passing of the other.

Born:
Kyn Shifters who are born, some are Pure Bloods—rare few bloodlines.

Bound:
An Amanusa, caught in a casted circle by a summoner who uses all their names, to enslave—body and soul—to do the summoner's bidding. If a name is missed, they become half-Bound.

Chindis:
Vengeful spirits of the dead, raised by witches, however can be done by anyone with the ability, controlled by their summoner. Torment victims and rip them apart psychically. Generally are spirits of those who died violently or before their time. Once vengeance is taken, they'll rest.

Cinar International:
European based corporation.

The Council:
The ruling eleven members of the Kyn, chosen from around the world and headquartered in Turkey.

Division:
Preternatural Crimes Division, a group of talented and/or psychic humans who work for US Government and assist the Kyn on supernatural crimes.

Feral:
Wolves whose animal nature has taken control. Tend to attack humans and those closest to them. Nothing of the thinking man is left behind.

Fey:
One of four Kyn races, Sidhe descendants.

Kyn:
The entire preternatural community, composed of all four houses: Fey, Lycos, Amanusa, and Magi.

Lycos/Shifters:
One of four Kyn races, shape shifters, generally predator animals.

Magi:
One of four Kyn races, made of witches and wizards.

Mated:
Emotional bond created when two shifters commit.

Mavericks:
Lone wolves who have chosen to leave packs and roam on own. Can be Born or Bitten.

Mirroring:
Ability to send part of yourself into another by merging two

magics, can add strength, but only as passenger. Empathic magic, deep level merger gives access to individual's mind/heart. Witches can mirror.

Sarielian Order:
The ultimate group of Wraiths, made of nine of the most dangerous Kyn of the world.

Shadowed Paths:
The walkways in Between, used when Shadow Walking.

Shadow Walking:
Ability to travel in the realm that exists between the waking world and the magical one.

Side:
A realm accessible to the Amanusa, not easily borne by other Kyn, completely unbearable by humans. A third plane of existence.

Sisna:
Sanskrit demon slur, lewd version of tailed demon or phallus-worshipper.

Soul Stealer:
Nomâhtsé' héõo' Adanta - Eater of Souls, a psychic being created by black magic from the remains of a soul, tied to summoner. Gains strength eating the souls of others.

Taliesin Security:
The public security company housing the Northwest Kyn.

Tachair:

Gaelic word for "light", Raine uses it for light spell.

Three-fold Law:
Witches follow concept: What you do, will come back to you three-fold.

Tracker:
Shifters who are outside Pack hierarchy, their duty is to hunt/execute rogue shifters and threats (internal/external) to Pack.

Witches:
Practitioners of natural magic/white magic who follow the Three Fold law.

Wizards:
Practitioners of spells, potions, tend toward dark magic, use science and rituals.

Wraiths:
Twelve member highly skilled collection of North American Kyn who serve as the ultimate police for the Kyn and human monsters. They are not publicly acknowledged, basis of Boogieman stories for Kyn, even human not sure if they exist.

88 Ivories:
Music/dance club in downtown Portland

CAST OF KYN

NORTHWEST KYN

Ryan Mulcahy
Head of Fey House,
Captain of the Wraiths,
Chief Executive Officer (CEO) of Taliesin

Natasha Bertoi
Head of Amanusa House,
Chief Marketing Officer (CMO) of Taliesin

Warrick Vidis
Head of Lycos House,
Chief Financial Officer (CFO) of Taliesin

Cheveyo
Head of Magi House,
Chief Information Officer (CIO) of Taliesin

Carys Iver
Chief Legal Council for Taliesin

NORTHWEST WRAITHS

Raine McCord
Gavin Durand
Xander Cade
Jamie Ryder
Axel Kayser
Niall
Gideon
Dorian
Chayton
Fahd
Kevin Sullivan
Killian

SOUTHWEST KYN

Rio Castle
Head of Amanusa House

Tala Whiteriver
Head of Magi House

Tomás Chavez
Head of Lycos House

KYN COUNCIL SO FAR...

Leopold DiMarcco
Zayn Aimeric
Corwin Westbrooke
Malachi
Antonia

SARIELIAN ORDER SO FAR...

Darius Abazi

KYN KRONICLES

Welcome to a world where the supernatural walks alongside humans, their existence kept secret behind the thinnest of veils. Now modern man's scientific curiosity is determined to rip that curtain aside, revealing the nightmares in the shadows.

SHADOW'S EDGE

Raine's spent a lifetime hunting monsters, but can she stop her prey from exposing the supernatural community one bloody corpse at a time?

SHADOW'S SOUL

When a simple assignment turns into a nightmare, can Raine and Gavin unravel old vendettas before they both pay the ultimate price?

SHADOW'S MOON

Compromise isn't in Warrick's vocabulary and Xander won't abandon the hunt. As the line between instinct and intellect blurs, will they survive the fallout?

SHADOW'S CURSE

When the queen of chaos locks horns with death's justice, Natasha and Darius set a dangerous game in motion, leading two predators into a lethal dance of secrets.

SHADOW'S DREAM

Tala can't forget the past. Cheveyo can't change it. As the dreams they shared linger, can they escape the encroaching nightmare before it's too late?

SHADOW'S FALL

A trail of missing Kyn leads a powerful new threat into Raine's backyard. Will she and Gavin be able to hold their own or fall under the weight of secrets haunting the shadows?

About the Author

"This story is an emotional roller coaster, from betrayal, anger, fear, love..." —InD'tale Magazine

Jami Gray is the coffee addicted, music junkie, Queen Nerd of her personal Geek Squad, Alpha Mom of the Fur Minxes, who writes to soothe the voices crammed in her head. Her series combine high-stakes urban fantasy and edgy paranormal romantic suspense into books you don't want to put down. Buckle up and get ready for a wild ride through the fascinating worlds of the Arcane, the Kyn, the PSY-IV Teams, and the Collapse.

Come visit Jami's website at **https://www.jamigray.com** and stay up to date on what kind of trouble she's getting into and when you can expect to join in.

amazon.com/author/jamigray
instagram.com/jamigrayauthor
facebook.com/JamiGrayWriter
threads.com/@jamigrayauthor
goodreads.com/JamiGray
bookbub.com/authors/jami-gray

www.ingramcontent.com/pod-product-compliance
Lightning Source LLC
Chambersburg PA
CBHW050957180726
48291CB00006B/1865

9781948884198